The Prophecy of Andarraine
Book One

UNBREAKING

Wynn Talley Perkins

ISBN ePub: 978-1-943924-42-4
ISBN-13 Paperback: 978-1-943924-41-7

Contents

This book is dedicated to

Dee and Wayne Talley

My parents, my support, my inspiration.

Thank you.

Acknowledgements

I would like to start by thanking those who, through their unending support, have most made this book possible: my husband, Ian Perkins, our two sons, Luke and London, and my parents, Dee and Wayne Talley. I'd also like to thank Sheryl Moody for her efforts in editing, and especially my publisher and fellow author J. Steven Young for his guidance and support. Thanks, too, to all of my early readers who include, among others: Rev. Lynda Sutherland, Lauren Hanson, Julie Berryhill, Khalil Perilstein and Lynn Wiggers. I am deeply grateful.

Prologue:

The world was a sheet of gray in front of him. The sky was joined to the lake waters by the torrential downpour. It had dropped suddenly from the low mist that had been clinging to the world for the past three days now, and all of it was gray. The landscape was cloaked in a wet twilight that rumbled, roared and crashed with every breathtaking flash from the dark gray storm.

Brody huddled under the porch, the waters lapping up to kiss his feet as the wind threatened to blow him loose from his sanctuary. The old rotting timbers above him were doing nothing to keep him dry as water poured between their widening cracks, forming rivulets and streams working to wash him into the waiting lake water. He pulled his knees closer to his chest. His poor woolen tunic was soaked through to his skin. The mud beneath his bottom was beginning to glue him in place.

The next flash revealed the churning waters in front of him. They reached as far as he could see to the right or left and were impossibly vast. Sitting next to that immenseness, Brody felt small and helpless. His father and the other men, not yet home from the day's fishing, were out there somewhere in the grayness.

He risked a glance up. The small house that he lived in with his family faced the Unbreaking, the cursed mountain that loomed up out of the lake and towered over the tiny village of Luring like a boot over an anthill. Only the poorest families lived facing it directly. Other villagers said that If you looked directly at the face of it, the old gods themselves would come in the night and steal your very soul away.

Another crash and flash brought the stone surface of the mountain into sharp relief. Brody swallowed hard and looked back down quickly. The lake water was pooling under his bottom now. Brody knew that he had to move. He knew that swiftly rising waters could reach the house and could rise so suddenly as to carry off the strongest of men. He knew this, but he didn't dare move a muscle. His breath was caught in the rising mist in front of his face. He knew his mother was calling for him above, but he could not hope to hear her over the storm.

He had been down at the little dock waiting for his father since the noon-time sun had been in the sky. And now that gray dusk was settling in all around him he felt that something terrible was upon the little family. His father had never failed to return from morning fishing. Their regular afternoon foray into the wide river beyond the lake had not happened today. The men had not returned to exchange large lake boats for smaller, swifter river vessels, and hope had now faded away that there might be any good explanation for their absence.

The fishermen of Luring often said that one day the curse of living in the shadow of the Unbreaking would come upon them. They'd say into their beer mugs that the old gods would claim all of Luring one day. Then they would laugh their hearty laughs and ruffle the hair of the younger boys who sat wide-eyed and unblinking at their feet. They said that the Unbreaking overlooked the edge of the world. Brody had often felt that the little fishing village of Luring was itself the edge of the world, clinging to the rocks trying not to go down with the falls.

Brody looked down. In almost no time he was sitting in water up to his waist. His knees were poking out of the top of the water where he held them fast to his chest. Another booming flash and he felt the water surge toward him again, getting still deeper. He wanted his father to come and help him, to climb under the porch and retrieve him, but he knew his father wasn't coming. Possibly he was never coming again.

Brody swallowed back tears realizing for the first time the water that soaked his face wasn't just rain water. He began to feel that he was floating just slightly with every small wave now, and terror began to replace the deep sadness that had rooted him here, under the porch watching the tiny dock, all afternoon. The next wave actually carried him a few inches and then put him back, the water was indeed rising more swiftly than he had ever seen it. Instinctively, he grabbed the lip of the porch overhead and pulled his bottom up out of the mud with a sickening squelch. With a jerk, his head hit the spongy boards above him. He glanced around and saw that water was running up around him on both sides and that the slick muddy hill that led up from the lake to his home was washing away. He had no way out.

What would his father tell him to do? He began to panic. He closed his eyes and tried to call up the image of his father: tall, lean, muscular. The smell came to him first. It was leather, stale water, pipe tobacco and ale. He could feel his father's arm reaching for him, the rough worn wool of his sleeve, his calloused hands. "Sometimes you just find a way," his father's voice said in his head recalling his answer just last winter when the food stores were running out early and mother was pregnant and sick and Brody feared that the season would be their last. "Find a way."

He grabbed the lip of the porch with both hands. But try as he might he couldn't pull himself over the edge. The water rushing in from that direction was fighting against him and kept dragging him back down and under. "Find a way."

Brody looked up. The boards above him dumped water over his shoulders and were creaking and cracking with the weight of the house. There were spots on the porch that were so rotten, the family knew better than to step on them. Brody reached up. Light and warmth and safety were just beyond those old boards. He reached his fingers through the largest crack, clinging to the rim of the porch with his left hand to keep from floating away. Only his head and shoulders were above the water now. He grabbed the splintered ragged edges with his small fingers and pulled with all his weight. Another flash and boom and the sound of the board breaking off was obscured. Blood ran freely onto his cheek and into his eye and mouth. Pain seared up his left arm as dirty water soaked into the fresh wound. Bracing for more pain, he lifted his freshly gouged hand back up through the new hole for a better grip, his face barely lifted out of the rising water. He braced the top of his head against the new opening and pushed up with all his might, clinging to the crooked, splintered edges as he thrashed against the rising lake. His mouth filled with water and he began to choke as he impetuously tried to roar out his pain and effort, the rotten board above him cracking and breaking across his head.

Suddenly he smashed through gulping air, spitting blood, and trying desperately not to hang himself on the new jagged opening. He opened his eyes, ignoring the sting of blood pooling into them, and saw the water beginning to lap up over the edge of the porch, where he waited with his head stuck through the sharp wood. Now what?

Still gasping for air and screaming into the storm, he forced his hands back through, curled his body up so that his feet braced against the lip from below, and pushed his shoulders through the now-mangled porch floor. It took all of his strength to pull his weight through the floor until his bum was resting on the porch. He sat hunched and bloody, feet still dangling through the hole, gasping, watching red and gray puddles swirling about him. He was still sitting in water. The lake had crested the porch and was advancing on the front door. He looked back. His mother swung the door wide, saw him and screamed. Lightning flashed and she yanked him from his perch and drug his exhausted limp frame into the damp cottage.

"Good boy, Brody," his father said from the deep recesses where only Brody could hear, "You found a way. That's what you have to do now, son. Just keep finding a way..."

Brody, who had been lost in a sea of gray, saw the world fade to black.

*   *   *

Adrik rested his back against the cool of the rock and breathed in deeply, sinking slowly down the cliff wall to sit, still and poised, on the jutting rock behind the small bit of scrub that was all the cover he could find. He estimated that he was still at least 60 feet off the valley floor, paused precariously on a four-foot stretch of sharp rock. Across the ravine below him, an odd collection of sparse evergreen trees grew up at strange angles fighting the rock wall for access to sunlight. Their roots twisted toward the angry river below dipping occasionally into the rock but otherwise forming a nearly petrified mass of knot that covered the mountain face.

Impossibly, however, something was moving along the mountain wall. The shadows darted in and out under the dying afternoon sun independently of the trees.

Adrik glanced back up and caught the eye of another figure crouching on the ledge above. Her pale blonde hair was glowing halo-like around her head as the sun caught in each strand and made them golden. Her blue eyes were cautious and worried, and Adrik quickly nodded his head upward at her, signaling her to back away. She was no good as a scout and shone like a beacon in the sun.

Adrik inched slowly, catlike, out to the end of the stone spike to peer around the barren shrub. Moving slowly, he could appear as shadow even to the most discerning eyes. His own hair flowed white, but was wispy and ghostlike and less apt to catch the light. His skin was black as night and shadow and possibly created from one or the other. His violet eyes, however, were no more good in daylight across this distance than any other elf's, though he'd never admit it. He leaned carefully forward and held his breath.

The shape moving along the face of the mountain across from him also paused. Wary that he had been spotted, and deciding quickly that it was more likely his companion that gave them away, he willed his aching muscles to remain as statue-like as he could tolerate. A breeze was picking up around him, and in the distance to his right, there was a low rumble of thunder. Great, he thought, right in our path. He could see the torrential downpour taking place just up and over the falls as he felt the first drops of drizzle land on his arms and neck.

He looked back just as the shadow across began to move again, and was suddenly three shadows. Humanoid he was sure, but he could tell nothing else. The official road was below him, running along the river that cut valley from mountain in the ancient past. He knew damn well why he was avoiding it. He wondered why his unseen companions across the way were avoiding it, too. He feared they may share common purpose, but doubted they'd find common cause.

He watched the shadowy figures move ahead until he felt certain that he was not being watched, then he risked a turn and moved back to the steeply sloping rock that led up to his companion. He climbed up until he was staring at her feet. Then he began to pull himself up onto the narrow ledge that was serving as a pass for the pair. The mountain continued to loom like a curtain of mud and rock above them, disappearing into the cloudy, now dripping, sky.

Adrik shook his head to say that what he had seen was not good. He surveyed the girl in front of him. She sat crouched on the path, with her back against the mountain looking up at him now standing in front of her. It was all the cover she could have managed. Her hair was very bright yellow, not truly white like his. Her skin was pale and milky in contrast to his pitch black. Her eyes were as blue as a cloudless summer sky. Her narrow, young face, however, was etched with worry beyond her years as she waited to hear what Adrik would say about these shadows.

Adrik knelt in front of her. "Three," he whispered, "and definitely men of some sort. Moving in the same direction as we are and with some speed."

She bit her lip and studied his even gaze for more information, but he had none to give. He felt his own gaze soften with concern as he watched her. Then he frowned and cursed himself inwardly. He had grown too fond of her, and he knew that was pointless.

"I take it you don't know what they are?"

"I can only tell you what they're not, Arisa. They're not official representatives of the king, which wouldn't make them friendly anyway, and they aren't friends because we have none. I can only think of two reasons someone would sneak up into this gods-forsaken land, and of the two, I can't imagine that bandits would be very prosperous. So we have to assume that we've got company."

Arisa nodded, dropped her gaze to the river below, and then looked back up at Adrik.

"Then the prophecy isn't being ignored," she stared at him with harder eyes now, "Someone else is paying attention."

"Well, we knew that, at least from my own homeland. The question is who, or who else. And given what happened to you, Arisa, we can only imagine what it may have done to anyone else who got their hands on it. Let's move on."

They scrambled to their feet, Adrik picking up his traveling gear and weapons as he did so. He carried a twisted black longbow made from hardened and cursed roots not unlike the ones of the facing rock wall. He also strapped a long, slightly curved blade to his back before fumbling with quiver and backpack and bedroll. Arisa carried only equipment and a pair of long daggers for her defense, but Adrik knew she didn't really need them.

Arisa had read the Prophecy of Andarraine, which had been forbidden as dangerous, and she had not walked away unscathed. She had been a new apprentice in the ancient library at Felwater's Rune Keep where the Prophecy had been hidden away for more centuries than could be counted by scholars. It came from an age where magic ran freely through the veins of the world and was said to carry that magic in each rune inked upon it. Scholars lived and died by the safe studying of the individual runes, copied ages ago separately. But no one had actually *read* the script as a whole in countless years.

Adrik smiled vaguely at himself at her stupidity for doing it. He smiled, really, because he suspected that in her shoes he'd have done the same thing. Reading and re-reading, copying and recopying tomes and tomes of philosophy, history and translation of each independent letter sounded ridiculous to the practical man that he was. No, she'd gone and read the thing as if it were simply another text, although he doubted it was that simple, and now she had problems...

Parts of the Prophecy itself were known after a fashion. That is to say, that versions of pieces of it were passed through the lore of all the races. Few believed it, some were zealots about it; no one, however, understood it. But Arisa, now, seemed to have glimpses of some of it, and it really wasn't good.

He stopped abruptly and she bumped into his back having been apparently lost in her own thoughts. He was quite sure that he'd heard the slip of footing on rock overhead.

His awareness of it was too late. Gnarled figures dropped onto them from an unseen perch above, like rotted trees turned into men. Where they landed their rough skin abraded and burned. Both Adrik and Arisa were thrown to their backs. Arisa rebounded quickly with reflexes that impressed even Adrik, leaping back to her feet with both daggers drawn. Adrik pulled his falchion from his back and cleaved the one in front of him with a powerful overhead strike. His foe stumbled backward but did not fall.

There were five of them. Two between the companions, one of which Adrik had just failed to fell. One behind each and a last which landed on Adrik's head as he was trying to make count. In horror he watched as his original victim sprouted vines that pulled itself back to a whole. He felt a strong tendril of vines reach around his neck from behind as blood sprouted across both of his legs once the new attacker rolled off of him. He could hear Arisa shrieking just beyond his view and thought the worst for her chances.

Adrik jabbed behind him with all his strength, both hands on his sword-hilt, in hopes of relieving the strangle hold the enemy had over him. His face and shoulder were burning badly now where the first one had landed and his vision began to blur.

"Poison!" yelled Arisa, her voice strangely hoarse, "It's poison!"

Adrik's jab had done the trick, he felt the vine loosen around his neck and coughing for new breath, he leapt to his feet giving himself a better view of the mended foe in front of him. It had no real face and nothing that could be called eyes. It appeared to be a twisting mass of the same limbs and roots that he had noticed growing across the ravine. Its odd mass had parted at the bottom third to form legs of a sort. And it sported four writhing thorny vines, ending in elongated thorns like claws. Adrik noticed this just as the world started to dip and rock. Poison. He had to act fast.

The two behind him got themselves upright while the first one lunged. Anticipating it, Adrik slammed his uninjured shoulder backward into his rising foes, causing the one in front of him to overreach and lose footing, tumbling off the cliff edge.

Fire erupted in front of Adrik's eyes at that moment. He saw with dismay the two vine-things that had attacked Arisa piled in a suddenly-burning heap on top of the spot where his companion had just been. Arisa was nowhere.

"Arisa!" he yelled and his voice caught in his throat, burning and sounding more guttural than he had sounded before. The rocking world began a slow spin around him and he felt himself stumble He knew he could not afford to lose his footing on such a narrow ledge. "Arisa!" He nearly growled this time and tasted blood in his throat.

The foe pinned against the wall made a try for Adrik's neck with one of its deadly vines but missed as Adrik ducked, but the other caught his face with a thorny claw that felt as if it tore his ear free. He kicked out at it as he yelled in pain and sent it, too over the edge. The two burning corpses went soaring over the edge as Arisa emerged from beneath them, clearly burned but still upright and fighting. Adrik dodged quickly as another ball of searing flame shot from her outstretched fingers and ignited his pinned target. Adrik pressed himself against the solid security of the cliff face and eased himself down to the ground as the spinning of the world sped up and blackness threatened to engulf him. He just made out the approaching form of his friend, before everything went dark.

That was five years ago....

Chapter 1:

24th Day of the 11th Month, 3rd Day of the Week, Autumn
Amusday, Renets 24

Tollie

Tollie looked out the window. She wanted to find inspiration for her day. She listened for the song of birds or the light dancing merrily on some piece of nature. She needed color, music, life to drift into her bower from the world outside.

Nothing.

The squat rectangular brick building that sat far below her window looked from here like a turd left behind by the ancient world's most boring mythical beast. Neat round bushes dotted their way around the thing as if someone sculpted fake greenery in a lame attempt to hide the turd. An unimaginative cut-stone walkway led in a straight line to the tower itself far below her window. The edge of the high stone wall that surrounded Tollie's whole world snuck out from behind both sides of the little brick plop and slinked away out of sight in both directions.

Tollie sighed loudly and laid her cheek on her folded arms that were all that graced her narrow windowsill. There was not even warmth in the light the window welcomed. Not this morning at least.

A knock at the door behind her roused her from her self-pity. She looked up, catching her reflection in the glass for a brief moment as she did: round face, dark curly hair, pretty features, eyes that looked to be cut from the same glass as the window. She did not even turn around.

"Who is it?" she asked as if today she might be surprised by a stranger, or at least an unusual-er.

The door creaked slightly open and, predictably, her maid said on cue, "I really do need to oil these dratted hinges." Tollie rolled her eyes at herself in the glass.

"Supper is prepared," the maid went on, "Will you sup in your room or would you like to join your Papa?"

The question caught Tollie slightly off guard. Her Papa had been dining in private for nearly 2 weeks now, although supper together had been their routine for many years before. She never particularly enjoyed dinner with her Papa, in fact she HATED it, but it would mean a grand adventure down to the dining room for the first time in a while.

"I'll come down," she pronounced.

She slipped herself from her perch on her small study desk that she had purposefully placed facing out of her window years before she came to realize that there was nothing out of the window to look at. She stepped off of its attached wooden seat and earned a disapproving stare from Maeve, the maid. Maeve's eyes looked Tollie up and down and the expression on her face did not change. If it could have made a noise on its own it would have clucked like an elderly hen. Tollie had her leather garden pants pulled up under her nightdress, but haphazardly so that the skirt of it was tucked on one side and hanging out over the waistband on the other. Under her very practical pant leg, her neat little dress boots were poking out, the quickest pair she could find this morning when she ran out to meet the post as it arrived, with a dollop of mud dried onto the toe.

"I'll leave you to dress then," Maeve commented, lips pursed, and she shut the door before Tollie could make to leave the room. What difference did it make? Her Papa wouldn't notice if she walked into the dining room naked which, at this moment, she had half a mind to do.

Tollie put her fists on her small hips and glanced around her prison cell. In fairness, she had a large room, half circle in shape. She had frilly drapes at the windows, well-made wooden furniture with fancy curves and such to it. Warm rugs, pretty tapestries, and a handsome secretary-style desk that had been made just for her. And she had books. They were everywhere, in fact. On the bed, the desk, the closet floor, the shelves, the rugs, everywhere. Strewn about with them were jumbled parchment, spills of ink, whiddled bits of broken wood, baskets, bottles, bags, and the occasional homemade paper flying toy, a craft she intended to perfect. She had a closet full of clothes, and a door that wasn't locked, certainly. Technically she had full run of the tower and all of the public portions of the library and grounds.

So why did she feel like she was imprisoned? She kicked through the detritus on her floor, vaguely searching for something clean enough to put on. She picked up a likely-looking rag which turned out to be a pretty lace-necked frock with an ink stain down the front. She sighed and threw it back onto the floor.

Well, for starters it didn't help that she hated books. She hated reading, writing, numbers and most definitely runes. Living in a tower overlooking a library made that pretty miserable. For seconds, she thought bitterly to herself and hearing her Papa's voice in her head correcting her grammar, everyone here makes me feel stupid.

Tollie lighted on a plain but clean gown of winter cloth still miraculously hanging in her closet and dressed hurriedly. When her uncarefully discarded clothing accidently landed on her old, unattractive study desk facing out of the window she stopped and knocked the offending item to the floor. That was the only piece in the room she had any respect for. It had been her mother's.

With no more thought for the things she left behind, she headed out to the landing. She spared not a glance for the door right next to hers as she headed down the hand-carved wooden staircase. She hated that place worst of all.

The dining room was four levels down past her Papa's room, his private study and, oh yes, his library. The dining room was large, round and set with large windows all around. The heavy oval table that dominated the center of it could have sat 16 people if given the chance, but Tollie had never seen it seat more than 4. Today 2 places had been set, at opposite ends.

Tollie shook her head and sighed. She meandered over to a window opposite on the tower from her own. Over here she could, at least, look out over the garden and the beautiful tree-lined walk that led out from the walls and down the road along the river. She could nearly make out the sparkle of the water from here. The tower guard marched in and out of here in a predictable routine. Still, Tollie would join them if given the chance, if only to see what lay at the other end of the path.

The door opened behind her and she heard the hurried footsteps of her Papa come in and take a seat. He said nothing and Tollie knew without turning around that he had his rather large nose in a book.

"Evening, Papa."

"Oh, evening, of course, Tollie, how are you my dear?"

"Lonely, Papa."

"Ah, good. That's good. Me? I'm fine just fine."

Tollie turned around. He hadn't even looked up. She found herself wishing that she had come down naked.

When the food arrived, Tollie paid very little attention to it. It was an elegant plate of something deliciously prepared, just like every night. She watched her Papa, her only company, as he continued to thumb through whatever volume he was immersed in, making notes.

That night, Tollie sat up in bed, tears running down her round face. She had a book open across her lap and a candle sputtering out its dying light on her nightstand. She looked toward the window. Many nights she'd gotten up, hoping to see something. But the roof overhang was just above her and so she couldn't see stars. The lights would be on in the windows of the turd house because the groundskeeper kept odd hours. Otherwise, the world outside her window would be dark. The book in her lap offered no support. It was a creepy old manuscript about lost spirits, a crown, and the arrival of the faeries in the Morrowlands. It was a "scholarly" work, her Papa called it, so it was thick and dry and hard to follow. Tollie's mind kept wandering and she couldn't get through a paragraph and still remember what she'd read.

But her Papa had set her to this project. "See if the work has any value," he'd told her. "I look forward to your report."

She sighed, and shut the heavy tome with a muffled thud. Her report? Her report would be that if young hafling girls were going to be forced to receive this kind of education, then scholars should be better storytellers, and that works such as these were wastes of one's precious lifetime.

She wiped her eyes and nose on her sleeve and glared down at the unforgiving book. She was her Papa's assistant. Technically he didn't need one. There was no one more brilliant anywhere in the shared free lands, which is why a hafling had the post and title of Lord Librarian. He was the first after all. An honor, he called it, to have the title and not be an elf. For Tollie it was a nightmare.

But she was expected to turn out just like him, and somehow her Papa had failed to notice that she wasn't. Begrudgingly, she reopened the book and tried to read more of it, falling instead into an uneasy sleep.

In her dream she was surrounded by a messy garden, and old crumbling garden walls. The air smelled strongly of roses and lavender and just the right amount of compost and mud. She ran through the garden pathways as they twisted and turned in every direction, cackling like the crazed small child she once was. She passed her Papa once or twice, sitting on a bench with a book, reading a story to her sister who sat with rapt interest in whatever it was. She bumped blindly into her mother, knocking her tray of cookies out of her hands and scattering them in crumbs everywhere, both of them laughing raucously over the mess. Still Tollie kept running and singing her song:

> "I am run with wind and light
> I am run with birds in flight
> I am run with mirth and might
> So I will run all day and night!"

But eventually something was chasing her. The dream became dark. The familiar faces vanished. First her mother's, then her sister's. The walls grew higher, the paths straighter, her sister's room next door loomed into her vision. She was being boxed in, trapped, and something was coming...

She woke with a start and the heavy book slid off of her afghan and hit the floor with a loud slam. She sat up, still panting from her run in the dream and glanced around the room. The candle had burned itself out. The moonlight caressed her mother's study desk and bathed it halo-like with a soft, dust-filled glow. In the dark, the mess of her room looked like the tangle of that old garden seen from a bird's view. Her startle settled back down into sadness. She missed that place. That's all it was. They had been a family there. Tollie turned over, away from the window and the desk, and willed herself back to sleep.

She awoke the next morning with a plan. She was tired of living a lie and of being ignored. She wasn't going to do what her sister did and just abandon him, but she had to get him to see her again. She decided to confront him.

This time she paid attention to what she was dressing in. She even picked up a few items of clothing and piled them by the door for Maeve to wash. She carefully chose a simple but pretty blouse and a plain, neat blue skirt. She knocked the dollop of mud off of her dress boot and put the pair on. She found her hairbrush in the closet under a lump of broken clay that had tried to be her first attempt at a vase. She knocked the clay dust out of it and pulled it through her hair, leaving slightly gray streaks in it that she couldn't do anything about. She tied it up in a loose blue ribbon and blushed her cheeks quickly in the mirror. Then she set off down the stairs.

Excitement was building in Tollie's chest as she checked for her Papa in his study and his personal library. She needed to ask him why: why had he suddenly dropped everything and moved them here? Why had he stayed after Mom died? Most importantly, she needed him to understand that she was not going to follow in his footsteps.

She stopped outside of the dining room, breath now rising in her chest where excitement had been. The image of her Papa's disappointed face, his pursed lips, his sad eyes filled her with sudden regret.

"Tollie?" His voice came from the dining room where he had chosen uncharacteristically to breakfast.

"Yes, Papa?" She peered sheepishly around the corner, a furious argument taking place in her own heart.

"Come and sit with me. I need your opinion on something."

"Yes, Papa," she answered him as she slipped into the room. He was sat at the far end of the table, propped up with extra seat cushions. His balding head shone in the morning sun coming through all the windows, and his reading glasses perched lightly on the end of his long nose both worked together to make him appear much older this morning than Tollie thought of him. *This job is killing him,* she thought to herself. *He really does need me.*

He had books and notes spread all around his breakfast plate, a spoon in one hand and a quill in the other. Similarly he had drops of egg on his notepad and ink on his lips. She grinned bemusedly and slipped into a chair next to him.

"Yes, Papa?"

What ensued was a vaguely intellectual discussion about the nature of the understanding of time throughout history in which Ellerby, Lord Librarian himself, little aging halfling with his mumbling speech and soft voice, asked his daughter a hundred questions which he answered and reanswered for himself. In the end, Tollie had said the same two words over and over, "yes, Papa," while Ellerby had an intense and impossible-to-follow conversation with himself. He ended his maddening discourse by telling her how proud he was of her and how grateful to have her by his side. He then dismissed her to her chores and, just like that, Tollie's big confrontation she was going to have with him evaporated with the morning dew on the grass below.

Tollie spent what was left of her morning tidying up Ellerby's personal library. She did not touch the large volumes of impressively illuminated treatises of royal bloodlines that he seemed to have laid out everywhere, but she put away those books that had been tossed aside or shut and left behind. She dusted, straightened his papers, refilled his ink, and informed Maeve that she would be having lunch out in the garden.

Dutifully, Tollie lugged the stupid old tome down with her. Any book that had ghosts and faeries in it at the same time just needed to be thrown in the river, she thought to herself. But she gave it another go anyway while munching on fresh autumn apples, salted pork and walnut bread under fading trees and amid neatly-cropped bushes.

There did seem to be something of a story to it, at least. There was this odd heroine who the scholar thought to be either a dark-skinned human or of a now-dead race. He also wondered at length about her age, settling for the vague "too young to die the way she did." Apparently she set a bunch of angry ghosts loose which did not seem to Tollie like a particularly heroic act, but apparently they had been her Papa's subjects in life and had been murdered. So, Tollie mused, they did apparently have good reason to be angry.

As the afternoon wore on Tollie made some notes that amounted more to a catalog of seemingly irrelevant topics that the author treated with inappropriate length. Tollie assumed this made them important points. The age of the girl, and her race, her uncanny gift for writing in runic script, and a long and boring section full of maps wherein the author tried to guess at the location where the supposedly evil army that the angry ghosts attacked had cursed part of a large forest. It seemed, to Tollie, to be somewhere in the Willows Kingdom, near the Breaking Mountains, but what did she know?

The autumn chill of late afternoon settled in around her and Tollie made to return to her room. She had not had the day she'd intended, but she had been productive for the first time in over a week. And maybe, she thought to herself, if I can get through this project we can finally have that talk.

As Tollie headed back toward the tower entrance directly below her bower window some 70 feet above, she saw someone else coming out of the door. Someone tall, even for an elf, and elderly. Still far enough away to duck behind a bush, she hid just long enough to see who it might be, if only to avoid being patted on the head and congratulated, "Your Papa's so proud, you know." She got that a lot and it made her feel ill. She was not a chip off of his block. She was a mirror for him, one he didn't realize he was looking into and therefore thought he saw another person.

Strangely, though, it was the old gardener, Harold, backing slowly out of the tower door, heavily laden with some burden. Mesmerized, Tollie watched in shock as he emerged with a towering stack of books from her Papa's library! He was barely able to walk under the weight of at least 7 large volumes. He paused and looked nervously up and down for viewers, and then trotted off at a wobbly pace toward the little brick turd-building he lived in and worked out of.

Tollie was horrified, but completely unsure of what to do. Elderly or not, Harold was human and therefore nearly twice Tollie's size. Plus she had a book with her that was a prize volume to her Papa's mind, even if she did want to see how well it might float. She waited for Harold to shut his door after one more suspicious glance around, and she made quickly for the relative safety of the tower door.

The bottom floor, littered with tables and benches for study, was dark and empty. Tollie took to the stairs at a run and, despite the weight of the book she carried, sped past the 4 little public offices on the first floor without notice, past the dining room, past the library and gasping arrived on the landing outside of her Papa's private study, doubled over and clutching an horrendous stitch in her side.

Her Papa's study door was closed so, politely and catching her breath, she knocked.

"What is it?" came Ellerby's irritated voice from within.

"It's me, Papa," she said breathlessly.

"Ah! Come in! Come in!"

Tollie entered the cluttered room with reverence and care. Here was a room cluttered with purpose and thought unlike her own cluttered carelessly and thoughtlessly. Books and papers strewn in here had been left panting and out of breath from their own workout first. They had not made it back to their proper place yet entirely because they lacked the energy to be put back. Tollie's room was recklessly strewn by abused objects, her Papa's objects were collapsed in an exhausted heap.

Ellerby recognized the book under his daughter's arm and lit up like she had not seen him do since her childhood, back when he had been a playful Papa fond of his playful child. He immediately went to take it from her and excitedly asked to hear her thoughts on the matters presented. Then he did something he never did anymore. He shut up and waited for her to speak, listening intently, eyes focused only on her. Tollie forgot about the gardener.

She didn't really have anything to say, and she had no where near finished reading the thing, but she was so enamored of having her Papa's attention, if only for that moment, that she dove into the subject matter anyway, bringing out her little page of notes and plowing through what little she understood. Ellerby, Lord Librarian, listened intently.

When she finished regurgitating her lame synopsis, silence fell in the room.

Ellerby studied her a moment, then asked, "But what do you think?"

Disarmed by the question, Tollie started simply with, "Freeing ghosts to go destroy an army doesn't seem very heroic."

Ellerby nodded, "A great deal of thought has been given to the deeds of that woman. Many believe her to be the last of a reign of terrible evil. That author, however, the one you're reading doesn't believe so."

"No," Tollie agreed, "He doesn't."

"But you do?"

"I don't know yet. I haven't finished reading it."

Ellerby nodded. He looked disappointed, and Tollie was crestfallen.

"Indeed." Ellerby continued, "you should not form an opinion until you've heard the man out. I'm glad you're putting such time and thought into this piece. It could well prove to be crucial to us."

Tollie frowned at her Papa as he went back to the notes on his desk. Nothing he said seemed to make sense anymore. She started to feel that what others saw as genius in him was becoming dementia.

"Papa?"

"Hmmmm?" asked Ellerby without looking up.

"Does she have to be good or evil?"

At this, the Lord Librarian looked up at his daughter again, a quizzical expression on his face. "What do you mean?"

"Well, if this was a real person, couldn't she just have been, well, real? Maybe she did both good things and bad things. Like most people."

Ellerby studied his daughter for several moments. Tollie stood in the silence of his stare feeling like she had, this time, come naked. Finally he spoke.

"We tend to, in the fullness of time, as it were, assign meaning and truth to the events of history. We like to think that good and evil fight a never-ending war with our...our...our mythological epoch that we all feel we are inheriting."

Tollie cocked her head to one side, trying to process his meaning.

"What I'm saying, Tollie," he began to clarify, "Is that it is easy to forget that the people of our past, especially our long ago past, were people, no more or less fallible than we. You are absolutely right, my lass, and more so even than the scholar whose work this is. She was most likely neither good nor evil. Hard as it is to accept, often even the greatest of our heroes and sometimes the worst of our villains were never more or less than people themselves. We color them, we do. With our own desire to inherit an epoch tale. Well done, Tollie! Well done indeed! I should have, myself thought of that!"

Tollie blushed. Then she smiled. She watched him as he scribbled some note or another with more earnest. Then he paused to shut her book and give it back to her. She nodded and happily took the book with her as she made to leave, stopping just shy of getting totally out of the door. She remembered the gardener.

Reopening the door she cleared her throat. Ellerby looked up.

"Papa, Harold, he was...well he was taking books from the tower out to his shack," she paused, not wanting to accuse him of anything, "Did you...did you know?"

Again, age appeared to fill Ellerby's features, causing him to look older than Tollie wanted him to be. "Don't worry about that," her Papa told her firmly, "Just leave that be."

Ellerby did not join his daughter for supper that night. Tollie insisted on eating in the dining room anyway which clearly annoyed Maeve. Tollie didn't care, though. She felt she'd earned it after her "brilliant" idea of the afternoon. She was still fully flush with having done her Papa proud. She even thought she could feel her mother in the back of her mind smiling at her from long ago. Tonight Tollie tasted the food, enjoyed the fine china and even indulged in a glass of elvish wine. The latter left her smiling even more broadly as she went up to bed to read.

Tollie slipped on her newly laundered nightdress, lamenting the tear in the lace at the hem. She didn't take good care of her things, she admitted. But this had been her mother's nightdress, and she wished she'd done better by it.

The dreaded tome was lying on her bed waiting for her, almost taunting her. It was the key to her Papa's madness, she thought, at least in its current incarnation. But however proud she was of her moment of enlightened morality, she still hated to read the damned book. She wasn't even halfway through it, and she knew her Papa had wanted her finished by now.

She exhaled firmly and climbed into bed like a reluctant lover. She heard her Papa's door slam downstairs and the loud scrape of his chair. It was unusual for him to be so noisy, but Tollie ignored it. She had to get through this one thing. For him.

As she opened the book a slip of paper fell from the pages and landed in her lap. She was sure that couldn't have been there before, as poorly as she had treated the book, anything hidden in it would have fallen out by now. Surely.

Carefully she unfolded it, noticing that it was smudged badly from having been folded before the ink was dry. It was in her Papa's handwriting. As if he knew, he dropped a book somewhere below her and swore loudly.

My Dearest Tollie,

I know these last six years have been hard on you. I pretend not to notice but I do. I had hoped to have the time to explain things to you more fully, but time is an elusive mistress, and no man can keep her. When things go badly, take the books Harold has and get them to safety. They cannot stay here any longer. If you cannot finish the story you hold, skip to the part about the faeries. That crown cannot fall into evil hands.

The last portion was more scribbled and was the part that was smudged:

You are right, you know, and I hope that you will remember me, too, as a person. Do not try to make me any one thing or another. But know, too, that there is evil in this world. Whether we want it to be there or not. And it often hides as regular people.

Love,

Papa

From somewhere below, Maeve screamed.

Tollie kicked the blanket off of her legs and ran for the landing. The screaming kept going, long and shrill and turned to words, "Guards! Guards! Oh, help us please! Guards! Come quick! Oh, gods," she sobbed, "Come quick!"

Tollie reached her Papa's study without remembering the steps in between. She stood in the doorway, unable to breathe, tears running silently down her face, her mouth open in shock. Ellerby's head was face down on his desk, a single trickle of blood running out of each ear. He was pale and unmoving and Tollie knew at once he was gone. As the guards crested the landing and yelled to sound the alarm, Tollie collapsed, unnoticed, just inside the doorway, and wept.

Brody

Brody Clorr shook out his wet hair on the banks of the lake. He was just no good at boat building. His dog, Fletch, yapped happily, swimming around after the ducks. The bottom falling out of *yet another* fishing boat had been no less than a grand adventure for the seafaring pooch. Brody sighed, wringing the hair that was laying wet against his neck in his fist. He looked out over the unforgiving lake, shook his head, and tried to wring the water out of his thinning tunic.

It had been five years since that fateful day when his world had been stolen from him. Five years since he had become a man too soon, at the ripe old age of twelve. Or at least he had tried. Today, he felt as much like a boy just pretending to be grown up as he had the day after that flood.

Only a few of the old families remained. Not that there had ever been many, but now there were fewer. Unfortunately their lords expected no less in taxes. Those who had no where else to go, families like Brody's, were forced to find a way. Find a way.

He looked out over the lake with eyes lowered. The Unbreaking still loomed above his vision, but he never glanced at it. Even for a moment. He knew that if anyone in Luring knew that he had looked at it that day, they'd blame him. They'd blame him and they'd see that he paid.

Never mind the fact that the men were already gone before he looked. Never mind that the flood had already begun. Five years later the people of Luring had not recovered. Because the men never returned. They were never seen again. Young Brody had waited for his father in vain. And the flood that nearly claimed his life, did claim the lives of 12 others and destroyed nearly a third of the little huts that had stood at the time. Brody's house had largely survived, but what repairs had been needed were accomplished through the efforts of a 12-year-old boy and a woman newly from child bed who was a weaver by craft. The house had needed to be re-repaired every year since. Now at 17 he still hadn't replaced his father's fishing vessels, though he built new ones twice a year it seemed, and he was barely able to help his mother support the family. Rista, his 15-year-old sister was now helping with the fishing, which was its own little private disaster.

But what could he do? He continued to teach Rann and Till, his younger brothers, to fish, but could not yet rely on their skills. Still, every little bit helped and when the boats he built were newer and therefore more sturdy than they would become, he'd take them out and hope for the best. He had to. He had to find a way.

Other than having looked upon the face of the mountain that day, one other thing had changed for Brody. He'd imagined his father had helped him in his hour of need. He'd thought he'd conjured memories of his father's words and smell and touch. But now, the dead seemed to follow Brody. It began as soon as he awoke from his terrible ordeal with the whispering that no one else could hear. He could still hear it if he tried, like someone waiting for him just beyond his vision. Often enough, it was several someones.

He shuddered.

He let out a long shrill whistle. Happily as if all life were full of joy, Fletch swam toward his master who smiled weakly down at him.

Fletch always made Brody feel better. Because when the full-fledged voices came, the ones that needed him desperately to do something for them, Fletch would bark at them. Brody didn't know if the dog sensed something change about his master or some other reasonable explanation, but it made Brody feel better to think that the dog could hear it. That way, maybe he wasn't losing his mind.

Of course, he'd do the things his father asked. Once his grandparents' voices could be heard, begging him to bring his younger siblings to visit their graves. Other than those, he didn't listen to the many requests. But it did make him feel better that Fletch would bark.

He shrugged it all off as often as he could. He often thought that if anyone could ever tell him what actually happened that day, what really had happened to his father, that he'd stop hearing the unsettled voices. He tried to convince himself nightly that the persistence of the voices was just his own mind, trying somehow to understand. But whenever he would challenge the voices, whenever he would ask them for answers, they were silent.

Brody looked up to the sky. It was bluer today than it had been. Being the stormy season, the sky was often indistinct in its hue. Today the fog had given way to a cloudy sky that shone brilliantly in the backdrop of its low-hanging load. The clouds were white and fluffy like a child's drawing, but still they threatened rain. He wished silently up to them that the deceased that paraded through his mind might have some advice on building the next fishing boat. That's really what he needed.

"It sunk *AGAIN*?" came the derisive voice of Rista, "How can you complain about *my* fishing when you can't even build a decent boat?"

She appeared next to him clearly still angry that he had refused to take her out with him this morning, but truly, he needed a break. Fishing was dull and monotonous, but at least before Rista had been a constant companion, it had been an *escape*.

Brody's good friend and usual companion, Tarfinn Kipp, came striding purposefully up the banks at that moment, which Brody felt relieved him of the responsibility of responding to his sister. She crossed her arms angrily over her chest and stamped her foot in the mud. Then she whisked herself around with a poignant whipping of her long light brown pony tail that nearly caught her brother in the face, and stormed back up to the house. Fletch followed happily behind her, yapping all the way.

Tarfinn, Finn for short, arrived and looked after Rista with a bewildered expression followed by a knowing grin.

"I thought you said she didn't want to come with us this morning," he teased his friend.

Brody hung his head, then looked out over the lake still keeping his gaze below the Unbreaking, "I know. I just needed to get away. Sorry. You were right, though. We could have used another fisherman, especially today. Even her."

"You know. She's doing better than you give her credit for," Finn started then shook it off. He clearly had something else on his mind, "Another storm's coming though." He nodded his head pointedly in the direction of the foreboding mountain without looking at it, like they all did, "Better secure your firewood. I see Rista did make herself useful this morning."

Brody looked back toward his home for the first time since returning from the disappointing morning trip and noticed now the impressive stack of freshly cut wood on the front porch. Fletch sat next to it, his tail wagging merrily. Brody's shoulders sank. Rista really had worked hard, probably all morning. He really didn't give her enough credit.

Moving toward the chore of salvaging Rista's morning effort, Brody found himself shaking his head. More things than one had changed since that horrible day five years ago. Now the storms plagued the area regularly. Where once the stormy season brought regular downpours and occasional floods, now storms swept out of the mountains, seemingly from the Unbreaking itself, year round. These were terrible storms that threatened to blow the very village itself away, and brought regular flooding no matter the season. Brody was old enough to remember that this had not always been the case, and while other men mused that the poor fishing anymore had to do with the curse come upon them at last, Brody felt that the frequency of storms and flooding had been as hard for those that dwell in the lake as for those that dwelt around it.

Shadows seemed to lengthen when the storms were about. No one ever said so, but Brody knew he couldn't be the only one who had noticed. Night was blacker, too, and never was there a moment when there was no cloud in the sky.

Brody reached the warm inviting interior of his small home just as the gusts of rain hit the world behind him. Fletch followed behind just a moment too late and got drenched in no time. He shook himself vigorously sending water spraying everywhere and causing Brody to shout. Then he curled up innocently by the fire and was asleep in a wink. Rista looked up from where she and Mother were weaving by the fire and exclaimed, "Oh, my firewood!" trying to leap out from under a mound of wool.

"I got it," Brody assured her pointing to the large pile just inside the door he'd been making while being entirely ignored for the last fifteen minutes, "and it's a good job, too. Thanks for doing that."

"I didn't do it for you," Rista plopped back against her chair sullen, "But I did imagine your face in every log," she added with a large grin.

Mother shot her a chiding look then glanced at Brody, "I heard the fishing was poor again? What's the plan now?"

Brody looked around the room, from his mother's worried eyes, to his sister's accusing stare, to his two younger brothers playing a game with discarded bits of wool from the weaving on the bare floor. There were two chairs by the fire where the women sat to weave and one square table pushed against the wall laden with the cooking pots. Across from the fire on Brody's right were the neatly piled bedrolls they all would use at night. Spare fishing nets and gear were piled under the house and secured with a strong old net Brody's father had made. That was it. They had sold everything they couldn't burn for fuel or eat, and still the fishing wasn't getting better. Their clothes were threadbare, but none of his mother's hard-worked wool could be for their use if they were to pay their taxes.

"Brody?" his mother tried to ease him out of his thoughts.

He shrugged, "Find a way," he stated with a mirthless grin, "I don't know that there is a plan."

"I'm surprised more people don't leave," Rista pondered.

Brody and his mother held each other's gazes. The truth was, anyone who'd had anywhere else to go had already left. This was it. Sink or swim. As it stood right now, Brody doubted anyone in the village would survive another winter.

Brody left his mother's gaze and wandered over to the small table, where a small pile of potatoes and radishes and a much smaller block of cheese would have to feed them for another day or two. Longer if he couldn't catch anything. Without another word, he grabbed a potato and a knife and began to make supper.

The storm lasted all night. Fletch was probably the only one in the village that slept through the night, and that was only because they'd finally taught him that he couldn't bark his head off at the lightning after everyone had gone to bed, so nighttime storms just weren't any fun for him. The next morning Finn picked up Brody and Rista in his larger lake vessel and they set out again while Fletch whimpered pitifully at the shore over being left behind.

The mood was somber and the friends were quiet. Brody and Finn had just yesterday strung fishing nets across the mouth of the falls. It was a dangerous venture, and one only the most experienced and able fishermen would have done in years past, but desperation had driven them to the very edges of their world for food. None of them wanted to think about what might happen if it didn't pay off. Quietly, Brody just prayed to his own ancestors that there would be at least *something* in that net to show for the work.

Finn left Brody on the left bank as close as he could manage the boat to the falls, then piloted himself and Rista to the other side of the lake. Once there he climbed out and left Rista with his boat. It was a gamble. These were the most dangerous waters on the lake, and that was the last fishing vessel Finn and Brody had between them. Nonetheless, Rista was no match against the falls herself, inexperienced as she was, and couldn't be asked to go into those waters to pull in the nets, so her job would be to keep the boat as close as she could and help them pull their catch aboard. There was no safe place to moor a boat at this end of the lake. Yesterday they had walked to the location with empty nets. Today they were hoping to need the boat to bring full nets in.

Only twelve other men remained in the village. One was a trapper. Three were too elderly or infirm to help with more than gathering firewood and gardening vegetables, although in truth they were all eating more garden vegetables these days than fish. Six still had swift river craft that they could carry up above the smaller falls that fed into Luring Lake and navigate the much more shallow, rocky swift waters above the town. And the last two were young: one just older than Finn and Brody and one just younger, but both were being taught to fish on the river by family members who still had those skills and those boats.

Fishing on the river had been better than on the lake, but not by a whole lot, and these men insisted that there was not enough to support any more fishermen. In truth, Brody knew, because Finn had told him, they had offered to teach the river fishing skills to Finn who refused because they were not going to teach Brody. Brody knew why, too. Five years ago, when the world in Luring had been turned upside down, Brody had come bursting up through the floorboards of his front porch. He had terrible scars to show for his ordeal, including one down the entire right side of his face that should have gouged his eye. He was marked, they thought: marked by the evil of that day and no one trusted his story of what he had been doing in the water. He may never have told them that he looked at the mountain, but he might as well have been jumping up and down yelling threats at the dark gods that must dwell there for all his fellow villagers thought of him. All, that is, except for his own family and Finn, who stood by his side and were now treated with the same suspicion.

Finn lost his whole family on that day. His father had been a close friend of Brody's father, and they had been fishing together. His mother and sister drowned when their house was washed out into the lake. Finn had been up above the tree line chopping wood. Brody had tried on many occasions to reassure him that all his being away had done was ensure his own survival, that he couldn't have done anything more. Finn, however, had always carried the burden that perhaps if he had been home...

"Both scarred," mused Brody to himself as he trudged along the slippery muddy banks. He was using the rock on his left to keep steady. It was soaked and slick but jagged enough to offer a handhold. The ground around this end of the lake was barely wide enough to place one foot in front of the other, and it was muddy and sloped. The water at his feet churned slowly out toward the middle where it became a rush of white water leaping and spitting in its excitement to ride over the falls not far ahead.

Brody hoped the net held up to the force. He'd knotted it himself, which didn't give him much comfort. His thoughts strayed to Rista. She was now 3 years older than he was when he had to take over as the man of the house. Part of him knew that he had to stop treating her as a child, and yet part of him knew that by all rights she still was, and should be allowed to be. He worked hard to keep his siblings from having to grow up as fast as he did, but he was failing them.

He stopped and looked up at the inevitable clouds drifting across the sky before continuing, choking back a lump in his throat. This was really why he didn't like to have her around, he knew suddenly. Because her trying to be an adult, too, reminded him that he had failed to let her be a child. But in truth, by trying to keep her a child, he wasn't teaching her how to grow up. And that was now his job, too.

"You're making it, Brody. Focus on the task at hand."

His father's voice called up on the wind along with his smell. Brody looked around and realized that he was nearing the edge. He had been lost in thought and could very easily have walked right out over the mountain and fallen to the road along the river below. He swallowed hard. Focus, he told himself. Pay attention now.

The white water would soon be rushing over his feet and he'd have to make it the rest of the way to the net across slippery rocks with no mountainside to hold on to. The water yesterday had tried with all its very impressive might to take him with it over the edge. From where he was standing now the narrow strip of muddy land swung back at a sharp angle around the water-cut rock he'd been leaning on. Heading that way, away from the falls, it became more firm and formed a wider, but still thin, rocky ledge that continued to run along the face of the mountain as it descended slowly toward Graffling Valley. To his right some of the rocks that walled the muddy basin of Luring Lake as it tried to tumble over the edge along with the water could be seen jutting out of the depths as the waters swirled over them.

Ahead of him he could clearly see the path of the falls dropping away below him into the swirling basin some 200 feet below. From this distance he could just make out the roadway running alongside the river that spilled out of the basin. The road disappeared somewhere below his feet and he knew that it wound precariously up through a cut mountain pass that deposited the rare traveler, or the less rare tax collector, into Luring village not far above his own home. That road, Brody knew, was well patrolled and not a place to be caught without the proper permissions. Past Luring, the cut pass turned away deeper into the mountains away from the Unbreaking, where the mountain lords had other communities that mined precious metals and gems somewhere far below the surface in the dark.

Brody shuddered. Staring over the precipice he was struck by its beauty. The spray was frigid and soaking him to the bone as he stood there, but he knew that many of the villagers that he had grown up with and that had left Luring had ended up in those mines. But here the trees growing out of the cliff face across the river were so green and the water was swirling white and clear blue. The fresh air, the crying hawk overhead all reminded Brody that he was still lucky to be who he was, and that not having had anywhere else to go, might not have been so bad. He breathed in the fresh, wet air and smiled a rare smile before he was brought back to his senses by someone calling his name.

"Brody! Damn you! Get out here! I can't do this by myself!"

Brody could barely hear his friend over the roaring waters though Finn was yelling at his loudest. He was already navigating carefully the rocks from the other side that would lead to their net. Brody nodded and waved. He knew he looked foolish, but wanted to convey that he had heard his friend. Then he steeled up his courage and moved his right foot onto a slick rock below the surface of the water.

As they made their way across, each step was a critical moment. The water seemed personally offended by their refusal to follow it to the waiting river below, and each footfall was tried dearly. Brody only had to make it about ten feet, and no where near the center of the falls, but even that much was treacherous. He knew the world dropped straight into mist-sprayed void to his left, but he didn't dare look down. There was no comfort to be had from his right either, as the lake that was so beautiful to him moments before, seemed an angry stampede to him now.

He glanced up occasionally to see his friend's progress. Finn had to go farther, but the curve of the mountain on his side made the water less fierce until his last five feet. Off behind Finn and up the bank a little way, he could see Rista in the boat watching them anxiously, and for the first time he wondered how in the world they thought they were going to get a full net over to where she was.

Finn reached the larger rock protruding out of the water on the edge of the falls proper where he had tied his end of the net. Brody watched with trepidation as his friend eased himself down so that he was able to grasp it. Brody had two more steps to go. He could see his own knot sticking up out of the water on an ancient twisted trunk that had served as his choice of anchor yesterday. Brody made a careful first step and heard: "WOOOOOOOOOOHOOOOOOOO!"

The sound of Finn's cry caused him to slip momentarily and he had to crouch quickly with an ungainly jerk to catch himself with his hands. Despite the frigid chill, sweat beaded up on his scarred face from the near fall.

"What the hell did you do that for?!" he shouted at Finn angrily. He couldn't look up at him to see what was going on. He was caught in a terrible position with both hands down and his nose practically resting on his right foot with his left stretched painfully back behind him where it had slipped off its supporting rock. He choked on the thick spray of water he was fighting not to inhale.

"Sorry!" Finn yelled, "You OK?"

In truth, Brody wasn't sure how he'd get out of his predicament, but he was too terrified to say so out loud. It wouldn't take the water long to push him over from this position, and Finn was on the wrong side of the falls to help him.

"Please," he muttered to his foot, taking in water as he did, "Please, Father, Grandfather, somebody..."

He felt his body swaying in the current and couldn't find an inch of himself he thought he could safely move. The shadows darkened around him. He smelled leather and ale and sweat, though maybe his own. The water seemed to slow. The air seemed to still. In a moment he managed to kick his left foot off its rock to meet his right foot while thrusting his upper body into the air with one motion. He couldn't even remember deciding to do it. It was as if he'd been pushed.

He stood for a moment catching his breath, panic receding into his chest, his heart pounding in his ears. And as suddenly as it started, the silence and shadows lifted and the deafening noise of the falls and the faint noise of his friend's shouts over them came rushing back, nearly knocking him over again. He stood there panting for several slow seconds before he looked up.

One more step and he was fifteen feet from Finn, perched right at the mouth of the small space all that angry water was churned into before finding freedom. Making it this far he looked over at Finn and gasped a relieved smile. Finn wasn't smiling back.

Still crouched by his own end of the net, Finn's face was as white as the river spray, horror etched across his features. Brody startled and chanced a look behind him to see what had upset Finn so.

"Finn?" he shouted.

Finn blinked and regarded Brody with clear fear in his eyes.

"What was that?" he finally choked out.

Brody frowned. "What was what?"

"That! What did you DO?"

"What do you mean? You yelled. I nearly fell over the edge, but I didn't. Thankfully. What's the matter?"

Finn stared at him a moment longer then composed himself.

"Help me here then," he said shakily, "I yelled because we did it!" Excitement was returning to his voice, "This damn thing's full and heavy!"

Terror was giving way to his own growing excitement, Brody grinned heartily and crouched down to help. Sure enough, as they began to untie the net it writhed and wiggled and jerked and was quite heavy. Both men had to sit on their respective rocks to hoist their catch above the edge so they could see. Joy flooded them both as they saw their net teeming with as much fish in one catch as they had gotten all summer. Both struggled with their balance as they tried to hang on to the heavy net, hoisting it up between them and laughing like fools. A whooping sound reached their ears and they turned to see Rista standing in the boat, a triumphant fist in the air and they laughed even harder.

It took them the better part of an hour to figure out how to bundle the net up like a sack so that Finn could carry it back to the boat, and then to get back across to where their footing was more sure. Brody was still smiling the broadest smile he owned as he reached the comforting grasp of the rock wall and the muddy slope that would serve as his path home. He looked back and waited until he he saw his now slower-moving friend reach relative safety with their good fortune slung over his shoulder and still dragging the ground. Rista was being cautious in her approach despite her excitement, and Brody was glad to see it. Now if they could only get themselves all back safely, there would finally be something to celebrate after so long.

He allowed himself a moment again there on the edge of the world, where he could see out across the vast expanse of the river valley below, the beauty of the falls which no longer seemed angry but seemed instead to celebrate with him, the blue sky dotted with white fluffy clouds, the mountains like sentinels against every horizon. He didn't know what other places there might be in the world, but in that moment, he was satisfied with his own place in it. This was surely a view not everyone would ever have. He breathed in the awesomeness of it and scanned the vista.

Something then caught his eye. Along the ridge that his own path would become if he turned to follow the mountain out over the ravine, there was an odd metal glint coming from within a tangled bramble he could just make out. It appeared to be gold.

Brody looked back to his friend and his sister. They had safely reached one another. Even from this distance he could tell Rista was smiling as they pulled the full net into the little boat. It would take them a little while yet to make it to him. He looked back at the tangled mass and saw the glint of gold again.

Brody wasn't a greedy man. It was a pointless ambition in this part of the world. But he was a practical man, and traders did indeed traverse these mountains selling the wares that the locals couldn't provide for themselves. Mother's wool, smoked fish, rope and netting were the usual things they had to barter with, but

Brody was aware that gold, even a little of it, would afford food and supplies for several winters. He glanced back across the lake one more time making up his mind. Finn was just climbing into the skiff, Rista laughing at him as he was surely trodding on dying fish. Brody smiled again at the thought, then set off on his own course.

He had to cling carefully to the rock wall to keep his footing around the precarious bend. Once he cleared the corner, he was on slightly wider, somewhat drier perching, but still had to hug the mountain face until it curved again to run parallel to the river below. There the path, such as it was, became rocky and wide enough for a man to walk comfortably along if he watched his step. There was occasional scrub and loose rock up here, but once the mountain cut away from the falls it dried up quickly, becoming a very different terrain.

The ledge sloped fairly steeply. This wasn't used as a path typically, and Brody knew from the tales of the older men in the village who had been out this way before that at the far end, this ledge narrowed to nothing while still at least 30 feet from the valley floor and quite a long way from the top of the mountain, which also sloped downward from this point, but at a more leisurely pace. With his left hand sliding along dry, caked dirt covering the rock cliff he realized quickly that his normal ability to measure distance was unreliable up here, and the further he walked, the tangled mass didn't seem to be getting closer.

Yesterday he had gone farther from home than he'd ever been, traveling to the very edge of his own world. Today he'd trekked even farther. He was just considering turning around and giving up the pursuit when he finally saw the thing itself begin to loom larger. Brody looked down. At this point he was only about 75 feet up off of the valley floor, but he'd been walking now for probably half an hour.

"Brody!" Finn's voice came from far behind, a panic etched in the tone. Brody stopped dead in his tracks, guilt welling up in his chest. It should have occurred to him before now that Finn and Rista would fear the worst when they came to retrieve him and could not see him along the edge. It should have, but it hadn't. Maybe this *was* greed he thought to himself. That he would pursue a hint of gold without a thought for the feelings of his friends. What was he thinking?

But the other side of him reminded him. You were thinking, it suggested, of your family and what the reality of gold might mean for them. Bringing back a full net of fish AND even a tiny speck of gold would see them through the winter and into the next one at least. That task was all he thought about any more.

Brody stopped and waited for Finn, remorse written all over his face. Finn didn't appear angry as he approached. Instead he came cautiously, looking as if he feared Brody had lost his mind.

"Where are you going?" he asked with trepidation.

Brody dropped his shoulders and looked at his friend with sincere regret.

"I saw something, and it turned out to be further away than I originally thought. Forgive me. I thought I'd be back around in view before you got there."

The look on his friend's face wasn't much better.

"Look, I'm really sorry. Why are you looking at me like that?"

Finn finally reached him. He'd moved more quickly than Brody had, but still it must have taken him some 20 minutes or more. Finn's eyes hadn't left Brody's face and the worry projected from them had remained intense.

"What happened to you back there?" Finn asked at last, "When you slipped in the water?"

Taken aback by the question, it took Brody a moment to remember what Finn was referring to. He furrowed his brow.

"You yelled. You said 'woohoo' or something and it surprised me. I slipped. It took me a moment to recover, but I did. Why?"

Finn stood face to face with Brody making the latter all the more aware of how much bigger than he Finn really was. Here was, Brody remembered clearly, the main reason the superstitions of everyone else never turned into anything more unpleasant. TarFinn Kipp was the biggest and the best fighter. It had been said that if he'd wanted to, he could have run off and joined the King's Army. No one else in town had his build or his talent. Up here, on this tiny ledge, overlooking the very middle of nowhere, the difference between them was immense.

Finn looked at him suspiciously, and went on, "So nothing weird happened there while you were down? Nothing any different than just getting up?"

Brody looked into his friends' eyes. What had happened? He'd asked for help. He'd nearly fallen. And somehow, help had come. Had Finn seen or heard something? He felt comforted when Fletch would bark, but Finn looking at him as if he'd grown an extra head, that bothered him completely.

"I don't know what happened," he admitted truthfully, "I guess I thought about my father just when I thought I was going to fall, and it was like... I knew what to do. Everything seemed to get quiet, then I was up and it was OK. Why?" then he smiled and tried to blow it off, "Did I piss myself or something?"

Finn's face softened. His mouth became crooked, but not quite a smile. "That would have been less freaky," he said, "No, forget it. So why are we here?"

Brody turned and pointed. The crumpled mass of bramble or whatever it was stood just 20 feet away now. There was definitely something gold wrapped about it like a medallion, and there appeared to be other metal caught inside of it, too. Down at the very bottom of the mass, Brody now realized, was a large strange sword.

They stared at it for a moment. Brody had been so caught up in his own thoughts he hadn't really seen the thing clearly, but now it was a curiosity indeed. It looked like two masses of tangled vine, that were vaguely humanoid in shape. One appeared to be crouching over the other. The crouching figure had a gold medallion around what would be its neck. It had a huge lump where its back should have been if, indeed, it were thought to be facing the lower clump. There looked to be two plain, but long, battle-worn daggers lost in the tangle. The mass on the ground underneath the gaze of the first seemed to sit with legs flayed on top of a large strange-looking sword. Smaller lumpy brambles resting beside it and a singular vine that appeared to grow right out of the cliff that had the shape of a huge bow. Finn grabbed Brody's shoulder.

"Slowly," he whispered, "Just back away. Quickly."

He was trying to pull Brody back toward himself. The hand on Brody's shoulder was trembling.

Brody took a step back and turned to Finn. He knew what the other thinking. The Bramblemen lived on the cursed mountain and sometimes were known to venture west into the odd forests across the ravine from where they stood. But Brody had never heard of a sighting south of the river, as they were now. Nor had he heard of them bearing jewelry and weapons. All of this he pointed out to Finn, who calmed a little but was still very much on edge.

Brody turned back to the odd formation in front of him and crossed the last of the distance to it. He felt more secure, to have Finn Kipp behind him, without a doubt.

The two...things....were faceless and only vaguely humanoid in their shape, yet something about their pose and possessions made them feel like dried out, mummified corpses. Brody reached to touch one and felt his hand pulled away by Finn. He glanced back and Finn shook his head. Brody looked back at the two. He found himself empathizing with them as if they really had been people. Then he realized what had Finn so guarded. The weapons, the medallion...what if these *had* been people? What in this world could have done *this* to *people*?

The two men back-tracked a little way and talked in hushed voices as if speaking over the dead. Although up close it was easy to convince yourself that your eyes were playing tricks on you, from 15 feet back they clearly looked humanoid.

"Do you think they're real?" Brody asked quickly.

Finn wasn't really looking at him, but past him at the bramble lumps. He shrugged, but not so that he seemed unconcerned.

"Finn?"

Finn finally tore his eyes from what to him was clearly a horror to behold. He cleared his throat and spoke, his voice sounded raspy and quite unlike his own as if he might be holding tears out of his eyes.

"There's a legend," he began quietly, "That high on the Unbreaking are a tribe of Bramblemen that have a poison. The legend says that the land up there is forested not with trees but with petrified *people* that look like frozen Bramblemen themselves. I've heard the trappers tell those stories, but even if they were true..." here he paused and looked deeply and meaningfully at Brody, "What would they be doing down here?"

"More importantly, Finn. Are these Bramblemen or are they innocent travelers? And do these little leaves sprouting from them mean that they're...alive?"

They both looked back at the two sad piles of thorny vine. They were dry and dying, but still had leaves growing in the shade of their own interiors. As plants, at least, they were still living.

"Well," Finn pondered, "Officially sanctioned travelers come along the road. Bandits usually traverse the areas below where they can hide and still ambush the road. It's hard to imagine why someone would choose this route. Innocent? Hard to say, but probably not. Alive," he paused, the look of horror deepening on his face, "I hope not."

"They probably didn't deserve this," Brody returned to the pair and bent over to study them, "They look sweet. This one with the gold medallion looks like it...I mean he....or she I suppose," he looked thoughtfully at what was really very blobbish, "was trying to help...er....the other one. The one on the ground."

He looked at it more closely, and saw something peculiar tangled in the vines. In what would be the raised right hand of the standing figure, Brody saw a tiny gleam of glass. This time when he approached and reached for the figure, Finn didn't try to stop him.

Brody ducked his head carefully between them, struggling not to touch them. He had to look very close to see what was there. It appeared to be a small vial of a shiny sky blue liquid. It was already uncorked.

"This is gonna spill when we move them," he pointed out to Finn who was approaching much more slowly now.

"Move them? Who said anything about moving them?"

Brody pulled his head out and looked at Finn.

"You really think we should just leave them?"

"Brody, no offense, but do you really think there's anything we can do to help them? We may end up just like them for our trouble, and then who do you think will help us?"

Brody had to concede his point. What could they possibly do? What risk was he taking when his family needed him so much? He didn't want to be one of those people who just looked the other way when someone was in need. There were too many of them these days. But there were also so many in need, and he was already responsible for his portion of them. This might just be that point where drawing the line and realizing defeat were the nobler things to do. He looked at the gold medallion.

It was an odd shape. He'd never seen anything like it before. It was a continuous line that began and ended as straight lines pointing left, joined at a hoop at the bottom. It resembled nothing Brody could think of.

"What about this?' he asked Finn, "This could buy food and supplies for a long time to come. Shouldn't we at least try to get it?"

Finn looked suspiciously at it, then back at Brody.

"I should try," he said quietly, "Your family needs you."

Brody looked at his friend again as if he'd never seen him. Finn had lost his whole family five years ago. He lived alone. He helped Brody with everything, and it should have occurred to Brody before now that he thought of Brody's family as something of his own. He truly had no one else.

Brody tensed. He refused to think of his friend as expendable. It suddenly made the bramble-things more frightening than they had been. Besides, Brody mused, he was the one that was untrusted. If Finn weren't around, he might not be able to do anything for his family anymore. Brody shook his head.

"No, my family needs you, too, Finn. People trust you," Brody sighed and looked at the medallion. He reached a hand up and tried to pull it over the thing's head.

The bramble figure rocked when he tried. It was light-weight, like dried out vines. It was attached to the ground and to the wall of the cliff by...roots he guessed, but the rest wobbled with the effort of trying to pull the medallion clear. He realized just as he got the necklace free, that he had spilled the contents of the vial.

He jumped back as the blue liquid spiraled out unnaturally, weaving its way around the arm and down to the rest of the form like smoke. Brody and Finn stumbled over each other to get back from it, nearly losing their footing and going over the edge.

The smoky bluish substance engulfed the whole mass of brambles. For a moment it hung there as if unsure what to do next. Then as quickly as it had spilled, it dissipated into nothing. Brody held his breath, the gold medallion in his left hand cutting into his palm where he was squeezing it. The jumble of vines shuddered, softened and fell over. When it hit the ground, it was a girl. She moaned.

It took the two men a moment to realize what had happened. She was more pale than anyone they'd ever met, with the most golden blond hair they'd ever seen. Her clothes were strange, light and soft and were dyed in blues and greens, very unlike the undyed wool and heavier clothing of the local people. She wore a pack on her back that was bleached leather, with embroidery across the front and she carried a soft, gossamer looking blanket rolled beneath it. Two ordinary fighting daggers had fallen from her tangle as she collapsed, and she was still grasping the vial. She squirmed for a moment and her hair fell across her face. Her ears were pointed.

The locals had heard tales of elves, far away in the distant reaches of the world that would be forever alien to themselves, but they knew almost nothing about them. Their own local lords were well-known in their dislike for other races, and only humans ever had official sanction in the highland kingdom. Elves were believed to deal in magic, and all magic was evil according to those that claimed to know. What would an elf be doing here?

Brody moved over to her. She was beautiful, angelic. He'd never seen anyone like her at all. Even the traders and trappers, the guards and tax collectors that occasionally came through were not as unique and amazing in their differences as this girl was. His people had deeply tanned, wood-brown skin. Their hair grew in shades of brown as did their eyes. Their clothing was simple and practical. Their builds were sturdy.

This girl looked fragile and translucent. Her skin seemed to almost glow in the sunlight, except, Brody now realized with a start that tore him from his reverie, except where she was injured.

He moved over to her and brushed the hair from her face. She was unconscious, and a faint bruise was sprouting around her right eye and temple, on the wrong side of her head to have come from her fall just then. She also had a gaping wound across her midsection that looked like a claw mark and was beginning to bleed freely again. Her arms bore small but serious burns and her clothing was singed.

Finn was stepping carefully over her now, squeezing between Brody and the ledge. He was pulling off his own tunic and pressing it firmly into the bleeding wound.

"Quick, Brody, look and see if she has anything in her pack for bandages!"

Carefully Brody pulled her pack off of her delicate shoulders. The leather was soft and strange. He opened it and found a smaller pouch laying on top, made of the same soft bleached leather. Underneath were rolls of bandages. He moved the pouch carefully and it clinked like glass. Gently, he laid it in the dirt beside him and began to hand the bandages over to Finn. Underneath he could see more gear wrapped in other cloth, a roll of rope and a small lantern.

Finn lifted the girl's shirt to tend to her wounds. Brody blushed and looked away, his eyes falling on the little pouch he had removed from her bag. He remembered the clink and glanced at the other form, still petrified if that's what you'd call it, sitting sprawled against the cliff. He picked up and opened the pouch.

Inside it were other carefully wrapped vials. Two contained something that looked like watered-down blood. One contained something that looked more like smoke than liquid. There were several larger vials that appeared to only contain water and there were three more vials of blue liquid like the one Brody had spilled accidentally.

While Finn worked on bandaging the girl's wounds, Brody took out a small vial and eased himself over to the other figure. As a second thought, he pulled the last roll of bandaging out of the girls pack and held it at the ready. Judging by this one's posture, he reasoned to himself, it was the more badly injured. Finn had just enough time to look up and ask, "What are you doing?" before Brody uncorked the vial and poured it over the vines.

He leaped back as the smoky effect unfurled around the figure and the lumps beside it. A backpack, a quiver of strange arrows, and a large black bow revealed themselves first. Then a male figure with snow-white hair and skin that appeared burned black at every surface toppled over sideways from where he had sat. He was utterly still.

Both human men reached for him at once, expecting him to have been burned beyond the hope of care, but when they touched him they found his skin to be soft, his features unmangled. It was as if he had been dyed rather than burned. They pulled their hands away simultaneously in shock.

Then his blood began to seep through his equally curious clothing. A pool of blood was forming, too, under the side of his face on which he laying. Rolling him over they found that the right side of his face had been scraped deeply, nearly skinned, and that the wound had nearly claimed the entirety of his ear. It wasn't serious, except that it was bleeding much more freely than it should. His legs were also bleeding from two deep cuts across his thighs.

Finn and Brody bandaged the two as carefully as they could and then began the arduous journey of carrying back first the girl and then the male. It was nearing dusk by the time they managed to get both bodies around the edge of the mountain wall that formed the bowl containing Luring Lake and its little fishing village.

From there, Finn carried the girl over his shoulder, past the dangerous narrow muddy slope into the rapids and laid her on the bank once it was wide enough. Brody watched as Finn started to head back for him and the male elf waiting nearer the falls. Finn stopped and looked back. Brody realized Rista and their mother were headed toward him in his boat, Fletch leaning on the prow with his front legs, wagging and yapping to herald their arrival. Brody stood furthest away from them at the edge, clinging to the rock and holding up the burned-looking male sandwiched between himself and the cliff waiting for Finn's return. The white water was lapping at his heels and his footing wasn't good, but seeing the approach of the small craft gave him the sense of relief he needed to finish out his wait.

Finn finally reached him. Brody was exhausted and ached from his neck to his calves. The weight of his charge seemed to have grown exponentially as he had waited while Finn had loaded the girl into the skiff and explained briefly to the women what had been going on. Finn was clearly wearing out, too, but seemed to be holding up better than Brody, having the stronger frame of the two.

The male elf proved to be more solid than the female, but still not as heavy as a grown human man despite his impressive length. Finn carried him, slipping and stumbling and struggling for balance while Brody followed behind. His load was almost as much of a challenge carrying the elf's belongings: the backpack, bedroll, large strange sword, larger stranger bow and quiver. Finn fell into the water with his charge just short of the boat, but managed to grab hold. He and the black elf were pulled up by Rista and their mother, to the accompaniment of more barking. Brody flopped exhausted into the boat just behind him.

The little boat reeked of fish, bringing Brody back the tremendous sense of accomplishment from earlier in the day. He smiled sleepily to himself as he swayed with the motion of the boat, petting his little dog absentmindedly and watching his mother and Rista examine the curious medallion between them. Then he sat up and helped Finn row the whole strange load all the way home.

Chapter 2:

25th Day of the 11th Month, 4th Day of the Week, Pre-Dawn in Autumn
Kylarsday, Renets 25

Kierra

Kierra watched her breath coalescing in front of her in the chill of the autumn dusk. She could hear the stomping and clanging of the enemy army gathering in the clearing just beyond the tree-line as she waited with near-crippling dread, crouched in the dew-damp moss floor of the woodland rise waiting for her first battle to start. Thunder rumbled in the distance as if to echo the clamor of wagons and other foreign horrors on wheels the invading army had brought to unleash on them. How had her world come to this?

She glanced around her at the anxious faces of the woodland willowelves, clutching bows, peering through the gathering dark, waiting for the bloody chaos that longed to spring free from the tautly tense musculature of the army lying in wait all around them. Any second, the quiet of the forest would shatter and war would erupt like volcanic fire vomited as pure hate from the weapons and the anger of those that lingered in fear just on the edge of it. Overhead, the thunder grew louder as a soft drizzle of rain began to fall through the trees. How, Kierra wondered, had we come to this moment?

As the elves crept silently into their ambush positions, the loud machinery of the human army clanged, banged and rolled ahead of them just unseen, larger, stronger but more clumsy. The terrified determination locked in the jaws of the people she knew to every side of her was the only testimony she had left now that survival loomed on the horizon for any of them. She glanced to the trees. Already bowmen were carefully drawing silent death across their strings. Light crept trepidatiously under the horizon, peeking only pale light through the thick clouds as if the sun feared that it may not be safe to remain in the sky any longer.

But even as the night approached, the light changed unexpectedly.

Suddenly, instead of the last golden rays peering through the trees, a strange silver glow streaked across and above the canopy, as if the stars had suddenly fallen from the night sky through the storm clouds and into the forest, catching everyone's attention away from their quarry ahead. As everyone looked up the sky flashed with a bolt of lightning so bright that for several moments Kierra was blinded by it. The clap of thunder shook the forest floor, knocking her momentarily off balance as lights popped in front of her eyes.

Suddenly men were screaming around her. Kierra rolled over to her knees and clutched the wet dirt of the ground with her non-bow hand. She stumbled awkwardly to the nearest tree and pulled herself up, steadying her bow and trying to clear her eyes. The light around her had turned silver everywhere and it appeared as if an odd silvery light was streaking straight for her.

She tried to raise her bow. Around her were screams and odd gurgles and the crashing of trees. Thunder boomed through the forest shaking the ground and threatening to knock her off her feet again. As she leveled her bow at the light rushing toward her, she saw faces in it. The light seemed to split into a row of horses with many riders, all clutching bladed weapons she couldn't make out, and all made of a light that half blinded and half sickened her to look at. The faces were at once whole and then again rotted and putrid. She could almost see them and yet see the trees behind them.

As they charged her mercilessly and the sounds of thunder and screaming built to a torturous crescendo in her ears, Kierra dropped her bow and dove instead for the soft, wet, living moss of the forest floor at the feet of the ghostly attackers. She was a few seconds too late. She felt the sickening light pass through her flesh as her breath caught in the eerie stillness. Her body felt as if it were stuffed with dense cloth, and yet there was a sharp pain somewhere in her lower body where a blade that was somehow cold to her soul but not to her flesh had clearly touched her and slid up through her skin. She felt her shoulder hit the ground and then her hip and head. The ground was wet and not nearly as soft as she would have liked. She felt the trampling of aeons pass through her as the screaming and thundering shook her and grew faint. Tiredness, bone-deep, welled up in her like never before and she felt a connection to the rock beneath her that called to her like peace and sanctuary. She gave in.

Eventually, she awoke. In the distance she could still hear the strange ghostly screaming that indicated to her that the army of undead light, or whatever they were, were not altogether gone. The darkness of the night was broken by a light that was still pale and silvery, and the storm flashing and thundering overhead was dumping chill, stinging rain onto the muddy ground where she lay. She looked for help. She called out futilely into a suddenly calmed world. The underbrush and ivy failed to conceal the seemingly endless sea of broken, lifeless corpses strewn everywhere about her. None responded. As if in laughter, lightening flashed overhead.

The world spun around Kierra just as it seemed to fill with darkness. She clutched her still-bleeding left shoulder as tightly to her as she could and limped through the dark undergrowth of the once-familiar forest. She could not afford to keep bleeding freely. She'd left the bodies of her comrades lying strewn across the forest floor. She'd looked for signs of life among them, but had found none. She continued to stumble and limp through the dark forest, nausea running up to greet her with every dizzying step. Her dearest ambition at that moment was to lay down and sleep, just to close her eyes for a moment, but she knew she had to keep going. To rest now would be to lay down and die. A whole army decimated where it stood, with no warning, no rally of defense, no thought but to scream. The horrors of the early evening drowned her weary mind, puling her down and back.

She felt the wet, cold earth reach up to her bottom. She blinked and realized that she'd fallen. Putting her good arm out, she hoisted herself up with difficulty to an uneasy stand. Again the dark forest around her tilted and threatened to spin as it grew colder much more quickly than Kierra thought was natural.

There were caves, well-hidden and deep enough to give some warmth. She had used them before and knew they were not far, but even as she thought it, her weakening legs offered her doubt that she could make it even that far. Without help, the young recruit was not going to live through the night. She thought of abandoning her pack and gear, but she feared that without supplies, she'd just die anyway.

She could see the bodies laying all around her, just as they had when she'd struggled up out of the bush where she'd fallen, all hacked down by a quick misty dusk and the sounds of ghostly horsemen. She could no longer even see the trees, just the dead, as if she were wandering about in a field of felled soldiers. She closed her eyes. She had to clear her head enough to stop seeing the corpses. She left them behind; it had to have been a quarter of a mile at least.

She opened her eyes, refusing to look down, and tripped. Hitting the ground hard, she felt her ankle twist beneath her weight and crumple under her. The pain reached to her knee, as she looked back and stared into the eyes of the corpse she'd tripped over. It was lying behind her, and not at all in her head.

Shocked she looked around. The scene was familiar and terrible, but quickly Kierra realized that these were not the men and women she'd left behind. These were *human:* an army of the enemy hewn just as her own friends were. The strange haunted cavalry that destroyed the evening in a matter of moments, it had not come from this army. This was the forest clearing where they had been gathering their machinery for war. The sudden army of death had not been their magic. Then whose?

Kierra shuddered sending more pain through her badly wounded body and another dizzy spin through the world. She heard a groan and turned with the instincts of a cat ready to bolt. A human soldier lay face-down a mere 5 feet from her hand. He was stirring ever so slightly and sputtering breath. She could barely see him in the dark.

Without thinking, Kierra crawled to him, no longer able to get up onto her badly damaged leg, and grateful for a fellow living being in the growing cold and terror. Whatever had done this to them, decimated two armies, had itself not been living. She could still recall the moment of nothingness that had engulfed her when she fell through the body of one of the lifeless horsemen as he wounded her. The air was not cold, nor was it warm. As she sank through his tomb-still form there had been no sensation, no sound, no movement of air. Silent and without temperature, what had slaughtered her companions had been magic from the very grave itself.

But now, here at her fingertips, the man's body was warm and he moaned when she lay her hand on his back to check for the rise and fall of breath. A small pool of blood had soaked the ground near his groin, but it didn't look like death's ransom. He stirred under her touch, and painfully rolled over to look up at her.

At first Kierra assumed the terror in his eyes still lingered from his confrontation with their ghostly attackers. But quickly it dawned on her that they were staring each into the eyes of the enemy they'd gathered here to fight. She'd been looking for a fellow survivor. Might he kill her instead?

The moment lengthened between them and Kierra realized that he was waiting for her own killing blow to fall, too weak to defend himself against her. His brow was swollen and deeply purple, and blood was caked dry on his face. The wound to his left hip looked nearly deep enough to have been stopped by bone, and although he had not bled out, he had bled freely.

"Um," Kierra started as she clutched her bleeding, aching arm, "I'm not going to hurt you." It was awkward, but she hoped it was reassuring. Her next statement would have to be, "I think we may be the only survivors."

The human looked at her incredulously and Kierra waited patiently for him to recall all of the horror of the night, to end up where she was. But Kierra knew that this was a soldier of King Olgar, a human from the new regime of the Mountain peoples. King Olgar had been very clear in his directive. He felt that all non-humans were evil and needed to be wiped out. Now here was one of his many armies, well within the borders of the willowelves' own kingdom. This reality caught up with Kierra and she stumbled backward two steps and fell on her bottom in the mud.

The human managed to prop himself onto his elbows with difficulty. He surveyed the scene of horrendous lifelessness all around him with shock and terror on his face. Then he looked back at Kierra, the young willowelf sitting in the mud watching him. She swallowed.

A strange screeching on the wind in the distance made the wind around them suddenly feel unnaturally still. For a moment the rain seemed to stand still in its tracks before returning even harder. The ground was rumbling again. Kierra looked to the human in horror. He shared her dread.

"They're coming back, aren't they?" he stammered at her, looking around through the now-earnest rain as the distant noises seemed to rise and fall in every direction.

"There are caves," she told him, "Not far..."

"Where?" he was clamoring to his feet. He returned the sword that was lying beside him to a holster on his back. Kierra gulped; it was almost as large as she was. He hoisted his pack up to his shoulder painfully and stumbled backward before catching himself. Kierra was watching him in horror. His strength was astounding. Willowelves were lithe and fast, but she could no more lift that sword than she could uproot a tree.

He looked down at her expectantly, the sounds around them growing.

She felt the rain dripping off of her nose, inwardly laughing at the fact that only moments before it was he that was waiting for her killing blow to fall.

"I can't walk," she admitted, admiring the wound to his hip and his ungainly, graceless, but continued ability to stand and move.

He looked behind him as if they might be ambushed and hobbled over to her. She instinctively recoiled.

"I'm not going to hurt you either," the words were a struggle for him. She looked into his face and could see that his pupils were uneven. He offered her a hand and she took it.

The pain that seared through her injured leg reached all the way to the underside of her injured left arm, even though she had not dared to try to put weight on it. He nudged his own good leg under her bad one and draped her bad arm around his neck. Kierra didn't protest. His body was more solid than any living thing she'd ever touched, like a tree turned to flesh. It was frightening.

"Which way?"

She pointed.

They lurched, and stumbled. Several times Kierra reached out her free hand to block a tree before they ran into it. Between injury, confusion, weight and his poor human reflexes, their journey was ungainly and painful and slow. Underbrush tangled his feet. Branches slashed into their faces. At least once, when they fell, the large human actually fell on top of Kierra, knocking all of the air out of her lungs.

By this point, though, she could see the first of the large rocks jetting out of the forest floor. They'd passed the field the humans had hoped to use as a battlefield and had reentered the woods on the far side where the trees were more sparse and the forest floor more scraggly with low scrub and thorns and berry bushes. Leaning away from them, like a large shy playmate guarding its toy, there jutted a huge bolder of granite from the dirt and rock of the moss strewn carpet fifty feet from them. Kierra knew that the toy it guarded contained the first and smallest of a series of caves in this part of the woods.

It wasn't too soon. The air was turning silvered. The screaming was growing louder, although this time, the unnatural screeching screams were not being drowned out by the screams of Kierra's own comrades. She could hear a strange, almost melodic, mournful sound to the pitch of the noise of death that was rising up again around them.

Kierra felt the human man lurch up off of her and hoist her up from her midsection.

"Shelter!" he yelled, his voice nearly being drowned out now, "Where is shelter?"

Kierra pointed to the jutting rock, "Climb the back of that thing. You see how it twists toward the front about halfway up? That ledge leads to a small cave opening."

He jerked forward, Kierra tucked under one arm like baggage. When he reached the rock, he flung her up onto it as carefully but as quickly as he could. The light was growing bright behind them. Kierra crawled with her two good limbs, dragging her bad leg and own small pack and weapons with elven alacrity around to the front of the cave, her new companion just behind her. She slid into its shallow mouth and reached out to pull him on top of her. The slant of the rocky hole allowed him to slide in freely and he stopped himself from landing on her again by bracing himself against the far wall. The cave, such as it was, was barely more than a tomb for the two of them, and could only have fit one or two more people, and then only if they were very intimate.

Kierra watched in horror over the man's shoulder as the ghostly army sped past behind him. She clutched his shoulders and pulled him in closer to her, hoping to keep his back away from their raised lances and blades. They were made of light and smoke and cold it seemed, and the expressions on what remained of their faces were gleeful, almost joyous. But Kierra knew that their touch was solid and that what they left behind was not something to be celebrated.

She looked into the human eyes that were directly in front of her. They reflected her fear and pain back at her like mirrors to her soul. She gripped his shirt more tightly, closed her eyes, and laid her head against his chest. She felt him lay his own head down against the rock floor of the small cave. And then she felt his upper arm wrap around her and hold her closer to him in a gentle embrace. Kierra began to weep.

Several long moments passed between them and the noise grew fainter outside again.

"What's your name?" she heard the gruff voice near her ear ask her.

"Kierra," she whispered into his filthy tunic.

"What?" he pulled slightly away and looked up at her. His pupils seemed to have worked themselves out somewhat, but his eyes were bloodshot and one was swollen. The man had been trying to adjust himself more onto his back in the last several minutes, too, and Kierra realized that he'd fallen into the cave laying on his damaged hip.

Kierra pulled away and tried to help him make room to get off of his wound, which was bleeding again.

"Kierra," she answered again, "Kee-aira, and you need to get off that hip..."

"I know," he groaned, and began to relieve himself of his pack and, to Kierra's mind, ridiculously huge weapon, so that he could roll over onto his back. He glanced out of the cave opening to where the ghostly horsemen had passed again just moments before. All of the plants looked withered and suddenly sick.

Kierra was pulling bandages and healing herbs out of her own bag and wondering if the same herbs that her people used to treat wounds were even appropriate for a human, but she assumed they were. Despite what seemed at times like insurmountable differences between them, Kierra was starting to suspect they weren't as different as they might have guessed.

"What about you?" she asked. He looked back at her, and noticed what she was getting out, "What are you called?"

"Keen," said Keen, "And it looks like there's a stream down there. You think we have time to fill waterskins before those things come back?"

Kierra looked at him. His lips looked parched. She offered him her water which he took gratefully and drank sparingly, "Thank you."

He looked at her guilty, "We'd been marching all day. I'd run out."

She cocked an eyebrow at him, wanting very much to point out that if they had not been invading her country, he could have avoided that particular difficulty. She left it alone.

Keen handed the waterskin back and looked back out toward the fresh stream twinkling innocently in the full moonlight, but thunder rumbled overhead again and Keen smiled, "Even better."

Keen set about to rigging a rain catching canister using a round tin container he was carrying for this purpose, while Kierra tried to tend to her own wounds and then, finally to his. She cleaned his head wound with rags she soaked in the rain that was pouring out of the sky again, and wrapped it in herb-soaked bandages, which apparently seemed odd to him, but which he let her do. He was much less inclined to let her see his damaged hip, but after he slipped out into the rain to clean it up himself, he came hobbling back with his pants barely pulled back on admitting that the wound would indeed need to be sewn shut.

With the rain now concealing the moon, Kierra had to light a small lantern, even with her elf eyes, to have a hope of seeing what she was doing now. His hip had sustained a really very deep wound, and Kierra was quite sure that an elf would not have rebounded from the blood loss from a wound like this like Keen had. She had heard other elves speak with fear about how hardy and resilient, and therefore hard to kill, humans were, but seeing it this clearly was daunting. It was nicer to not be Keen's enemy.

She sewed his wound shut and giggled to herself as he blushed almost as much as he grimaced from the pain. He marveled to her about how quick and neat she'd been.

"Elf," she answered him. Darn right, she thought, we may be more frail, but we're fast with reflexes you can't hope to match. It's the only way we can ever stand up to people like you. Another part of her, though, that was softening to him, thought, but I wish we didn't have to. You don't seem so bad.

The world outside turned silver again, and the now-familiar screeching began to return. Dread filled Keen's face as he looked into Kierra's. He reached quickly for his nearly full rain water container, pulling it into the shelter and replacing its cork. The two of them huddled into the back of the cave, and Kierra realized that Keen's pants were still not fully back up around his waist. She put her head on his shoulder and tried not to laugh. Here in this shared nightmare, Keen was no longer frightening.

They began to realize that they may be trapped for an unknown amount of time in a very small space. After this third pass of the deadly undead army, Kierra and Keen took inventory of their shared supplies. Using Keen's rain catcher and their two waterskins, they would be able to store a good supply of water overnight. Between them, if they were careful, they could probably survive up to four days on the rations they were carrying. Kierra thought they should be able to survive a week, but Keen clearly needed to eat more than she did.

Their shelter was small. They could do little more than sit or lay down. Keen was carrying some small pieces of charcoal they could use to make a low light, low heat fire on which to cook if they could catch anything, and Kierra knew she was quite good with her bow, but they needed to be able to anticipate the time they had between the waves of ghostly undeath before she could venture out to hunt at all. Certainly, they hoped the nightmare they were caught in would end by morning, but they had already realized by this point that it would be foolish to make that assumption.

It was Keen who noticed that each time the army rode by it was larger. It was a somber recognition, but both feared that it was swelling with the fresh victims of each new successful ride. Kierra tried not to think about the people she had known who had just earlier that evening been breaking camp with her in a pre-dusk fog that was threatening rain and war.

They laid out Keen's bedding closest to the wall and Kierra's next to him so that he would not roll over onto to her as a result of the slope of the cave floor in the night. They had thought to take turns sleeping, but both injured and trapped, with intermittent passings of an army of ghosts, they little thought they would be found by chance. Kierra knew, and she suspected Keen did, too, that they were probably making a mistake, but the truth was that they were both too exhausted to stay awake any longer by the time an uneasy darkness finally crept back into the forest after a fourth passing of ghosts brought an eerie and unnatural silence with it.

Kierra pulled her blanket over her freshly bandaged shoulder. She could feel the warmth and strength of Keen's body just behind her as she faced the pressing darkness of the forest beyond the cave opening in front of her. Their packs and gear were stacked like a wall along the front of her body up to her chest so she could just peer out from behind it. She had her weapons in front of her and knew Keen's were behind him against the wall. She felt him put his arm around her. She hadn't expected that, but it was warm and friendly and she didn't protest. In fact, she was really grateful. She leaned back against him and reached up and grabbed his hand against her chest. At that moment, she wasn't really sure that they weren't the only two living things left in the world. How much death had been spread by whatever this was that had happened? She couldn't lay here and think about that. She closed her eyes, and let the darkness and her own exhaustion take her.

The next couple of days passed in much the same vein. The very next day was the hardest, as injury and exhaustion peaked for both and grief and panic rose very close to the surface several times. Kierra was careful not to let her anger over the invasion by the humans itself come out at Keen, but at her most honest, she was only keeping it in check out of fear. In part, she still harbored fear that he might lash out at her in response. More and more, though, she was developing the simpler fear that he would turn away from her. She needed him, even wanted him, to stay more than she wanted to express any resentment at his nation.

But it gnawed at her. How much did he agree with his king? Would he do it again? When this was all over, would he, Keen, go back to trying to wipe out everything that she, Kierra, loved most in this world? She had to keep pushing those thoughts aside and keep moving forward toward the next day, and then the next, as the rule of the ghostly mercenaries continued to linger over the forest. It may not matter, she chided herself. The things I love may not be there anymore for him to destroy...

For three days they made their food stretch as best they could. Kierra had spied a nest of rabbits at the foot of a tree just at the base of the rock, eight feet below the opening of their cave. Like themselves, the little things were hesitant to come out, even for food and water. She almost hated to end their lives knowing how it felt to be crouching in a hole fearing the horrors that rode by several times an hour, hoping to survive death's onslaught of the forest. But Kierra knew she couldn't think like that. By the end of the third day, their rations were running low and those rabbits were their best chance of another meal. Her leg was just beginning to show any sign of healing at all, and not much at that. Her shoulder, however, was healing well enough for her to start thinking about the use of her bow.

Keen's face was beginning to look almost handsome, but Kierra wasn't sure if that was because the swelling was receding some or if it was just because she was becoming so accustomed to him.

His hip was no better, and she feared he might develop an infection in the wound, as deep and dirty as it was. She tried to help him keep it clean and the leg as straight as possible, but it obviously caused him significant pain and by their third day together, it seemed to be hurting him more instead of less. He wouldn't say so, though, and she didn't ask. He seemed to feel the need to be a provider and caretaker for the pair, and didn't like to admit to his woundedness. Kierra found it strange, but tried not to offend him. She wondered if he thought of her as child-like because she was smaller than he himself was, but, then, he didn't talk to her like a child, so she brushed that thought aside. Not an elf, she kept reminding herself. Just not an elf.

Her own left leg was cut along its outer length. The wound wasn't deep, but it was long and had been a hard blow that had knocked her leg crookedly under her as she fell. The muscles in her upper thigh and the joints of her knee and ankle all burned and ached and much of the leg was badly bruised and swollen. Still, it didn't seem to be broken and Kierra hadn't lost a lot of blood, so she followed Keen's lead and tried not to complain or ask for too much help. She assumed that was the expectation of his culture, and she was OK pushing on. They needed to be doing that anyway. He was sweet, though, and seemed willing to help her more than he wanted help for himself. Maybe he, too, was realizing that her way of dealing with injury was different. She was curious about him, but didn't know how to talk to him without offending him, and she was so scared of chasing him away.

So it was on that third day in the evening as they were eating a second meal that Kierra brought up the idea of hunting in the morning.

"Hunting? Is your leg up to that? You'd only have like fifteen or twenty minutes AT MOST!" Keen was incredulous.

"I won't need it," Kierra assured him, "There's a rabbit hole I've been watching. This morning they came out for water just before dawn, right after the ghosts went by. I'm assuming they'll do it again tomorrow, and I'll just have my bow ready this time. It's just a brace, a pair, but we can't cook much more than that up here anyway. I'll climb down and get them. It won't take more than five minutes. The other thing..." Kierra was watching him. He seemed surprised. His perception in the dark was not what hers was, and she was starting to think she might be making him feel bad, but then woodland living was what she was born and bred for, so she couldn't help being gifted at it, "The other thing is that the rain hasn't been as prolific today, and we might want to consider trying to get down to the creek..."

He nodded, "We'll need the extra water for stew if we're going to make rabbit meat stretch..." He was glancing out toward the stream. Kierra followed his gaze. She suspected that he wanted to volunteer to be helpful, but they both knew that even injured, she was fastest, so she cut him off, "I'll go." He looked crestfallen, but nodded. She added, "You be ready with those weird charcoal briquette things so you can cook these things. She smiled at him. She had hoped to help him feel useful, but the look he was giving her told her that he was uncomfortable. She grimaced at him. She didn't know what to say. His dilemmas didn't make sense to her.

That night Kierra lay awake, long after she should have been asleep, worrying about her relationship with Keen, which seemed a strange thing to be doing even to her. He was laying behind her in his usual position, his warm, strong body supporting her smaller, more frail one. His arm was draped protectively over her, and she was grateful for his living presence and his warmth. The autumn night air was cold in the forest, and her healing body seemed to be more prone to its chill. More than that, his company, his steady breathing, his reassuring presence, felt like hope made manifest in some solid rock-like form that she could cling to in her desperation. She needed him. She wanted more than anything for him to need her in return. She didn't want to make him feel unwanted or less than useful. She understood deep in her being that they both needed a sense of good spirit to survive this terror. She resolved to get past the food shortage, and then to try to figure out how to help Keen find his spirit. She smiled to herself. She grasped his hand and felt him squeeze hers back. He was also awake. Don't worry, friend, she thought. We're going to make it through this.

But the next morning didn't go quite as she had planned. The ghostly army rode by just as the rabbits were venturing out, which ruined Kierra's hunting plans. Worse, she'd been perched just outside the cave mouth when they came and had jerked suddenly back inside, re-injuring her shoulder somewhat. Although by evening her shoulder was better, they were also using the last of their food which made her rabbit-hunting plans for the following morning a more desperate proposition.

Keen had been kind in caring for her damaged shoulder. He seemed more willing to look after her injuries than to have her look after his. It was a little strange, and she didn't how she felt about it. Did he think she'd hurt him? Surely after everything they'd already been through together he knew better than that.

Kierra spent most of that evening watching the rabbit hole for any sign of movement, hoping the little morsels would venture out for an evening forest stroll, but no such luck. They were indeed going to have to bank on a last minute successful morning hunt. Keen seemed to be watching Kierra as she watched the rabbits. She would dearly love to have known what he was thinking about her, but she didn't dare ask. She was too afraid that he still thought the same kinds of things that all of his kind seemed to think about elves. At this point, she simply had to trust him. She had no choice.

That night, laying in his arms and drifting off to sleep, she reassured herself. If he meant me any harm, she thought, surely I wouldn't have made it through the night many times over by now. And with that passing thought, she agreed to let go of her paranoia about him. After all, he'd really been nothing but nice to her. He watched her strangely at times, yes. He seemed uncomfortable with her doing things for him, yes. But he'd been nothing but nice, and truly, he'd saved her life.

Jesp

"Sorry I'm late," the old groundskeeper stammered, wringing his hands as he walked, "The Lord Librarian needed me this afternoon. He's been worrying me so."

"Anything interesting?" Jesp asked, doubting it would be. She rode along, perched on Harold's shoulder.

"'Fraid it might be," he answered, nervously glancing around the garden, "Can't say, of course...none of my business really..." the old man trailed off.

Jesp frowned. The old human man had been the groundskeeper at the library since he inherited the job from his own grandfather as a teenage boy. Probably no one knew the place better than old Harold did. His job was very secure, since neither the faeries nor the elves would let the other hold the position, the compromise that was Harold's family line had helped keep the fragile peace for centuries now. The story was that an ancestor of Harold's, barely a man himself, had broken up what was about to come to war between the two over who had the right to keep up the Garden. He did this by pointing out that he'd taken care of it while they were fighting. Of course that wasn't everything, the treaties that comprised the peace between the Garden Fae and the Morrowelves probably took up their own dusty chamber in the library. Jesp didn't care much. She liked the elves more or less, at least she liked the guards. She tried not to think about the ones *inside* the building. They were too creepy: hunched, silent, pale and as dusty as the books they dwelled on. It was foreign in the extreme to a faerie that anyone would spend so much time indoors. Of course, Jesp couldn't read, so the lure of books was completely beyond her.

But as the only child of two of the Garden's gardeners, Jesp liked Harold. His shoulders were broad and comfortable. He didn't try to impress with big words and academic rambling. He cared about the Garden and didn't mind when faelings played in dancing circles around his nose or in his old boots. It was a thoughtful man, Jesp thought, that always checked his boots for faerie children before slipping them on.

The cobbled path wove itself lazily along the river. The trees that reached lovingly over it protected it from both the sun and the threats that lay across the seemingly innocuous waters. There was a faint humming coming from all around, a tune just out of earshot. The air was filled with the gentle fragrance of whatever ancient breed of flower grew in the vines, hugging the old trees like lovers. The Garden was its own magic, and had a starkly different feel than the straight lines and high walls of the Library itself. The beauty of the Garden was in its unkept *feel* even though it was, in fact, kept very well.

Lore in this part of the world had it that the trees were sprouted from old wand wood, when magic was everywhere and the peoples of the world were unafraid to wield it. It was believed, also that the fae races sprung out of it and still inhabited its strongest domains. Funny how all the boys Jesp had grown up with seemed to have a different idea of where future faeries should come from, she thought to herself.

It was also said that the elven races had been split apart by magic: the same magic that seeped up out of the very land and sprouted new faeries. That superstition was at the root of the tension between those races, according to these same wise folklorists, rarely felt except in the separation they maintained from one another. Even in such close proximity as the Garden and the Library, they had very little to do with each other.

Harold crossed off of the path and into the Garden proper. The grass was neatly shorn, the flower beds carefully weeded, but none of it had a manicured or "designed" feel to it. Trees grew at odd angles, flowers sprouted where they wanted to, and junipers and azaleas competed for attention in unruly clumps everywhere.

And everywhere faeries flitted in and out of the leaves, sat on flowers and ringed the trees. Faeries didn't live in dusty old brick buildings, and didn't understand why the elves did. They wove platform decks and bowl-like umbrellas out of the softest vines, hidden deep in the underbrush, behind thorny branches, or nestled in the most overgrown trees. Jesp and her parents were quite comfortable at night sleeping in their old juniper bush, and Harold graciously kept the poison ivy out of it, without disrupting anything. Harold was good for the Garden.

Evening was settling around them bringing with it chilling breezes off the river. Cold always seemed to come from that direction. So did dark. As the sun was setting in the west now, shadows seemed to rise from everywhere across the river, to the east. Jesp shuddered.

Harold had come straight through the heart of the Garden and cut back left toward the road again.

"Over here?" he asked Jesp.

"Yes, just there," Jesp answered pointing to an area of disturbed ground and rocks just at the edge of a flower bed where someone or something had been digging. "We need to know if you did that," she informed the old man.

Harold knelt carefully by the disrupted ground so as not to dislodge his passenger. He looked carefully at the freshly dug hole and furrowed his brow.

"Me?" he said at last, "I wouldn't have left this mess."

"Well, we thought if you'd been called away for something and hadn't gotten back to it yet..."

"No way. I don't do no digging in the autumn," he hesitated, chewing on his tongue. He lowered his voice to a whisper, "Did they find anything?"

"No," Jesp whispered back, "This plot is one of the decoys, but it's the fourth decoy that's been disturbed in a month."

"The fourth?!" Harold exclaimed out loud, causing Jesp to slip. She caught herself on her light wings and landed back on Harold's shoulder as he stammered apologies, "Why didn't anyone tell me?"

"Now, *that* I don't know," Jesp admitted though she suspected strongly that no one had taken the others seriously since they had been put back nicely, "But this one happened in a hurry by the looks of it."

Harold breathed in deeply and started chewing again. Jesp couldn't follow him to wherever his thoughts were leading him, but she smelled trouble, and knew he smelled it, too.

"I'll leave you to it, then," Jesp said after a few long moments, "I've got a watch to get to."

Harold said nothing, but nodded, and Jesp flew off and up into the trees.

A single elven guard marched along the road ignoring the faerie music and the company, her blond hair flowing behind her in the gentle early evening breeze, lost in her own thoughts. Jesp watched her, unseen from above, musing over her own speculations at the elf's thoughts. She snorted quietly to herself when the elf tripped over an archaic root protruding through the roadway. She didn't mean to resent the elf, but resent her she did.

Jesp sat high on her perch among the branches overreaching the path and watched the elf disappear north. The second guard on last evening watch would be headed this way shortly, then. Jesp sighed. If that girl, the one who watched her captain so dreamily rather than attending to her duties, was on watch this evening, then the next guard Jesp would see would be the captain of the Tower guard. Jesp admired him for taking a lowly river patrol shift with his other duties.

As the crisp, clean young captain marched proudly into sight heading south, she overcame the urge once again to fly down to him and join him on his patrol. Her wings fluttered nervously behind her as she leaned in to see him more closely in the growing dark. Well, not him, but his weapons. He had a beautiful sword swaying on his belt that Jesp was sure had to be an heirloom. His shield, currently on his back, was blue and silver and painted with the Tower crest. He had a small hand crossbow bouncing off of his thigh on the far side of his belt and Jesp knew the quiver hung just below his shield. She hoisted her own small quiver higher onto her shoulder. Hers were much smaller, but hers were poisoned.

"There you are!"

The voice from behind and above her startled her out of her tree. She fell two inches before her autumn-colored wings caught her on the breeze and brought her back to the branch, face-to-face with her visitor.

"Kyrt!" she yelled, puffing her chest out in full annoyance, "What did you do that for?"

Below them, the captain paused and glanced up at the sound of angry, but tiny, voices. He shrugged and kept going. The faeries didn't notice.

"You know, sitting up here watching the elves isn't going to turn you into one," he teased.

She had nothing to say to that. She didn't expect him to understand, and she couldn't explain. She hated that particular rumor and was tired of hearing it. She got as much as she could get out of her glare before turning and flying off as fast as she could. In point of fact, she was pretty darn fast.

"Hey!" Kyrt called after her, "You're leaving your post!"

Jesp stopped, fluttering just over the heart of the garden. It wasn't like her to run from her post like that. She turned around.

At that moment, Kyrt speeding after her, slammed into her front side and both of them tumbled out of the air landing with a thwack on an old wisteria branch and breaking it clean in two. They both caught themselves in the air before they hit the ground. Kyrt was blushing furiously. Jesp glowered at him as if she could set him aflame.

"Sorry, Jesp, I..."

She didn't wait to hear what he had to say. She flew at top speed back to her tree. It was her job to watch the way across the river at night, and even though she often felt that the elves had this covered better than she did, her job was to raise the alarm in the Garden if ever anything should happen. The elves wouldn't bother to do that. They'd forgotten what a sacred site the Garden was, and they'd most certainly defend the library first if defense was ever needed.

Kyrt caught up to her and she refused to look at him. The stars were coming out overhead and twinkling merrily at her like they knew something amusing and weren't sharing. Jesp frowned at them.

"I guess you won't be happy to hear that I've volunteered to join you up here," Kyrt mentioned quietly.

Jesp did turn and look at him then, shock all over her face, "What do you mean?!"

"Well, since the recent disturbances in the gardens, the elders thought they ought to double the night watch. So....I'm your partner now!" He grinned brightly at her, but his eyes shown fear. Jesp stifled a laugh.

"Then next time I abandon my post, don't follow me," she teased. Kyrt relaxed.

"Yeah, OK. Good point."

"Do they really think anything's going to happen?"

"Well, someone's obviously been digging up the decoys," Kyrt reasoned.

Jesp nodded, though really this fact didn't bother her much. Faeries may not be known for their genius, but they were good at deviousness. Generations ago, several had learned how to read and write just so that they could plant false information in the books in the library. The elves, after all, seemed to think that anything, once written down, was indisputable fact. That's where the decoys came from. 8 different locations in the Garden were given credit for being the hiding place of 8 different "sources of faerie magic" or some other nonsense. But as far as any of the fae knew, the truth about the Garden wasn't written down anywhere.

"If they're digging up the decoys," Jesp reasoned, "Then they're relying on the books, which means they'll never get the truth."

Jesp hated little more than when people had their *facts* wrong. Faeries don't spring from magic. The elven races were not likely split by it. There was no ancient source of Fae magic buried in the Garden. Books weren't always correct. And, despite all the rumors, Jesp didn't secretly want to be an elf. These things bothered her. They bothered her because they were wrong and people believed them anyway.

"If they're digging up the decoys, then they're looking," Kyrt responded, "And we all know how dangerous *that* could be. What if the real information *is* in that Library somewhere?"

"I doubt it."

"Why?"

"Cuz...only the faeries know, and we're not stupid enough to write it down."

Kyrt nodded, but he looked worried. He paused, clearly considering something. When he looked back at Jesp, his gaze was more playful.

"Look, everyone says you want to be an elf. But...do you?"

"No," she insisted.

"So, what is it then? Maybe I'd like it, too. Then at least you'd have company."

He grinned at her. She considered him for a moment. Did she really want his company? She exhaled, a hint of exasperation in her breath. Her parents were obviously aware that faeries didn't spring up out of magic places. They kept encouraging her to spend more time with Kyrt. It annoyed Jesp, but at least he wasn't as bad as some of the others.

"I just want to join the tower guard," she confessed.

Kyrt frowned at her, watching her intently.

"Why do you care?" she asked him, looking away and then turning back to hear his answer.

Kyrt didn't have a good answer for that one. He bit his lip nervously. It made Jesp chuckle despite herself. He smiled back.

"I guess, it's just, well, you're not like everybody else. And, and..." he paused and watched her for the glare. Jesp realized it had faltered. "And, I like that. You're just not boring....OK chasing you around when you're in a tiff isn't exactly fun...." he rambled then caught himself, realizing he wasn't heading in the right direction. He looked back at her for a clue as to how he was doing.

Jesp watched him. Words weren't her strong suit. And she didn't know how to tell him nicely that she wasn't into boys right now. The truth was, she was into *weapons*. Weapons she couldn't wield. Shiny, bladed weapons and painted shields. To Jesp, they were better than flowers or jewelry, and certainly better than boys.

She turned away, staring across at the darkness of the river, "But I can't join the tower guard, so it doesn't matter."

"Why can't you?" he asked innocently, but Jesp stared at him as if he'd just produced a baby troll.

"Uh...I'm a little *small*," she informed him, "And, in case the fact has eluded you somehow, they only let *elves* in. And despite popular misinformation, I do not want to be an elf!"

"Do you want my opinion?" he asked earnestly.

"Not really."

Silence. She didn't expect that. She expected him to keep on going.

She stared a moment longer and caved in, "Oh all right, what's your opinion?"

There seemed to be some sort of commotion taking place at the end of the road, near the tower. Jesp and Kyrt ignored it.

"They'd be lucky to have you, and you should ask. After all, I don't think any faerie's ever tried. How do you know what they'll say?"

The commotion was getting louder and several guards were running in and out of the library tower. Jesp considered the commotion for a moment, watching for a cue that she needed to react, too.

"Or start your own Garden Guard."

Jesp snapped at that point, "We're *faeries* Kyrt! What the crap kind of guard unit would *that* be?"

"Well, hopefully not one that sits in the trees all day moping over passing elves. You want to live this life? Then find a way to live it, because you're not really doing anything this way but feeling sorry for yourself!"

Jesp stared at him open mouthed. She knew he'd finished a little more angrily than he intended, but she couldn't argue with him. Then it hit her.

"You already knew, didn't you?"

"What do you mean?"

"You already knew what I was going to say."

He sighed. "I don't know how much of a warrior you'll make, Jesp, but you'd make any lookout proud... I figured it out."

She paused and considered this, "How?"

He blushed, but her eyes bore into him and he confessed, "I've been watching you."

GONG

A loud horrible bell noise split the night and nearly unseated the two faeries.

GONG

The elven guard that had just come off shift came running back into the grounds.

GONG

"GO!" Jesp yelled at Kyrt, "Alert the Garden!"

"You think they can't hear that?!"

GONG

"GO!"

"What're you going to do?"

"See what's happening!"

GONG

Kyrt flew off and the ringing silence that fell over all the grounds was more deafening than the bell. Jesp pulled her crossbow over one shoulder and tightened her quiver on the other. Then she flew off at an alarmingly fast rate straight for the Librarian's tower. People were shouting and rushing around. The strict quiet and order of the Library was gone. Scholars and students were filing out of the main Library building and main tower in complete chaos. Pandemonium reigned and no one seemed to know what was going on.

Jesp wasn't going to join the problem. It was obvious at a glance, that no one down here had a clue in this world. Torches were being lit in the darkness and in the wandering crowd they gave the impression that the base of the small tower was on fire. Jesp was about 20 feet over their heads and had been completely unnoticed. She looked up at the tower. This was the smaller tower, 80 feet high and brick. It was the official residence of the Lord Librarian. Someone was screaming near the top. Jesp headed up.

The flickering, dancing lights coming from the windows seemed inappropriately jovial. As Jesp flew up the outside of the tower, she heard it more clearly "Help! Please help! Guards! Guards!"

Through the fifth floor window Jesp could see a mass of milling bodies accomplishing nothing. She flew through the window, over their heads and straight into the room beyond. It was a cluttered, book-filled room, but there was no doubt what the commotion was about. Ellerby, Lord Librarian was slumped over a desk, dead.

Jesp stared at his limp form for a moment, lost in shock. Ellerby was as much a stranger to her as anyone at the Library was, but he was someone the faeries were fond of. As a halfling, he hailed from a race that lived in more natural surroundings typically than morrowelves did. Although book-lovers and scientists as much as the morrowelves, halflings did not build big towers and windowless buildings to educate themselves in. As such, they had not lost touch with what Jesp would describe as "the more natural races" like the rest of the library staff had. Almost 6 years ago, when Ellerby first came to the library, he and his wife Lynhop would walk frequently in the Garden, and several of Jesp's kin had the opportunity to meet them.

A faint high-pitched noise reached Jesp's ears over the general chaotic din. A weeping in the corner of the room. Flying over and through the mass of elves, and even being swatted at, Jesp found a crumpled heap of a girl weeping in the corner. She was so small compared to the elves that she was going unnoticed and was in danger of being trampled.

Jesp landed quietly on the bookshelf beside her and spoke softly in her ear,

"Miss? You're going to get stepped on. Miss?"

The curly mop of dark hair was streaked with clumps of gray dust, although the young woman's clothes seemed tidy.

"Miss?"

A tear-streaked young face looked up and, noticing the faerie, startled.

Jesp knew at once who she was, although she couldn't have guessed her name. Lynhop had had twin girls and they looked just like her.

"You really should move out of here," Jesp said as gently as she could.

The young halfling looked around the room as if seeing the commotion for the first time. She nodded slowly, in a daze, and began to crawl out between the legs of milling elves. Jesp flew around and through them, being swatted several times, trying to keep up with the girl. She caught phrases as she went like "head bashed on the desk" and "must have known the killer," "definitely murder" and "just like 6 years ago." But Jesp was only halfway paying attention. Ellerby's shocked daughter had reached the landing and was heading up. Jesp flew straight up into the stairwell to follow her.

Up two flights of stairs to one of two doors on the top landing, Jesp followed the girl quietly. She entered the room behind her as the girl flopped face down on her bed and wept in earnest.

Jesp landed on the footboard and looked around. This was easily the messiest place she'd ever seen. She didn't particularly like things perfectly neat and tidy, unnatural she'd call it, but this place needed weeding, pruning, and some fragrance at least. Less books and more windows, Jesp thought, that's what it really needed.

Jesp hopped down onto the bed and tried not to enjoy herself too much walking (stumbling, bouncing, half-crawling) the length of the bed. It felt like walking on a cloud, and Jesp, who'd never seen the point of furniture, thought she'd like to have one. She reached the girl's head, stopped, and carefully wiped the grin off her face.

"Miss?"

The poor, red-eyed girl turned to look at her, then frowned.

"Are you supposed to be here?"

Jesp considered this a moment. She'd never had any desire, really, to come into the building, not unless it was going to be the armory she would see, but it had never occurred to her that she might not be allowed. Jesp typically considered the world to be open if you dared, but the elves probably didn't see it that way. They had big ownership issues.

Jesp shrugged and stayed her ground, though the bed was bouncing slightly with every move the halfling made and Jesp was privately enjoying the ride.

"Who are you?"

"Jesp," Jesp answered and then for clarification added, "I'm a friend of Harold's."

"Oh! Harold!"

The halfling girl flung herself off the bed and dove for something on the floor. This sent a wave of bounce up through the bed knocking Jesp up, into the air and into the wall with a thud. The room went dark. Jesp was vaguely aware of a spinning sensation and then...nothing.

*   *   *

The light was bright in her face and it was making Jesp's head pound. She was lying on something hard and her left wing was tangled in something. Her legs felt like they were made of lead and when she tried to roll over, she couldn't do it.

"Now, there, little one," the voice was Harold's, "Easy going. You've had a shock."

Jesp moved her hand to her aching head and tried to raise it up off of the hard wooden surface she was lying on. Her tangled wing throbbed, but remained tangled. She looked back at it and gasped.

"Yes, little one, it's broken, but it's not bad. I've splinted it with spider silk and it should heal fine. No flying for a few days, though, I'm afraid."

Jesp tried to focus on the old man. The light shining in her face seemed to be coming from beyond him, and she could only see his dark silhouette. There was someone else in the room, though, someone smaller. And then Jesp smelled smoke.

"Mmmmmm, smoke...." she mumbled. Her voice sounded far away to her.

"Yes, I'm afraid so. You're lucky to be alive. You both are. Luckily, Tollie here brought you out before the fire got to you."

Jesp sat up and tried desperately to focus. "Fire?" She searched her memory. Weeping halfling, fluffy bed, rock solid wall, nothing. That was what she remembered.

"All those elves wandering around with torches around the books," Tollie sobbed, "They burned the tower to the ground!"

'Well, not quite the ground," Harold sighed, "But close enough. Several guards didn't make it out. Horrible tragedy all around last night. If that huge storm hadn't rolled out of the south, more than the tower might've been lost"

Harold was shaking his head as he moved around the room. The room, finally, was coming into focus and Jesp tried to clear her head enough to take it in. She was laying on a long, narrow wooden table like a workbench. She had been laid on a clean rag on the only clear spot on the table which was littered with small bottles full of dried herbs and liquids, random tools, flower pots and potted plants. A table just across from hers and parallel to it held neatly stacked pots, pans, wooden dishes and cans of food. The space between the two was almost too narrow for Harold to move around comfortably, a thing which he was trying to do as he poured something that smelled like it had been in the sun too long into a little thimble from the other table.

"Now, here, drink this...slowly," he cautioned, handing her the thimble.

Jesp sniffed it and immediately felt dizzy again. She looked up at Harold like he was crazy.

"Trust me, Jesp. That'll make you right or make you hurt less or both." He smiled toothily.

Jesp looked down the length of the tables. At the foot of the other one there was a human-sized bed positioned along the wall. The Halfling was sitting on it. Her hair was a mess, her white blouse was smoky and gray and her neat blue skirt was singed. She was missing a boot, too, Jesp noticed since her little legs dangled far enough off the floor that Jesp could have stood on Kyrt's shoulders under them. There appeared to be a trundle on the floor next to it, with a disheveled blanket and a huge book laying on it. The open door was beyond it blazing sunlight into the room.

Jesp sipped at the horrid beverage. It made her feel instantly like she had tinkled all over her legs and feet: warm and wet. The sensation spread and the dizziness became...pleasant. She smiled at Harold who nodded.

"There you go. Back to new soon."

Harold moved to the end of Jesp's table and sat in one of two wooden chairs against the wall across from his bed and looked at Tollie.

"So, have you thought anymore?" he asked her as Jesp sipped and got drunk.

"All I do is think. What did he mean? And why didn't he just talk to me? I don't even know who to trust."

"Yes you do. You just want to trust someone closer, bigger, or more, but if you're honest with yourself you know who you can trust"

"You mean Tallie..." It wasn't a question.

"I know that empty room next to yours has caused you a lot of grief for the past two years. You and your sister may not see eye to eye on things..."

"She abandoned us!"

"But she wouldn't betray you, and that counts right now, Missy. Besides, I think you know why she left better than you want to..."

Jesp watched them in silence going over the events of the night in her head. The Garden, the decoys, her conversation with Harold...

"Harold?" Her voice sounded week and odd. Her head felt very very warm and slightly fuzzy. She looked at the thimble in her hands. It was half empty. She put it down.

Harold got up and came back to where Jesp was laying.

"Harold? You said the Lord Librarian had been worrying you yesterday afternoon. What was that about?"

Harold glanced back at the halfling girl before answering.

"We was just discussing that. Books," he said and placed his hands on his hips, looking very seriously at Jesp when he said it. Jesp resisted rolling her eyes. Of course, books. "Ellerby wanted me to keep some books out here for him. Tollie here was just looking at some of the titles, and I gotta tell ya, Jesp. This may be related to the reason we met earlier. Seems Ellerby knew someone was up to wantin' to know more about your kin and that there Garden."

Jesp looked across at Tollie and their eyes met. Hers were puffy and tear-stained. Jesp's were probably blood-shot. But both eyes contained needed questions and answers, and Jesp knew this journey had only just begun.

It was already afternoon before Jesp had woken up. Harold agreed to go and find her parents and, yes, Kyrt. Jesp regretted adding his name as soon as she had, but she knew he'd be worried. Harold told her Kyrt had raised the alarm in the Garden last night, and that anyone that tried to enter it after that got shot full of tiny needle-like arrows and sleeping poison. 6 elves and a cat were the total count, but the bottom line was that the faeries would protect that space when needed, even if they seemed frivolous most of the time.

While Harold was gone Jesp and Tollie had a quick conversation which amounted to neither wanting to tell the other what was going on first. Jesp wasn't about to tell *anyone* the secrets of the Garden, no offense meant. Harold only knew because an ancestor of his somewhere along the way found out and passed it on. Tollie didn't want to talk about the books or her sister, and otherwise she couldn't imagine what was happening.

When Harold came back, Kyrt was with him. Jesp tried to pretend she wasn't glad to see him. She thought she was starting to like Tollie until she uttered the phrase "You guys are cute together," causing Jesp to pretend to vomit. Kyrt laughed. Jesp smiled. She was drunk, after all.

Jesp's parents were in an elder meeting, so a faerie had to be sent to tell them the good news. They all had assumed that Jesp had been lost in the fire, since no one had seen her since. Also, another decoy had been dug up between the time that Kyrt and Jesp had gone on duty and Kyrt's raising the alarm in the Garden. Worse than that, he said, someone also dug somewhere closer to the truth.

"What truth?" Tollie asked innocently.

Harold cleared his throat loudly, gave the faeries a meaningful look, and announced that he would fetch supper. Tollie, Kyrt and Jesp waited in uncomfortable silence.

After a meal of berries and cream during which the human and the halfling also ate pork, Harold struck up a conspiratorial conversation that made Jesp choke.

"Here's the thing," he started, "I know I can trust all o ye, even if you don't know each other. So, I'm breakin' this kegger wide open. Old Ellerby wanted me to keep some books for him so his youngun here could get 'em to safety when needed. 'When needed' I thought then and I think now meant 'once I get killed.'"

At this pronouncement Tollie gasped audibly and set down her plate with a clang. "I'm sorry to be so blunt, but we really don't know what time's left."

"Left?" asked Kyrt. "What's that supposed to mean?"

"Truth in a nutshell is this," the old man went on, "Almost 6 years ago the Fire Titan flew over the sky east of here. Far east. People shrugged it off. Just a comet. But right after, the old Lord Librarian was murdered in his sleep. This chapper that thought he was going to get the post started making some odd changes, especially among the guards. But then the Council of Librarians suddenly brought in this halfling for the job instead. Ellerby was the only one they could find that was smarter than the other guy, and they had to prove someone was smarter to avoid giving that one the keys. The guy left, thankfully and things calmed down...for a bit."

Harold lit up a pipe. The smoke made Tollie and Jesp both cough and Jesp realized her lungs felt scratchy. She really had been in a fire. Harold apologized and put the pipe out, lighting a candle instead to chase away the gathering dark.

"I don't want to take long, cuz I think you all should leave tonight."

"Leave?" sputtered Jesp, "We can't leave! Someone's trying to dig up the Garden!"

"Yes," Harold sat back and studied Jesp for a while, "The Garden is no longer safe."

"Then we have to defend it," Kyrt insisted and Jesp felt a rush of gratitude towards him immediately. She felt like the world was losing sanity around her. You didn't leave when things were in danger. Not important things. The Garden needed protecting, not fleeing.

"The Garden has to be kept safe," Jesp insisted simply to Kyrt's nods.

"So does the library!" shrieked Tollie.

Harold shook his head no. "It's not the land or the building that needs protecting and it's neither the Library nor the Garden that folks wanna steal," he stated plainly. "To protect things that really matter, you'll have ta take 'em away from the places where they are, where folks know they are."

"Away?" Jesp interjected, "No one knows!"

"Someone knows, Jesp, or they wouldn't be digging."

"Knows what?" Tollie asked, "That the crown is there?"

A silence louder and deeper than the one left by the bell last night settled on the faeries. The room spun slightly for the drunk Jesp. *This can not be.*

Harold took in the silence, let it sink in for everybody.

"These places are only protected 'cause of what they contain," he went on, "And that's also what makes these places dangerous. You hafta get these things to safety..."

"What things?" Kyrt asked, "There's only one thing."

"In the Garden," Harold agreed, "The Library, however is another matter."

He looked meaningfully at Tollie whose eyes widened as if she'd been slapped, but in slow motion.

"But that was stolen! Erased! When we were betrayed 5 ½ years ago!"

Harold shook his head. "And you could not have gotten to it anyway. But your father has picked out books the traitor needs. And the Library no longer has them. The secrets of the Garden'll likewise hafta be rescued. Before they're stolen. I have a cart out back. I suggest strongly that you leave tonight."

Jesp was in a daze. Could Harold be suggesting what she thought he was suggesting? Dig up the crown and steal it? Betray everyone and everything?

But she wouldn't be betraying anything, would she? Not if she was doing exactly what she was supposed to be doing and keeping it safe. She looked at Kyrt whose eyes shown with the same fears and questions that burned in her. Harold and Tollie were both watching them.

Finally Jesp spoke, "How did you know about the crown?"

"I didn't exactly. My father left a book in my safe keeping for me to read, and it mentions it, only...only I haven't finished reading it. I guessed, but if I can guess that that's what's there, someone who reads more than me can figure out what it's for and how to get it. If you want to protect it, Harold's probably right," and at this Tollie swallowed hard, clearly trying to get up her own resolve, "It can't stay wherever it is."

Jesp nodded. "So it is written down after all." It was automatic and she didn't even know what she meant by it, but Kyrt took it as a sign. He flew out of the cabin.

Jesp made to leave with him, but stumbled and fell. Harold, deftly for his age, caught her and righted her back on the table.

"Careful, Little one. You can't fly for several days, remember?"

Jesp watched in horror as preparations were made for this insane journey. Harold and Tollie began shoving books into bags and crates and rolling them in blankets to sneak out to the waiting cart. 12 books made the journey out disguised as supplies and rags. Then they started packing up hurried knapsacks. Dried oats, dried fruit and syrup. Pork jerky and salt-cured sausages. Liquor for pain. A small bedroll for Tollie. Feed for the mule. Then Harold packed up several glass vials and jars carefully in a crate and told Tollie to leave them to the faeries. Jesp knew what it was. Harold helped preserve the ingredients they used to poison their weapons. He thought they'd need it. It was a sobering thought.

A couple of hours had passed and Jesp's life seemed to be turning on its end. Her parents came by while the packing was going on. They had a tearful reunion and Jesp didn't want them to go. She wanted Harold to pack her up in a pocket and carry her to the juniper bush to heal. She wanted him to leave her alone so she could pretend that the world wasn't changing all of a sudden.

But in the end she stayed silent. Harold told Jesp's parents that he was sending her to town with a supply run so a more adept healer could look at her wing. Her parents were frightened, even offered to go with her, but Jesp faked a broad smile, told them they'd spoil her fun, then admitted that Kyrt was going. Relieved and delighted, her parents left. Jesp felt an unfathomable emptiness fill the space where they had been, and she feared it was the last she'd see of them. Glancing at Tollie, she knew the halfling understood more deeply than Jesp wanted to imagine. Jesp looked away.

Kyrt returned finally, heavily laden with a filthy, mud-caked old burlap sack twice as big as he was. Harold's eyes widened and he nodded reaching for the sack. But Kyrt jerked it away and said, "Uh uh. This is still being protected by the fae, even if it's only two of us."

Jesp realized she hadn't been breathing in that moment, and exhaled.

Harold backed away and nodded. "Of course," he said, "I understand. Leave it with Jesp then and grab weapons for the two of you, spare quivers of arrows particularly. I've already packed the herbs you'll need. And hurry."

Clearly exhausted and out of breath, Kyrt lugged the muddy, molded bag up to Jesp and flew out the door again. Jesp realized then that she had no crossbow or arrows anymore. She pulled herself up, eying the other two, and waited nervously for Kyrt to return.

The weight of the thing laying next to her was palpable in the silence, even though it was barely touching her skin. An incalculable number of generations of Fae, all the Fae of the Garden that had ever been, had been there only to protect this one thing. And now it was lying serenely next to her, filthy and smelly, and very very heavy on her conscience. Why was she stealing this from her own people? What had they done? The chances of a traitor or infiltrator among them was almost laughable. And though they were little and often flighty, they could be quite dangerous when necessary. So why do this?

Because, said the voice in the back of her head that had kept her mostly quiet all night, if the Library is overrun, the Garden will be, too. There are too many potential enemies and no allies. Secrecy was what kept it safe. Not faeries, not really. We just watched it to make sure it stayed secret. And it hasn't.

Kyrt returned, and that was it. Harold carried Jesp to the cart behind the rectangular brick building. It was half full and covered with a tarp. He'd placed a leather satchel full of soft rags so that it hung just inside the back and out of sight, and placed Jesp in it. Kyrt landed on a secured box next to her, hauling the dirty burlap sack with him and letting it come to rest on the floor of the cart, between two sacks of feed. His eyes locked with Jesp's and it wasn't playful between them anymore. Nothing this serious had ever happened in their lives, and they silently promised each other that they were in it together.

Tollie climbed into the front of the cart.

"You know how to drive it?" Harold asked her.

Deep breath and a nod, Jesp could just see the top of her curly head from where she was peering out of her satchel.

"You know where you're going?"

Tollie looked up at Harold but didn't answer.

Kyrt spoke up, though. "Remind us why you're not going?"

"Because I'll be missed and then we'll be followed," he answered simply. "Tollie is believed to have died in the fire. And, meaning no offense, the folks at the library won't realize you and Jesp are gone."

Jesp found her voice at this point, "Where *are* we going?"

Tollie dropped her head and wiped her eyes but didn't answer.

"I told Tollie not to tell me. In case I'm....questioned."

Jesp didn't like the sound of that pause, but she said nothing else. With a snap and a jerk that set the satchel swaying slightly the cart rolled forward and out the back gate.

*   *   *

The three days that followed were long and restless for Jesp. She drank a lot of liquor mostly because her wing hurt badly, especially the next day. The satchel swayed slightly and Jesp alternated between sleeping and feeling seasick. Kyrt remained dutifully perched on or near the crown and took care of Jesp, too. At least with seeing that she had food and water. It was discovered in an embarrassing moment the first day that Tollie would have to help Jesp occasionally, as Kyrt was unable (and Jesp unwilling) to get her down out of the satchel to pee.

Tollie drove about 3 hours that first night before the exhaustion was too much for her. She parked off the road in a copse of trees and slept in the back of the cart while Jesp and Kyrt kept watch. For three full days and three full nights they went on that way. They spoke very little except for practical things. Tollie drove most of the day and cared for the mule. Kyrt stood watch at night and cared for Jesp, who by the third day felt like a mule. The faeries still didn't know where they were going, but knew for sure by now that they couldn't go back.

As they were stopping to sup and let Tollie rest at the end of their third day, Tollie finally broke the silence.

"I'm surprised you haven't asked where we're going," she acknowledged over yet another meal of sausage for her, oats and syrup for the fae.

Kyrt looked up at Jesp drunk in her satchel. Jesp shrugged. She just wanted to be whole again.

"We don't know much about the world outside of the Garden. If you told us, it probably wouldn't mean much," he admitted.

Tollie nodded.

"I don't know many places either. Right now I'm heading to my childhood home. It's probably dumb because if anyone realizes I'm alive, they'll probably think to look there, but, well, it was the first place I thought of and we left in such a hurry."

"Is anyone there?" Jesp managed to ask although she thought her speech sounded slurred.

"I doubt it. We took my mom back there to bury her when she died four years ago. It was all overgrown and rundown. Rats maybe. I wish..." Tollie started choking on tears before she gained enough composure to speak again, "I wish I could've taken Daddy there..." she buried her head in her arms and finished between sobs, "but...he...burned...in the fire..."

Tollie said nothing else after that and eventually cried herself to sleep. Jesp stayed up with Kyrt for a while and had a whispered conversation with him before turning in herself.

"OK, so what are *we* going to do?" she asked him.

He looked at her thoughtfully then glanced back at the sleeping form of Tollie before answering, "We might as well stick together. We need each other I think. We certainly can't leave her."

Jesp looked at Tollie's silent form, breathing deeply after letting out so much pain. She knew the halfling felt more lost than she, Jesp, did. Jesp had family to return to, and Kyrt by her side. Feeling that rush of affection for Kyrt, she blushed.

"What is it?" asked Kyrt.

Jesp turned back to him. "Nothing," she lied, "I just feel bad for her."

Adrik

Adrik woke with a start. The night was deep and silent around him. He felt around him. He was laying on hard wood in his own bedding. As his eyes began to sort through the shadows, he saw figures sleeping around him, some even children. The air was chill, but not unpleasant. Where was he? He tried to lift himself onto his arms when pain and dizziness brought the memories flooding back to him: the fight, the vine creatures, the poison, Arisa...

Ignoring the pain, he leaped silently to his feet. The world tried to spin on him, but he could steady himself. That was an improvement at least. He glanced around at the forms littered about the floor. Arisa was next to him. He knelt and found her clean, bandaged and breathing. He was himself also clean, bandaged, and pant-less in his own long tunic.

He looked around. They were in a hovel that was wooden in construction and smelled strongly of mildew and fish. There was almost no furniture and the other bodies surrounding him appeared to be a family. It looked like the man and the woman were not sharing bedding. There appeared to be another female, maybe nearing adulthood. She had the shape of a woman, but not the size. And two smaller figures bundled tightly in their blankets who could have been either gender. They all had the same dark tousled brown hair deeply tanned complexions, and were all apparently human. A small, lean mutt of a dog by the dying fire lifted its head to watch him, ears perked.

Adrik found his pants folded neatly next to his blankets and pulled them on quietly. Then he crossed the room silently on his elf feet. He reached the door, intent on determining their location, but it squeaked loudly as he opened it. He cringed and several bodies stirred behind him. He glanced back at the dog who seemed undisturbed by his leaving and was settling back into sleep. He slipped out into the night.

He found himself on a small, rotting porch with a poor repair in the center that creaked ominously beneath even his weight. He reached the loose rail and stared out at the night. His elven eyes discerned the scene quickly despite the dark. He was on the edge of a large lake dotted about with other hovels and shacks with small pitiful fishing vessels moored and tied around its edge. More importantly, though, was the large dark stone of a mountain that loomed in front of him. It was imposing over the tiny village, like the lake was a box that was open and the mountain was a lid that could be slammed shut at any moment. As he stared, he'd have sworn the breeze picked up around him as if in caution. It was the Gatewell. The mountain he and Arisa were searching for. The one the Prophecy said had ended the reign of evil more than a millennium ago. Ended it, but may have been a major part of it, too.

The door creaked open behind him. He'd expected it. He'd heard the heavy footfalls of the adult male human following him slowly out, gracelessly, and the little dog's paws pattering behind. Adrik shook his head and smirked. He should be grateful to these peasants he reminded himself. He couldn't imagine how they'd managed to save them, but clearly they had.

Adrik turned to face the man that arrived behind him and was surprised by his youth. He'd expected a man old enough to have fathered the children in the shack, but this one was barely a man, if that. He was shorter than Adrik, but broader in the shoulders, with shoulder-length wavy brown hair and a wicked scar that sliced the right side of his soft brown face over his eye. Adrik felt himself back against the rail, aware suddenly that he was uncharacteristically unarmed. The young man's visage was startling in the shadow of night.

The human youth stopped and looked at him, more curiously than angrily. He was tall and thin, gangly, and clumsy-looking. Adrik chided himself for feeling threatened by a scar. The dog happily leapt off the porch and went chasing merrily after a squirrel without barking.

"I'm guessing that my companion and I owe you our gratitude," Adrik stated, remembering why it was that he usually let Arisa do the talking, "So....thank you." He tried a warm, friendly smile but suspected strongly that his own sense of feeling ridiculous was mucking it up.

The youth stared at him curiously a moment longer and then seemed to remember to have manners.

"You're welcome," he whispered, glancing back into the hovel to be sure no one was being disturbed, "How long were you up there?"

Adrik considered the question realizing that his head was throbbing slightly now. What did he remember? The fight. The dizziness. The word "poison", he didn't even remember now which one of them said it. He remembered Arisa coming toward him, he had fallen he thought...And now they were here. How long *had* it been?

"I have no idea," he admitted, "What day is it?"

The boy didn't seem to know how to answer.

"Okay, what *month* is it?"

The youth seemed puzzled by the question. He furrowed his brow, thought a moment, then answered, "Well, it's been a year since the last major flood, 2 since the Lords sent men into the mining region with orders for ore for more weapons, 5 years since the fishermen vanished and the storms began, 6 since the fire demon was in the northern sky...."

"Fire demon?" Adrik cut him off. He'd been listening to the dribble about meaningless events with patience, he thought, but the fire demon meant something to him, "You mean the great red comet that went over the foothills and plains north of here in the spring?" Adrik felt a panic rising in his chest he tried to keep down, waiting for the answer.

"Yeah, it was early spring but it was spring. It looked like a dragon attacking below the mountains. And two years before that the stars on that horizon had turned orange for a moon cycle. In the autumn."

Adrik stared at the young human in horror. There were parts of the Andarraine Prophecy everyone knew. Well, he mused, most everyone. He suspected that the boy with whom he was having this conversation may very well never have heard of it. One was the return of the elemental comets. It was the advent of the fire comet streaking over the foothills in what was at that time to his *east* that had started he and Arisa on their journey, *7 months ago*. "How long ago did the fire demon...do whatever?"

"6 years ago, well, just over 5 ½ years. Almost 7 months to the day before the great storm that stole all the men and unleashed all the other storms. At least, that's what they say happened."

The young man shrugged. Of course, thought Adrik, 5 years off course and I have to figure it out with someone who doesn't even know the days of the week. How priceless.

Adrik sighed, "OK," he tried again, "You say there was a bad storm?"

Adrik was trying to picture that fateful day in his head. Praying to gods he resented in fact, that the youth had his time line wrong. Something. But he remembered in the distance, the black clouds and rumbling thunder that were in their path had they managed to continue forward. It looked bad and he had hoped that they'd avoid it.

"Yeah," the youth said, "It flooded the village and the fishermen," he paused and looked sad, "They never made it home that day."

Adrik recognized a point in the conversation where someone like Arisa would chide him for not expressing sympathy. Biting back his own sense of its pointlessness he attempted, "Sorry. I take it you knew these fishermen." Please say no he added to himself, so we can move on.

"My father was one of them, they were most of the men from our village."

Drat, thought Adrik, now I'll be stuck with the story. Head it off....

"Um.....I'm so sorry....so tell me about the storm," he hoped he wasn't sounding insensitive. He really really wished Arisa would wake up.

The young man looked at him, head cocked to one side.

"OK, but then I'm going back to bed unless you need something. I've had a long day. Who are you anyway?"

"Oh, my name's Adrik."

"And you're an elf, right?"

Adrik pursed his lips, unsure of how to answer that. It only just at this moment occurred to him that he was incredibly lucky to have been discovered by an uneducated and probably illiterate peasant family. Anyone that Adrik would consider to have any sense would have killed him rather than have helped him. He stared at the young man, momentarily afraid of how he should respond.

"Uh. Yeeesssss. I'm an elf, so the storm? I hate to keep you up..."

"All right, Adrik the Elf, I'm Brody. Brody Clorr. Welcome to Luring," the young man paused, Adrik tried to look patient, then Brody went on, "Five years ago or so the men didn't come back from their usual morning fishing trip. They'd gone around the bend in the lake and were out of sight of the village, which wasn't unusual, but they always came back near noonday to switch to river craft."

Great, thought Adrik, the fishermen story. Why do I have to deal with this?

"Anyway, they didn't come back, and after they'd been missing several hours this terrible storm blew up out of season. It flooded most of the village," at this Brody looked down at his feet, then back at Adrik, "Most of the survivors left. There aren't many of us here now, but I can't imagine that it all matters very much to the two of you, really. Why do you ask?"

Maybe, thought Adrik, the boy has more sense than it appears.

"We saw that storm on the horizon the day we were attacked," he said and he turned back to look at the Gatewell.

"No! Don't!"

Brody had lunged and grabbed Adrik from behind, pulling him to the floor of the little porch. Adrik was caught uncharacteristically by surprise. He leapt to his feet prepared to strike. Brody rolled off of him breathlessly and looked startled at Adrik's quick return to his feet.

"Don't look to the Unbreaking! You'll bring the curse down on us all!"

"The what?"

"What's going on out there?" the sounds of people stirring hurriedly out of bedding and heading toward the door reached their ears, "Brody?"

Adrik glanced to the door still alarmed and breathing hard. Brody remained seated on the porch floor watching the elf in equal alarm.

"S'alright, mom! Go back to bed!"

The porch door creaked open and the younger female stuck her head out. Beyond her Adrik could hear her younger siblings being put back to bed.

"What the? Oh wow!" came the girl's voice as she stared at Adrik in fascinated surprise, "You really *are* an elf!"

Adrik relaxed. These people were harmless.

"Rista come back to bed!" came the mother's voice. "Let the men be!"

Rista's face twisted in annoyance. She stared a moment longer at Adrik, clearly not able to see him well in the dark and turned back into the house.

The boy called Brody watched her head back inside then turned back to Adrik. Then he said more quietly, "That mountain there," he nodded his head to the Gatewell without looking up at it, "is cursed. If you even look at it, the curse will come down on us all."

Adrik studied him a moment, cocking an eyebrow and stifling a smirk. The arrogant side of himself, which he conceded was a large portion, wanted to brush this off as peasant superstitious gibberish. Another part, however, *knew* the Gatewell was cursed and wondered what useful information about that might be gleaned from the peasant superstitious gibberish. A bright flash nearly blinded him in that moment and the rumble of thunder that followed came directly from the direction of the Gatewell.

"Get back in the house!" Brody commanded, leaping to his feet. He then did something unexpected and jumped down off of the porch into the night. Adrik expected to hear a splash. It had appeared in that moment that Brody had jumped right into the lake, but when Adrik looked over the rail, he saw the youth running with surprising speed along the bank toward a tiny shed-like shack some 40 feet away.

The next flash was even brighter and was immediately coupled by a deafening crash. The hair on the back of Adrik's neck was standing, and his elf senses told him this was no ordinary storm. Lights were flickering to life in hovels all around the lake and Adrik could tell by the screams and scrambling noises he heard, that people were running for higher ground. What had he done?

The storm raged the rest of the night and proved instantly to Adrik that the mountain was nothing to be toyed with. It woke the whole household, even Arisa, and Adrik was genuinely glad to see her. Brody had returned before the storm actually struck with another young man about his age but bigger and built like a mountain himself, his dog following excitedly behind him.

The smell of smoke increased with every flash. The screaming that could be heard all around the lake was terrible. Arisa's eyes shown with terror. Her sense of magic was much more acute than his. The flickering quality of the growing light outside told them that a terrible fire raged somewhere out there but none of them dared go near the door to look. The water came up under the door and rose fast around them. The mother grabbed the two smaller children, both boys Adrik had realized at some point. Adrik helped Arisa, who was still very injured and weak, and they grabbed their own packs, weapons and supplies as quickly as they could. The other three gathered a pair of large heavy chests, some fishing equipment and a ladder from the corner and they all climbed up through a trapdoor in the ceiling and onto the rain-soaked roof. The girl went back down for the dog and only just made it back up the ladder in time. It was slick up there and terrifying, with no shelter or protection. Looking around, Adrik knew there was none to be had. Fire lit the trees on the north side above the lake looming over the upper falls. The only noise around them were panicked screams and the now incessant barking of the dog in the girl's arms. The lake had risen to such a height, that no structures could be seen. The small group Adrik was with scrambled from the roof into the trees above them and watched in silent horror before dawn as the roof of the house itself was washed out into the lake and into the darkness.

The littlest of the boys had fallen from his mother's grasp in a moment of undecided panic and only Adrik's elfborne reflexes had saved the child as he sprung from one tree to a lower branch on the other, batlike, and intercepted the boy in midair. As the storm finally dissipated, the sky shown the deepest most violent purple to herald daybreak that Adrik had ever seen, and even the dog had gone from barking to whimpering. Adrik was sitting the lowest in any of the trees, clutching to a boy that could not have been more than five winters in age, their feet dangling into the water of the risen lake. Around them there was utter silence, smoke and water.

Adrik looked above him to the others of their small group. Not far above him in the tree to his immediate right, the mother clung to a tree trunk with her second-smallest child sandwiched against it, looking out across what was once her village home. Above her in the same tree, Arisa and the family's daughter held each other above the chaos, a fishing net dangling from their branch and a pair of fishing poles, one broken, tangled in the lower branches of the tree just at Adrik's height. The small dog, now silent, was squeezed between them. Somehow the two young men had hoisted one of the chests into a tree ahead of Adrik and had it balanced between them just above his head. There had been a terrible moment in the last hour where the other, heavier chest had narrowly missed Adrik and the child as it dropped over their heads into the waiting waters of the lake.

The boy in Adrik's arms looked up at him. His eyes asked questions the child didn't know how to word. Adrik stared back. These people had nothing. Now they had less. They'd saved he and Arisa and he may have destroyed everything they ever knew. He continued to stare back. He didn't know what to say.

As if in answer to their pressing dilemma, and before Adrik even realized that they had a new one, a small boat banged sideways into the mother's tree.

"Grab that boat!" She yelled down. The noise sounded loud and out of place in the eerie silence around them.

Adrik could just reach the boat with his feet. He nearly let the child slip when he did. He grabbed the boy by both wrists and lowered him into it, then dropped lightly down beside him. Even with his elven reflexes he nearly lost footing. He was certainly not used to boats. He held fast to the trunk of the tree he left knowing full well that if this boat floated out into the lake, he and the child would be lost. He could no more navigate a skiff or swim than he could take back the moment where he had looked at the mountain. He looked up at the young men for advice. They were locked in conversation about the chest and how to deal with it from where they were. Adrik's eyes next sought out Arisa. She was looking...oh no! As he looked up he realized that Arisa was staring right at the cursed mountain!

"Arisa!" he yelled to her desperately, "Down here!"

Arisa pulled out of the thoughts she'd lost herself in and frowned down at him. The girl named Rista was trying to untangle the net from the tree and wasn't paying attention.

Adrik glanced over to the mother and saw that she was making her way down to the boat. She dropped in beside him and reached up to pull her other son down from the tree. She looked nervously at Adrik and then smiled.

"Do you think you can get us over to the edge?" she asked as she settled down between her boys.

"Uh..." Adrik looked about. "OK"

Adrik fumbled his grip from one tree to the next pulling the little boat along, but ultimately getting them over to the side. The mother unloaded herself and the two boys on the steep muddy banks and sent Adrik back for the others. Adrik grimaced, wondering why this woman would think he knew how to do this, but feeling too guilty to refuse. When he made his way to the tree under the two young men, the girl Rista had untangled the net and helped them suspend the chest by it between their two trees.

Adrik looked around worriedly and saw that Arisa was hanging on in her original position watching Adrik play hero, still clutching the dog, a mischievous twinkle in her eye. Adrik narrowed his eyes at her, but was truly glad to see her coming around to herself after all they'd been through in recent memory.

The three humans in the trees lowered their chest in its net to the waiting boat. Adrik wondered what possessions people such as these had to cherish so much that they'd risk their lives to save it, but decided it was none of his business. The chest landed with a thud that nearly caused Adrik to lose his footing. He heard Arisa giggle and he risked a glance up to glower at her, grateful he hadn't the complexion to blush. Rista climbed down into the boat on top of the chest and she and Adrik made it once again to the side. This time, however, Rista steered, and the trip was smoother. Unfortunately, and stupidly Adrik thought, her mother made her get out with the chest and sent Adrik back out again. On the third and last trip, the two young men helped Arisa and the dog very carefully into the boat, both blushing, Adrik trying not to laugh.

But the situation was far from laughable when they reached the side a final time. They had each other, a chest full of unknown treasures, Adrik and Arisa's weapons and bags which could be fished from the trees, a boat with no oars, one good fishing pole and a net. There was nothing else, as the violet sky turned blood red, settled into orange and began to fade to colorless gray-white as the sun rose. Everything was utterly still and silent. Then the mother began to quietly weep. All of the humans looked lost and Adrik tried to swallow his growing sense of guilt as he sat apart from the others, trying to look away.

It was Arisa that pulled him out of his reverie. She'd placed a bandaged and burned hand on his arm and held his gaze when he turned to look at her.

"You were magnificent back there," she spoke softly to him, "Especially when you caught that little boy when he fell. But you seem less pleased with yourself than I'd expect." She smiled gently, watching him as he chose not to rise to her insinuation of his arrogance.

Adrik glanced back up at the family, all huddled together, all lost in their separate mourning.

"Did you know that looking at the Gatewell was a magically cursed act?" he whispered to her.

She furrowed her brow.

"No, did you?"

"Not until after I did it," he swallowed as he admitted his involvement in this.

"Then it's not your fault. You didn't know. Besides," here she glanced back to make sure their conversation was private, "I can't imagine that no one has ever done it before and that it just destroyed their entire village this *one* time. There was more to this storm," she swallowed, "I fear it was me."

He looked at her, eye to eye, with confusion.

"You?"

"You know I don't know what my magic's capable of. I was unconscious. I don't know what I may have done."

"You snored a little," Adrik teased. He knew she'd done no such thing, but it amused him. She grimaced at the thought, "But you didn't do this either."

He paused and looked across the water.

"Did you see how dark the shadows got?"

"I thought that was you."

Adrik shook his head. "For several moments I couldn't see it was so dark. That's never happened to me before."

"I saw something else," she whispered even lower, "The one that's tall and thin instead of big and scary..." Adrik nodded that he knew, "He had spirits to help him. It was brief, just as we fled from the roof to the trees, I saw them."

"Evil spirits?"

Arisa shook her head. "No just dead ones. They didn't feel evil, just creepy."

As the day brightened a small band of other survivors reached them. All of them had lost everything. Only the family that Adrik and Arisa had been with had survived intact. The revelation that the elves were present was a subject of sudden intense fury and blame, but the one that called himself Brody reasoned wisely with them that if they had been the source of the curse, those that had taken them in would be the worst off, not least affected. Adrik had to give the boy credit. He didn't mention Adrik's looking at the mountain and breaking their taboo, and he maintained sensible, reasoned calm in the face of their accusations. In the midst of the uproar, however, Adrik did learn that he had been scarred, "marked" they called it, in the terrible storm five years ago, and had been the subject of their suspicion then, too. Did they know about the spirits on some level?

The bigger guy had made reason more acceptable to the small desperate group, by standing between Brody and the rest and generally being very threatening about it. Adrik learned that his name was Tarfinn, and that he had apparently been put in this position with regard to his friend before.

Arisa sat apart from the humans and watched them work things out on their own. Adrik was used to this sort of thing. Shadowelves, such as he was, were not trusted by any race outside of their own. Not even among their own, in point of fact. But morrowelves, such as Arisa, were very highly regarded by most races. It had come as no surprise to Adrik that they couldn't get permission to take the road along Graffling River into the Highlands. The people of this country were notoriously superstitious and unwelcoming of outsiders, especially outside races. But Arisa had genuinely believed that diplomacy would prevail. This sort of thing shocked her.

So she watched the humans, and Adrik watched her, and eventually the thing came to a stalemate when tired, exhausted, devastated and hungry they simply wore themselves out arguing about it. It was at that moment that Brody revealed the contents of his chest, Adrik nearly fell over in surprise. It was fish. A chest full of stinking, freshly caught fish. His greatest treasure was food. Adrik was struck by how truly simple these people were.

The small band that remained of a once-probably-ancient fishing community was 26 including the unwelcome elves, plus a dog, which meant that the group that Adrik had survived with was almost a third of the survivors. Others seemed to have worked that out, too, because the arguments over Brody's past and the presence of the elves did not commence after lunch. There was Adrik, Arisa, Brody and his mother, Tarfinn, Rista, the little boys Rann and Till, another mother who'd saved only one of her three children, a pair of twin boys about Rista's age who'd watched their mother and brother drown, a young man older than Brody and Tarfinn, an elderly man with dirty hands who'd saved his two young grandkids but not their mother, a young father and his daughter who was between Rista's and Rann's ages who had already been alone before the storm, a couple with a teenaged-boy and a younger one who'd lost the elders in their family, a young man with a toddler whose pregnant wife had "just nearly made it," and a young couple expecting their first child. Clearly, Adrik thought darkly, this ordeal was not yet over for these people. He realized as he thought it, that the fact needed to be addressed.

He cleared his throat. Begrudgingly, it earned him the attention of those who had been content to ignore his presence. Brody, Tarfinn and those he thought of as "his" group looked up as well.

"Look I don't mean to make a bad situation sound worse," and here Arisa visibly braced waiting to jump to his defense, "but we've half a day now, maybe less, till dark and no shelter. Is there anything near here?"

Arisa relaxed and nodded at him. He shot her a look that said, mockingly, he resented her lack of confidence. She smiled.

Tarfinn shook his head as the others, their situation dawning more harshly on them now, looked around at each other for hope.

"The next closest town is a mining camp, up the mountainside here about four days' journey," Tarfinn was explaining to him, "If we head down the mountain to the river road we can reach a larger settlement but at twice the distance."

"Graffling Fort?" Arisa asked innocently glancing sideways at Adrik with a grin. They'd wanted to hang Adrik there. It was the second time in his life that Arisa had broken him out of a jail cell. He grimaced at the reference. Tarfinn, however, not noticing the exchange, continued.

"But you're right. Wherever we're headed we should get going."

The discussion that ensued was more level-headed than the first one was and concerned the choice of destinations and whether those that that wanted to go one way should simply separate from those who wished to go the other. That idea was dismissed quickly. All together was definitely the best chance any of them had. No mention was made of the elves and they did not engage in the conversation, feeling that ultimately it would be a very minor decision in their own lives. The choices hinged on what work might be available in each location and which previous members of their village had gone before them to each place.

Brody resolutely DID NOT want to end up working in a mine. Tarfinn agreed and seemed to be considering an army life if he could get down to the fort, but the other adults liked the possibility of a smaller community and the support of old townsfolk. Brody looked crestfallen and Tarfinn angry. Adrik, looked around at the children's scared faces and tried to reconcile himself with the thought of them having to work hard labor in a thankless mine somewhere. He tried to swallow it. It wasn't like him to give a damn, and now was a bad time to start, he told himself.

One thing was certain. There was nothing left for them here. They'd tried for five years to rebuild and move on, and it had come to this. Sink or swim, they were saying. Find a way. Adrik listened to them banter these phrases between them as if they were now a joke. 'Find a way out' seemed to be the only option now.

Arisa moved over to Adrik and whispered, "Our intended path lies in the other direction. You don't think to go with them do you?"

Adrik shot her a withering look.

"And who will protect them? The old man? Or the pregnant woman? Oh, I know," he said, an evil gleam in his eye, "Brody will fend off attacks with his fishing pole, is that it?"

Arisa looked at him sympathetically, "Well, well, well," she said, "I knew there was more of a heart in the shadow somewhere."

He scowled his best scowl at her, but she was right. It really wasn't like him to feel involved like this, but he did, and he had to think it was good for him somehow. This compassion stuff was something he'd been asked to learn, by Arisa of course.

He looked at her for answers, something he never did. She shrugged, "It'll put us eight days out of our way, but it's ok with me."

And Adrik realized he hadn't told her. The realization widened his eyes, and she asked, "What?"

"Arisa, we were on that mountain ledge five years."

"Five years!? That's impossible. Why would you think that?"

Her response was so loud it startled the peasants out of their conversation and caused them to look nervously over at the elves.

So he told her, ignoring the humans who drifted back to their conversations gratefully. He told her about the comet and about the storm. He was brief and whispered quietly, but when he was through he realized that the rest were still paying attention anyway.

She looked around self-consciously, "Well, then, I guess eight days really *is* no big deal, but, Adrik," and she leaned in very close so as to not be overheard. The humans tried to pretend to not be listening, "Have there been any more comets?"

"Not that were seen up here I don't think," he smiled to himself as he remembered last night on the porch, "I think it would have been mentioned."

"How can you be so sure?"

"Trust me," be smirked to himself, recalling with mild annoyance Brody's long list of meaningless events over the years.

The rest of the day was somber. Another decision was made to make for higher ground and camp, spending the rest of the day preparing for travel. It was Arisa's suggestion that she made privately to Rista who then suggested it to the group at large. A dry and reasonably flat expanse was found some way up the mountainside, where a view of the road could be had without being easily spotted the other way around. The ground was muddy, but there was nothing for it, and Arisa pointed out to Adrik as he was grumbling about it that they were lucky it was even flat given the terrain.

The women, except Rista, along with Orwyd, the old man, watched the children while the younger men, elves and Rista scavenged for everything they could salvage. Their timely little rescue boat was split apart for firewood with an ax Tarfinn had found quickly, which allowed the women, also, to dry what cloth goods had been found. Adrik was sorry to see it go, though at least part of his reservation was the overwhelming smell of fish it gave to the fire.

The afternoon was a success such as it could be. They found more pieces of salvageable wood in the form of floating furniture and ruined canoes. A sack of apples was recovered along with three uprooted tomato stalks bearing fruit. They found the bedding from one whole bed that, although soaked, could make enough travel bedding for all of the children if they were kept together.

The best and most exhilarating moment of the day came when the dog found an infant alive in the water and barked until it was seen and rescued. The child was immediately taken in by the mother mourning for two she had lost. That rescue spurred a sense of searching for other survivors which lasted later into the night than Adrik thought it should, and turned up no others. Several bodies were recovered, some lost family members of the survivors, and the decision was made to tie something heavy to them and give them back to the water. Adrik was privately glad that none of the missing children were found, as even he didn't think he could stand to see that.

That night they smoked the remaining fish and, under the circumstances, Adrik was glad they'd gone to so much trouble to save the huge chest of fish. It was enough to get them all where they were going and well into the winter season, though Adrik didn't think he could stand to eat smoked fish for that long. That night's supper was freshly smoked fish and fresh, albeit waterlogged, tomatoes, finished off by the last find of the evening, an untapped keg of ale from a dead neighbor's reserves. Even the little dog ate well, and Adrik mused over the little thing's luck. Had the fish not survived, he might have been supper.

The night was long and uncomfortable. Arisa had insisted that she and Adrik give up their own bedrolls to the children since theirs were wet, and had promised them to the pregnant woman and the other young mother thereafter. Arisa and Adrik shared a watch, as did Brody and Tarfinn, then the only three young men who were adults and not also trying to keep a motherless toddler asleep took a last one. Nonetheless, Adrik didn't sleep a wink. He'd pointed out to Arisa that their sleep was being guarded by unarmed fishermen, and he suspected that Arisa had one eye open as well.

The next two days were miserable. They climbed along what passed for a road up into the mountain. It was wide enough for carts to travel single file, but the ride would be terrible. The way was rocky and steep, and the children could not climb far without needing to be carried. The villagers were not accustomed to hard travel, and were doing barely better than the children in their pace and stamina. Even the dog was visibly exhausted. Despite the fact that elves in general did not usually possess the stamina of humans, Adrik and Arisa danced up and down the path around them, Adrik scouting and Arisa sensing. Arisa had insisted several times to Adrik that things still did not "feel right," but could elaborate no further. Adrik impressed the children with his speed at climbing trees and by shooting a circling bird out of the sky in one shot. That night, at least, they didn't have to eat fish. Their camps were small and crowded, but each time were all the level ground they could find.

Brody was silent for the two days except when he just couldn't avoid having to say something, and even then he seemed to say as little as possible. Tarfinn, who Adrik had learned to call "Finn," stayed by his side and said very little more. Rista spent time with the elves when she could get away with it, but it made Adrik feel like he had a little sister again, and thinking about his youngest sister filled him with regret. Arisa mothered Rista which didn't seem to suit her, and by the end of the second day she had retreated to her mother and younger brothers.

As they set up what passed for camp on the third night, they were barely more than halfway to their destination and moving more slowly than when they began. Adrik hadn't really slept at all for three nights, and had been petrified for 5 years before that. He approached Brody and Finn who seemed more receptive to speaking with him than he had expected and convinced them to split their shifts with he and Arisa. So Adrik took the first watch with Brody, and decided to finally get some sleep when his watch was over.

With everyone asleep, Adrik sat apart from the little group hoping that Brody would join him. He wanted to tell Brody that he was sorry. He needed to know if the young man blamed him for what had happened, but Brody took up a sensible position opposite the camp from him and so the opportunity was lost.

Adrik fell asleep quickly when Arisa and Finn got up to watch. He tried not to think about what he considered to be the uncovered third watch, because he really wanted to sleep through it. His last comforting thought before sleep finally claimed him was that even unable to fight effectively, the three men on third watch could at least keep their eyes open and call for help if it were needed. And even if they failed that, Fletch was an accomplished noise maker.

It was needed.

Adrik woke with a start to the sound of shouts and barks around him. He sprung deftly to his feet and drew his bow with alacrity.

"What is it?" came the shouts, "What are they?"

The little dog was pointed, hackles raised, into the woods and was barking a fierce, growling bark.

Adrik looked around. The three fishermen who had been on watch were staring blindly into the darkness around them where a growling seemed to come from everywhere. Finn emerged with his chopping ax. He held it comfortably, Adrik noticed, like a man who knew how to use it. Brody was quick to his feet, too, and Adrik realized that Arisa had given him a dagger. But none of them could see and they were making for torches.

Adrik glanced into the trees and saw Arisa do the same. As he looked, the first of a pack of ragged looking wolves leaped for the nearest startled child. Adrik let loose a fast arrow and the stricken wolf landed next to its prey. Arisa threw her remaining dagger into the first wolf she saw and Adrik took two more out with his bow. Finn had managed two with his ax and Brody had garnered the presence of mind to gather the rest of the humans around the children in a protective circle. There was a flash like lightning from Arisa and two more fell. Then one jumped Finn while he was pulling his ax from a third corpse and Adrik shot it, but not before it had gotten a bite out of him.

It was over as fast as it had started. Starving and with too many mouths to feed the whole pack had fought to the death. But the villagers had only had one injury, and Adrik was relieved at how fortunate they were. Wolves in better health would not have gone down so easily.

Finn was bandaged and found to have a significant but not devastating injury to his left arm. No one else was injured. The children and their parents were terrified, but the one thing that had changed for the better, Adrik was glad to see, was that the elves, Brody and Finn were no longer treated as outsiders but as heroes. Even Fletch was getting some credit for the barking alarm and was looking very proud of himself, too.

The next day was spent skinning the wolves, smoking their meat, and preparing their hides to be tanned. It was a windfall for the villagers. It gave them more food to carry them farther and something tangible for them to barter with in their new home. 9 large wolf pelts would be worth some supplies if not shelter for the desperate group, and despite the fear, there was some joy in the day.

That night another storm blew up more wild and more terrible than even the one before. From this height they watched its fury unleashed in the lakeside area and the lower valley. Here on the opposite mountain, the night was dominated with torrential downpour and an impressive light and sound show, but the true devastation of the storm was contained within the mountain bowls and ravines. No one slept. They stayed huddled together, many of the children insisting on snuggling with Adrik, who tried not look put out. Arisa tried harder not to laugh at him.

They all watched, wondering how much worse it could have been, worrying that at any moment it might come their way. Adrik and Arisa, unconvinced now that the mere viewing of the far mountain bore any bad luck, saw clearly that the storm originated from and lingered the longest on top of the Gatewell itself before descending into the Luring Lake ravine.

It was just before dawn that they saw it: the thing Adrik and Arisa knew would come. Just as the storm seemed to be dissipating it streaked across the top of the mountain they all feared. At first it looked like a shooting star, but then it lingered in the sky getting longer and brighter until it appeared that lightning had become a constellation across the eastern sky, and still it got brighter. Just before the sky started to lighten and cause it to fade, it looked like it might touch the top of the Gatewell. Even the villagers were watching, their taboo forgotten.

"What is it?" whispered Till who had decided that Adrik was his special friend since their time together in a tree so many days ago. The whole group seemed to hold its breath for an answer.

Adrik thought briefly about his response and decided on the truth, "It's the Water Comet. Like the Fire Demon six years ago, only this one's worse."

Chapter 3:

2nd Day of the 12th Month, 2nd Day of the Week, Autumn
Rothsday, Shilirs 2

Keen

Kierra was perched by the cave mouth, bow in hand, her whole body taut and alert. Keen leaned against the far wall gripping the hilt of his zweihander across his lap watching her as much as he could in this darkness. As the strange light of the spirit army cast its eerie glow across the opening of their shared stone burrow, he could make her out as a dark, still shadow against the wailing gloom. He wanted to suggest that she back up. He worried that she was too close to the gap, but he'd never met a woman like her before. She kept wanting to take care of him instead of things being the other way around. She'd even saved his life, really, by showing him to this cave. He wasn't used to it. It made him feel...odd.

But she was good at everything she tried, and she was so fast. Even on that badly messed up leg, she could get around better than he could up here. He'd heard elves were quick and far more able in the forest than humans, but she was embarrassing. And then she kept suggesting that he do female chores like cooking and collecting water and taking stock of supplies. He really liked her. He couldn't help it. But sometimes it was like she was mocking him.

As the wailing lights flickered past he watched her twitch to a slightly more alert pose, her bow at the ready. He'd heard about elven bowmen, but since the battle they were about to fight with the elves had never happened, he'd not had the chance to see it for himself. He gripped his own weapon more tightly. He doubted she'd need it, but he'd be ready if she did. As much as she kept doing for him, the last thing he was going to do was to fail to be prepared if she got into some kind of trouble. He hated himself for the thought, but he found himself hoping just a little that she had just a small bit of trouble he could help her out of.

Yesterday, she'd been ready like this, too, but the weird spirits had lingered past daybreak, and the rabbits hadn't come out. They couldn't afford for that to happen this morning. Keen was truly afraid that if Kierra couldn't snare these rabbits this time, she'd actually try to go out hunting. He cringed. He was the man.

It should be he, not she, taking that kind of risk.

A strange light flickered in the sky above them. Oh no, thought Keen, what now? Kierra's still form twitched again as she glanced up at something streaking across the sky above them. From where he was in the back of the cave, Keen couldn't make it out. It seemed to linger above the trees like lightning made still for several long minutes. He could tell Kierra was watching it warily, although her motionless body remained poised for the sudden doom of rabbits.

Her still form seemed to twitch a third time and then suddenly... an arrow loosed from the string of her bow, and almost faster than his eyes could follow, she'd loaded and fired a second. Just as quickly she leaped down from her perch and into the darkness below.

He lurched forward keeping his blade tipped to the side. She'd already grabbed her kill and had turned to come back up to the cave by the time he'd reached the lip to look down. Damn, he thought. Elf fast. She wouldn't be quite as fast climbing back up the eight feet or so with her bad leg. She handed him up two dead rabbits and two bloody arrows and made to start her climb when the light changed suddenly again.

She looked quickly back to where the ghost army had just gone and Keen followed her gaze. They were heading back! But how? Could they have seen or sensed her? They'd never come back before.

Kierra looked up at Keen in a panic and reached for the lip of the cave. Keen tossed his weapon and the rabbits back behind him and grabbed her by both wrists, hoisting her up and into his lap almost as easily as he had relieved her of her catch, marveling at her light weight again as he had on the battlefield when he'd half-carried her in the first place. He wrapped his arms around her and they both fell back against the far wall as the now-familiar wailing ghosts raced past, this time in the wrong direction.

He looked into her terrified eyes, his arms encircling her as she sat draped, much less gracefully than usual, across his lap, both of them breathing heavily. He felt a twinge of guilt for having wished to have to rescue her. She rested her forehead on his shoulder and breathed out loudly. He pulled her in more tightly and she didn't resist. Elf or not, he was really quite fond of her. He laid his cheek against her hair. Despite the fact that neither of them had bathed in several days, her hair was still fairly soft. He smiled. Of course it is, you overly-perfect strange little creature, you. And then he added to himself, I'm glad you're OK.

She looked back up at him, "Thanks," she murmured. Then she looked back out into the dawning morning. The ghosts were lingering, as if they were searching for something they had sensed but had no way to find. She looked back into his face and gulped. He nodded. There were many things he didn't understand in this world, but right now, fear was something he understood just fine.

Keen and Kierra watched the ghosts. They didn't seem to move with much purpose or thought. It was more like watching smoke that was trapped in a bowl trying to waft out to freedom. Even when their faces turned toward the cave opening, they gave no indication of sight.

The faces themselves were horrible. Some were skulls. Some were half rotted. Many, though, were both elves and humans and appeared more recently dead. At least once, Keen thought one looked familiar. It made him physically sick and he must have recoiled. Kierra turned to him.

"What is it?" she asked.

"Nothing," he answered. He couldn't bring himself to say what he was thinking out loud. It made it too real. He shuddered.

Kierra watched his face a moment longer and then turned back to the spirits. He often wondered what she was thinking about him when she did that. As little as he'd been helpful so far, she must have thought him to be much weaker than he really was. He wanted to make a better impression on her, but speed had been more useful to them so far than strength. He wanted to make it up to her.

Eventually the spirits moved on. Keen felt Kierra's body relax in his arms. He liked the way she felt in his arms, though he'd certainly never say so. She turned to him, worry written all over her face.

"Now," she said, "about that water."

Keen was shocked, "Surely you're not going back out there now?"

Kierra shrugged, "If I get into trouble, you'll pull me back in again, won't you?"

Keen wasn't sure if she was teasing him or not, "Of course I will," he answered somewhat defiantly.

She nodded slowly glancing back out toward the stream in one direction and then back the other way where the ghosts had just gone, breathing deeply, stealing up her courage.

"But maybe I should go..." Keen suggested. He didn't know why he suggested it. He wasn't as fast as Kierra, but he hated not feeling useful. He just couldn't stand waiting around while she did all of the dangerous stuff.

She frowned at him, "Why?"

Well, that was an ego blow.

He shrugged, "My turn?"

She smiled, "You can't be fast enough, besides," and this time she reached up and kissed him unexpectedly on the cheek. Keen felt himself blush, "I couldn't possibly pull you up the side of the rock if you got into trouble. Why shouldn't we play to our talents?"

After that kiss, the only talent Keen suddenly wanted to play to involved Kierra not going anywhere at all. He pushed that thought aside. "OK," he agreed, "I guess I'm just bored."

"An undead army threatening our very survival and you're bored?" she smiled. She was definitely teasing now, "I don't ever want to visit your country." She grinned at him broadly and pulled away.

She was looking down at the stream glinting in the sunlight. He could tell she was gathering her courage. He hated to let her go, but he conceded that they needed that water, and she'd be faster than he was at getting it. He realized he was still gripping her arm, albeit loosely. He let her go.

Apparently taking that as something of a sign, Kierra slipped quietly down from the safety of their perch, landing lightly on her elf feet and glancing nervously in both directions. Keen handed her down both waterskins and she ran like a scared doe for the far stream, reaching it so fast he'd hardly seen her feet touch the ground. She bent over the water and Keen longed to feel the cold fresh wet of that creek on his own skin, but much more than that, he longed to have Kierra back to safety. She filled one skin and then the other, the minutes dragging out for Keen as he held his breath and watched back and forth in each direction. Then he saw what he feared: the light changed abruptly back to silver.

"Kierra!"

She'd sensed it, too. Her head jerked up and she darted from her hunched position like a scared rabbit, corking the second skin as she ran. The wailing grew as the light did. Keen leaned out and over the edge as Kierra reached her hands up to him desperately. The armies of the dead were upon her as her hands reached his. He could see the scream of frozen pain and horror that failed to leave her throat as it deformed her face. Her body wrenched and pulled. He yanked against the tide of death.

Keen fell backward into the cave with Kierra on top of him. It had felt as if he'd torn her in two. The wailing of their foe had turned to a screaming just outside their entrance, but the dead could not understand where their quarry had gone. Kierra's blood ran freely across Keen's lap, but her crying, agonized voice had returned and she was panting breath.

He turned her over quickly to assess the damage, thinking nothing for her modesty as he ripped her tunic and leggings looking to stem the tide of red that was covering her front. The gashes weren't deep, but they were everywhere. She appeared to have been clawed by hands that ended in daggers. Kierra gripped the front of his tunic, breathing heavily into his chest as he used her own torn clothing to press into the worst of her new wounds.

Slowly, her bleeding stopped. Keen used some of the new water to clean her up before wrapping her abdomen and legs in the last of their clean bandages. The floor of the cave was a bloody mess of elf blood mingled with rabbit, and the metallic smell was sickening. Kierra seemed weaker than she should be from these new wounds alone, but then then she had just sprinted faster than he could have, which must have worn her out. She was still recovering from earlier injury and neither of them had eaten or slept well for days now. Still, she seemed already to have paled as if she'd lost more blood than it appeared she had.

Keen helped her to change into her one spare tunic from her pack. Her skin was cool and damp, and she didn't look healthy at all.

"Kierra?"

She looked up at him with eyes that seemed strangely distant.

"Talk to me. Are you OK?"

She blinked, and gripped his shoulder again, laying her head against him for support.

"I don't know."

"Were you poisoned?"

She paused, "I don't think so."

She looked back up at him and smiled weakly, "I'm just not as strong as you," her smile faded, "Elves just can't take the kind of damage that humans can." She looked around at the mess on the floor around them, "Or lose the same amount of blood..." She laid her head back down against him, "I feel sick..."

Now Keen was worried. All along he'd been judging her condition based on his knowledge of humans. It had never occurred to him that she would be more fragile. She seemed so much more strong and able than the women he knew back home, at least in many ways. She wasn't as sturdy, but she was so competent in the forest and so brave in the face of these horrors. Keen just couldn't imagine his mother or sister-in-law in this situation. But Kierra was thinner, lighter, paler and just wound more tightly than a human. Keen cursed inwardly for not realizing that she was also more frail. He held her weakened frame helplessly in his arms, willing her not to die as her pulled her closer to himself. He couldn't tell her how he had come to feel about her, but he was starting to admit it wordlessly to himself. He certainly couldn't fail her in this moment.

Gently, he laid her down on his own blanket, out of the bloody mess and started to clean up the cave floor so that he could begin the process of preparing the rabbits to be cooked. Yesterday he resented being asked to cook and would have recoiled physically if she had asked him to clean. Right now, he just wanted to give Kierra some sustenance, some strength, and he couldn't look at all of Kierra's blood. Angry tears were sprouting from his eyes as he beat the rabbit gut and elf blood out of the cave. He tried not to let Kierra see his face. He had to save her.

That night was restless. Kierra's breathing was thin and rattled at times. Keen gave up on sleep early in the night to stand vigil over the wounded elf. His own wounded hip was starting to show signs of re-injury or infection, but he hardly cared about that except that it was becoming harder for him to move around, and he knew that if it fell to him now to leave the cave for any supplies, he'd be even slower than usual. Reality cloaked him like the thick darkness of the night. Without Kierra's speed and skill, there would be no surviving this undead menace.

Deep down, he wasn't sure he wanted to. He'd failed her, and he'd only been here in the first place to kill her and others like her. Why? Because he'd been told they were evil. Elves. All elves. Evil to the core and possessed of magic that would destroy our world if we didn't destroy them first. Keen watched Kierra's timid breathing in the cool, damp cave. Murder is what it is, Keen thought to himself, just a justification for murder. And in that dark, silent, dread-filled moment, Keen sat up praying for Kierra, and wondering what his king was really up to.

Morning dawned and Kierra opened her eyes. Keen practically jumped up from his post by the entrance and bumped his head on the cave ceiling.

"You OK?" Kierra asked innocently with a smile.

"If you are," Keen smiled back, rubbing his head.

He knew he had to look a mess. He hadn't bathed in days. He'd spent most of yesterday cleaning up blood and then cleaning dead rabbits for stew. Then he'd cleaned up Kierra's vomit later which hadn't made him feel any better about his ability to contribute to Kierra's well being. Now he'd been up all night, too. He didn't even want to think about what he must smell like, but the sight of Kierra opening her eyes and finding the strength to smile was enough to push all of that out of his mind. He bent over her and stroked her head. Her hair was no longer soft. She was sweaty and cool and still looked pale. Nonetheless, she was breathing better than she had been in the night, and her lips and nail beds had better color.

"Is there any stew left?" Kierra asked in a voice that sound too gravelly for her own.

"I didn't think you'd liked it," he chided as he got up to light the small charcoals he heated their food with.

She smiled weakly, "Not funny. I ate too fast..." Her voice trailed off behind him as he began to move the pot of stew onto the small fire. He turned quickly to check on her, but she was still watching him. She had a somewhat glazed-over look in her eyes, but her eyes themselves were still blinking.

"You had me worried last night," he confessed.

"Me too."

"I hope we get more rain," he told her as he stirred the soup.

"Hmmmm?"

He looked back over at her watching him, a hungry look now making her gaze seem more natural. Good, he thought as he added out loud, "Because I don't think sending either of us back out for water is a good idea."

Kierra turned her head slightly toward the cave opening sadly. "No," she admitted.

Keen was able to feed Kierra a healthy amount of well-thickened broth slowly, and she seemed to gain some strength from it. She slept most of the rest of the day, but her breathing and her color were much less alarming after she ate.

While Kierra slept, Keen decided to try to use her bow. It was light and required much less strength to pull than the one he had used to hunt at home. In a way, that made it harder to aim and manage than he expected. Still, with her sleeping, he could only embarrass himself so much.

Not wanting to waste her arrows, he tied a long length of his own rope to one. He knew that he would lose a great deal of accuracy with this drag, but then, he wasn't counting on having very much of that anyway. He waited until he saw what he was looking for: the flock of geese that seemed to fly over each afternoon, probably moving from nesting grounds to watering holes and back again. It was a large flock, and he only had to hit one bird on one trip there or back again.

His first shot went wild and startled the geese sending the birds everywhere. He recovered the arrow quickly and fired it again at a confused low-flyer still seeking cover. This time he was successful enough. He clipped the bird's wing and sent it hurdling out of the sky. It landed on the ground at the base of a tree in full view of his perch where it thrashed wounded and unable to get out of harm's way. Keen pulled his arrow in again and fired it one more time, this time skewering the goose and managing to pull it in by the rope.

He was just lifting it triumphantly, and he thought fairly quietly, over the edge of the cave entrance when he heard a voice behind him say, "That was magnificent."

He turned around, slightly embarrassed, hoisting the small goose up by its ankles. Kierra was laying on her side watching him and grinning.

"Well, I'm no archer..." he stammered.

"Neither am I," she said.

He was astonished, "What do you mean, 'neither are you?' Of course you are!"

Kierra furrowed her brow. She still looked pale, though not nearly as bad as she had. Keen realized that he might have sounded a bit more angry than he had intended.

"No," she said carefully and quietly, "I'm not. I just carry a bow for protection. I'm not an archer."

"Boy, I'd hate to meet a real elven archer then," Keen said earnestly, and he knew he meant it. Kierra gave him a pitied look, but said nothing more about it. What she did say was, "But archer or not, that really was a great idea. I wouldn't have thought of the rope."

Keen blushed. He realized she hadn't been teasing him. She'd meant the compliment. He tried to smile, but knew it came out awkwardly, "Thanks. There's nothing left of the stew but broth, and there's not much of the rations left either."

"Any sign of more rain?" she asked.

He looked up at the cloudy but dry sky, "No."

She sighed, "How much water is left?"

"Most of one skin."

"A day at most."

Keen looked back up at the sky. He couldn't see it well through the forest canopy, but his best guess was that the clouds were moving off rather than gathering in. He doubted they could count on any more rain. He looked down to the little stream. If his hip wasn't in as bad of shape as it was, he might be able to make it down there for one skin's worth of water at a time, he thought. But as it was, he was struggling to drag his leg around the cave and was starting to wonder if he could even walk at this point, given the opportunity to stand up properly. The truth was that they had about a day to figure out how to get water before their situation became truly desperate.

Keen looked back at Kierra and their eyes met. The severity of concern in her stare told him that her thoughts were not far from his. He nodded, but then he turned to cleaning his goose.

The goose made an excellent supper, and there was just enough rabbit stew broth left that they used no water that evening. Keen set up the rain catcher again just in case, but with little real hope of collecting any.

The night passed predictably. The wailing army of restless ghosts continued to hunt for living prey sporadically. Kierra seemed stable enough that

Keen slept more than he had the night before, although the throbbing in his hip prevented him from sleeping as well as he needed. At one point in the depth of the night, a light drizzling rain did fall, but it amounted to less than an inch of accumulation in the collector. Still, they shared it over cold goose for breakfast.

The pain in Keen's left hip was terrible now. He could no longer sit still or lay comfortably in any position. He felt his body rocking slowly in place as he ate breakfast. Kierra, who was sitting propped against the wall watched him nervously. He grimaced as he shifted positions again and again, the sensation of red-hot pokers pressing into his bones becoming unavoidable now, and the lingering ache now extending into his back, groin and as far down his leg as his shin. The swelling had gotten so bad he'd had to loosen the ties on his pants now a third time. Kierra was steadily improving. Keen was glad of that. He himself, on the other hand, was slowly declining.

"I've had a thought," Kierra said, still watching him cautiously, clear worry etched in every line on her pale face, "but it's probably suicide. Can you still walk?"

He looked back at her, biting his lip, trying to hold in the growing agony. He'd love to walk. He didn't know if he could or not, but the part of him that was growing desperate just wanted to stretch, to move, to uncurl, to do anything to change position and to have more space even though the more rational side of him knew that none of that would actually treat his injury.

"I doubt it, but I'd try. Why?"

"I should have thought of this before we got this bad off, and now I don't know how much my stupidity may have cost us, in which case, I'm sorry. I'm not cut out for this sort of thing, really..." She had tears in her eyes, and Keen couldn't fathom how she could say such a thing. She was so clearly cut out for this sort of thing. He frowned at her. That probably didn't help much. She went on anyway, "This is just the first, and the smallest, of a series of caves. It was the one we could get to, obviously. It occurs to me now...probably too late," she looked down, forlorn, and to Keen still a bit beautiful, "We should probably try to get to the next one. And then maybe the next...if we make it, that is. If we can get from one cave to the next, we can get closer to the stream..."

Closer to the stream....Keen felt his own gaze glaze over. What wouldn't he give to bathe his burning, aching leg in cool water? Of course, he still wouldn't have time for that, but still, just to move...He realized that Kierra was right. It was probably suicidal by now. They should have tried this days ago, but they couldn't turn back time. This was what they had to work with. They would have to try it. He lifted his eyes back up to meet hers with determined purpose and nodded solemnly. They only had enough water for a day. They had to get to that stream in that amount of time or they would die anyway. Thinking about it like that made it much less crazy.

"How far to the next one?"

"I'll show you...as soon as it's safe."

They waited until the screaming hoards of death passed by next and trepidatiously stuck their heads out of their cave. It was eight feet down to the forest floor. Looking straight out to the left it was a little more than a hundred yards to the stream, but looking in the same direction but up and over the rock that sheltered them, a larger rock sat lower into the ground a mere hundred feet away. Even from here it was clear that the space between the rock itself and where it should have met the ground was just wide enough to slide into.

"How deep is that?" Keen asked her, eying the narrow opening nervously. He could certainly get into it, but even with his pack on he'd be too wide.

"It's easily twice as big as this cave," she answered, "Maybe bigger. It gets really damp in there when it rains, obviously, but clearly we're not expecting a lot of that or we wouldn't be moving. My mother grew up not far from here. I've played in these caves as a child. Even in heavy rains, that thing doesn't flood. It's safe." She grinned at him, "That's the best snowball fort there is, right there."

Keen smiled nostalgically. He and his brothers always built their own snowball forts. How did he and an elf have that childhood passtime in common? He knew he was developing a sadness about the way he was looking at her. He could tell by the uncomfortable way she glanced away. He kept watching her anyway. She really wasn't so different from him: not in any of the ways that mattered.

And right on cue, the light turned silver and the wailing started. It was getting old and bothersome. The pair ducked back into their familiar and, by now, very smelly cave. While they waited for the noisome army to pass by they quickly gathered up their gear, packing everything as tightly and as lightly as they could.

They agreed that on this next pass they would merely test their ability to escape and not try to make it all the way to the new cave.

It was a good thing they did. Kierra made it down just fine, but couldn't get back up without help, and began bleeding again once she made it. Nonetheless, she felt fairly sure that she could sprint to the new cave and roll in. Keen on the other hand landed badly on his bad leg. He had no trouble using his arms to pull himself back up, but by the time he had, the undead were back looking for the disturbance of the living again, and Keen wasn't sure if he could walk. He had barely been able to stand.

Still, they knew they had to try. They hatched a new plan. Kierra didn't like the new plan, but it was Keen's plan and he insisted on it because they had to get closer to the water. He gave Kierra as much of the gear as she thought she could carry and still run which amounted to her pack, lantern, bow, quiver, blanket, the "dirty bowl," which was the extra bowl they used as a bedpan, and the extra waterskin and rations. Keen left everything out of his pack he didn't need which was most of it, but he kept his cooking supplies and the rain catcher, his messkit and bedroll, her lantern oil, and one spare tunic he still had, mostly in case they needed it to make bandages. He then took some of the ruined cloth leftover from clothes they were wearing when they were injured and wrapped the tip and lower length of his blade and then used what was left to pad the hilt as best he could. He was going to use his huge sword as a crutch in the hopes that he could hobble just fast enough. Kierra was worried stiff.

"What I need for you to do," Keen told her looking her dead in the eyes and trying to sound as sure of himself as he could muster, "Is to get there and roll in quickly, so that you're out of my way in case I can get there."

"IN CASE????" she exclaimed exasperatedly, "What if I don't find that acceptable?" She was positively mutinous. Keen smiled. He really did like her.

The wailing was beginning to quiet again. They needed to move.

"I'm not getting any better or any faster. The water's not getting any closer. Unless you've got a better idea, then you need to go...now."

Her bottom lip quivered defiantly, but she grabbed her appointed supplies, kissed his cheek again and slipped past him and out of the cave. He had to not think about that kiss. He had to move immediately behind her. They'd sense her right away. Too late, it occurred to him that maybe he should have gone first.

Keen dropped carefully onto his good leg and leaned onto his trusty zweihander. The sword was strong. It gave him confidence. The pain that shot through his skeleton was terrible, but it was nothing compared to the terror he suddenly felt being out in the open. Kierra was gone in a flash. Keen concentrated everything into putting the sword into the ground one step at a time. One step at a time. Step. Step. Step. One movement in front of the other. Move. Keep Moving. Forget the searing pain. Step. Step. Step. Move. The. Sword. One step. Then another. One. More. Step. Then one more. Like digging over a distance. The light was turning silver. One. More. Step. Keep stepping. Just keep stepping. He wasn't even looking where he was going, so he glanced up and realized he was off in his aim. Halfway there, but he needed to veer slightly to his left. Step. Step. Step. Dig. Dig. Dig. Move. Move. Move. He could hear the wailing. He looked up again. Kierra was diving into the cave. Good girl. You made it. Step. Step Step. Keep moving, Keen. Just keep moving. Dig. Dig. Dig. The air was turning cold.

"KEEN!"

He could hear Kierra. He opened his eyes. She was within reach sticking out of the hole. He threw his pack off to her. The light was blindingly silver. The wailing drowning out all sound. He dove for the ground, dropping his sword under him.

Everything was muffled and sharp like he was rolling in wool lined in daggers. He tried to scream but he could feel something wet gurgling up from his throat. He began to fall through a sickening wet hole until he was met with a

THUD

He opened his eyes. Kierra was staring down at him horrified. Above him the silver light of the wailing ghost army was pouring in the opening of the new cave. He tried to speak, but started to choke and tasted blood. Kierra's eyes widened. She reached desperately for her pack as Keen's world went from bright silver to dark black.

When he woke later he was laying on Kierra's blanket, the smell of leftover goose warming on charcoal coming from somewhere near his feet. He could still taste blood in his mouth, but it wasn't as fresh. The light seemed more normal. The ceiling was farther away than it had been for days. He looked around.

This was definitely a larger cave, easily twice as big, but darker. The opening was much smaller and this one was mostly under ground. It smelled damp and mossy, but that was a significant improvement over the smell they had left in the old one. Kierra was indeed at the end of the cave nearest Keen's feet cooking. He smiled. She didn't usually cook for him. He tried to sit up, and the sound startled her. She turned around.

"Oh, goodness! You're awake!" she exclaimed and rushed to his side. She laid a gentle hand on his abdomen and looked worriedly into his face, "How are you?"

Keen had to stop and consider the question. His hip hurt like crazy, although it was so much more comfortable to be able to stretch it out. He felt sort of beat up all over, like he'd been in a bad fight, but he didn't feel particularly injured anywhere. He was dizzy and weak, and his chest and throat burned a bit like he'd inhaled hot air. That last thought was odd, since the air had felt so cold. And that, too, was odd as he thought about it, because he hadn't remembered it being cold the day of the battle when he'd encountered these things before. With all of this running through his head, he must have started to look odd, because Kierra started to look concerned again.

"Keen?" she prodded gently. She took his hand in her own.

"I think I'm OK," he answered finally, although he realized that his voice sounded hoarse, "I just feel really beat up."

Kierra offered him the waterskin and he drank gladly. It was hard with as bad as he felt to refrain from drinking too deeply. Kierra didn't even caution him. She looked parched, but she said nothing. He offered it back to her when he finally stopped himself, but she shook her head. The skin was already half gone, Keen realized. They'd need to move again, and maybe another time after that to even hope to be close enough to the stream to have ready access to water. This wasn't over.

They ate in near silence and made solemn preparations for the next move. The next cave was a little closer, but the entrance was on the other side of its hillock than the one facing where they were currently, and there was a short climb up a few rocks to get there. They only had to go about 60 feet, but the four or five foot climb around to the cave mouth had both of them worried.

This time Keen left first, and Kierra let him get a good head start. She still passed him, but he was nearly in the cave before the army arrived and only suffered a tear in his backpack on this second trip, which was much less worrisome. What did worry them both, however, was that by the time they made it into this cave, which was much more open and felt much less safe, Keen really could no longer put any weight at all on his bad leg and he was spitting blood again.

They rested that afternoon before moving one last time into a strange cave made up of a hollow of rock and a tangle of two trees' roots all nestled together. This shelter was only slightly larger than their original, was slightly subterranean, with an opening about half the size of what they had had before. It was only about fifty feet from the last cave and a straight shot across the forest floor. Keen had to lean very heavily on his zweihander to make it, but he did it. He was slower, but the army had only just arrived as he got under the new shelter which had put them just over halfway to the stream. And although Keen didn't like the idea, Kierra decided that she would go to the stream and fill one waterskin after that. After all, she reasoned, she'd managed two from twice the distance before.

"At more more full health," Keen reminded her.

"I'll grant you," she admitted, clearly exhausted, "But this is half the distance and half the water. And I think it makes more sense than us trying to move you again on that leg. Besides, the next closest cave is as far from here as the first one was, and I don't think we're up for that, although if we get to where we can make it, that'll put us just 50-60 feet from the stream. We could survive there for a long time, if we could just get there."

Keen nodded. If we could just get there.

As dusk settled about them, Kierra returned with the thing they needed most: water. She'd beat the ghastly army by inches it seemed, but she'd filled the empty waterskin. They'd make it another day with what they had. Keen resolved to try to kill another bird the next day if he could, if only to keep convincing himself that he was contributing.

Keen and Kierra cuddled up together in their new home. They were parched, bloody, sweaty, dirty, swollen and goodness knew what else, but they were still alive, and by the looks of it, they just might stay that way a little while longer at least. They had each other, and for that, Keen was very very grateful.

Keen woke the next morning with a renewed sense of gratitude for his life and Kierra's companionship. It took him most of the day, given his deteriorating condition, but he did manage to snare another bird. This one was just a small duck, but it was food. Kierra ran out in the afternoon and filled the skin they'd emptied in the last day. The pair began to make plans for an eventual trip to the last cave, but Keen was in no shape to try it today, or tomorrow for that matter.

Keen did take the time during that day, while sitting patiently and watching for ducks, to observe the maddening menace that had been stalking them all of this time. He noticed that not every group that passed by was the same. The more rotted and skeletal looking spirits seemed to be enacting a battle between themselves, but killing anything that got in their way. He watched a cavalry charge that seemed to be unaware of the trees. He watched lines break and flee, only to be routed and then reform and march back. He could not see the whole of whatever they would call their "battlefield," but as the groups of ghosts ran and rode back and forth, he was beginning to form a whole picture anyway.

But on top of that were bands of newer-looking spirits. Some were still grotesquely rotted, but some looked like the ghosts of the recent dead. These groups seemed to merely be roaming back and forth in a violent haze, searching for something. The two sets of spirits, the battle participants and the roamers, seemed to be completely unaware of each other.

He shared his observations with Kierra who seemed less interested unless the information helped them with their ordeal. Keen wasn't sure that it did, but he definitely found the whole thing curious.

"Was there ever a battle fought here like this?"

Kierra thought for a moment and answered, "The field where you guys were setting up your attack," and at that Keen noticed her eyes darken at him briefly, but he didn't mention it. He already felt guilty. "It's been called by a lot of names, but all them seem to refer to war or death. I grew up calling it 'Massacre Field,' but I've also heard it called 'Battleground Park' and 'The Warrior's Graveyard.' I think it's official name is 'Bloodless Grove' according to the lore keepers in Willowmark. Anyway, no trees grow there, no matter how many acorns fall. But it looks grassy and healthy and beautiful, and It fills with flowers in the spring if no armies are marching across it," and again Keen noticed her look toward him change, "But something bad must have happened there. A long time ago."

"But no stories of it being haunted?"

"Not that I've ever heard. Truthfully, it's an obvious sort of place to have a battle if you're going to have one in the Willows at all, so I just assumed..." She let the thought hang in the air.

"Assumed?" Keen prodded.

"Well, yeah. I just assumed that it had probably been a battlefield before. Maybe many times, But the Willows hasn't seen real war like this in over a thousand years...not on our own soil at least."

"Wow. A thousand years?"

"Over."

Keen studied her for a moment and then returned to his task. Learning the history of the area was somewhat fascinating, and hearing Kierra talk about it made him that much more aware of how he'd almost helped to destroy her home.

One other thing changed between them finally. For the first time in their now 8 days together, they finally began to talk a little about themselves over an evening meal of poorly roasted duck and stream water. It seemed somewhat surreal to Keen to think about home, family and a life beyond these woods anymore, but even stranger to think about an elvish family, home, hearth and friends waiting for his strangely perfect little companion at the end of their ordeal together.

"No, I'm not an archer," it began. Keen had made a comment yet again about killing the duck, but not having been an archer as Kierra was, "I've told you that." She was smiling and shaking her head, but clearly somewhat exasperated. "My brother's mate is a scout AND an archer, and quite a good one," she went on, "Do you know how much she would laugh at you calling ME an archer?"

"Well, you're better with a bow than I am," Keen protested marveling inwardly, also, at her use of the word, 'mate,' "What are you, then?" His voice was still unusually deep for his own, but he was able to use it more freely.

"A singer," she answered simply, and Keen nearly spit his food out.

"A what?" he exclaimed.

Kierra eyed him defiantly.

"I thought you were in the army," he choked.

"I was assigned to the unit for assistance," she said defensively.

"What kind of assistance?" he asked, now really wondering at the word 'mate' and blushing.

She shot him a curious and incredulous look that clearly told him she had no idea why he was blushing, for which he was extremely grateful.

"Do you have any idea what a treesinger is?" she asked him.

He raised his eyebrows. "Nope."

"I had a feeling," she responded, "Well, for starters, I could help you heal that leg if I were whole myself," Kierra paused, clearly weighing what to say.

Keen, too, weighed how to hear her words. He suspected strongly that he was about to hear things that a week ago would have alarmed him significantly. Now he was reminding himself that he would trust, and in fact had trusted, Kierra with his life, so he needed to remember that, no matter what she said next.

She seemed to be watching the pained expression on his face pretty carefully before she continued, "All natural life has an underlying vibration, like music. I can sing that. I can," she paused again, but this time it seemed to Keen that she was trying to find the words to explain rather than the courage, "...tap into the...like attune to the underlying melody of your leg trying to heal or of a plant trying to grow and I can...encourage it along. I can...hear how one living thing is connected to the next living thing and the next and the next after that so that when I sing I can get a simple message across a great distance to someone to whom I'm very connected to emotionally. I'm a treesinger. It's a sacred art...and no, it's not magic, so don't even go there. We just understand nature differently, more deeply, than most people do..."

Kierra looked down and trailed off. She'd hit a touchy subject for herself, and Keen understood that he was not invited to argue that last point. He didn't. It made him uncomfortable, but he thought it was strangely exciting, too. He didn't know how he felt, but not knowing how he felt was becoming a familiar sensation around Kierra. So, instead he went for a safer topic.

"So, you have a brother?"

Kierra looked up, all traces of worry gone. That suited Keen fine. He didn't need to have the difficult, weird conversation. Someone else can sort that stuff out. He can talk about brothers. He had those himself. He knew about having brothers.

"Yes. Joran. He's an officer in the military, which is where I got the idea to volunteer. Well, not *from* my brother so much. In truth, he was mortified. But my father, my brother, and my brother's lover are all in the military. In fact so are my cousin and *his* lover, so when they were looking for treesinger support for new units it seemed to make sense to me to volunteer. My brother nearly had a conniption, though."

Keen smiled. He didn't understand the magic/not-magic thing, but the rest of this was sounding like anybody's family. She really wasn't as weird as she sometimes seemed. And he liked her. He just couldn't shake that at all.

"Why?" he asked, suspecting he could guess at the answer.

"Mostly because he thought I'd get myself killed. Joran doesn't have a lot faith in my ability to do much on my own."

Keen tried not to laugh. She's so amazing. She can do just about anything. But her very normal-sounding family included a very normal-sounding brother that probably had no idea.

"What about you?" she asked him, "Have you got a sibling?"

"Two brothers," he answered, "One older. One younger."

"Wow! Three! That's a large family!" she exclaimed, clearly impressed.

He recoiled slightly. "No it's not!" he protested, "My mother's the youngest of 12 children and HER mom was one of 14!"

Kierra choked on her duck at that point and required assistance from Keen to get it out. When she was finally breathing again, Keen learned that Kierra had, in fact, never even heard of a family larger than 4 children and would have considered that tremendous. Apparently the elves were struggling to merely maintain their population from one generation to the next.

"That's what makes war so devastating...well one of many things," Kierra concluded eventually, "We really don't bounce back well. We never have."

They spent that night curled up together as usual. Keen laid awake longer than normal wondering about Joran and his lover and what they were like and wanting very much to tell them how capable and amazing Kierra was. He also cradled Kierra a little more tightly than he normally did. He wasn't sure, but he thought he heard her crying.

Tollie

On the fourth morning, Tollie woke with a start. She'd been having her nightmare again, only this time, the garden was flooding and her father and sister were trapped in the rising waters. Tollie didn't feel like a little girl anymore; she felt much older, older in fact, than she really was. Just as her father fell into the abyss, she heard small voices shouting:

"What the hell was that?!"

Tollie became aware of the cart, the hard boards of the driver's bench under her aching back. She missed her bed, but tried to go back to sleep anyway. A dream where maybe she could still save her father was a better place to be right now.

"Crap! It's getting bigger!" the small voice was male and urgent. Tollie thought it odd that she was still dreaming.

"That may be moving slower, but I think it's bigger than the last one!" a small female voice added, sounding scared.

Tollie opened her eyes. How was she supposed to sleep when her dream was being so loud?

"This is bad..." the first one muttered. It was Kyrt, "Tollie! We gotta get out of here!"

Realizing the voices weren't in her dreams, Tollie scrambled out of her knotted blanket, kicking and swearing, panic rising at the thought that something was wrong. Struggling to her feet she knew immediately that the light wasn't right. Lights seemed to be popping in front of her eyes and she could hardly focus. Turning toward the source, she realized there was a light show taking place on the horizon to the far southeast. It looked as if all the stars had gathered on one horizon and melted into an angry serpent, stalking the horizon as it grew. The air felt slightly charged and threatened to electrify the pre-dawn dampness.

She felt something land lightly leaf-like on her shoulder. Gentle as it was, she jumped anyway. Kyrt caught the air on his wings and settled back onto Tollie's shoulder.

"What is it?" he whispered, unapologetic for startling her.

Small footprints stumbling on the cart behind heralded Jesp's arrival.

"It's the Water Titan," Tollie gulped. "The prophecy. It's....happening."

As dawn broke, it cleared the image from the sky, but not from the depths of Tollie's soul. She felt a deeper cold than she ever had in her life.

Her body ached all over, but she forced it back into the now-familiar position of driving the cart. She realized sadly that right now she'd give anything to be back in her tower room with everything the way it had been, just five days ago. But she couldn't linger on that right now. Every part of her hurt from driving a hard wooden cart for so long, but she'd have to do it again, and keep doing it, for at least another day or two. She took a deep breath.

"Jesp get down from there!" Kyrt yelled as Tollie, raising the reigns to nudge the mule forward, realized that Jesp was still clinging to the board that separated Tollie's seat from the back of the cart. Tollie put the reigns down again and turned to look at the faerie.

Jesp was clinging to the cart for all she was worth, a fearful expression on her face as she realized the cart had nearly lurched forward and she still couldn't fly.

"Sorry," Tollie stammered, picking Jesp up carefully and putting her back in her satchel. It was rather like caring for a wounded bird, except that wounded birds probably went in their nests and didn't need to be carried to a private bush on occasion.

Jesp looked up at her with that drunken look Tollie was accustomed to from her. "Thanks," she squeaked. Tollie nodded, glanced at Kyrt and then back at the horizon. A terrible storm was gathering in that direction now. Tollie felt a lump in her throat. She wasn't fond of storms.

Setting off at last, Tollie took mental stock of where they were and what she knew about this road. They'd been careful thus far to camp in remote places and to drive straight through populated ones, but knowing what was looming behind them, Tollie desperately tried to think of an inn or stable she could reach quickly. She really didn't want to get caught in that thing.

Her mind raced with information she'd gleaned from the library over the last nearly six years. She realized that although she'd been slow to learn it, and reluctant at that, she'd picked up a lot. She tried not to think of her own lacking knowledge as what remained of her father's legacy, but she still wanted to make him proud and knew he needed her now more than he ever had.

The sun was warm, but the breeze threatened the cool of a spring storm. She remembered that the Water Titan was sometimes referred to as the Storm Titan. It was also called the Titan of Death. Tollie tried not to dwell on that title, but was willing to bet quite a lot on the fact that the storm that was coming was going to be really really bad.

She was right. The wind blew up before she reached the edge of the town she'd sidetracked off to. Small voices yelling in the back forced her to stop and get Jesp down from her sack. The wind was rocking it so violently it was threatening to come loose from its hangings and Jesp had vomited all over it. Tollie simply sat Jesp in her lap and kept going, the drizzle giving way to stinging rain as thunder loomed distantly and flashing clouds raced to catch them.

Tollie pulled into the farthest outskirts of Stable Glen, a border town between the Morrowlands and the Meadows, between the kingdom of the morrowelves and the unkempt wilds and neat villages of the halfling, gnome and elfling populations intermingled beyond it. In the distance, even in the gathering dark of the storm, the huge mountain range to the far north, innocuously called the Barrow Hills, were visible holding up the far horizon.

Stable Glen housed and bred the horses the Morrowelf border patrol used. It had been a stroke of sudden insight Tollie had that she silently thanked her father for. It was a place littered with stables where she hoped they could hide and wait out the madness that was breaking loose overhead.

She reached the nearest breeding farm as the rain became truly torrential. She was worried that Kyrt would get washed out of the cart if she kept going. She found herself cradling Jesp against the wind and rain like a small kitten. She stopped at the steading and ran in. She offered the farmer and his wife a few coins for a chance to wait out the storm in a stable or barn. Tollie didn't mention the faeries in case anyone was looking for any sign of the crown being moved.

The older elf and his wife were genial and, making excuses about Tollie's cart getting stuck in the mud in the pasture, insisted she take a guest room instead. It was a tremendous stroke of luck for the trio. The guest room was on the back of the house with its own entrance. It was small by elf standards, but plenty large enough for the three of them. Tollie stuck a faerie in each pocket and shoved the crown into her bag of clothes and ran them inside. It was a testament to how bad the weather had gotten that neither faerie protested at her taking temporary charge of the crown.

She left the faeries and her bag on the generous bed and ran back out for the books. She made several trips as the storm grew louder and nastier, but eventually got all of their supplies inside as well. The farmer took their mule to a dry shed nearest the house and gave it some feed before trekking back through the sloshing mud. Tollie took the muddy bag out of her suitcase and spread the books out all over the room to dry them out. All in all, Tollie was exhausted by the time she collapsed wet and cold on top of the quilted bed covering.

A slight bouncing near her face prevented her from falling asleep laying sideways across the bed. She peered out from behind tired eyelids to see Jesp and Kyrt walking, bouncing, dancing? Whatever they were doing on the bed they were also starting to giggle and bounce higher.

Tollie was too tired to be irritated, too tired to be amused either. She felt washed up and wrung out from her soaked cloak right through to her grief-stricken heart. What she did mutter was, "Be careful, Jesp. You don't want to end up like last time."

Tollie did eventually get up and shake out the damp blankets she had laid on. She shared the warm and hardy grain and vegetable stew that the farmer's wife brought in, smirking mischievously at the faeries for having dived under the pillows to avoid notice. She changed into dry clothes after insisting that both faeries turn their back, helped Jesp find a moment of much needed privacy in a potted plant, and fell fast asleep as soon as her head hit the pillow. She didn't even pay attention to where the faeries ended up.

Tollie was mildly aware of the fact that the storm raged all night. But she was only aware of it inasmuch as it made her sleep that much more deeply. Normally she didn't like storms, but there was something about her gratitude for not being out in this one that made her sleep like she hadn't in ages: dreamlessly.

Tollie woke with a start as the predawn grayness settled around her room through its two huge windows. Something wasn't right. She could hear the rain still coming down pretty hard outside, but the huge booming thunder of the night before was quiet. But that wasn't it. Tollie rolled over. On the pillow next to her, a garden glove and an old knitted scarf were crumpled in heaps and breathing. Wait, no, she could see the brown curly tufted hair of Kyrt sticking out of the glove, his blue and silver wings just visible folded in behind him. The breathing scarf, then, was easier to explain.

What had woken her? She searched her memory for a sound or clue. Something was wrong: all of her senses told her so. But what.

"Kyrt?" she whispered.

She heard the faerie start to stir with a "hrmmph," when suddenly

CRASH!

There was a women's scream, suddenly muffled, and then the farmer yelled, "Let go of her!"

The faeries scrambled out of their nests with a start and Tollie jumped out of bed as the sounds of struggle became quickly louder.

"Quick! Hide!" Tollie whispered urgently as the door crashed open.

Tollie had barely made it out of bed. The two faeries had dove under the mussed covers she'd left behind and were essentially invisible, but everything else: the books laid out to dry, the muddy old sack containing the crown, even the faeries' weapons, were laid out in clear view.

Tollie looked terrified up into the muddy and triumphantly angry leather face of a human thug. Another, slightly cleaner and elven, was behind him in the doorway.

"Ah, a halfling for company, Farmer Scop?" the elf growled, "Your tastes have worsened."

The human grabbed Tollie roughly by the upper arm and dragged her out of the room and past the stairs outside the door that led to the farmer's private rooms. She clammered her feet desperately for a foothold to avoid the scraping of the rough boards against her bare legs, but the human was moving too quickly and was too intent on being rough.

In the large fireside sitting room that dominated the lower floor of the farmhouse stood a very clean and eerily dry elf wearing much richer clothing than the four thugs that were in the room. The two Tollie hadn't seen yet, both human, were tying the struggling farmer and his wife into chairs with gags. The look on

Farmer Scop's face told Tollie that the knots were far too tight, and his arms were clearly pulled too far back behind him. Tollie watched as a tear leaked out of one startled eye before she was thrust hard into a small wooden chair with her back against the stairway and tied just as roughly. The pain in her arms and shoulders was as intense as fire and as immediate as the jerking that threatened to break them.

"Please," she muttered before something was shoved into her mouth that tasted vaguely of oil.

"Sorry little Miss," said the clean elf calmly, looking down at her with an almost hungry look across his face, "But we can't leave tale-tellers here. Scop should have warned you that he'd crossed me before he offered you a bed. Pity," he concluded without any sense of the word.

The one thug that was an elf hit the farmer squarely in the face and then repeated the abuse. His wife strained for all she was worth against her bonds, clearly screaming and crying into her gag. As the second blow landed on the farmer's face, Tollie realized with horror that the three humans were dumping oil all over the furniture. Panic rose in her chest as the realization of what they were planning washed over her like a muddy wave. She glanced back at one who had gotten out of her sight just in time to get a face full of the oil he was pouring over her head. A second bottle of oil was dumped on the farmer's wife, and one more punch clearly broke Scop's nose. The men backed off at a gesture from the clean elf who looked more menacing than anything Tollie had ever witnessed.

Pulling a box of matches out of his jacket pocket, he looked at the bleeding Farmer Scop and said with a mildly amused smile, "No oil for you I'm afraid. With any luck, you'll live long enough to watch these two burn first."

Tollie tried to scream, tried to struggle. She realized she'd just been sitting there and these men were going to KILL THEM.

The thugs gathered behind their boss, clearly excited to watch the fire start. Their leader, now smiling broadly selected a match from his box. Tollie was now trying to pull her shoulders out of their sockets to get loose. Her face was soaked in oil and tears and the scream that was lost in her head was pounding on her temples to get out. Her arm joints felt like they were being dissolved in lava, but Tollie jerked anyway. Across the room the farmer and his wife were doing the same, the farmer clearly trying to plead through his gag.

The matchstick emerged. Then the man's face changed to one of mild surprise. He muttered "Wha..." and fell to the ground.

The stunned silence that followed didn't last long. Two more men, both human, fell just as suddenly as the last two began drawing weapons. Looking up at the hanging lamp, the last elf yelled "Faeries!" as two small dart-like arrows flew over Tollie's head from the staircase behind her and hit the elf in the side of the face. He went down as soon as his eyes registered what had happened. The last man took a huge swing at the lamp with a hammer, smashing it into bits of soft copper and hot candle wax with a huge crashing noise.

"Kyrt!" yelled Jesp's voice from overhead, but a small dart flew up out of the rubble and struck the man's hand as it was heading back down for a final blow. The hand dropped just short of the wreckage and the hammer broke the floorboard inches from where Kyrt was emerging, shakily, from under a copper wax pan. He looked up at where Jesp must have been, on the stairs behind Tollie, and passed out.

"NO!" yelled Jesp from somewhere slightly farther down the stairs than Tollie had first heard her, "Kyrt!"

Tollie watched with fascinated horror as Jesp came running around the bottom stair a moment later, skidding in oil and tripping over debris. Tollie tried to yell to her for help, but she was too focused on one thing: the small faerie-shaped lump in the middle of the room.

Tollie had oil running into her eyes and burning so badly she had to shut them. She could tell she was still screaming, but had lost all conscious control over it. She had lost feeling now in her hands and her neck was starting to feel like it was tearing. She tried to scream louder, unable to lean forward to let the oil run out of her eyes without further torturing her neck. After another long moment she heard Jesp's familiar small voice near her feet yell, "Stop kicking!"

Obediently Tollie tried to become as still as she could, though the impulse to writhe was overwhelming. She felt a small sawing motion between her ankles and was surprised by how quickly the thick ropes dropped away. A moment more and Tollie dared try to open her eyes to see where the faerie had gotten to, accepting the searing oil in hopes that her shoulders would soon be relieved. She didn't see Jesp anywhere but eventually heard her on the staircase behind. She shut her eyes and started to moan unintentionally when she finally felt the sawing motion at her wrists. Then a small pair of feet walked up her aching arm and cut the final rope.

Tollie's arms sprang out from her sides fiercely, unwittingly flinging Jesp back to the bottom of the stair. Tollie couldn't see her. She couldn't see much of anything but blurred popping lights as she pulled the rag out of her mouth and got unsteadily to her feet. She knew Farmer Scop and his wife were still in agony, but dutifully she checked on the faeries first. Both were stirring. Jesp looked dizzy and was moving slowly, but she was moving. Kyrt had sat up, but didn't seem to be able to stand. He looked up at Tollie panting, horror still in his eyes as Tollie went to untie the last two intended victims. Then she did the bravest thing she was capable of. She fell into a sobbing heap on the floor.

"I'm going for the authorities," came the voice of Farmer Scop. Tollie could hear the big people moving around the room. The faeries. She looked up quickly to where they had been, terrified that she'd let them get stepped on.

"Now, there, dear," came the voice of the farmer's wife. Tollie could see that she bending over the spot where Kyrt had been sitting moments before. She sounded like she was talking to a child, "Where did you come from?"

Tollie dragged herself off of the floor. Every bit of her ached, her eyes burned, she felt slimy and had been shaken to her very core. But she wasn't about to let the well-meaning elderly elf talk to Kyrt like a small child. Tollie herself hated that, and Kyrt and Jesp had just saved their lives.

She reached the pair of them as the elf reached down to lift the clearly agonized Kyrt off the ground, "There there, little one. We'll get you fixed up."

"Um, ma'am," Tollie stammered, "He's a full grown male. He's not a child."

Kyrt looked at Tollie. His face was strained with pain but his eyes were grateful.

The elf blinked at Tollie for a moment and said, "Oh, I'm sorry. I didn't mean to offend."

This made Tollie feel bad. She hadn t meant to be rude.

Tollie crossed quickly to where she had last seen Jesp, leaving the farmer's wife to carry Kyrt over to a serving board sitting under the front window. She was muttering something about seeing that he was patched up.

Jesp was still standing at the base of the stairs, clinging to the bottom of the rail. She looked scared and breathless, but whole. Tollie knelt down to her.

"Thank you," and at this Tollie choked on tears determined to come pouring out, "I don't even want to think about what nearly happened there. We owe you our lives." And again Tollie was bawling. It seemed she had so much to cry about anymore. There was just too much to keep in. She sat next to Jesp and wept. She was vaguely aware of conversation going on across the room, but she just couldn't participate. Her father was gone. She had no home, no foundation. Her body ached and she was just injured and nearly murdered. No one who had known her even knew she was still alive. Had they even looked? Or had they just assumed she was dead, shrugged their shoulders and went on with their lives? And her father....Tollie couldn't even bury him. At least she'd have liked to have brought him back to rest next to her mother, but she couldn't even do that. All she could do was cling to the stair rail and cry.

Farmer Scop arrived back at some point with the authorities. Tollie got up and allowed herself to be questioned. She was in a trance. No one registered for her. She didn't see anybody. She nodded or shook her head or answered in short meaningless phrases like, "No, I don't think so," or "I don't remember." The only time she was alert at all was when an elf wearing a tabard, which may have described them all really if she had paid attention, asked her where they were from. This jerked her back to her senses with urgency.

"Hilltop Market," she lied quickly, "We're headed home from Ash Lake University." She wasn't sure where the lie had come from, but it was a good one. It would explain the books, at least. Hopefully, they'd have no reason to go through their things and find the crown.

Tollie watched numbly as the still-sleeping would-be murderers were locked in chains and carried out to a waiting cart. Apparently there had been other deaths in the area attributed to these men, but nothing that could be proven. The guards were thanking the serving board for their part in saving the elderly couple. Tollie looked around and realized Jesp was gone.

"Jesp?"

"I have the little ones over here, dear," the lady elf responded, "I've got them patched up."

Tollie crossed to the table. Kyrt was laying down. His legs were both bandaged heavily. His wings were folded under him and he was staring blankly at the ceiling taking very long blinks. There was an empty thimble sitting next to him. Jesp's torn wing had been unwrapped and looked much better. The pattern across it was no longer aligned properly, like a torn picture on paper glued back slightly crooked, but the brilliant red, orange and gold coloring of it was vibrant again where it had been so pale after the fire. Jesp was holding Kyrt's hand in her lap, sitting cross-legged. Her head had a tiny bandage around it, but she had a fierceness about her now that Tollie had never seen in her before. Jesp was angry.

The farmer's wife looked down at Tollie as the last of the thugs were hauled roughly out the front door. She had a black eye sprouting dramatically across a third of her face and her good eye was bloodshot. Her hair was caked with oil. Her dress was ripped and she had her shoulders hunched forward so she could move her arms without disturbing them. She looked a terrible mess, and Tollie knew she must look the same.

"I'm Ella, by the way," she said simply, "I don't know that I introduced myself before. Do you need anything?"

A new life, Tollie thought bitterly, but shook her head no.

"We owe you everything," the farmer said from behind her, choking on his words. "Your little friends here really saved the day. We can never repay you."

He moved into Tollie's side view but she didn't look up at him. She lowered her head and shook it again. She was staring at her friends, for now she realized they were exactly that, and started crying softly again. She felt that if she spoke, surely everything in her being would explode out uncontrollably in some wet tragedy. She had nothing left to offer anyone.

Ella put a gentle arm around her shoulder. "Let us make you a warm bath," she offered. "I know I'd like one." She was crying, too.

At this Tollie nodded. She looked down at Jesp and their eyes met. Jesp's expression had turned to concern; Tollie's was apology.

The day passed in a haze for Tollie. She bathed dutifully when presented with a tub of warm clean water. She scrubbed the oil off of her skin and out of her hair. She redressed and allowed her oil-soaked clothes to be laundered by Ella who seemed determined to keep moving as if nothing had happened. Jesp had agreed on their behalf to stay another couple of days. Tollie learned that Kyrt's legs were possibly broken, but hopefully not. Jesp had banged her head hard enough to black out, but seemed OK now. Tollie hurt everywhere, inside and out. She was in such shock she was useless to anyone. she only ate when something was put in front of her, and even then, she didn't know what she was eating. Jesp started fussing over her after a couple of hours, concern clearly setting in. Tollie didn't acknowledge it. She was almost completely despondent.

Ellerby had been a good man. He had given up the life he had loved with his family to do something for the greater good. But his wife had died in their new home. One of his daughters left him. The other never understood. Then he died, murdered. Tollie had faced the prospect of being murdered. Was her father as terrified as she had been? Did he suffer, too? Did he even know what happened? Would Tollie ever know for sure?

As dusk settled in around her in her large quilted bed a thought finally hit her. Wordlessly it emerged, more a certainty of purpose than an idea. She sat up quickly and unexpectedly, causing Jesp to jump. She got up and looked over the books until she found the one: the one her father had asked her to finish reading. Suddenly, it was all she wanted to do.

*   *   *

Tollie had stayed up all night reading. The faeries had been given their own bed of sorts by Ella who had cleaned out a small drawer, lined it with a pillow and given them a knitted towel for a blanket. She'd made Kyrt some kind of pain potion that had honey in it and smelled strongly of lemon and liquor. He snored all night, though it was hardly a distraction to Tollie.

At some point in the night, Tollie came out of her shock enough to feel bad that she had not done more to help Scop and Ella. They were both more injured than she, and she had not been the one that had saved them. Nonetheless, she had allowed them to care for her before themselves, and she was blossoming some regret there.

The next two days went by without much ado. Tollie alternated all of her time between reading, helping Ella with chores, caring for Kyrt (although Jesp was doing the most of this) and sleeping. Everyone was recovering from some amount of injury or another except for Jesp, who was fine by the next day and had even begun flying again. Tollie's long excursions into the tome her father had given her had taken on new meaning and therefore new interest. She could hear his voice in her head, reading to her like he did when she was young, and finally, she got wrapped up in the story itself. It was a bizarre story, mostly because the author didn't know it himself. Tollie had to admit to herself that she liked the made up kind better, where the author knew all the details and could share. Nonetheless, it was a story full of twists and turns and Tollie finally began to understand what was going on. Maybe. A little.

Tollie watched the faeries together with a small pang of jealousy. As much as she had developed more of a "team spirit" since arriving in Stable Glen, they were much more "together" than Tollie was and it made her lonely. Still, she had her book, her father's voice in her head, and a new-found resolve to find Tallie, the only family she had left.

By the end of their third day there, and their second full day of recovery, Jesp flew over to Tollie's bed after supper and perched patiently on the top of her book. Tollie finished her paragraph and looked up.

"You've been staring at that an awful lot since we got here," Jesp mused. "Is it going to help us? Because I think we need a plan."

Jesp looked back over to the drawer where Kyrt had rolled over snoring in his sleep. She pressed her lips in concern then turned back to Tollie.

"This is the book where I learned about the crown," Tollie explained, "And it's the one my father wanted me to read before he died. And, yes, I think it's going to help. As for a plan," and here she paused to consider the faerie. Up to this point Tollie had thought of herself as in charge. If she was honest with herself, she really only felt that the faeries were along because Harold had respected their right to stay with the crown. She really hadn't considered them relevant or even useful. They were another burden she had to look after. She felt terrible about that now. They'd saved her life. They'd saved the books and the crown. They'd proven that they were potentially more useful than she herself could be. Yet here she was about to dictate the plan to Jesp, still making all the choices for the group.

"Yes?" Jesp encouraged her out of her reverie.

"I had planned to head to Brewhall, where I'm from. I wanted to go there partly because I wanted to visit my mother's grave and at least bury *something* in honor of my father. But I'd also hoped my sister might be there. When we were younger, my parents ran the school there and it was really good and had an excellent reputation. My sister was angry when my parents left it for the Library job, so I was kind of hoping that might be where she ended up."

"OK," Jesp started, "I understand that this needs to be a family time for you. But have you thought any about where we're going to go with the crown?"

Tollie looked at her, wondering if she should point out that this really shouldn't be Tollie's decision. Instead she went on, "My sister was the smart one, like my father. I was hoping that if I could get as much information as I could and then take it to her that she'd have an idea of what we should do next. Other than you, Kyrt and Harold, she's the only one I trust." Here she paused and considered what to say. The idea that this should be up to Kyrt and Jesp was nagging at her, but deep down, Tollie really didn't want to be dissuaded from looking for Tallie. She wanted to find her sister more than anything. So she decided for somewhere down the middle, "Once we find my sister and get her advice, I guess it's really up to the two of you."

Jesp nodded. "You're from the Meadows, right?"

"Yes, Brewhall, just over the border."

"There are other fae there. Unless we decide to do something with the crown, I think we should find another faerie settlement to hide it in. That's worked for nearly two thousand years, so it seems good enough to me."

Tollie considered this. Really it hadn't occurred to her to just take it to another safe place and hide it again. Why not?

Because, said a voice in her head that sounded a lot like Ellerby, it's resurfaced for a reason. Something's going on.

"I can't shake the feeling that there's a reason someone's looking for it. The Titans are loose again: two so far. I think it may be time for the crown to resurface. After all," she added, her voice quickening as ideas started streaming into her tired brain, "There's got to be a reason why it was never destroyed. Someone obviously thought it would have a purpose again."

"It's dangerous," Jesp said simply. "Someone may not have been able to destroy it. In the wrong hands it could be worse than the right person not having it, if you know what I mean."

Tollie thought about that for a moment, then she had another sinking feeling. More prejudice and sense of superiority were about to be wounded. She'd assumed that the faeries didn't really understand what it was they had. Suddenly, she realized that this was a ridiculous assumption.

"What do you know about the crown anyway?" she ventured quietly.

Jesp glanced nervously toward the bedroom door. It was shut. Farmer Scop was out, broken nose and all, helping a mare foal. Ella could be heard coming and going from the kitchen out back to the herb garden through the window of their room, but she was too far to hear a quiet conversation.

"In the Garden we sing songs," Jesp started, "The serious and sad ones are long and full of history, but it's mostly irrelevant stuff about lineages and places where faeries live. It's stuff we need to know if we're ever out in the world like this," and here she looked around the room as if to include the whole world in it, "After all, the world's an awfully big place for the likes of us."

The look on Jesp's tired face told Tollie very clearly that the largeness of the world and all the ways in which someone so small could become lost in it, weighed very heavily on Jesp's mind lately. Jesp went on:

"If you want to know what really matters to faeries, you listen to the frivolity." Jesp sighed and settled down onto Tollie's lap, between Tollie and the book. Tollie understood this to mean that here is where you pay attention to what I am saying. She laid the book down flat and looked Jesp straight in the eyes.

"They say faeries are good at deception, and we are. People assume we just play tricks and make jokes and that it means nothing, but..." Jesp considered Tollie here, and Tollie was very careful to look quite serious, "But that's just part of the deception. Listen, really listen, to the songs of faelings: the ones that sound ridiculous and meaningless. That's where you really learn our secrets."

Jesp studied Tollie's face sternly.

"Wow," Tollie tried, "That's....shockingly clever."

"And very secret Tollie. Never repeat this please."

"You have my word," Tollie assured her.

"And more importantly than that...and here I'm really really serious in a way my kind usually aren't..."

Tollie nodded.

"Never ever ever write any of this down."

Tollie thought about this for a moment. Of course. The books. The crown would have been totally safe. No one would ever have taken the faeries seriously enough to know that they were hiding something of this magnitude, and hiding it competently, except that someone wrote it down. Then someone found the reference and wrote speculations. And someone else included references to the speculations in a history somewhere, and before long, the secret was available if you knew what to look for. Tollie nodded slowly. Jesp was absolutely right.

Jesp sighed and started to sing. It took Tollie a moment to realize what she was listening to, then she gasped audibly. She knew this story:

"Hey ho with a mite and mo

A hey diddle diddle and a pig's big toe.

Lady fair with gold in your hair

How'd you make the ghosts all go over there?

Widdle widdle wee and ticky ticky tee

Twas long ago and you'll never know.

Faelings dance and faelings prance

But lady dark had them all in a trance.

Beeeeecaaaauuuuuuse...

With a circle of gold I can never get old

With a staff of silver I can rule for ever

Gold on my head not under my bed

And you can't hurt me so wee wee wee.

But lady dark all happy as a lark

You let the gold go without any mark

You set away the silver with nary a shiver

And into the well you you did choose to dwell.

And we all ask why (this part was spoken by Jesp in a squeaky tone)

Beeeeeecaaaaaaause

Hey ho with a mite and a mo

A hey diddle diddle and a pig's big toe

My dad had the gold and the silver old

But someone had him and me so bold

If I wore the crown I wouldn't frown

To die in the well it wouldn't let me fell

The ghosts they moan and the ghosts they groan

But when I diddle dee they were all set FREEEEEEEEEEEE!"

Jesp ended with a silly swooning fall and a high-pitched 'free', clearly meant to indicate to an uneducated listener that this was merely children's fun. Tollie, on the other hand, was suddenly less uneducated.

"Oh my..." was all she could manage.

A very drunk Kyrt had managed to fly in a meandering pattern, lopsided over to where they were talking. He was frowning when he sat down, bandaged legs out in front of him, next to Jesp.

"Why did you sing that?" he asked Jesp accusingly in a conspiratorial whisper, "That's not for anyone else's ears. You know that!"

Tollie couldn't tell if he was worried or angry, but one thing was for sure: right here in front of her, the frivolity of the faeries was being completely unmasked. This was suddenly not jovial love-struck Kyrt. Jesp had torn down a veil and Tollie was peering into another world.

Jesp sighed and looked very seriously at Kyrt, "Because the crown's fate now rests with her as much as it does with us, Kyrt. If I'd known you were awake, I would have talked to you about it first. I've been chewing on it for two days now while you've slept, and I didn't want to leave out of here tomorrow without talking to Tollie. I'm sorry."

Kyrt nodded slowly and very seriously. Then he turned around to face Tollie.

"Did any of that make sense to you?"

Tollie looked down at him. With his legs protruded out in such straight lines he looked a little silly, but the fire in eyes had no silliness in it. Inwardly, Tollie was shaking her head. All those years the morrowelves had been studying, writing, reading, searching, and little faerie children were dancing around in the Garden outside singing songs that would have told them what they wanted to know, if they had listened.

"Yes. Um, a bit," Tollie paused to see what reaction she'd get. Jesp sat down tenderly next to Kyrt and laid her forehead on his shoulder. She looked weary and sad. He put an arm around her head without looking away from Tollie's gaze.

Tollie nodded and went on a little more confidently, "The crown belonged to the last Queen of Andarraine. Or...well it most likely belonged to several rulers of Andarraine, but she's the one who's remembered for having it. The book I have says she gave her crown to the faeries and then went and released a bunch of angry spirits of murder victims," and here Tollie was brutally reminded of having nearly become one of those herself recently. In fact, her father *was* a murdered spirit now. She trembled for a moment, then caught Kyrt's unnervingly steady gaze and continued, "And, um, the angry spirits laid waste to a whole army and then cursed their forest, or something like that. Most of this book is about the faeries and the Garden, but just mundane stuff about it, and about the history of the founding of the Library. It was built on the spot where the Queen of Andarraine originally summoned the Titans, although the author doesn't think that part's true." Tollie bit her lip, "It's really a bit confusing."

Jesp was looking up at her again, sorrow all over her face for the betrayal she felt she'd carried out. Kyrt still had an arm absentmindedly around her. They really were cute. Tollie shook that last thought from her mind.

Kyrt spoke, "Well the song's not confusing if you know how to look past nonsense like a faerie does. In plain English," and here he looked at Jesp whose eyes widened in apparent terror, "The crown was her father's and not hers. It kept the wearer from aging or being injured. She gave up her life to set those spirits free, something she couldn't do if she had the crown. She did it because she and her father were being controlled by someone else. That's the song, and don't look at me like that, Jesp. You started it."

Jesp was staring at him in horror, but she didn't say a word.

Tollie continued to stare while searching her memory for other relevant bits from the book.

"At one point the author says that the last King was forced to give his crown to his daughter. He says many historians have taken this to mean that the daughter somehow forced her father into either naming her his heiress or else abdicating to her during his lifetime, but the author wanted to suggest something more innocuous, like he was forced to give it to her because he didn't have a son, or because he'd made a deal or something. But if they were being controlled...." she drifted off, searching for implications to all of this that she couldn't quite catch. It seemed that all wisdom was fluttering just out of her reach...like faeries.

"So, someone is looking for it because it will allow them to never age and to be uninjurable?" Tollie asked the room at large, albeit quietly as Ella had come back into the house.

"Actually," sniffed Jesp who had a large tear running down her cheek now, "Another song we sing has an old king in it who grew 'very very old over a long long time,' so my mother always said the crown made you age slowly rather than not age at all."

Kyrt nodded, "My grandmother said the same thing. And that *other* song," and here he looked at Jesp and shook his head. She immediately buried her head in his shoulder and quietly began to cry, "mentions a 'silver scepter to rule the land.' They are magic items that helped the ancient kings of Andarraine rule. If the Titans are coming back and someone wants the crown, someone wants to rule again. And I don't think that sounds good. From what our songs tell us, Andarraine ruled all the races from the South Mountains to the Barrier Hills and beyond, however far that is. It includes us I know for sure."

Tollie nodded. Here she realized that the fae knew words they didn't understand. They got the *concept,* but didn't know how they fit in the world.

"The Barrier Hills are those mountains that you can see to the north from here. They're more often called the Barrow Hills or the Barrowlands now. I'm not exactly sure why. And yes, the South Mountains are a long way off past where we came from. That's called the Breaking. That's essentially the whole continent."

Jesp looked up, tear-streaked, and croaked, "What's a whole continent?"

Tollie smirked, but not in an unkind way. This was easily the most interesting conversation she'd ever had. "It's all the land you can get to without having to get into a big boat and going over a lot of water. Any direction you go in, if you go until you hit water so wide you can't see across, you're still on this continent. And my understanding is that at its height, Andarraine did rule the whole thing. Some scholars speculate even more."

"Wow," said Jesp, forgetting her misery temporarily, "Is that a good thing or a bad thing?"

"That's just it," Tollie realized aloud, "I think that's the question my father was trying to answer."

Brody

The next day they got moving again. Brody had said almost nothing to anyone since the argument that led them on this route. He dreaded the idea of mining. He'd spent his whole life in fresh air and water and hated the idea of being underground. He didn't even like the idea of being inside if he didn't have to be. He knew they were lucky to be alive and luckier to have even as much as they had, but that didn't stop him from feeling like his life was over.

The events of the night before had shaken everyone considerably and now there was an overwhelming sense of wanting to get where they were going. At least most of the little group felt that way. Brody could have put the event off all year.

He went to sleep that night uneasy, thinking over the sum of his life and feeling rather sad about it. His triumphs were few, although his last great catch was now supporting what was left of his village and he was proud of that. They'd given him credit for helping out when the wolves attacked, but he wished he'd fought like Finn had. Finn and the elves were amazing. As he drifted off to sleep, his thoughts strayed to his father: to the grim knowledge settling about him now that he'd never really know what happened to him, and to wondering if, despite it all, he'd have been proud of Brody.

He dreamed that he was underwater, but able to breathe. It was cool and wet all around him and really very pleasant. Somehow he could see that view from the falls that had so exhilarated him less than a week ago. He was under water and on top of the world at the same time. He wanted it to feel great, but everywhere was sadness. He felt like the waters were the tears of his people, flooding the world as far as he could see.

He looked back toward where his village was and he saw him: his father standing at the bottom of the lake. He swam as hard and as fast as he could, a young boy again, having been waiting by the dock for hours. He was without scars, without age, anxious and delighted.

He reached his father and they embraced warmly. His father's smile was genuine and warm and shone with the pride that Brody so longed to feel from him.

But Brody frowned, feeling undeserving.

"Why can you not accept my love and my pride, Brody?" his father chided.

Brody hung his head and wept. He started to tell his father of all the terrible things that had happened in his absence, including what an awful fisherman he, Brody, had turned out to be, but his father brushed his story aside laughing. He placed both hands on his eldest son's shoulders.

"I don't have long here, Brody, and there are things I have to say," his tone was serious but not scolding, "You were never meant to be a fisherman. Your life is greater than we ever were. Don't consign yourself to this life you don't want, but do not think ill of those who do want it. What happened to us that day has everything to do with that comet that hangs in the nighttime sky even now. Speak to the elves. Tell them we've spoken. Tell them you've been touched by the Water Titan," his voice was getting more and more faint, Brody could no longer feel his father's hands on his shoulders, "You were drawn to them as they have been drawn to their own paths. Tell them about me..."

Immediately Brody's breathing failed. He was underwater, far underwater, and needed air desperately. He began to swim up and up and up and around him he could hear whispers in the water:

"You are ours now. You belong to the water. You belong to the heart, to change, and to the dead. Stay with us now. You are ours."

He could see the light above him, but could not reach it. He was lightheaded from the effort and his strength was failing.

"You are ours now.....heart....change....death....water"

He awoke suddenly coughing and gasping as if he had nearly drowned. Fletch was licking his face and whimpering lowly.

It was second watch. Finn hurried over to him, full of concern. The elf-girl, Arisa, watched from across the camp. Near her, he saw the dark elf, Adrik, stir for a moment and relax again.

"What the hell was that?" Finn whispered to him after being assured that Brody was OK.

"A dream," Brody panted, "Nothing more"

Finn considered him a moment, then spoke cautiously, "The shadows were thick around you. Darker than anywhere else and darker than they were before or after. It was the same when you fell at the falls. Brody," and here he glanced around to be sure that no one was listening. Arisa turned away, "What's really going on?"

Brody stared, horrified, into his friend's eyes. He didn't want anyone to know. He dreaded being proven to be as strange as everyone said that he was, but he had to give Finn and their friendship credit. Finn was worried, not frightened. Hopefully, he was up to the truth. He certainly deserved it.

"I don't know. I thought I had been imagining it, but it's getting more powerful, and stranger..." Brody really had no idea how to tell his friend the truth. He wasn't even entirely sure he knew what the truth was. He sighed, "Sometimes I can hear my father's voice. Sometimes I can even smell him. Once I heard my Grandfather, too. I thought it was all in my head, but Fletch can sense it. He barks when the voices are around."

Finn looked at him, his expression one of mingled fear and concern.

"What do they say?"

"Well, just now, my father told me that what happened to him had something to do with that comet thing," Brody nodded his head to where the new comet was still visible in the night sky tonight, "And that I need to talk to the elves about it. Finn, I don't think," and here he paused for words but could come up with none better, "I don't think I'll be staying in the mining camp when we get there. I think, maybe, there's something I'm supposed to do. Will you look after my family?"

"Hell, no," Finn's answer was startling and blunt and shocked Brody completely, but he continued, "Look, I don't want to become a miner anymore than you do. These other men," and here he glanced around at sleeping figures, "They're content with the idea of steady work, but I want something more. If you're not staying, neither am I. I have nothing here. I just, well, I have nothing anywhere else either, so I stay."

Brody looked at his friend as if he'd never seen him before. Here he, Brody, was feeling sorry for himself over and over again always forgetting how much he had to be thankful for. He nodded at Finn. It was a relief, in fact, to think that whatever purpose there might be for his life, he'd have Finn there.

"Thanks, Finn. I'll need you. I don't know where I'm going, but I know

I'll need you."

Finn nodded, and without another word returned to the spot where he'd been carrying out his watch. Brody settled himself back onto the ground, his mind racing. But exhaustion won over and he drifted back into an uneasy sleep.

Dawn came too soon for Brody, but he rose quickly anyway, trying to chase sleep away while hanging onto the dreams of the night. He needed very much to remember what his father had said to him. He needed now to get answers. He needed to speak to the elves.

But shortly after they awoke, Brody got a surprise. They all ate and packed up what little they had for the day, excited at the anticipation that they should reach their new homes by dusk. Everyone was thrilled at the prospect of putting the journey behind and, despite knowing that there would be hardships in rebuilding, of finally starting to do just that. The twin boys had an aunt and uncle that had moved up here a year ago that they hoped to see, and the expectant couple had family, too, and were looking forward at last to seeing them. But Brody had not expected the announcement that Arisa made once all was packed and ready.

"You are sure," she asked the men at large, "that you will complete your journey this day and will not need to camp another night?"

Orwyd pointed to a flat expanse above their heads to the southeast, just below the mountain peak.

"That's it right there. If we were any closer we could wave. The road up there's not straight and it's steep, but it's not more than 4 or 5 miles and the road will get better in the next one or two."

Arisa looked up to ledge and nodded, "If you're sure, then. This is where we'll leave you. If we might be so much trouble as to ask a favor of all of you before we go? We'd rather you didn't mention that we were here. We're...uh..." and here she glanced at Adrik who watched her with a steady gaze, "Not really supposed to be here," she finished lamely.

This spurred a round of suspicious muttering, but Orwyd spoke up in defiance of the younger men, "You have our word, and thank you for saving all of our lives."

Adrik nodded. Arisa smiled, and that was it. The elves made to leave back down the way they'd come.

Brody shot a desperate look at Finn who had moved to help Orwyd begin the trail, wincing when the older man accidentally grabbed his injured left arm. His time was now, he knew. Any chance of a private, secret conversation was gone. Finn nodded at him.

"Wait," he said quietly as the two elves passed him heading in the other direction, "I'm in need of your counsel before you go." Brody thought his words sounded lame, but, then, he felt very strange about the whole conversation he was about to have. He was acting on a dream, but he knew he wasn't ready to give up on a life above ground: a life he thought of as free.

The elves paused, as did everyone else. He looked up at the others and said, "I'll catch up," then added with a grin, "Most of you are slower than me."

Finn interjected, "I'll stay with you," and handed Orwyd off to Rista, making his way back down to where the other three stood, cradling the wounded arm. Fletch stayed happily wagging his tail between them.

Adrik looked wary and Arisa curious, but they stopped and waited. Brody swallowed. Now he'd have to tell these strangers how crazy he was, which was harder than telling Finn in the night had been. Brody felt reckless and fearful but excited, too. His life was about to change forever, more even than it had so far, and he could feel it in the depths of his being.

Once it was just the four left, three turned expectantly to Brody who noticed that Adrik in particular looked apprehensive.

Brody sighed and began as cautiously as he could, which really wasn't very, "Look, I think that...that...my destiny, maybe mine and Finn's" he shot Finn an apologetic look, "lie more along the same road as yours than theirs," and here he indicated the villagers who were still visible making their slow way up the mountain. "I don't know how, but there are some things I have to tell you, and ask you about, and...and I'm not sure where to start. Finn, any chance you thought I was crazy before is about to be confirmed, so if that bothers, you," he smiled lamely at his friend, "Now's the time to close your ears."

"I told you; you're not leaving me behind."

Brody nodded and placed a hand gratefully on his friend's shoulder, "OK."

Arisa suggested that they sit. Adrik looked mildly annoyed but obliged, plopping his gear in a dry patch of grass beside the road and then sitting next to it. He looked up at Brody with raised eyebrows. Fletch deflated the arrogant look immediately by jumping into the elf's lap and licking his nose. Arisa, chuckling at the dog, offered a clean stump to Brody as Finn deposited his heavy frame next to Adrik, dwarfing the elf and reaching to pull Fletch into his own lap. Arisa sat on a large rock a little deeper in, causing them all to turn toward her. Then everyone looked at Brody, a mix of interest on their faces. Brody started having second thoughts and seriously considered "Nevermind" before realizing it was too late for that.

"OK. I was told to tell the two of you something, but," here he paused feeling quite stupid, "I don't know what it means."

"OK. That's fine," Arisa encouraged him, "We've come across a lot we don't know what it means," and she turned a friendly smile to Adrik who rolled his eyes and nodded.

"Not to be rude," Adrik suggested, "But do go ahead with it." He was looking undignified wiping dog slobber from his face.

"Apparently I've been touched by the Water Titan, and I was drawn to that path like you were drawn to yours," Brody hoped that meant something to them because he didn't want to have to explain. He got both immediately.

Arisa and Adrik exchanged meaningful glances and spoke at the same time.

"That explains the shadows," said Arisa.

"And who told you to tell us this?" asked Adrik.

Finn's gaze was steady. He looked neither accusing nor understanding, but unflinchingly at Brody, stroking Fletch's head with his good hand as he listened.

Arisa and Adrik exchanged glances again, apparently sorting out between them in some silent fashion which should go first. Adrik prevailed. He looked at expectantly at Brody for an answer to his question. Brody sighed.

"My father."

"Isn't your father dead?" Adrik insisted, and Arisa shot him a disgusted look.

"That," she enunciated meaningfully at Adrik, "Explains the shadows."

Adrik nodded at her and leaned back against a tree.

"Shadows?" Brody asked, happy at the idea that anything explained anything in the conversation so far.

Arisa nodded and sighed, "I noticed, the night of the flood, that you were assisted by....spirits. Ancestors maybe?" she tried not to alarm him, "Or...well, you tell me."

Brody relaxed a little. At least they seemed prepared to believe him. Finn's face remained stony.

"You saw them?" he asked her excitedly.

"Just the shadows, but I knew what it was."

"I've seen the shadows, too, Brody," Finn reminded him, "Twice now."

Brody nodded and refrained from saying, 'yes, but you didn't know what they were.'

"So," Brody changed tactics, "Does the message mean anything to you?"

Arisa studied him a moment before answering. "Possibly. Does it mean anything to you?"

Brody shrugged. "Nothing that seems substantial to me at the moment. I can't hardly put it in context."

"Well, the Water Titan is the proper name of that comet that we've been seeing the last two nights," she started, "At least I think that's right."

She glanced at Adrik who was now watching her as intensely as Finn watched Brody.

"Being touched by it would mean that you've inherited water...um...powers."

"Powers?" Finn interjected and Adrik looked suddenly very guarded, "Like *magic* powers?"

Magic was evil. They'd been told that all their lives. Brody didn't feel that he, or his father for that matter, were the least bit evil. Even though he suspected the word magic might come into it, he didn't like hearing it.

"Magic is just a word," Arisa replied diplomatically, causing Adrik to roll his eyes, "The fact is the Water Titan has allowed you to do things, maybe see and hear things, maybe more, that other people can't."

"OK," Brody started up again wanting to leave the more delicate nuances of the conversation alone in favor of concrete answers, "So what does it have to do with you? Anything?" And here he found himself hoping that it did, hoping that the gateway into his new more exciting life was about to be revealed to him. He realized with a start that he really had no intention of following the others up the mountain. He thought suddenly of his mother and his siblings. They would be expecting him, and suddenly now he realized he may never come. That thought filled him with tremendous sadness.

"I don't know for sure," came the answer which revived him a bit, "But the Water Titan itself is very relevant to us. Was there anything more to the message? Have you perhaps taken it out of context?"

"It was a dream, actually, last night. I was back at the lake again, underneath it, and my father was there. He was at the bottom. He said I was never meant to be a fisherman, that I'm destined for greater things. He said that what happened to him and the other village men that day five years ago, was tied up in the coming of the comet and with whatever the two of you are up to. He said I needed to talk to you and he told me to say that specific message."

Even Fletch was watching him closely now. A breeze stirred around them and they sat momentarily lost in separate thoughts.

"What did happen that day?" Arisa asked at last.

"I wish I knew," came Brody's answer, "The men went out fishing like they always did. They always came home for lunch and switched from lake boats to canoes to take up on the river in the afternoons. But noonday came and they never arrived. By afternoon a terrible storm came down from the Unbreaking and destroyed a lot of the village. The storms have been frequent and intense since then, much more than they ever were before."

"What's the Unbreaking?" Adrik asked.

"The mountain I told you not to look at. That's its name."

Arisa looked curiously at him "The Gatewell," he told her, "It's the Gatewell."

Arisa slid down off of her rock to the ground so that she could lean against it.

"That could be our answer, Adrik," she seemed to be speaking to the trees now, "If we could find what happened to the fishermen, it may lead us to other answers."

"Well, if you're going after those answers," Finn now spoke up, solid determination in his voice, "We're going with you."

The four looked at each other, sizing up the group as a whole. Fletch sat up and licked Finn's chin.

Arisa and Adrik held each other's gaze longest, after the general exchange of gazes that had gone around the circle. At last, Adrik turned his eyes away and shrugged.

"OK," said Arisa, "That could be very useful. But, what about your family?"

Brody nodded, excitement welling up in him again.

"I do have to see them safely to the new village and make sure they'll be safe." It was what he most wanted after all. Not to leave them waiting with no answers like his father had, but to let them know first. It would be hard, but at least they'd know. And, he realized with a lump forming in his throat, Rista could take care of them. "I cant just leave from here. Can you wait?"

This, to Brody, was the pivotal moment, but it past quickly. "Yes," Arisa agreed, "I don't see why not, though we should get farther off the road."

"It's agreed, then," said Finn with a smile, "But I'm wondering if you're going to tell us what exactly it is we're up to?"

"That'll take a while," said Adrik sarcastically.

"Adrik's right," agreed Arisa, "We'll climb deeper into the woods here and find a suitable camp. We'll meet you here, or one of us will anyway, in four days time. That'll give you two days to spend with your family and to pack. And here," and with this she offered, quite unexpectedly, a golden coin in his own currency. Brody stared at it in shock. His people used coins from time to time, but mostly worked on barter. He'd only ever seen copper coins before, though the rumor of silver and gold varieties was not secret.

Brody shook his head. "I can't take that." They'd already returned her medallion to her.

"Yes you can," she said firmly, pressing it into his palm before he could withdraw, "You've saved our lives, which are priceless to us frankly. And if you're going to help us further on our quest, then it benefits us both that you feel your family is secure and that you be well supplied for the journey ahead. Heck, we could use whatever supplies you could bring back to us as well. Even if you only go as far as to discover the truth about your father."

"Fathers," Finn spoke up, "Mine, too. I just can't talk to him anymore..."

"Fathers," Arisa corrected, "You may still be gone for weeks. If you stay with us after that, or if turning back proves not to be an option, you could be gone much much longer. Years, possibly."

"Think of it," said Adrik with a wry grin, "As an investment we're making in you."

Brody and Finn looked at each other seriously for a moment, and Brody pocketed the coin.

"But you have to realize," said Adrik standing, "That you may not come back at all. Where we're going is far more dangerous than walking up this hill has been."

"Where *are* you going?" Brody asked.

"Into the Unbreaking."

Finn and Brody watched the elves make their way west, deeper into the woods and the steeper more dangerous terrain.

"Into the Unbreaking?" Finn whispered to Brody.

Brody shrugged. He couldn't shake the feeling of elation, whatever the dangers they faced might be. After five years, they were finally going to investigate their fathers' disappearance. And after losing nearly everything, they were at least not going to sign up for mining work. He felt he could tackle the Unbreaking on his own at that moment, but he knew it wouldn't last.

They were just beginning their trek up the road after the villagers when they heard a loud rumbling noise behind them. Finn had his axe out and Brody was ducking into the trees before they heard the creaking of carts and the cursing of men. Backtracking they found a trader caravan of three wagons making the torturous journey up this last leg of the mountain road.

It turned out to be another stroke of good fortune. The merchants offered to pay Finn and Brody to help them and their mules push and pull their wagons up the path. Accepting the chore, however, slowed them down even more and they didn't catch up to the villagers before they reached the mountain camp. Brody knew that Finn was in excruciating pain shouldering his share of the burden being wounded, but he didn't embarrass him by mentioning it.

"Camp" was not an accurate term they realized when they arrived. Here was a more sturdy, larger, well-kept village. The structures were neat and in good repair, built from thick wood and stone. There was a shop, a blacksmith, a baker, even a small tavern and brewery. Sheep and goats wandered the central area which was bordered by little homes ringed with small barns and a few kitchen buildings.

Finn and Brody were greeted warmly by their own who were standing in the village center giving account of their ordeal to concerned villagers and long-unseen family members. The twins were locked in embrace with their aunt, who Brody knew. And the pregnant woman, Kala was engaged in conversation with her sister who had married into a family up here. The traders immediately joined in the conversation after catching their breath and wiping their collective brow. They had been shocked at the destruction of Luring, which would have been the most recent stop for them before reaching this *town*, which is more of what it was than a village or camp.

Directly across the town from where they were standing was a clear blue mountain lake that immediately had the effect of making Brody feel more at home. It was nothing as large as Luring Lake. Even from here he could see the other side clearly, but the presence of water made him feel more comfortable. There was a wide path that led up to and past the lake and Brody could just make out the mountain maw that served as a mine entrance.

Brody noticed that Finn's arm had begun to bleed through his bandage and sleeve again, but luckily Kala's new brother-in-law was something of a doctor. The stitches he provided for Finn made Brody cringe to watch, but Finn seemed to have better use of his arm almost immediately.

The town was called Kipping, apparently after an ancestor of Finn's that he'd never mentioned. The townsfolk were amused to learn that a Kipp descendant was in their village once again. Brody's mother and Rista were not surprised to hear that Brody and Finn weren't staying, but there was too much to do in too short a time to dwell on the sadness of the moment. The shepherd was delighted to hear that there was an experienced weaver moving into town as he had been paying traders to carry his wool down to Luring. He offered Brody's family the space over his barn for a short term residence. It was dry, sturdy and bigger than their previous home. It had a wood stove instead of a fireplace and smelled strongly of the animals, but under the circumstances it was better than hoped for.

They sold the wolf skins to the traders and split the money. Between that and their wages for helping to get the carts up the mountain, Brody and Finn had another half gold to supply themselves and Brody's family with. He bought his mother and sister the wool they'd need to make good bedding and clothing for themselves and the younger boys. He got them also a pair of chairs and a small table, some cook pots, several sacks of garden vegetables, jars of spices, and firewood. Most importantly, he bought the shepherd's own loom from him for his mother's use. He and Finn then bought themselves some rope, two sacks, water and aleskins, a lantern and oil, a cook pot, two messkits, and two camp rolls for bedding. They also bought two hand axes for fighting that Finn would carry so that they could leave the wood ax with Rista who would use it. Those axes were the most expensive items they purchased. Brody also cut a strong walking stick that could double as a weapon if he needed it to.

Brody arranged for the local shopkeeper to take Rann as an apprentice and he made his mother promise that she would find other work than mining for Till if he, Brody, wasn't back by then. She agreed. The miners were hardy and stable folk, but had the definite air about them of men who had to beat their living out of the world, and Brody, however offensive it may sound to these good people, did not want that life for his brothers.

Finn went hunting the second day and killed an elk, while Brody was making arrangements for his family. He struggled to carry it back with his bad arm, but was so caught up in the triumph that he managed. He skinned it and began the tanning process that would provide him with some leather for protection in a fight. He'd have to finish the painstaking process on the road, but tanning was something Finn knew how to do. They left the meat with Brody's family and in turn carried some of the smoked fish and by now salted wolf's meat with them for their journey. Brody's mother baked them some thick bread, a loaf apiece, that would keep several days, and before they knew it both their money and their time was spent. Fletch seemed to sense that something was wrong and Brody could hear him whining even after he'd left the barn.

It was exhilarating to be setting off on a new life, but sad to leave an old one behind. Brody wondered briefly if he'd ever see his family again, but pushed the thought from his mind. Having Finn with him buoyed his spirits and they set off back down the hill and toward whatever destiny awaited them.

Chapter 4:

6th Day of the 12th Month, 6^{rth} Day of the Week, Autumn
Isilsday, Shilirs 6

Kierra

Their ninth day together seemed to dawn more brightly than their previous mornings had. Kierra woke up stiff and sore, but knew that what she felt had to be nothing compared to what Keen was going through by now. She'd had her near brush with death that Keen had so tenderly nursed her through already. Now she feared that Keen himself was heading into a very bad place indeed with his wounded hip that she was not yet whole enough herself to help him heal.

The bright sunlight felt like hope to her anyway. They had two fairly full waterskins and half of a cooked duck. And although it had only been two days since Kierra had her run-in with the strange screeching undead, she'd regained strength quickly. Keen had recovered quickly from being trampled by them, too, which seemed remarkable to Kierra who'd watched in horror as he'd choked on his own blood. The injuries that seemed to be lingering were the ones they'd gotten first. Were the spirits losing their power?

"How do you feel today, Keen?" Kierra asked as this thought occurred to her suddenly. He didn't look so good. She was almost immediately sorry she asked.

"My throat's better. My hip, not so much," he answered through gritted teeth.

If Kierra could just heal her own shoulder and leg enough from that first day, she might still be able to sing well enough to make a difference. The truth, though, was that if he had developed an infection, there would be a point of no return eventually. She had to help ease his body toward healing it before it had gone too far toward failing, and she had no hope of doing that while her own body was working on itself.

She pushed that back out of her head and returned to the thought she'd been having before, "It doesn't seem like these more recent injuries were as devastating to heal as the first ones were. I wonder if the spirits are losing potency."

As the idea hung in the air between them Keen sat up, an encouraged, hopeful expression dawning across his handsome face.

"That's true," he began thoughtfully, "I had more contact with them physically this time than I did when they got my hip, but I'm definitely better off..."

Kierra nodded, "And the blow two days ago nearly killed me, but here I am just two days later essentially fully healed from it, while the wounds in my shoulder and leg which were lesser injuries still linger. This menace may be ending, Keen. It may be over soon."

She smiled at him, but she only half meant it. She longed for freedom from these caves and from this plight. She longed for fresher air, fresher food, ready access to water. She longed for another treesinger to sing her wounds toward better healing. And more than any of it, she longed to see her family and friends and to tell them that she was alive and well. But she knew in her heart that it would mean goodbye forever to Keen. There was no where in the world they could be together, not even as friends, and certainly not as lovers. And if Kierra was completely honest, she wanted the latter arrangement. But, she could never have him, and their time together would likely soon be over.

And when it was, Keen would have to make a choice. Home for him was a place where elves were hated, and he was in the army where he would be ordered back over the border to kill again. Kierra hadn't thought about it before, but she wondered now how many battles he'd fought in, and how many elves he'd already killed. She wondered if that bothered him now, and she realized that a wet tear was rolling down her cheek as she thought all of these things while staring deeply into his dark brown eyes. She didn't look away. What would he say?

"Well, that's good, isn't it?" he looked at her quizzically and reached up, brushing the tear away with those strong hands, "What's the matter?"

She smiled weakly at him, "Nothing. I'm just tired."

He nodded and held her gaze a while longer before looking away and down at his dirty boots, "Yeah," he said in a muffled voice unlike his own, "I'll miss you, too."

She kept watching him, and eventually he looked back up at her. She wanted to jump into his arms. She wanted to beg him to stay, or at least to suggest that maybe there was a way that he could. But even as she began to have those thoughts she knew better. She dropped her gaze from his. Her own people didn't exactly hate humans like his people hated elves, but they had never really accepted outsiders into their sacred forests.

Before the wars had broken out they had traded at the borders with humans and other elves, but it had been many generations since they'd even allowed other elves into what they called the "Sacred Trust."

Keen had saved her life. Her family would probably understand. Her village might even take him in, but beyond that, there'd only be trouble for Keen in the Willows. He'd never be free. He'd always be an outsider. It wasn't even fair for her to ask.

She felt his hand on her shoulder and looked back up into the brown and now watery depths of his eyes. They were full of friendship and worry, and she liked to imagine more than that. She gripped his arm, closed her eyes and laid her head against his hand. It was rough and weathered like he was, but so familiar now. She could feel the tears coming more earnestly. How ever was she going to let him go?

The familiar silver light and screeching madness broke the silence of the moment. Kierra opened her eyes and looked across at him to make sure they were both safely tucked inside as they needed to be. Avoiding this lingering danger had become such rote by now, she hardly tensed at the sound anymore. And briefly she marveled at what a person could become accustomed to. She watched Keen's face and wondered how long it would take to become accustomed to his absence.

A new fear began to well up in Kierra. What if she had bonded with him by accident? Would he even understand what that meant? The concern must have shown on her face because immediately Keen responded to it.

"What's wrong?"

Kierra came out of her reverie. She'd been staring into his eyes, but not really seeing him. Now she looked at him honestly and swallowed. She didn't know how to put her feelings into words anymore and was too scared of what he might say. The army of ghosts was loud outside, and nothing she needed to tell him was best said shouted over their screeching. So, instead, she leaned forward, wrapped her arms around his neck and climbed sobbing into his lap. He sat stunned for less than a second before he pulled her in closer and began to rock gently as she cried. If that didn't tell him what he needed to know, then he just wasn't going to understand.

They didn't talk much the rest of the day. If Kierra had admitted much, she'd have had to have admitted that she was embarrassed by the events of the morning. She wished she could ask Keen how he felt about what had happened between them. She wished she could ask him how he felt about a great many things. But she continued to lack the courage and time was running out. By dusk that evening the pair had clearly realized that the span of time between undead army rides was significantly longer. That evening, Kierra easily got down to the stream for more water and had no trouble getting back, and Keen got out of the cave and stretched while she did it. The ghosts came back later, but they didn't do it in any hurry. Their ordeal was nearing its end.

They finished their duck over the course of the day. And for the first time they started to make some more daring plans. Kierra wanted to wash their clothing the next day and maybe hunt. Keen wanted to try to make it to the stream to clean his wounded hip and rebandage it. It was exhilarating to be thinking of doing so much and they began to warn themselves that they may be thinking too big too soon. So instead, they decided to set off first thing in the morning for the last cave.

Kierra woke the next morning with a new determination to start moving on with her life. She'd spent much of the night lying awake recovering from fitful dreams about Keen, war, his family and hers, and the family they could never have together. So by the next morning, Kierra felt that she had played out too many of the possibilities to have any left to cling to. She had to let him go, and she had to start doing it right away.

They got their things together in relative quiet other than the necessary conversation to sort out belongings, pack and give directions. Keen could tell something had changed between them. He kept giving her worried and confused looks, but he didn't ask her any questions. Things had been awkward since she collapsed in his arms the day before, and since Keen wasn't the talker of the two of them, Kierra was banking on the idea that she wouldn't have to explain if she didn't bring it up. She hated treating him this way, but soon she'd never see him again.

The thought brought the tears so close to her eyes, that she choked and had to blink them back. No, she couldn't have this conversation. Not with him. She'd have it at home. She'd talk to her mother, or her grandmother, maybe, or

Rana or Nira, even Joran, but not Keen. She couldn't talk to Keen. After all, at this point, either he'd say he didn't share her feelings which would devastate her, or he'd admit that he did, which would have the same effect.

They waited for the ghosts to pass, and it took far longer than they expected, even after yesterday's re-appraisal of their movement. In fact, it took hours. They moved to the last cave without incident. Kierra helped Keen walk. They took their time. The final cave was formed where the land dipped down on one side steeply to allow the water to run alongside it, cutting a large jutting rock nearly in two. The stream had only been visible from the caves before where it tumbled out from behind the large boulder. But out here in the open, the large rocks tumbled away from it on one side like a petrified cascade opening finally into a cave mouth. It aimed away from the water, but the journey around the rock face to the babbling brook was not more than 60 feet, if it was that.

The cave itself was fairly small, but not the smallest they'd used, and it was clean and safe and the closest they'd been yet to fresh water. No sooner than they'd made their way to its shelter, Kierra braved the short distance down to the water's edge.

At this end the water was a little deeper and swifter than the spot where she'd been filling the skins. She took her bow this time, and moving with the grace and reflexes of all her kin, she was rewarded with several decent small fish in a short period of time. She could not have spent this much time even yesterday. She waded briefly into the cool waters and splashed its refreshing chill onto her dry face. She wanted to laugh out loud with pure joy at the sensation of simply being alive, but she didn't give into the impulse. She knew that not far away from her, her own dear friend still had not had the chance to feel this water. Not to mention that he might worry if he heard her call out. She giggled quietly to herself, and then grabbed the arrow where she'd strung five little fish and headed back to where Keen already had a pot waiting. She cocked an eyebrow at him.

"I knew you'd bring back something since you left with that bow, being the best not-an-archer I've ever personally met," he smiled at her, "That's a decent catch."

"It still doesn't beat your goose," she laughed back, "So, you still win at not being an archer, but, yeah, it'll feed us a meal. I was down there a while. I suspect you'll be able to go and clean your wound on the next pass if you want to."

He raised both eyebrows at her. The hungry look in his eyes had nothing to do with fish. There was no doubt about it. Kierra knew in an instant that he wanted to feel that water as badly as she'd wanted to shout about it. Maybe more. She didn't blame him. It was wonderful.

The next pass never came. They had not known it when they sat waiting hours for the army to race past before moving to this last cave, but that pass was the last pass. The ghosts were gone. They waited the rest of the day for the spirits to ride again, holding off Keen's trip to the stream, sure that the army would show up again no sooner than he stepped outside. And as badly as he was walking, he just wouldn't get back inside fast enough. But they never came. And so, by nightfall, they were no longer just making plans for a bath, they were making plans for a final departure. It was all Kierra could do to keep from weeping.

The next morning was somber. It drizzled briefly, but gave up and let the day get on with its business. There was a light mist that clung to the ground as if the forest wanted to give the smallest creatures the chance to have some extra cover in case they were all wrong about things returning to normal at long last. 'Normal,' Kierra reminded herself, had always been a life without Keen, but now she felt that a life without air would be easier to face.

She watched him pack what was left of his things while half-heartedly arranging hers into her bag. Each item now carried a memory: the lantern she used to see by when she'd stitched his wound, the pot she'd used to heat food for him after their harrowing escape to the second cave, the small bag that had contained herbs she'd used to wrap his head wound. Her thoughts wouldn't shut up and leave her in peace to pack, and she realized that her face was wet with tears again. She was grateful that Keen had his back to her. Surely he'd be glad to be gone from all of her sobbing, she thought.

But then he turned around. His eyes looked blood-shot and he sounded like he had a cold. Kierra chanced a smirk at him. He smiled sweetly at her and brushed her matted, filthy hair out of her tears.

"I hate to ask," he started gruffly, "But now that we're free, I really do have to think about getting out of here."

Kierra nodded glumly. She hated it, but she knew he had family and home elsewhere, in a place where she could never follow him.

"Well, it's just that it's occurred to me that I'm an enemy here," he paused and grimaced. Kierra looked up at him. Surely he didn't intend to return to the army? Surely he couldn't. Her consternation must have shown through her stare, because he continued, "No, it's not like that, I just mean, what if more of your army come through here?" Kierra realized he looked scared. Suddenly she was worried, too. She hadn't thought of that, "I *have* to get out of here, unless..."

"Unless?"

"Unless," he sighed, "You think I should be arrested, or brought to justice or whatever..." he swallowed and looked down at his lap. Kierra just stared at him, "In which case I've decided to accept that." He looked back up at her with a steady tear-filled gaze. He meant it. He'd accept her judgment against him, if she passed it.

But Kierra shook her head at him without dropping her eyes from his.

"I don't know what you've done, and I don't want to know. But you saved my life. And more than that...I don't think I could hurt you if I tried..."

He smiled at her. "If it makes you feel any better, I only just joined the army. This would have been my first battle, so...other than show up and almost die, I'm not sure I have done anything."

Kierra nodded, relieved, and smiled, "That does make me feel a little better. Especially if you promise me you're not coming back," and here she stopped because the words were painful, "Even though I hate to never see you again."

Keen reached for her, but Kierra pulled away, "No, don't. I can't. I'm sorry."

He nodded. "I understand. I'm sorry, too. I wish things were different. No, I'm not coming back. I wouldn't have a choice. In fact I don't, but I can already tell you this wound in my hip is the end of my military career whether I want it to be or not. And believe me when I say that I do. I'm grateful for the way out. I'd let them lock me up or hang me before I'd let them send me back here. I swear."

Her lip was quivering again. Inwardly she was cursing at herself and trying to think of anything else. The best way to get him out of here: what *was* the best way out?

She dried her eyes and looked out at the water.

"Follow that stream in the direction of its flow. It'll lead you out to the Shil'Arinn near the fork where the Graffling River becomes the Fel. You'll have to find a way across, though. The river is swift and wide and deep there, but it's the quickest way to your border, but Keen..."

She looked at him, all the dangers he was still facing raced through her head. She wanted to escort him the whole way, but she thought that was probably foolish. She wanted to know if he'd make it home. She wondered if she'd spend the rest of her life wondering what had happened to him after today and knowing deeply that she would wonder. She had to give him the best advice that she could, so that she could ever sleep again.

"The Shil'Arinn and the Graffling are both lined with archers and they're patrolled regularly. You need to be really careful as you approach the main water. Don't ignore the trees. Elves don't wander around on the ground and we don't hide our ambushes low either. Look up often. And if you get caught, tell them you were given passage by a treesinger and give my name. Not all of them will let you go, but they'll at least think twice before they kill you...I hope. How are you going to travel on that leg?"

He sighed. "I don't know," he admitted, "I may have survived one thing only to not make it out of the forest after all, frankly."

She started to reach for him this time, but stopped herself. He smiled.

"I have no choice but to try. It's the only choice or hope I have."

"Let me do some hunting for you before you go. At least that way you'll have food for your trip."

He smiled, "Thanks. I was still hoping to get a bath before I left, so there's some time. You sure you don't mind?"

"Not at all. I wish I could do more actually," and she meant it. She was starting to wonder whether or not she would get into trouble if she escorted him to the border. After all, if she was letting him use her name on the grounds that he had saved her life, then what was the difference? As she left to hunt some small game for him to travel with, she was even becoming excited about the idea. It wasn't far out of her way really, and then she could be sure that he'd make it at least across the river. Whatever happens to him in his own country she couldn't take responsibility for, but surely he'd be safe there.

She turned and made for higher ground, up and over the rocks that had made their home last night. She knew there was a small collecting pool of deeper cool water not far up stream at the base of a short falls. She and her brother and cousin often played there while visiting her grandparents as children, and it was usually full of fish and frequently visited by small animals seeking water. Kierra wasn't much of a hunter for an elf, but she knew she was better off than Keen was. She made for the spot, anxious for a bath herself, and confident that she could return with a decent stock of rations for the both of them to reach the Graffling River's edge with.

She reached the pool. It was as clear and blue and beautiful as she remembered. Kierra hadn't been up here in several years because her training had taken her so far away, it seemed, for so long. In reality, Willowmark isn't usually far from here, although it's location changes, but for many years it had seemed worlds away to Kierra.

Quietly, she slipped out of her filthy clothing. It felt good to be finally free of them. She wasted no time jumping quickly into the frigid water which sent a shiver like a burn bone-deep throughout her frame immediately. It was wonderful. She could feel the slither of fish just just under the surface flee in every direction as the bubbles of her breath escaped her growing underwater smile. She didn't open her eyes until she emerged gasping the crisp chill of the autumn into her protesting lungs, laughing joyously out loud as she did. Her feet barely reached the slime-covered rocks closest to the edge and her head was constantly battered with icy spray from the falls filling the pool before it cascaded out, pushing and shoving its way into the little stream that made its way down into the woods to become Keen and Kierra's saving grace for the past week. Kierra could only have dreamed of the wonder of this moment last week, and she thought of Keen and hoped dearly that he was finding the cooling water of the stream below her as refreshing to his body, but she had to shut that thought out. Thinking of Keen's body in water while she was up here naked was just a bad idea.

Kierra pulled her horribly soiled clothes into the water with her. She had nothing but rocks to use for soap, but that would be a better washing than they'd had for a long while, and she was grateful for it. She washed her clothes quickly and thoroughly, realizing that she had hunting and fishing to get to quickly if she was going to get Keen out of here in a timely fashion. Besides that, her teeth were chattering, and what had started out as a delightful experience was becoming dreadfully cold and Kierra was realizing that she had no way but cold autumn air to dry off.

She climbed, shivering, out onto the rocks and begun to wring out her soaking wet but now-clean clothing. Pulling them back on was a chore in the ridiculous and she managed to scrape a good bit of dirt back into them. Still, she figured she couldn't possibly smell as bad as she had before.

She was finally pulling on her boots and reaching for her bow when it hit her. It was a sudden sensation like she had never experienced before. It started like something had simultaneously gripped her around her heart and knocked the wind out of her. But in an instant she had a name for it: Keen was in trouble. She knew he was in grave danger. All of her senses were perked, heightened. Everything around her was acute: sights, sounds, smells. Her whole body had tensed to spring without her becoming aware. She was barely breathing. Her bow was in her hand already. She had no memory of picking it up off of the ground, and she knew with a homing instinct exactly what direction he was in. There was no question. They had bonded. And he needed her. Right now.

She sprang up and over rocks and through underbrush without paying attention to what she was jumping over. Small animals scurried for cover under step. She didn't care. Her heart pounded in her ears. She could hear her own steadying breath. She could feel a panic that wasn't hers. It was his. Something was wrong. He wasn't in pain. He was afraid. He wasn't alone. Oh no. She ran faster.

She reached the stone that hid the cave where they had slept. She could hear voices. She didn't stop to listen. She didn't care what they were saying. She leaped over the entire structure like a deer fleeing a predator, bow in one hand, bag in the other, fury on her face. They were not going to take him from her.

She hit the ground hard. Her leg was still not fully healed. It didn't catch her. She rolled awkwardly, but she jumped up and kept going. By now she could see them and they could see her. There were five willowelf soldiers. They had Keen on the ground with his hands behind his back. His shirt and boots were off. His pack and weapons were by the stream. His face was full of shock as he watched her run toward them. Their bows were drawn on him, but they didn't look prepared to fire.

Kierra stopped, mustering all of the righteous indignation she could channel through her panting breath and the catch she now had in her side.

"WAIT!" she shouted as she doubled over panting, "Stop!" she was clutching her side, struggling for breath. The air was so cold, "I gave....him....permissh....per....permissh..."

"That treesinger?" one of them asked Keen indignantly.

"Permission," Kierra finally stammered out wheezing in the frigid air.

Keen nodded innocently at the soldier.

"You can't..." Kierra continued to insist.

"Well, that at least confirms your story," the soldier continued, apparently ignoring Kierra who really wanted her indignation to show through with better effect.

"...arrest him..." she persisted.

"You're still under arrest," the soldier confirmed, continuing to ignore Kierra, who finally began to catch her breath and her attitude.

"Hey!" she panted a little less breathlessly, "I have every right to grant him right of access!"

"Not if he's a soldier!" the young elf stated firmly, wheeling on her, his eyes glaring with fury as if he was accusing her now of something heinous. His lips pursed and his nostrils flared and it was quite clear to Kierra that, as far as he was concerned, she'd crossed a line.

But the overwhelming sense of danger hadn't passed. What this man in front of her didn't know, in fact neither did Keen, was that she had accidentally bonded to him. And because of that, she knew that Keen wouldn't survive this encounter if she shied from his anger. She summoned her own fear and turned it into power, right from the depths of her toes. She felt it broiling like fire in her belly. She imagined it shining like fiery beacons from her eyes, imagined it turning the tears that had been forming there to steam. She'd practiced this technique in Willowmark, and it was effective. The man instinctively recoiled.

"This man saved my life," she stated slowly and carefully, "And I have the right to grant him passage. Not because he's a soldier. Not because he's a human. And not despite those things. And certainly I am not restricted by those things, but because the act of saving a treesinger from war grants pardon. Period. That law hasn't changed in two thousand years, and you will not unilaterally change it right now just because you don't like the particular person who happened to save the treesinger this time. I and I alone have authority to vouch for him and I do. Now BACK DOWN."

She had mustered all of her authority, but she knew it was dampened, literally, by the fact that she was dripping wet and snotty. She resisted the urge to wipe her nose. She was also resisting the urge to glance over to Keen. She could feel him watching her. She wanted so badly to smile at him, but she was determined to stare this jerk down.

She felt the danger loosen. Her breathing eased. The pulsing in her ears released. The tension in her chest remained tight and her muscles were still tense. His death was no longer immanent, but this path still led to a bad place for Keen. She hadn't won yet.

"You'll have to take it up with Wythir[1] Kethran," the soldier stated simply, and Kierra's heart sank. Kethran's name was well-known to her. He and her brother had been at odds before and mostly over issues like ethics and the use of torture. Kierra felt the blood run out of her face. She felt faint. Of all patrols to have captured Keen, why Kethran's men? The last time Joran and Kethran had a disagreement it had turned very public and had gone very badly for her brother. So badly, it had gotten him sent to the front lines and nearly gotten him killed.

The men were yanking Keen up and the anguish registered on his face when his weight hit his bad leg.

"He can't walk on that leg!" Kierra protested, her bonded instincts kicking in like fiery goosebumps as the pain rattled Keen's frame.

The soldier smiled at her, "He'll manage." And without further comment, the elves gathered up Keen's belongings and began to try to force him to march away from the water. The agony of walking on that leg would have been obvious to anyone, but Kierra could feel it without watching. It was in the pit of her stomach and riding across nerves in her skin. For her it wasn't pain exactly, but she'd never felt anything as equally uncomfortable that had to be called something else.

Kierra had no other power over these men than she had used, and Kethran

---

[1] Pronounced "Why-theer:" literally "Guardian." A low-ranking officer; leutinent

would be less swayed than they had been and she knew it. What was worse, she knew in her deepest instincts that they were walking Keen into a terrible and short future. She had to stop it somehow. She hated to get Joran involved. Kethran had already cost him plenty, and this was a human besides, but he was a human that had saved Kierra's life and to whom she was now bonded. Joran was the only hope she had.

But Kierra wasn't whole. Reaching Joran wouldn't be easy. Another side of her knew, however, that reaching across a distance was the easiest connection to make, and that saving a bonded mate gave her extra reserves she'd never had before. She stepped over into the cooling waters of the stream. Waters connect so many things. It's so easy to sense...

From the water to the roots of the trees, and from there to the birds and to the sky. She could feel the deep ground and all of the life that dwelled there, tunneling along. All of these things: tunneling insects, rabbits, birds, butterflies were moving toward....

Home.

And above that same ground squirrels and even wolves seemed to feel her presence. The petals blowing on flowers and branches of bushes bent in one direction. The breeze carried leaves and bees all in one direction:

Home.

And with all of it, she could send a simple song. As she sensed all of it moving toward the place she needed it to go, she stood in that stream and sang in the old Elven tongue:

E' Van tu'il, A Van il'tu
An tu shil fil, Il shil wan ru
May fara van, may willa shy
Endya lan, Endya thy
Fil'il shil, Dya tu
Halla trill, Trilla vu
Wa'el el wa, Wa'el wa el

Van tu'il, An tu shi! par'il vani.[2]

Joran

She let the song hang in the air. The soldiers had stopped. Two had turned around. So had Keen. His face was dripping with sweat. He was in terrible pain. Nonetheless, the expression on his face was pure awe. He'd never heard a treesinger sing before. Kierra couldn't do a lot of things as well as other elves, but she could sing to the forest. She looked him in the eyes with all the love she had for him, which was a tremendous amount now. She tried to tell him silently that she was going to help him.

She knew he didn't know the words she had sung, not in Elvish or in English, but the others did:

> "If you sing to me, I will sing to you
>
> What your heart hears, My heart first cries.
>
> As the bird sings, As the trees rise,
>
> Across the deep, Beyond divide,
>
> Hear my heart reach out to you,
>
> Feel the beat that pulses through,
>
> All we are, All are we
>
> I sing to you what your heart has sung to me..."[3]

———————————————

[2] Pronunciation Guide:
> Eh vahn too eel, ah vahn eel too
> Ahn too sheel feel, eel sheel wahn roo
> may fahra vahn, may willa shy
> en-dye-ah lahn, en-dye-ah thy
> Feel sheel, dye-ah too
> hah-lah treel, trilla voo
> wah ell ell wah, wah ell wah ell
> Vahn too eel, Ahn too sheel pahr eel vahn-ee

[3] Literal Translation:
> If sing you me, then sing I you
> What your heart hears, my heart once cries
> As birds sing, as trees rise
> Over/out-reach the deep, over/out reach divide
> Hear my heart reach you
> Feel the beat beating through

The leader whipped around at last, "Joran?" he demanded incredulously, "And how may I ask do you know Wythir Joran?"

"He's my brother," Kierra answered innocently.

"Fantastic," the soldier spat, "Of course he is."

In her mind's eye she could see him. He'd looked up from something, startled, and said her name excitedly. He'd thought she was dead. Of course he had. He'd have gotten word by now what had happened to the unit she'd been assigned to. Her last vision of him was that he was leaping up from whatever he had been doing and yelling for someone. He was coming. He'd heard her. She couldn't be sure what he'd do for Keen, but her big brother knew she needed him and he was coming.

Kierra continued to stare down the soldier in front her with all the certainty of someone who knew that reinforcements were on the way. Her sense of impending dread remained, but it was waffling. She looked the man dead in the eyes: You will not win.

All/we all/we are, all/we are all/we (all and we are the same word)
Sing you I, what your heart for/on behalf of me sang.

Jesp

The past two days had been surreal for Jesp. She spent a good bit of time caring for Kyrt, which was weird in and of itself. He was gracious, and not overbearing or flirtatious about it, and Jesp appreciated that. Kyrt had been very brave. When Tollie had been jerked out of the room by those *men,* she, Jesp, had stood dumbstruck for several heart-pounding seconds. It was Kyrt that flew over and shoved the crown out of sight, Kyrt who grabbed their weapons, tossing Jesp hers while she was still on the bed, and Kyrt that helped Jesp down to the floor and suggested that she go up the stairs. And then, of course, it was Kyrt who'd almost been killed.

Jesp had always known that she gave him a harder time than he deserved, but it had never occurred to her that one day he might not be there. Kyrt was something Jesp just *expected.* Then he'd nearly died playing hero when playing hero had always been Jesp's fantasy.

And, yes, she knew that Kyrt was enjoying having her take care of him. She felt bad for him; if he hadn't been so badly hurt he could have enjoyed it more. She knew he'd had that thought at least once. If Jesp had to guess, Kyrt's favorite moments were when Ella would bring in two teacups of bathwater and prop a recipe book between them on the nightstand for privacy. They would joke back and forth about the meaninglessness of having to write down instructions for food, all the while being separately naked together. Jesp was just grateful that Kyrt couldn't see how badly she was blushing during those moments.

Jesp had other things on her mind, too. So many in fact, she'd begun to see why people who went looking for more information needed to have bigger heads. Her little one hurt quite a lot. She even found a point where, briefly, she realized why it might be useful to write something down.

Also, while all of this was going on, they got a little more information about what had happened and why. The elf that had attacked them had been forcing the local breeders to sell to him for half price. Farmer Scop had refused. For that, the bandit and his fellow trouble-makers were going to execute them horribly.

Jesp couldn't shake that. It was beyond her to peer into that kind of mind, and it made her wonder about the person who might be looking for the crown. If someone looking for cheap horses would do *that*, what would someone who wanted to rule a continent do? Her parents and Kyrt's family, their old friends and neighbors flashed through Jesp's mind and made her shudder.

Of course, Kyrt had gotten the opportunity to tease her for a little while just after everything happened. Though he grimaced as he mocked her, he had not missed the chance to point out that she had unmercifully compared the responding elf officers to the captain back home that she used to watch. She sniffed in disgust. Kyrt should have known. That wasn't the way *her captain* would have handled the situation.

They had already had *two* deaths in the community, and many people had already pointed the finger at this culprit. But there was nothing that could be done, supposedly: no proof. This officer, if you could call him that, just hoped that something would come along and rub his nose in the truth. Hmph, thought Jesp. That's not the way the elves handled things at the library.

"Are they better looking at the library too?" Kyrt had teased.

She'd be mad at him for it if he hadn't been hurt. Darn him. She smiled, "They certainly look better than *you* do right now."

Despite all of the teasing, the library, especially its Garden, weighed heavily on Jesp anymore, but in some ways it was easy to ignore the pangs of guilt and worry while enjoying the strange comforts of the Stable Glen farmhouse. The events of their first morning here were things Jesp would never be able to forget. Still, the truth kept her awake at night that she had abandoned her own people to whatever fate might chance upon them. She may have thought the leader of the town guard here to be an incompetent simpleton, but he had, at least, stayed in his community to try to help. Jesp had taken everything her people stood for and fled. She didn't even warn them that the danger might have been bigger than they thought, and now she wasn't sure she even grasped how huge the danger was herself. Increasingly, she felt like a traitor rather than a hero. How foolish had she been to think that she could ever have belonged in the Library Watch?

They'd been gone a week now with no word from home and still no way of knowing if they'd ever see it again. Despite the silent fears and misgivings, they set out again at last that very next morning. Ella had packed them supplies, especially food. Scop had made minor repairs to the wagon and had taken excellent care of their mule, which had been named Harry after its original owner. The farmhouse had been cleaned up and no longer reeked of lamp oil, although not all of the repairs had yet been made. Scop's face was still spectacularly splashed with blue, green and purple from his healing nose, and Jesp wondered how he could see out of his puffy eyes. Nevertheless, his smile was warm and genuine, and Jesp hated somewhat to leave.

Their first stop after hitting the road was the local courthouse. The three strangers to town had been asked to come and give testimony about what they had seen. This irritated Kyrt and Jesp who thought the whole process was a mockery, but Tollie insisted that a civilized community always provides everyone with a fair trial, to the best of its ability. It was hard for Jesp to believe that such a trial could be fair to the victims, but Ella and Scop had come down the day before and given their account, so Jesp felt they had to at least confirm the couple's story.

The courthouse, such as it was, looked a bit like an old barn that had been made out of better materials. Specifically, it was crafted of smooth, gray stone and thick, dark wood. The wide doors through which the public entered looked very much like the doors through which cattle might be driven, but scaled down to the appropriate size.

Apparently the elf that had tried to make a halfling-sized bonfire out of Tollie just days before had hired some more educated thug to try to say that he hadn't done it. The idea of it made Jesp fume. According to his *defense* Farmer Scop had staged the whole thing as a negotiating tactic to get the "honest tradesman" to pay a higher price. Jesp thought he ought to have to protest his innocence while tied to a chair with an oily rag in his mouth like the farmer had been forced to do.

Ella had sewn Tollie a cute little dress to wear that was yellow with an interlocking pattern of sunflowers around the trim. It was definitely elvish, but Tollie didn't complain. Jesp thought she seemed embarrassed about crying so much when everything happened, but Jesp didn't blame her for that. There had been decidedly too much scary in their lives recently. Tollie also seemed quite beside herself at having been rescued, but as Jesp reminded her repeatedly, Tollie had rescued Jesp from the burning tower just over a week ago. Secretly, Jesp just wished

It had been Jesp that had done the rescuing this time.

The inside of the courthouse was wooden, and decorated in the flowing carved artwork and trim that Jesp associated with the library. The people inside were dressed in the same kinds of clothing the elvish librarians and professors wore. Everyone, that is, except for the town guardsman. Jesp may not have liked him at first, but he was there in a uniform with a sword and shield, and Jesp considered that to be proper elvish attire. After all, it was what she would wear if she were an elf.

There was a table at the head of the room with three dour-looking male elves sitting behind it, watching them as they came in. The captain of the town guard was standing just behind the shoulder of the one on their right. There were chairs filling the room facing the front table and a little more than a handful of townsfolk elves were seated in them looking very serious. These people were dressed like Ella and Scop: they tried to be decorative, but didn't own cloth as nice as the front-table-people owned. Tollie looked like the child of any one of them walking into the room, dressed like a townsfolk. The image was likely not helped any, Jesp mused, by the two faeries flying in behind her, especially since one had his legs bandaged completely straight like a poorly-made child's doll. The man sitting on the left side of the table smirked.

The trial itself, such as it was, was pretty simple. The man in the middle of the table asked them to tell what happened. Tollie told her version first and while she was trying to tell her story, the man to the left kept asking her questions to make her second guess herself or to make her sound stupid. The man to the right would argue with him and try to encourage Tollie along. The man in the center seemed to have the job of listening, occasionally telling the other two when they were crossing a line although, to Jesp's mind, he let them cross the line, run up the street from it, dance a jig on the other side of town and make ugly faces at the line before he would decide they'd actually crossed it. Jesp fumed through the whole affair.

It didn't get any better when Tollie was done, either, because they went to close out the trial as soon as she answered "yes sir" to "is that everything."

"Hey, wait a minute!" Jesp yelled, "We came to talk to you, too!"

Left-side man tried to prevent this as "highly irregular" and called Jesp and

Kyrt "uneducated and illiterate." Right-side man didn't seem to know how to defend them either, which may have made Jesp even madder. It was at this point that the town guardsman redeemed himself by speaking for the first time since the event itself happened.

"If we consider ourselves a civilized society, then we have to allow the voices of all races, do we not? I may not have *your* education, Lord Greening, but I recognize an intelligent witness when I see one, and I'm not aware that this court recognizes racism as a defense."

Jesp and Kyrt smirked at each other from ear to ear. They knew instantly what they were going to do.

For the next hour, the two faeries flew through the air in a grand reenactment of the events of the attack, complete with sound effects and Kyrt's dramatic fall from the sky. Their story was met with gasps and even shrieks from time to time from the audience. And they did what faeries do: they embellished. By the time they were done there had been a duel to the death, a confession to the other murders, and a moment when the main bad guy had visibly pissed himself. Left-side guy, apparently named Lord Greening, couldn't get a word in edgewise. Every time he tried to ask a question one of them would say, "we're getting to that..."

Their dramatization ended in a standing ovation. Even Tollie stood up on a chair to applaud as the faeries flitted about, bowing to everyone they could reach.

Lord Greening insisted the entire testimony of the faeries be thrown out as "clearly theatrical," but Jesp could tell by the twinkle in the center man's eye that the damage had been done. And what's more, it had been fun. It was the first time Jesp had felt like a fae all week.

Ella and Scop arrived that afternoon for the verdict which followed another two hours of "deliberations" behind closed doors between the three men. The guardsman took a quiet moment during that time to thank Jesp and Kyrt. Apparently, Lord Greening was the attorney hired by the wealthy bandits, and he'd done a really good job of discrediting every one of the village witnesses including Ella and Scop, who looked like idiots with bad memories when he got done with them. Jesp glanced back at the pair of them sitting in the back of the room, her anger rising again.

Eventually the scumbags were led into the room in chains and pronounced guilty, to the clear shock and surprise of their leader who then fired his attorney on the spot. They were sentenced to hang and led away to much applause. Jesp and Kyrt circled the courtroom bowing again and then circled Scop and Ella's heads in honor while the pair of elves laughed appreciatively. All in all, the three left Stable Glen in better spirits than they had enjoyed so far during their trip, though they left later in the day than they had planned.

Kyrt and Jesp were settled into the back of the cart, the muddy bag that held the crown wedged between them. Jesp leaned against a small keg of ale and Kyrt sat on top of a small bag of supplies packed by Ella that contained one of her china cups for the faeries to bathe in. They were using the surface of the muddy bag to play a game in which they tried to get their own fist on top of the other's. They were laughing merrily.

Eventually Stable Glen was just a distant memory belonging to the road, and Jesp poked her head over the back of the front bench where Tollie was driving. She and Kyrt had just realized that Tollie had been silent for the two hours or more since they left.

"How about that trial, huh?" Jesp mused at her, hoping for a smile.

Tollie was silent.

Confused, Jesp looked back down at Kyrt who flew clumsily, still drunk from his pain concoction, up to join her.

"You OK, Tollie?" Jesp tried again.

Tollie sighed.

"You know," she started at last, "When you were telling me about how faeries tell the truth?" she was speaking quietly, conspiratorially, "How when you really listen to the playful stuff, you can hear the real stuff interwoven in?"

Jesp shot Kyrt an apologetic look. Kyrt looked very serious for a drunk faerie.

"Yeah?" Jesp agreed tentatively.

"Well, two things really. One, I really hope no one figures that out. I really do."

"Well, they haven't in over a millenium, have they?" Kyrt pointed out.

"Well, no offense, but I don't think they were listening before. But today in the courtroom...you guys really really said too much, and EVERYONE was paying attention to every word."

Kyrt and Jesp looked at each other in shock. They'd played, like they would have at home, with story-telling faerie-style. It wasn't something they did for big folk. What had they included? They started reviewing their story in their heads, silently, while watching each others' faces grow increasingly horrified in the slow seconds that followed. Jesp had admitted that Kyrt had hidden their treasure before leaving the room. They had mentioned the Garden. They'd called Tollie the Librarian's daughter....what had they done?

The silence between the three lingered a painful few moments longer and then Jesp, shakily, asked, "What was the other thing?"

Tollie thought a moment and answered, "Well, you guys embellished a lot..."

"We needed to. Those elves weren't listening!" Kyrt insisted, "They were being swayed by that attorney person, and he was flat-out lying!"

"I know," Tollie agreed, "But it made me wonder. How much embellishing do you think your ancestors did in those songs? How much can we rely on that information do you think?"

The faeries were quiet. They didn't have an answer for that.

Dusk was gathering about them reflecting the new mood in the cart. Tollie sighed again and pointed out that they'd stayed in Stable Glen longer than she'd hoped and couldn't quite reach the border of the Morrowlands before dark. Nonetheless, their accidental disclosures in the courtroom hanging heavily between them, they decided to keep going at least as far as the border. Jesp and Kyrt settled into an uneasy sleep in the back while Tollie kept driving. When she woke them several hours later, it was dark as pitch around them, and what they could make out of Tollie's features were practically aged with exhaustion.

Kyrt and Jesp got up to watch over Tollie while she slept, her child-like form curled into a ball among the softer supplies in the cart. The faeries sat on the back of her bench watching backward across their wagon and talking quietly about the things that had kept them up long after they had tried to go to sleep.

"Do you think anyone knew which garden or which library?"

"I suspect that if they put those two things together and cared to figure it out they could."

"And our treasure?" Jesp asked gulping, "I can't believe I said that."

"Well, it's done now."

"If Tollie gets killed in all of this, I will blame myself," she confessed, "I really would have made a *terrible* guard."

"No, you wouldn't, Jesp," Kyrt soothed.

"Yes! Yes, I would!" Jesp was in tears now, adamantly whispering her painful confession to him, "I got myself knocked out in the tower fire! I spent most of our trip drunk! When the bandits grabbed Tollie I froze! And then, as soon as I had an audience, I just spilled our secrets to a group of elves I'd never met! I'm a horrible horrible...."

"Person?" Kyrt asked innocently.

"I guess so, since I'm not anything else. I guess I'm just horrible at that! And I'm a horrible friend, too. I keep getting you and Tollie into worse messes!"

Jesp sobbed as quietly as she could so as not to wake Tollie, but it was hard. She'd fantasized for years about who she really wanted to be in the world, and now she was needed and she was letting everybody down. She felt like a mule again, only this time she was uninjured and sober.

After a few moments, Kyrt spoke again, "I've just been following your lead, Jesp. I would never have had the courage to do all of this without you for inspiration..."

Jesp let that statement settle into the silence for a moment. It wasn't much, but she was starting to realize that she really did, even despite herself, like Kyrt.

"Thank you," she whispered.

"You're welcome."

"I'll try to stop being so lame," she muttered with a teary grin.

"You're not lame..."

"You guys are both lame," Tollie mused, "If your goal is to let someone sleep..." The tone in her voice let them know she was smiling.

"Sorry."

"Sorry."

The rest of the brief night passed in silence. At first, just a rabbit or two passed by, but as they sat there Jesp realized their scenery really had changed. The neatly cobbled roads of the Morrowlands had given way rather drastically to a winding dirt road. The grass on either side was almost as high as the cart. The quiet of the elvish night, often pockmarked by a cricket or other pleasant noise, was replaced entirely by a raucous cacophony of nighttime croaks, chirps and chitterings all around them. Fireflies were everywhere and every time one blinked its beckoning light, a host of other flying insects became visible. Twice the faeries had to duck as hunting bats swooped overhead and a circling owl in the middle of their watch made the pair particularly nervous. Elvish gardeners and border patrols clearly didn't exist in the Meadows, and it was both beautiful and terrifying. Jesp felt very very small.

The next morning dawned bright and as loud with the noises of wildlife as the night had been. Birds sung, toads croaked and grasshoppers chirped and jumped everywhere about them in the golden wild-wheat fields that lay around them in every direction. Tollie even seemed more unfettered, humming to herself as she ate breakfast and prepared to take up the reins again. Even though the grasses surrounding them would have engulfed Tollie, Jesp could easily picture her wading out into them. At last, Tollie seemed to be at home.

The day began with a pack of dogs chasing the wagon, most of which Jesp and Kyrt knocked out with well-placed arrows. Otherwise their trip prominently featured a circling hawk that seemed to be eying the faeries hungrily, some passing halfling children running up the road with a wheel and a kite, and, as dusk settled in around them again, the largest fireflies the fae pair had ever seen. This part of the world may have been called the Meadows, but for Jesp and Kyrt it was a jungle safari.

Dusk brought with it a squeel of joy from Tollie who saw the turn off up ahead that would lead them down to the town of Brewhall. An hour later, they were turning slightly north again to bypass the town proper and head out to the remote cottage Tollie's family had once called home. Jesp noticed clearly that Tollie was practically bouncing in her seat. Jesp caught a lump in her throat as she tried to imagine what it would be like to be returning home after having been gone so long and realized that she may never get the chance. She glanced sadly at Kyrt whose sorrow-filled eyes seemed to share the same thought.

Happily Tollie turned the wagon around a last bend, gleefully exclaiming that they'd be able to see her home just around the corner. It was finally more dark than dusk, but Tollie seemed to think that her sister was likely home with lights lit in the house. They turned the corner, and the mood changed at once.

Initially they couldn't see anything, which depressed Tollie almost immediately as it dashed her hopes for a cheerful homecoming. But then the smell of old smoke and burnt grass reached their nostrils and Tollie slowed the cart down. Something wasn't right. Fearing an ambush, Tollie agreed to pull the cart over behind an ancient elm tree and wait with the crown while the faeries investigated. It was Jesp's idea, but she feared she was trying to be a little too brave. There had been a lot of faerie-eating wildlife so far in this area, and Kyrt wasn't yet fully whole and healed.

Once the cart was pulled to the side, the fae made Tollie swear a solemn oath, or at least one that felt solemn to them and was loosely based on the one Tollie'd been asked to swear in the courthouse at Stable Glen, to defend the crown to the death. Tollie clearly thought this was a bit much and insisted on adding the books to the promise, but she assured them that she got the point and wouldn't let anything happen to it. When she accused them of stalling, Jesp swallowed hard and they left.

What they discovered was the still-smoking ruins of an old cottage behind a hill. What remained of a walled garden was little more than ash with a few small gravestones peeking out of the ruin to one side. A small ash tree near the center still had the remains of a child's swing hanging from it, and something had been painted on the tree which, of course, Jesp couldn't read. The pair landed on a branch above the swing sadly, dreading what they would have to tell Tollie and deciding that they should look for halfling remains in the rubble before going back.

They were just taking to their wings to do this when

SLAM

With a hissing screech that shredded the silent night, a dark cat jumped out of nowhere to the branch where the fae had just been seconds before. It swatted out at the now fleeing faeries and caught Jesp squarely across her front and side, tearing the very bottom of her good wing. Her wings lost their catch of the wind and she felt herself plummeting. The cat, having overreached its swipe at Jesp, fell with her. The cat hit the dark ground first and leaped up to its feet immediately jumping for Jesp who had barely caught herself on her wings above the cat's head.

"Jesp!" Kyrt came shooting down out of the sky toward the cat as Jesp barely dodged its claw. She got her bow off of her shoulder and knocked an arrow. Screeching its indignation, the cat made for another leap. Jesp remained stationary in the air and let an arrow fly just as the cat became airborne, but its trajectory had been good and it collided with her even as it lost consciousness. She fell backwards with the cat on top of her and landed hard on the stony ground, cushioned only by the thick layer of ash that coated everything. Her back bent upward and the wind knocked out of her as the heavy form of the now-sleeping cat landed on top of her with a sickening crunch.

A moment later the cat slid off of her and she gasped welcome air while still laying across the unforgiving rock. Kyrt, having just hauled the cat off of her, grinned toothily in her face. Jesp panted for a moment, and then something even more unexpected happened. Unable to contain himself having found her alive, Kyrt grabbed Jesp and kissed her on the mouth with such passion it knocked the wind out of her again. He carried her gasping form back up to the tree branch and laid her across it gently.

"Sorry," he stammered, "I thought I'd lost you that time. That was really really brave, by the way."

Despite the dark, Jesp could tell he was blushing. She grabbed him and kissed him again, pressing the upper part of her body as firmly against him as she could manage. She was tired of pretending anymore. She could no longer imagine a life without him.

A moment or two later, they were staring into each others' eyes, panting, each looking for a clue as to how to continue. It was a voice from above them that brought them out of their moment together.

"Nice and all, but you two are going to get yourselves killed out here."

Jesp and Kyrt jumped into the air, grabbed their bows and looked up. Four faeries were lounging on a branch above them looking both amused and bored. The moonlight shining through their wings revealed colors unlike the Garden fae possessed. In the strange light of the moon, their faces appeared to be painted in bright colors, but Jesp wasn't entirely sure. These fae were odd.

Nonetheless, they didn't stick around to talk about it. Just as Jesp and Kyrt got their bearings enough to start asking questions, the four flew off together in an odd diagonal formation. Jesp noticed that each was carrying a bow and quiver, but also had daggers on their belts, which was odd enough as no fae Jesp had ever seen even wore a belt. They were dressed in what looked like scraps of cloth from halfling and elvish clothing rather than the more neatly crafted gossamer wrapped garments of their own clothing. They did not speak another word to Jesp or Kyrt as they flew off into the strangeness of the night.

Kyrt and Jesp found Tollie right where they'd left her. Her eyes widened in fear as she saw them and Jesp realized that they were both filthy and had torn their clothing. Jesp was bleeding also. Tollie's expression didn't lighten any, either, when she saw their faces. They didn't have good news.

After hearing about the brief adventure, which neither faerie told very dramatically and in which neither mentioned the kisses, Tollie insisted on taking the wagon up to the house herself. She found the cat and identified it as a kitten named Fluffy they had had 6 years ago when they had lived there, and she insisted on rescuing it.

"You do realize that it wants to eat us," Jesp scolded angrily, "And that it nearly killed me," she added pointing at her bloodied midsection which at that moment was still very painful.

"I'm sure Fluffy was just playing. He's not a mean cat."

Jesp turned incredulously to Kyrt open-mouthed. He rolled his eyes and shook his head, then a made a quick gesture with his hand across his neck making it very clear that the cat's life would not be long for this world if he went after Jesp again. Jesp smiled. In fact, she struggled against the urge to jump back into his arms. It was weird thinking of Kyrt like this, but Jesp was really enjoying it more than she would have expected to.

The tree concerned Tollie the most. After reviewing the painted words on it, her eyes got very large indeed and she climbed immediately back into the cart.

"Let's go," she insisted hurriedly, and without waiting for the fae to get secure, she started off back down the road with a jerk of the reins.

They rode fairly quietly back toward Brewhall; quietly, that is, once the faeries stopped cursing about being flung back into the wagon on top of the poisoned cat when the reins had been snapped so suddenly. They crested a hill and found themselves looking down on a surprisingly large valley town nestled neatly in the hills below them. From here it was clear that two buildings dominated the village. One, the largest, made up the very edge on one side and was very regular in its shape and solid in its build. The other, only slightly smaller, looked like it had been haphazardly added to over and over again without an overall plan. This one sat on the hill looking down on the town itself. In the center of the town, was a particularly tall narrow building that the rest of it seemed to be built around. The village had a cozy look to it, like a well-manicured garden of shrubs and hedges with a small tree growing in the center.

"Before we get down there," Kyrt spoke into the silence, "Are you going to tell us what the tree said?"

Jesp waited curiously for the answer. She'd been so upset about the cat, distracted by her injury and annoyed at the rough driving that she'd forgotten to be curious about the letters on the tree.

"It said 'You have nowhere to go.'" Tollie answered simply and quietly.

"OK. That's not good," Jesp sighed.

"No," Tollie agreed, "It really isn't."

The road wound down to the left and entered the hamlet on the far side from the largest building, the other one looking down on them from their left as they made their way into town. From the hillside opposite the strangely shaped building, Brewhall had looked larger than it turned out to be. Not that it had fewer buildings, just that everything was smaller up close. Of course, all of it towered over the two faeries, but these were buildings clearly built for and by halflings, not elves. An elf would have to stoop to enter any of them, and would have to sit on the floor inside to not be brushing against the ceiling. It made Jesp feel slightly less small. After all, she was barely larger than the palm of an elf's hand, but was as big as Tollie's head just from chin to scalp.

Tollie kept her head down as she trod the mule and cart through town. By this hour, there were very few lights on and no one in the streets. The clambering of the wooden wheels on the main dirt path seemed inordinately loud in the sleepy village. At the far side of town, she pulled over to a three-story building shaped like a triangle that rested in the shadow of the large edge-defining building. The lights were still on on the lower floor and loud cheerful singing was coming from inside.

"This is a popular pub," Tollie explained as she helped Jesp and Kyrt into her pockets, "With rooms for rent. I figure we'll be in less danger in public than in private tonight."

"What's the big building there?" Jesp asked. It looked foreboding and really huge compared to the tavern.

"That's the Brew Hall itself. The town was named after it. They make famous beer...and a lot of money."

Jesp looked up at the mountain of a building and thought about how many thimbles full of beer it would take to fill such a place. She grinned broadly.

Inside, the large room was full of mostly drunk, mostly male halflings, sitting at tables brooding, dancing on tables merrily, wandering between tables conversing, and some were ignoring the tables completely by sitting with their legs through the balcony rails or on stools at the bar. Many heads turned as Tollie came into the room, and a few nudged their buddies in case they hadn't noticed her. Curled up in Tollie's pocket, Jesp readied her bow.

"Do you have a private room left, Miss?" Tollie asked the middle-aged halfling woman behind the counter.

"Yes, one, but your faerie friends will cost extra," she answered bluntly.

Observant, thought Jesp, but I guess she has to be.

"That's fine. How much?"

Tollie settled up for a small private room on the top floor and two bowls of vegetable soup and a loaf of bread to be brought to the room. Then, ignoring the enthusiastic drinkers all around her, she took her key and headed up the stairs. There were only two small rooms at the very top of the inn, and Tollie opened the door to the room that would look out onto the street. The steep slope of the roof defined this room and there was only one small bed and a nightstand inside. There was also a small window with shutters that would latch from the inside.

Tollie deposited the two faeries on the bed and went back down for gear. She agreed to stable Fluffy with Harry for the sake of the fae. Kyrt asked her chivalrously if she needed an escort back downstairs, but Tollie said no. She was home and really not worried about the locals.

"It's the foreigners I'm worried about. I'd feel safer downstairs with the townsfolk drinking than up here where someone I can't trust might be in the room across the hall."

And with that, she left the faeries and locked the door behind her.

"Cheery thought," mused Jesp.

"Yep," said Kyrt.

The pair locked eyes a moment too long and then, forgetting that Tollie would be back quickly, jumped immediately into each others' arms. Jesp had never been with a man before, but something about Kyrt just felt like coming home, which is exactly what she wanted to feel by now. She had only meant to kiss him, but neither could hold back anymore. Somehow Kyrt had kept her so wrapped up in the experience, that he had Jesp's clothes completely off before she gave the moment any conscious thought. She blushed looking up into his heat-filled eyes, and proceded to to flip him over and remove his clothing, too. He didn't protest. Making love to Kyrt turned out to be the most natural, honest, and joy-filled experience she could have imagined. She immediately wanted to do it it again. Maybe fae did spring from magic after all.

They made furious, passionate love twice more on top of the bedspread. Neither of them particularly interested in lingering in the moment so much as relieving themselves finally of everything that had been pent up between them for far too long. It wasn't until they separated, panting and giggling, that either of them realized that they had left the crown downstairs in the wagon.

Tollie chided them for this very fact when she returned with it a little over an hour after she had left and asked them what in the world had gotten into the two of them. They looked guiltily at each other, but didn't answer. They'd barely gotten their clothes back on as she was unlocking the door.

Tollie had also brought both their teacup and their drawer pillow from Ella's bag, the small faerie-sized bandages Ella had made, and another bag of clothes for herself. Then she'd lugged two big bags of the books all the way up the two flights of stairs. She'd just gotten back to the room when supper arrived.

Kyrt and Jesp spent the night together in the nighstand drawer, freshly bathed and Jesp bandaged from their run-in with Fluffy followed by their run-in with each other. Tollie stayed up late into the night reading by candlelight. Somewhere in the wee hours of the morning the faeries were startled awake by the slamming of the large book and a single exclamation:

"Finally!"

The following morning the three finished their bread from the past night and, although Tollie was still half asleep, she seemed happier this morning than she had the night before. They checked out and Tollie asked the young man behind the counter about who was running the school.

"Tallie," he told her, "Ellerby's daughter, and she's gotten herself into a fair bit of trouble with the local brewer's guild, too."

"Oh?"

"Yeah. Apparently a lot of them got their education by coin for a long time, but Tallie says they can't do that no more. Now you gotta actually read books and study, not just be rich. She's made enemies, but I heard the school has a better reputation for it."

"I bet it does. Ellerby didn't sell out like that did he?"

The teenager shrugged. "I can't afford the time to go up there anyway, so I never knew much about it."

Tollie thanked him and left a few coins on the counter and the three of them left, Jesp and Kyrt on Tollie's shoulders this morning.

When they reached the wagon, Fluffy was groggy and able to eat some breakfast Tollie provided to him, but then he fell back to sleep. Jesp and Kyrt gave each other meaningful looks as Tollie baby-talked to the monster. That cat wasn't going to be happy when it woke up.

Tollie drove them up to the haphazardly shaped building on the hill and parked the wagon right in front of the ornate double front doors. These had words carved all over them, but they looked like they were supposed to be there. Tollie didn't pay any attention to it and just walked straight in. The faeries flew in behind her.

A furry, eyeless ball of floating fluff flew down from the banister above the warm, wooden grand foyer they had walked into. It made neat little circles in front of Tollie's face as if to make her stop.

"Ah," said Tollie, "Would you let Tallie know her sister's here?"

The thing sort of seemed to Jesp to have cocked its head, such as it was, to one side and then flew back up and over the railing of the upper landing. Shortly afterward a halfling woman that looked exactly like a better groomed Tollie came rushing to the rail.

"Tollie?!" she exclaimed excitedly! "Is it really you?!!!"

"In the flesh," Tollie answered, grinning slightly.

Tallie ran down the stairs with her strange furry floating friend following just behind her. She slammed ungracefully into Tollie, throwing her arms around her and nearly knocking her over onto the hard wooden floor. After a moment, it became clear to Jesp that Tallie was crying.

Pulling away from her sister, Tollie looked into her sister's tear-streaked face and asked, "What is it Tallie?"

"They'd told me you were dead," she stammered, "I got a notice that you and dad had both been killed in a fire. Oh Alura! Oh, Goddess!," she wept, "I though our last conversation would be...would be that fight we had....oh, I couldn't stand it!" She threw herself bawling onto her twin sister again, then pulled back and asked, "What about dad? Is he with you?"

"No," Tollie began to tear up, too, looking into her sister's loving eyes, "And it wasn't the fire that killed him either. Can we go somewhere to talk?"

Jesp and Kyrt decided to wait out in the cart, indicating as delicately as they could to Tollie that they wanted to stay with the crown. Tollie seemed to understand and held the door open for them to get back out. When the faeries made it back to the cart, however, Fluffy had finally woken up completely.

He was growling a low growl at the approaching fae and preparing to pounce. Jesp and Kyrt looked at each other, rolled their eyes, and shot the cat again, knocking it out right on top of the crown.

They spent the rest of the morning trimming its claws to nothing and filing its teeth while Tollie wasn't there to protest. They also took some time after eating some of the snacks left over from Ella's as a lunch, to mix up some more of the arrow poison. If Tollie was determined to keep Fluffy around, they expected to need it.

They didn't see Tollie again until well into the afternoon when she and Tallie emerged together and began unloading the cart ("What have you done to Fluffy now?") into the school building. Tallie had offered them a small suite upstairs which included two rooms, one with sitting furniture, and a privy, which had to be explained to the faeries. Jesp eyed the window boxes outside the sitting room and said, "So, I guess that one's our...what did you call it?"

"Privy, and yes, I suppose so," Tallie laughed, "Sleep tight."

Adrik

"So, have you thought any about what to tell these people?"

It was just after dawn on the fourth day and the elves were expecting to meet up with their human companions that evening. Adrik had grown increasingly nervous about it as each day progressed. Who were these men, and what did he and Arisa really know about them anyway? Adrik's gratitude for having been saved from petrification had worn off by this point. He couldn't be careless with trust just because he felt indebted to someone. He didn't, anyway. He'd saved the littlest boy in the family in the flood and fought off wolves while escorting the peasants from one pitiful existence to the other. Then Arisa had even given the two men more money than they'd probably ever seen in their lives. Adrik didn't feel that he owed them anything anymore.

But it was true that the lanky one had something going on with the spirits. Arisa had *seen* it and, morrowelf or not, he trusted Arisa. And the big burly one was good with that wood ax. Adrik couldn't help but wonder what the man might do with some real weapons and some actual training. But Adrik didn't have the time or the patience to be a teacher to a couple of peasant fishermen. Not when he felt the fate of the world on his shoulders. Normally he'd chide himself for being melodramatic after a thought like that, but it really was possible, even probable, that they did have the fate of the world on their shoulders.

Arisa looked up from the fire she was tending and furrowed her brow. "What do you mean?"

They'd spent the last 2½ days finally preparing for their journey again. Adrik had found a stream and refilled their water skins and washed their clothing and bedding. Then he'd spent a day hunting. He'd felled 8 geese, two rabbits and a boar, and then gotten irritated with Arisa when she greeted his great success with "Yes, there's a lot of wildlife up here, isn't there?" as if it took no skill whatsoever to spend a day bringing her back food for several weeks.

"I mean, the humans are coming back tonight and they're going to want answers to their questions. I just want to know what we're going to tell them."

"Well, first I'm going to apologize to them for the terrible butchering job I've done here. If they'd have been here we'd have more meat from these animals, and new leather to boot."

She smiled up at him knowing full well her lack of seriousness on the matter would irritate him. He scowled. She'd spent her time taking inventory of their belongings and supplies, *meditating* of all things, drawing runes and script out on paper she wouldn't let him see, and then butchering meat....badly. Now she was trying to recreate the method by which the humans had preserved those wolves by smoking them, and already one of the geese had caught fire. Adrik crossed his arms and began tapping his foot impatiently.

"All right," she humored him, "What do you want to tell them?"

"As little as possible. We just need to figure out what that is."

"Well, I daresay we don't know much more than that ourselves. Why don't you want to be honest with them?"

He glared at her. He hated it when she treated him like she was teaching him manners and virtue.

"What?" she asked innocently.

"Why do you put it like that?" he asked angrily, "Like I'm being dishonest instead of cautious? You haven't known these people any longer than I have, and they come from a superstitious, magic-hating, racist kingdom. You really don't think they could turn on us? Decide they have more loyalty to their own lords than to us? Do you know what ransom they could get for our lives? You never believe me that people aren't as nice as you are!"

She pursed her lips and sat back from her crouching position, "OK. Maybe we shouldn't have trusted them so quickly. We did have to make a fast decision there. But we've agreed to bring them along. Don't you think it's too late to decide not to give them the answers we promised?"

"No," he answered her flatly, "I don't. They want to figure out what happened to their people, their beloved fishermen or whatever." This derision earned him a scowl from Arisa, "They have no idea of the scope or magnitude of what we're doing. Not yet, anyway. Not until you offer them full disclosure and we find out the hard way where their true loyalties lie. After all, their own king is definitely an enemy to our mission."

Arisa sighed and started poking at the meat on the rack above the fire, biting her lip.

"Well, maybe that's where we should start with them," she said finally.

Adrik sat down near the fire. Properly smoked or not, the meat was beginning to smell delicious and they had not had breakfast. Arisa noticed the hungry look on his face, and smiled. "I cut plenty of bacon," she offered. Why don't you cook that up since you do it so well."

She uncovered about three pounds of beautifully cut bacon she hadn't begun to smoke yet. She may not have known what to do with geese and rabbit, or even the rest of the pork, but she could cut bacon, and she could calm his temper that easily, too. Arisa just knew how.

He smiled sheepishly at her and she returned the expression. He pulled the small flat iron he carried and stuck it in the fire under her smoking rack. Soon the air was filled with the delicious smell of cooking bacon and he cared a lot less about what Arisa did and did not say to the humans.

After breakfast Arisa renewed the conversation. He knew she would, so he just waited. She liked to let a matter cool before discussing it. She hadn't learned yet, he mused to himself, that letting him cool down didn't change his opinion or keep his temper from resurfacing. But, whatever. As long as they came to an agreement before they had company again, he could wait.

"So, here's my thought, Adrik, now that I've had some food and time to think about it. Brody has magic. We may have to help him come to terms with the *word* magic, but he has it and so he isn't going to be any more welcome in his own king's court than we are. What's more, if anyone finds out he has magic, his whole family would be in danger. I think we if can impress that upon him, we can trust him. But then there's Finn, and I don't know what to think about him. But I doubt we'll be able to talk to Brody without Finn, and it would be rude to try."

"So, let me get this straight, you want to intimidate him into being reliable?"

Adrik smiled at her. She stared helplessly at him.

"No," she insisted after a pause, "I just thought that if he understands the risks he's taking more fully, that he'd be less likely to turn on us, since that's what you're worried about."

"And that's not the least bit manipulative."

"Well, what do you want me to do? Wait till they show up and say, 'Sorry, we've changed our mind. You can't come'?" Her voice was rising now and her face was flush, "We need them. They know the area! They know the local legends! And Brody is in communication with a dead spirit that may have in his final act triggered the Water Titan for all we know! Didn't you say that your Queen believed that she had purposefully triggered the Fire Titan? We discounted that claim, but now I'm not so sure. So, what do you want?" She bit her tongue and looked back at him, breathing a little harder than necessary.

He'd done it now. He'd made her mad. He hadn't pushed her to actual anger before. He had wondered before, in fact, whether or not she even had a temper. He felt guilty again. He just didn't seem to be able to stop himself from giving in to what many people would call his nature.

"Sorry, Arisa," he said quietly, "I really don't mean to be an ass. Unfortunately it comes naturally." The truth was, he hated that fact sometimes.

She studied him for a moment and finally said, "Don't be so hard on yourself. You're a better person than any I've ever met."

This statement shocked him completely. *Him?* She must have found someone else to talk to in the last five minutes. His dismay must have shown on his face because she laughed.

"No, I mean it, Adrik. You don't give yourself enough credit."

"Is this one of those pep talks you give someone where you tell them they're already something you want them to turn out to be? Because that won't work, I assure you."

"Adrik, really. Look, I come from a culture where the standard of behavior is to strive to be a decent and compassionate person. You come from a culture..."

"I know where I come from," he shot back angrily.

"...where cruelty and sadism are the norm. You were taught to value power and control and to revel in other people's pain. You've told me so."

His temper was rising now. He didn't need a lecture about how horrible he was any more than he needed a pep talk that overlooked his personal flaws. He was about to explode at her when she continued.

"So, for you to make the choice every day to be a good person is harder than for me, and yet you do it. You've turned your back on everything you've been taught to try and be something good, with no direction and no instruction and no intuition for it. If truth be told, I don't know if I could have done it if our positions were reversed. You're the better person of the two of us," and at this she looked down and blushed, "It's an honor to know you really," she said in a small voice.

He stared at her for a moment, incredulous, his temper receding like a bladder losing air. What was she trying to accomplish with this? He struggled with his own identity every day, but he didn't see how the struggle itself made him any better. It seemed to him just to be a struggle.

He sat there speechless for several minutes while she went back to wrapping up the meat she'd managed to smoke properly and starting a stew with the meat she'd merely cooked instead. He continued to watch her, waiting for the request, the reason she was buttering him up. It didn't come.

He ate his slightly burned duck stew in silence. He'd done little more than stare at Arisa now for a full hour, and she was starting to glance at him nervously like he might just explode. Finally, with lunch cleaned up, she tried the conversation again, but very tentatively.

"Um, did you want to talk about the humans anymore?" she asked him, every word laced in caution.

"No," he answered simply, "I don't guess there's anything to discuss. Partial truth won't get us anywhere. Just watch your back, though."

And he left her there staring after him as he walked back to the road to wait for the humans, his head still ringing with the compliments. He'd tried hard to be better than he was born. But it had all started out of a need for vengeance. It was really just a way for him to lash out at all the pain and cruelty of his childhood. It happened that way sometimes. You got evil humans and other elves sometimes, and sometimes you got a shadowelf who turned to decency because he couldn't take it anymore. That was how Adrik saw himself: as someone who just hadn't been able to take it and decided to get back at those that had hurt him for so long.

He'd never met anyone like Arisa before. She saw past him, saw past the parts of him that he couldn't see past. But what she couldn't see, he reminded himself as he reached the road, was that it was her that kept him going, that kept him trying. He relied on her strength of character to keep up in himself what he often feared was no more than a charade.

Adrik wasn't alone with his thoughts for long. The sun was still high in the eastern sky over the mountains when he heard the unmistakable sound of conversation on the road. Soon he could make out Brody and Finn happily discussing fishing in some new lake and whether or not Rista would still end up a fisherman. He rolled his eyes, but then, maybe it would have been nicer to be that *simple.*

Adrik leapt out from his hiding place and enjoyed their startled jumps. He chuckled and they laughed, too.

"I'm glad you're here," he told them, "I did some hunting and Arisa thought she could butcher and smoke the meat like you did." He rolled his eyes and they smiled.

"Lead the way," they said.

The afternoon passed in friendly conversation. The humans set up salting racks for the meat and took the boar carcass and salvaged everything. Adrik had nearly decided to become a vegetarian after watching them make a simple sausage with the last parts they could do nothing else with, and had promised himself that he would not be partaking of the snout, ears or feet no matter how hungry he was. But the smell of his supper cooking later in the day chased those convictions out of his mind. He and Arisa had survived the 3 months they had traveled together on trail rations and food that he hunted for but that they couldn't cook well. They'd taken turns trying, and frankly Arisa was the better of the two. To a point, meat cooked over fire is meat cooked over fire, but this was fresh albeit messy sausage, seasoned with their freshly-bought spices and evenly cooked over spit. It was on another level entirely from the food they'd been eating. It might be worth the risk of having them along, Adrik conceded once his belly was full, just for the food.

In addition to sausage-making skills and some potatoes and onions that garnished the meal nicely, they'd also brought ale. And it was over this ale, that the conversation, so recently laden with details about the new village and the welfare of those that had survived, turned at last to more serious matters. Adrik would have been perfectly happy with a round of 'did everyone make it? Yes? Good,' and moving on, but Arisa had asked about each child, each new home, the village layout, their shopping and even asked for details about the tanning process they got to working on after supper. Apparently Finn was looking to make himself some "protective clothing" as he called it. Adrik doubted that the pieces of leather he'd begun to tan would cover much of him, but didn't say so. He needed new armor himself, and was hoping Finn would turn out to have some skill in making it.

"OK," said Arisa finally, "We need to make plans for the next leg of our journey." She looked pointedly at Adrik who promptly refilled his mug with ale and deposited himself comfortably at the base of a tree, picking sausage bits out of his teeth. Sensing no opposition from Adrik, Arisa continued, "Should we start with you telling us what happened on the day your fathers went missing, or do you have questions you need answered first?"

It was a bold way to start to the conversation, but Adrik still said nothing. He felt like a guard on duty or an eavesdropper or both. He was listening, but he'd decided this was Arisa's show. She'd stroked his ego, he mused to himself, which earned her the right to lead.

"Well, unfortunately," Finn started seriously, a piece of new leather slathered in smelly oil in his hands. Adrik thought it looked as if he was re-skinning it, and wondered if there'd be anything left when he was done. The oil stank, and he wished the man would cook some more sausage to cover the smell, "I think we've told you everything. To tell you the truth, until Brody's dream, we didn't know it was anything more than a random tragedy. I'm not sure what else to tell you without knowing what you're trying to find out."

Arisa nodded and looked at Adrik who merely stared back, finally electing to offer a shrug for support.

"Boy, I don't even know where to start. With me I guess. OK. Have you ever heard of the Prophecy of Andarraine?" she asked the humans directly. Boy, thought Adrik, right into the heart of it.

"Like the Kingdom of Andarraine?" Brody's voice sounded edgy and Adrik sat up protectively.

"Andarraine was supposed to be a really evil kingdom of humans that lived in these mountains a long time ago. I don't know if that's true or not, we don't get a lot of information up here, but that's what we've been told," Finn added helpfully.

"And magic, too," Brody added conspiratorially, "They supposedly had evil magic."

Adrik was starting to like Brody less.

"Well all of that's largely true," Arisa told them, "Except that despite what most of the world believes, Adrik and I don't think magic itself is inherently evil. Well, we're not the only ones, actually. But we believe that magic is a tool like any other. Completely neutral. Like an ax. You can cut firewood with it, or you can commit unspeakable acts of violence with it. Either way, good and evil don't exist in the ax. A tool is only as good or bad as its wielder. I mean, Brody, do you feel like you've become evil just because you've been infused with magic?"

"No. And that's something I really need to understand, too, because I don't believe that my father is evil, either, and I'm going to be pretty stubborn about that."

Adrik relaxed a little.

"Exactly, and that's fine. We don't think you or your father are evil, either."

It was like listening to a parent talk to a child, Adrik thought to himself, but Brody was relaxing as she spoke to him and that made Adrik more comfortable, so he decided not to interrupt.

"What we know, which isn't much I admit, is that the Kingdom of Andarraine was terribly evil and lasted for over a thousand years. It was destroyed, no one knows for sure how, two thousand years ago. We know that magic was commonplace in our world before that, but that it largely went away when Andarraine fell. And, yes, they used it, and they used it for evil purpose.

"There is a prophecy, and no one knows the whole thing. I'll come back to that. But most people know that it says that the Kingdom of Andarraine will return when magic does, so you can see why people associate magic with evil. Except that I happen to know that what the Prophecy really says is that magic will come back, heralded by these comets and that it will be a turning point for our world for good or for evil, but I can't convince anyone of it except Adrik. I really don't think it says anything at all about the Kingdom of Andarraine itself coming back, although I do think it says something about royalty, or a throne."

She finished, a bit breathlessly, and waited for a response.

"And how do you know?" asked Finn.

Again Arisa shot Adrik a questioning look and again he offered no help.

He wasn't good at this explaining stuff and got frustrated easily. So, he wasn't going to get involved in this unless he had to.

"Because I've read it," she told him.

"But you said no one knew the whole thing," Brody reminded her.

"Yeah, that's because I can't remember it."

This statement was met with stunned silence from the humans, and Adrik felt that he needed to come to Arisa's rescue at this point.

"Well not exactly, Arisa. It's not like you were told a story and don't remember how it goes. That wasn't normal reading you did, and it messed you up pretty badly."

Arisa sighed, "Yeah, it's definitely not a normal thing that happened, but all of that amounts to a longer story. Maybe we would should sleep and talk while we journey tomorrow?"

Adrik had to hand it to her. She had indeed tried to limit what she said, but, then again, he knew it was physically tasking for her to discuss it. After all, she had been essentially cursed. He watched the humans digest what had just been said, waiting for their response. He had a full belly and had drunk more than his share of the ale. He was sleepy now and happy for the conversation to be over. He'd even participated in it. He congratulated himself for that.

"That still really doesn't explain why you're traveling to The Unbreaking," Brody finally pointed out.

"Or how finding out about our fathers will help with anything," added Finn.

Well, damn, thought Adrik. Now would have been a good time for them to have been as dumb as he'd originally assumed they were. It was a good thing, though, he reasoned with himself, that they weren't, since he'd have to rely on them for the foreseeable future.

Arisa nodded, looking tired and turned her gaze to Adrik, obviously hoping for help with the story.

"OK," said Adrik taking over, "I'll answer what I can, but it's a symptom of what happened to her that she can't talk about it much or for long. What do you know about the Elven races?"

"There's more than one?" Brody asked helpfully, with a grin. Adrik and

Arisa both glared at him. He tried to rally a bit, but didn't help himself much in Adrik's opinion, "I mean the two of you look really different, but I hear that humans can, too, if they're from different places, but we're all the same race. Right?"

"Well, in truth," Arisa breathed. She was looking very tired, but this part of the conversation shouldn't make it worse, "That's not a bad point. We do consider ourselves to be separate races, but that has at least something to do with the fact that most of us believe that our inherent natures are very different. But frankly, Adrik himself is proof that it isn't nature but culture that separates us really."

Here we go again, he thought.

"There used to be five races of elves, but there are only three or four now. I'm a morrowelf. We're lorekeepers and scholars mostly. Adrik's a shadowelf. And there are also willowelves, who are dedicated to the preservation of nature and wild places, especially their ancient forest. Sorry, Adrik. You go ahead."

"So what are shadowelves known for?" asked Brody and Adrik stared at him a moment before answering.

"Mostly torturing people for fun," he added with a broad mocking smile.

The humans glared at him horrified and Arisa chided him.

"Adrik!"

"Sorry, but, well?"

Arisa shook her head, "Like I said, Adrik's proof that we aren't necessarily ruled by those roles."

"So you weren't kidding?" Brody pushed the point.

Adrik answered by removing his linen tunic. Underneath the blue-green cloth, his body was a mess of scars: some ritually created, others the result of punishments he'd received over the years for terrible crimes like arguing with his mother. There were stripes across each of his ribs, burns in patterns across his stomach and the unmistakable evidence of frequent vicious lashings across his back. Arisa gasped. He'd never shown his body to her before, either, but he'd gotten annoyed again. He did that so easily.

"Any other questions? Good."

Satisfied at their shock, he re-clothed himself and went on with what he wanted to say.

"Our *Queen*," and this word he spat with venom in his voice, "Said that she found a way to bring the Andarraine Prophecy to fruition. Well, she wasn't Queen yet when she said that, but she is now. Or, well, was five years ago. Hey!" he added with excitement, "Maybe she's dead by now!"

"We could only hope," agreed Arisa, "But I doubt we'll have been so lucky." She was laying out her bedding and removing what of her clothing she wouldn't be sleeping in. Adrik always watched her do this. He imagined her body was pristine, unscarred, pale and soft. He shook the thought out of his head and then shook again to rid himself of the annoyance that tonight there was an audience again. Though he would never admit it to her, he liked being alone with her, even though there was no more to it than there would be tonight. He'd die of shame to admit that he sometimes thought of her like that, but he did, every night.

Brought back to his senses he looked back at the humans.

"She announced that she would bring powerful magic back to the world and lead the shadowelves in a war over the other races. Well, she went on this quest with a selection of other shadowelves and when they finished whatever it was they did, the Fire Titan had appeared in the sky. At the time I didn't believe, and many of us didn't, that she'd really *done* anything. I thought she'd just figured out when that comet was coming, and made it look like she'd done it. But now I'm not so sure.

"Anyway, something changed in the world that day. The Queen, which she became immediately on her return, and two others had magic powers when they returned. They had developed different aspects of fire magic. Well, no one has wielded real magic since the days of Andarraine as far as we know, so the one thing I *did* believe was that the Andarraine Prophecy was coming true.

"Unfortunately, Arisa, telling my part of the story doesn't really answer their questions. Arisa? Arisa?"

He looked and Arisa was curled up in a little ball on top of her bedroll like a cat. He went and covered her up then suggested that the three of them split watches for the night. They agreed and went to bed.

Adrik stayed up for three more hours. He banked the fire. Put the last of their things away, and thought long and hard about everything that had happened in what seemed like such a short amount of time. He'd decided he couldn't live under Queen Kajiri's rule. But he'd known he'd never be welcome in the world anywhere. No shadowelf was, but they'd made sure of that themselves. He had the information about what had happened. He had some knowledge of what Queen Kajiri was now planning. He'd hoped that knowledge would buy him another life. And it had, actually. It had just taken some trouble, first. The important thing to him was that he was never going back. Never.

Adrik would have slept well with Brody on one watch and Finn on the other, but Arisa moaned and mumbled all night worrying him. Nonetheless, she was up before anyone in the morning and Adrik woke to the delicious smell of reheating sausage. As soon as she saw he was up, she sent him for water.

Adrik returned to find the humans awake and in deep conversation with Arisa. Realizing immediately that it was about him, he set about to cleaning himself up and pouring the last of the ale in four glasses. He knew what she'd done. She'd woken them to give them a chance to express their concerns about him while he wasn't in ear shot. She meant well, and he had a hard time staying mad at Arisa for long, but it felt like a betrayal. After all, she was the only friend he had in the world, especially now that he'd abandoned his little sister. Arisa was the one, in fact, that was slowly but surely teaching him what friendship was.

He gave her a look intended to project his hurt feelings to her. It was manipulative, but he didn't like this situation. She gave him a pitying look, cocking her head to one side, and he melted anyway. Damn her.

"So I'm sure you've used the time to catch them up on the whole story now, so I don't have to hear it again?" he chided her, waiting to see what she would claim to have been discussing.

"No, Mister Bruised Ego, I was telling them the same thing I told you yesterday about how much more decent you are than us for having done all that you've done."

Ouch.

The humans were giving him curious looks, then Brody said, "I guess the truth is that if someone more educated than me had found you on that ledge, they'd have killed you before you woke up. Well, for the record, I saw what kind of man you were when you saved my little brother in the flood. I don't need to know anything else. But, Arisa's right, you know, your path's been way harder than ours. I don't think anyone has the right to judge you."

Ouch again. OK, ego in check. Damn them all.

"Thank you is the correct response," Arisa informed him smirking all over her pale, thin face.

"I'll remember that next time you have an 'Adrik's Wonderful' conference in my absence," but he smiled when he said it, which ought to be enough for anybody. He was soooo glad right now that it wasn't possible to see a Shadowelf blush, because his face had gotten very warm, "But you're telling me that these poor gentlemen *still* don't have their questions answered?" He was really grinning at her now.

She pursed her lips suppressing a grin and handed him a plate of sausage. She fixed plates for the other two and then herself tossing him looks and shaking her head all the while. Then she settled down to eat and told Adrik, "You may finish your tale now, minstrel."

He nearly choked on his sausage.

So, Adrik explained that he'd heard of the Rune Keep: that it was supposed to be the place where the Prophecy itself was kept, if in fact there was such a thing, along with all known lore pertaining to it. He had decided to go there with what he knew, hoping for sanctuary but found none. It was over the river and just inside the Morrowlands, and they would hear nothing of what he had to say because of who and what he was.

"So they threw me in their dungeon for the crime of trying to save the world, and they're supposed to be the good guys," he finished with great relish.

Arisa clapped enthusiastically as he finished and he bowed mockingly to the small group's laughter.

"OK, I'm done," he then announced, "I'm sure Arisa's dying to tell you how she saved me and all of that dribble."

"What? You think I'm proud of that?" she laughed.

The group got their things together and began on their way down the mountain. They knew they'd make far better time going than they did coming. Not only was downhill going to speed them up, but they no longer had an old man, a pregnant woman and several small children to slow them down. They hoped that by nightfall they might make camp near where they had fought the wolves, returning to Luring the next night. Adrik teased Arisa that this arrangement *might* give her enough time to tell the humans what they wanted to know before they set off toward the Gatewell.

On the way down the mountain, Arisa picked the story back up again, but cautiously, avoiding the parts that would call up her strange weariness as much as possible. First she determined that the humans had not heard of the Rune Keep, so she decided to start there.

"The legends are true. The original Prophecy of Andarraine does indeed lie hidden away in the bowels of the deepest part of the Keep, although the Elder Librarians deny it. I was an apprentice there, nothing more. It's written in runes, does that mean anything to the two of you?"

The humans shook their heads.

"I don't know if you're familiar with the laws around here," Finn explained, "But it's illegal for anyone to learn to read or write, own a book, ask for or receive information not relevant to their local obligations, or travel. We thought we were doing good to know what an elf was and that Andarraine was evil."

Adrik smirked. They'd known the kingdom was oppressive and that it's Lords detested everything outside of their own petty and tyrannical worldview, but they'd just told a morrowelf that books were illegal, and he knew she'd explode. He counted it down in his head. 3..2..1

In fact her tirade was still ongoing when they paused to eat some fresh carrots the humans had and some of the trail rations the elves were carrying in what would pass for their midday meal. Adrik doubted Arisa had ever met anyone who couldn't read before and at some point during her long dissertation about the evils of forced ignorance, the two men had sheepishly admitted that neither of them had ever seen a book before. Or paper for that matter, though they'd heard of both.

Adrik just shook his head, smiled to himself and watched them from the rear. He was keeping an eye behind them as they went on. Arisa was just insisting that whenever they *did* return from this trip of theirs, she was bringing the village of Kipping a small library and dared the local lords to mess with it.

But lightning was flashing overhead at this point, and Adrik realized that it happened each time she got good and irate, so he finally stopped the amusing conversation. The sky then proceeded to drizzle steadily for the rest of the day, but no more lightning was seen once Arisa quit her rampage. When Brody and Finn realized that she was causing the lightning that time, they looked almost as startled as they did when Adrik had taken off his tunic, so he steered the conversation back to the point so they'd better understand what to expect from Arisa. At least, as much as you could know what to expect from Arisa.

"OK, guys," Adrik picked up the thread now, wanting to keep Arisa on an even keel for a little while, "What do you know about runes?"

He knew he was egging them back to literacy topic slightly, and they were glancing nervously at Arisa as they answered. He just found it all so amusing and stifled a snigger.

"Uh, nothing," they conceded.

"OK. Runes are like symbols that you draw. They each mean something. Most represent a whole word or concept, but any can be used instead as individual letters. The problem with reading them, however, is that each is infused with its own magic and you sort of ingest or absorb that magic when you read the rune. It's like the gold one around Arisa's neck, the Rune of Journey. When she looks at it, knowing what it means, it gives her some magical protection on the road. Technically it would work for anybody whether they could read it or not as long as the person who *inscribed it*, basically meaning they drew it, understood it. So, Finn for example, you could wear it for protection, but if you made a copy of it for someone else, since you can't read..." he paused long enough to see Arisa bite her lip, "The one you made wouldn't work, even for Arisa. Although," he added as an aside, "She could make it work by tracing it or something, couldn't you?"

"No, but someone who can actually inscribe this rune could. It's not one I've mastered. Each rune requires independent study to be able to do all that."

"Ah, OK. See, she's the expert here. Not me."

"No one writes in Runes anymore," she continued, "Except to inscribe one, maybe as many as three, for some simple purpose. And even historically, a permanent inscription costs the inscriber so much of themselves, people only ever wrote very short passages in any permanent form even when magic was commonplace. That's one of the things that makes the Prophecy so incredible: it's the longest runic inscription ever found. Reading something runic that is more than a short few words or concepts is powerful magic, and it's the only magic really left in our world, unless you count alchemy or astrology."

Adrik risked an amused glance over at the humans. He knew darn well they had no idea what either of those two disciplines were, and he wondered if they'd elect to point that out to her. They did not.

"My people believe that they *study* magic, cataloging it as history but nothing more. But I've come to realize more and more that in some ways we *practice* magic, even though we swear we don't. But I didn't understand how dangerous it would be to read a longer runic script. I was, as I said, only an apprentice.

"But when the comet came, the Fire Titan, I knew something was wrong. I asked my elders and betters what it meant and if the Prophecy mentioned such an event. The Keep *exists* to study the runes of the Prophecy to be able to warn the world when it was upon us and to advise us all how to prevent it, but none of them would do that. I thought for a while that they had become complacent in their scholarly lives, but I began to suspect that a certain few of the Elder Keepers and Librarians might be up to their own purposes. The runes are, after all, arguably the most powerful magic we have left, maybe the only magic, and all knowledge about them is kept there. I don't know why it doesn't seem to concern anybody that someone looking for power and personal gain would be drawn to that path. Actually, I guess that's not fair. The willowelves have been trying to warn us about that for years. But, we hold scholars in such esteem among the morrowelves that I think we've decided that they're morally infallible, which they're not."

The rain was coming harder now and the path was becoming slick. They had to abandon Arisa's latest topic of interest in favor of more practical discussion about their journey. They decided to take to the treeline for stability, knowing it would slow them down, but as the downpour threatened to become a deluge they had to stop. The rain was so loud they couldn't really keep on talking either. They spent a miserable night in which everything was soaked and they were themselves so muddy as to be unrecognizable from one another. Sleep would have been hard to come by anyway. Each watch saw movement in the trees. Nothing came close enough to warrant warning the others except as watch changed, but none felt secure not knowing what might be out there. Whatever it was, both Adrik and Arisa, whose vision was better under the circumstances, noticed that they walked upright and struggled not at all with the slick, muddy conditions. They also made no sound as far as elf ears could detect, and that was more worrisome.

The sun peaked through the clouds briefly as it rose, teasing them with warmth, light and the possibility of fire-cooked breakfast, before it hid away again allowing the rain to dominate the day. Miserable and wet as they were, they each kept to their own thoughts, bundled in their own cloaks and blankets, individually willing the day to end. They passed the point where the wolves had given up their lives in a last bid for a decent meal and were another four miles down before they gave the day up and looked for a campsite. Finn and Brody proved to be quite as able in the woods as Adrik, though much louder. It was Finn that found the godsend that heartened them all finally. It was a small cave. Small, but large enough for them and their gear to camp inside. And more importantly it was dry.

Finn volunteered to try to collect wood for a fire, though he didn't have much hope of finding anything dry. Still, he came back more quickly than expected and summoned Adrik outside to look at something he'd discovered.

Not far from the cave, Finn had found a slightly larger cave, set more precariously over a precipice. There was definite evidence that it had been used very recently and the tracks around it were strange indeed. Knowing that Adrik was an able tracker himself, Finn had asked his opinion of the tracks.

Finn looked more alarmed than Adrik thought was called for, but he didn't ask the man why. The tracks were alarming enough. They appeared to be thorny in places, and narrow and light in others. The rain had made a mess of them and Adrik couldn't be sure, but he guessed bramblemen and elves. He couldn't tell if there had been a fight or a friendship from the mess of tracks, but there was no blood or bodies which suggested the latter. Adrik could make no sense of the find and asked Finn his thoughts.

"Well," the large man answered with the same sick shock on his face, "If they were elves they were your kind. So, I'm gonna be rude and suspect they're up to no good."

"What makes you think they were shadowelves? This is an awfully long way away from our homelands."

"Did you see what they were eating?"

Adrik had been so perplexed by the tracks he'd done no more than glance into the cave. He'd noticed the leftover meat discarded and the pit still set up, but hadn't looked at either one. He did so now and his heart sank. It was a human child, and knowing his own compatriots, it had probably been cooked alive.

Finn was vomiting outside and Adrik nearly joined him. Shadowelves for sure, he had to admit, and he hoped sincerely that it was no one he knew. Either way, he thought bitterly, he was going to see them burned if they met, and he had a feeling that they would.

Chapter 5:

9th Day of the 12th Month, 2nd Day of the Week, Autumn
Rothsday, Shilirs 9

Keen

The next two days were some of the worst Keen could remember, although they continued to promise to get worse. The elves kept him chained to a cot in a tent he'd rather have never known existed. The dirt beneath his flimsy bed was caked with blood, and the place was cursed with flies. And on every post and a few small tables were hung or strewn a variety of twisted, spiked, bladed or clamping iron implements of so many shapes and varieties that Keen had worn himself out trying not to think about what all of them might be capable of. The small potbelly stove near the cot provided some welcome warmth since he had no blanket, but the presence of iron handles protruding from its flames suggested that it, too, had not been placed for his comfort.

He couldn't be angry really. His own people were notoriously cruel in disposing of elves that were captured, a fact about which he was reminded immediately upon his arrival. So, for two days he'd had just enough range of motion to slide over to a bedpan clumsily but to do little else.

And he'd met Kethran. He understood now why Kierra had lost all color to her face when his name had come up. That elf was crazy. And one thing that was clear was that Kethran didn't believe for one moment that Keen didn't know anything about troop movements or other tactical plans his king or officers had in this war. Kethran was quite sure that given enough pressure, Keen was likely to start remembering all kinds of things that he, Keen, currently was refusing to share. Except, of course, that Keen knew nothing of the sort, and couldn't for the life of him think of anything even remotely useful he might offer to tell the terrifying elf in exchange for his life, or even for a swift death which, looking around the tent, might be the best he could hope for.

Another thing Keen was absolutely certain of, though, was that he owed everything he still had left to Kierra. He hadn't been allowed to see her since she'd sung that enchantingly beautiful song by the stream two days ago: the last time he'd probably ever be free. More accurately, she hadn't been allowed to see him, but he'd heard her. She wasn't far away, and she hadn't stopped giving Kethran and his men every ounce of heck she had in her which, Keen smiled to himself, was quite a good amount of heck. Bless her. And that was why, although Keen hadn't been allowed to get up, or to smell fresh air, or to see Kierra, he hadn't suffered anything worse than to lie here amid the flies and stale blood and worry about what might be coming next...yet.

A tear rolled down his cheek. He remembered her song. He had never heard anything so hauntingly beautiful in his life. It was as if the sunlight had suddenly transformed into sound. Whatever happened to him now, his life was worth having heard that voice. More tears were flowing. He didn't care. He loved her. He wished he had ever told her. That was the regret he'd die with. She'd deserved to hear him say that: just that he loved her. She was so beautiful, so perfect. He had only come here to kill things, and she had stopped and saved him and then sang that beautiful song to save him again. And she was still here, yelling at people and stomping her little perfect feet in the dirt trying to save him. He smiled through his tears. He wanted to laugh at the memory of her leaping like a gazelle with more grace than he'd ever seen, all the way over that cave, then falling on that bad leg, then turning it back into an acrobatic kind of roll, then gasping for air while she was trying to yell at soldiers, but then pulling it all together to sing that song. He was smiling up at the dirty tent ceiling. The sun had risen again. They'd come in with bread and broth and more threats and questions. He tried not to care. He tried to hold onto his vision of Kierra at the stream: his one perfect memory of her.

Kethran came back. This time he came with two others. Keen swallowed hard and wiped his face. They looked grim and serious. Keen figured this was coming. It hadn't sounded like Kierra was doing much more than stalling them and making them angrier.

"You've had plenty of time to think by now. We've been more than generous," Kethran stated simply, his angry, insane eyes boring hungrily into Keen's. Keen swallowed again, his mind racing. What could he possibly tell them that they would accept? Rationally Keen knew that the answer was nothing. Even if he came up with something, Kethran would take it as a sign that Keen had held back and immediately press him for more. Keen could feel himself beginning to shake no matter how hard he tried to control himself. This path was inevitable. He kept staring helplessly into those merciless eyes. He could feel tears starting to form again. He wanted to at least appear brave in the face of this, but he was losing control of himself all over as the seconds passed between him and his jailors.

"Well?"

"I've told you," Keen choked his voice up out of his still-parched throat, "I'm more than willing to cooperate with you in any way that I can, but I'm nobody in the army and I don't know anything about the things you're asking me about. I wish I did. I really do. I can't think why you'd think I wouldn't tell you everything I know," he added this last bit clearly looking around the tent at the assembled horrors that had been left purposefully in his view.

"Get him up," Kethran ordered.

Keen's eyes darted to the two elves now advancing on him. Instinctively he glanced around at the various assembled nightmares wondering which ones required him to stand. As they were unlocking his manacles he looked back at Kethran who had backed up to make room for his comrades. He was watching mirthlessly, a calculating and cold expression locked on Keen's face. Keen knew that elf could use any instrument in this tent and not flinch. He had a passing thought as his manacles released and he began, gratefully, to sit up for the first time two days, which itself ached everywhere and was its own torture, that he hoped they'd moved Kierra far enough away that she wouldn't have to hear any of this.

Keen felt like they were peeling his skin off of the cot. His skeleton creaked as it tried to remember how to bend and support him again. Every part of him ached from being left with such limited mobility for so long. It had been bad enough while he was there, but it was far worse now that he was moving. And his hip felt like it was breaking as they moved him roughly from laying to sitting to standing.

As Keen's weight hit his bad leg he screamed. He had no control at all anymore. He wasn't sure which hit the ground first: his frame or the vomit, but both tumbled forward with splattering velocity. And Keen kept screaming. He'd lost just enough feeling laying on the cot to not have realized how bad his hip had gotten. He rolled over onto his side and threw up again.

From outside, he could hear Kierra scream, too. He could tell they were having to restrain her. She was pitching a fit. She'd heard him. He hated that. He tried to pull himself together. He didn't need to make her suffer. She'd been through enough over him.

He gripped the dirt and closed his eyes panting. He hoped he'd rolled out of his own sick, but he wasn't even sure. He could feel the boots of one of his tormentors preventing him from rolling completely onto his back but he was up on his better side. On his left, everything from his armpit to his toes was agony and he didn't dare move his left arm which he had curled up against his raised side. This, of course is what they grabbed.

"Get up."

The boot nearest him kicked him immediately in his injured hip. He screamed again, wishing for the first time that they would use anything else in this tent on any other part of him. Breaking him in half would have been easier to bear.

They yanked him up by his injured shoulder. Keen managed not to scream this time, biting his lip until he tasted blood instead. He had been ready for it. He got his weight onto his better side and prevented the sudden lurch onto his left that had been unavoidable from the cot. He was still breathing heavily through his mouth and staring wide-eyed at Kethran once he reached his feet. His eyesight had become blurry. He was quickly learning what the phrase "blinding pain" meant.

At this point Kethran spoke again. "It has been brought to my attention that it isn't healthy for us to leave you tied to a cot any longer." He grinned a rare smirk that didn't reach his eyes. Keen gulped. "So, we're going to let you spend some time over against the post instead. For a change of scenary we hope you will find memory stimulating. Let us know if you think of anything."

"Kethran, if you'll just give me a way to be useful to you that I can contribute to, I'll tell you anything you want to know. Seriously. But I don't know anything about troop movements or plans! I don't!"

Kethran nodded, and turned around and walked out of the tent.

Outside, Kierra immediately demanded to know what had happened, and Keen could hear the sadistic elf standing just outside the tent explaining calmly to her that Keen had been gotten up out of bed, but that his leg was hurting and that was all. Behind him, one of the elves holding his arms sniggered.

Secretly, Keen wanted her to believe Kethran. Not because the horrible officer deserved any credit for his sincerity, but because it was becoming increasingly clear that there was nothing Kierra could do for Keen, and it would be easier for Kierra, and probably Keen, if she just went on with her life. This was going to be bad enough. Keen dreaded the things that were about to happen, but he was starting to dread even more listening Kierra listen to them happen.

The two elves moved him roughly over to the center tent post. Fortunately it wasn't far, because they were certainly not giving him any opportunity to be careful about his leg. He gritted his teeth and muffled his groans enough that he didn't think Kierra could hear anything. They manacled his hands behind him so that he was facing the entrance to the tent. He could see the shadow of Kethran outside the flap still arguing with Kierra who still seemed convinced that at some point, someone would check to see that he, Keen, had not been harmed after having saved Kierra's life, and that Kethran would be held accountable if he had. Was that why they were still taking their time?

He was still lost in his musings over that, his weight distributed between his good leg and his back up against the pole, when he was caught completely off guard by the next phase of their plan for him. One elf next to him quickly kicked his bad leg back behind him while the second shoved him downward by both shoulders onto his good knee from behind him. The manacles easily allowed his arms to slide down the length of the pole forcing his left hip to bend in and under him. They then secured the manacles to his good ankle so he couldn't get up, trapping his bad leg between the pole and the manacles. Keen banged his head on the pole as he screamed and then nearly choked as he tried to dry-heave with nothing left in his stomach. Outside the tent, he could just make out Kethran physically preventing Kierra from rushing into the tent as Keen, gasping for breath against the sensation of having just been ripped in half finally blacked out.

Keen had no idea how long it lasted. He was in and out of consciousness. He was vaguely aware of his back arched grotesquely away from the tent post, his head writhing almost against his shoulder blades. He lurched forward a few times trying to throw up the contents of a still empty stomach, but he would just pass out again. Every thing was spinning. As he would lean forward, sweat would drip off the end of his nose making him feel sick again and forcing him to throw his head back against the post again.

Nothing below his neck felt human. Everything about his body was stretched and broken and burning to the point that he couldn't consciously identify it all. But he knew exactly where in the tangled mess of himself his hip was. It pulsated and ached and seared louder than any of it and every time he he concentrated on it he had to lurch forward again to try to be sick. The cycle was never-ending, maddening and surely, surely it would kill him. Please. Each time he woke up he cursed inwardly at his own strength and stamina. Just die, Keen. Please just die.

His breathing was jagged and painful, but he suspected it was too deep to be dangerous. Please come back. I'll tell you anything. But I don't know anything. I'll make something up. Please.

Eventually, after what seemed like years, he heard someone enter the tent. He couldn't really see. Too much sweat had run into his eyes for him to open them. He lifted his panting face to them anyway. He couldn't speak. He couldn't beg. He knew he was crying. Surely they'd get the point. I'll think of something. I'll wrack my brain. I promise. Please.

"You lying bastard!" the elf exclaimed.

Keen was shocked. What now? What could he possibly have done? He felt his pained breathing forcing itself in loud pants. It was the sound of his fear, he knew, but it quckly turned ragged again as he continued to try not to scream or dry heave. They could have lit him on fire. Keen wasn't sure he'd know the difference any more.

Someone else was coming in and moving behind him. He heard the tumbling of wooden wheels just outside. What was that? Fear was welling up. He didn't hear Kierra anymore. Or did he? There seemed to be a faint sobbing somewhere. Please don't make it worse. I can't take any worse. I can't. He tried to open his eyes.

Dimly he could see enough light to know the tent flap was open. Several people were gathered just outside and there something large out there. Keen blinked. A wagon maybe?

He felt the manacles drop and two elves were grabbing his arms and starting to lift. He braced for what he knew would be terrible, but he was grateful anyway. They lifted him surprisingly gently and gave him time to get his weight onto his good leg. As the blood and tension shifted, the leg went numb and Keen finally felt some small relief. He almost threw up again. He blinked furiously and managed to wipe his face, looking around.

The men that had hold of him were dressed like Kethran, but had compassionate faces like Kierra. In fact, both of them looked something like her, especially in the eyes. Outside by the wagon, Keen could see that Kethran himself was fuming.

"Can you walk?" the one to his left asked.

Keen nodded. He didn't know if he could, but he was ready to try.

Outside, Kethran was spitting angry.

"I'm taking this all the way to Willowmark, Joran!"

Joran. Keen knew that name.

The elf to his left spoke, "You do that, Kethran. And while you're there you be sure to tell them how you lied about not torturing him, how you struck a treesinger, and how you decided that the law that protects treesingers and those that save them from war no longer applies to you. You make sure you tell them all of that while you're there, because you can be sure that we will!"

Keen stopped. A little of what was going on was getting through to him. They were trying to help him move forward, but he was trying to pause. "He..hit Kierra?"

Joran smirked and looked at him, "She's fine. But let's get you out of here before Kethran figures out how to stop us," he whispered.

Joran and the other similar-looking, but quiet elf helped Keen slowly out to the waiting wagon and eased him up into the back of it. Keen laid down and pressed his good hip up against the side rail. The very back was open and his feet nearly hung out. Keen didn't care. Even though he was laying on his back, he grabbed the side with both of his hands and lay there panting with pain, exhaustion and gratitude looking up at the sky for the first time again in days. There were a few fluffy clouds dotting an otherwise brilliantly blue sky. Keen squinted his eyes against the brightness of it. It seemed suddenly surreal that the world outside his private chamber of horror could still have been so lovely.

Kierra arrived swiftly dragging Keen's things. She could barely lift his sword into the wagon next to him. She gasped when she saw him. She had clearly been crying, but the tears started fresh when their eyes met. He knew he had to look terrible, and he didn't even have the strength to smile at her. He imagined his attempt probably made him look constipated. He was so relieved to see her. She climbed into the wagon next to him, shaking her head at his condition, tears running freely down her lovely face.

"I'm so sorry," she managed to croak.

"Your sister's a traitor!" Kethran yelled after them as the cart jerked forward finally taking Keen away from this nightmare.

The quiet one who had been with Joran and who was now apparently sitting up in the front of the wagon somewhere near Keen's left shoulder turned back and shouted, "And you have no honor, Kethran! This is how the shadowelves fell! Not by magic, but by forgetting that there are certain things that are beneath decency that can't be justified by any ends! Evil will always be evil, Kethran! In anyone's hands, evil is evil!"

Kierra looked impressed. Apparently the quiet one didn't usually say much, to judge by the look on her face, and Keen was enjoying looking at her face. He'd missed it.

Kethran wasn't done. As they turned out of the camp and moved under the shade of the waiting trees of the forest, he yelled at them again, "You're all traitors!"

"Original," Joran mused from directly behind Keen. Joran must have been driving, "He seems to be stuck on that one argument."

There were about twelve elven guards flanking them. That had probably helped whatever arguments Joran and the quiet one had brought to bear. As he was looking around at them, he felt gentle hands on his sore, abused body and a soft familiar voice said, "Don't worry about them. They won't hurt you."

Kierra was leaning over him, full of love and worry, and Keen decided to take the moment finally to say the one thing he'd decided he'd regret not saying if he'd died. He swallowed hard, felt his head swim momentarily. Kierra's eyebrows knitted with concern.

"You OK?"

He nodded. "I love you," he whispered simply.

She smiled wetly, one hand still on his arm. With the other, she brushed his hair back. "I know," she whispered back.

"I heard the bastard hit you."

She chuckled. "He slapped me. I'm fine. Now be quiet and let me sing. I'm finally well enough..."

"If he's your mate, shouldn't you have been able to sing for him before?" asked Joran from the front.

Keen had to reach behind him to steady himself on the back rail because the whole world seem to spin at this comment. He'd just about closed his eyes ready to hear that wonderful singing voice again, when suddenly his eyes were wide open and he wondered what new drama might be waiting for him in Kierra's family.

"What?" he stammered.

Simultaneously, Kierra answered, "He doesn't know about that."

"Know about what?" Keen insisted, still terrified. He remembered his sister-in-law's leering brothers at his own brother's impromptu wedding. This he didn't need.

"How can he NOT know about that?" asked Joran incredulously.

"Hey! I didn't touch your sister!" Keen insisted desperately, twisting around to try to see what was going on behind him. The quiet one was clearly laughing quietly in his seat with one hand over his eyes and his other hand out in front of him for support.

"I thought you said..." Joran started.

"It was an accident," Kierra protested.

"An ACCIDENT?" Joran exclaimed causing the quiet one to double over into his lap with laughter, "How in the world was it an ACCIDENT?"

"What was an accident?" Keen asked Kierra desperately, and she looked down at him guiltily. He tried to raise both eyebrows at her to say, please don't get me trouble with your brother. He wasn't sure she was getting the message.

Kierra looked back at Joran and continued, "I'm not even sure it was mutual."

Joran stopped the wagon and turned fully around in his seat. Keen tried to sit up, but couldn't. This, at least, ended the discussion.

"Don't do that!" Kierra persuaded him, "You need to lie down."

He looked at her exasperatedly, "What I need is for you to not upset your brother while he's helping us get away. Pretty please?" And he laid back down.

The quiet one looked over at Joran still quietly giggling, but the wagon started moving again.

"Sorry," Kierra agreed, "I wasn't trying." She glanced back up at the front of the wagon, "I guess I'm good at it."

Keen also shot a glance in that direction, "It's a talent little sisters are born with," he assured her.

"Yep," came a voice from the front.

"Anyway, what I said is that we'd *bonded,* or that I bonded with him. I don't know if it was mutual. I never said he was my mate." Kierra continued quietly, looking down at the floor of the wagon and blushing.

"There's very little difference," Joran argued, "And it *can't* be mutual. Humans don't bond. They don't even mate for life."

"Wait! What?" Keen felt strongly that he needed to get a far better handle on this conversation than he had and he really just wished that the whole thing would just go away. He had many lovely and even enticing ideas about Kierra, none of which he wanted to discuss with her brother or whoever this other elf was, and more to the point he was quite sure that if any of them had ever actually happened he would have remembered it well. And it would certainly have been mutual. Plus, he certainly intended to marry someone one day, so he felt somewhat insulted being told that he wouldn't mate for life. But more than any of it, he really didn't feel like talking about anything right now. He really just wanted to pass out, not to have to defend his and, more importantly, Kierra's honor.

"Humans often take more than one lover before they settle on their final partner, don't they?" Joran asked matter-of-factly.

Keen felt very defensive. He certainly didn't want Joran asking him personally about his own love life if his having had one was going to upset Kierra. She didn't deserve that, and he wasn't sure that he, Keen, did either. He answered, "But we do take a final partner, though. One for life. We marry. At least we do in my country, and we stay with that person for life. At least we're supposed to, and I certainly would." He wanted to make that absolutely clear. If there was a place in this universe for he and Kierra to be together, then it would be for life. He was absolutely sure about that.

"See?" said Joran simply.

The quiet one was no longer laughing. In fact, he added, "Not the same at all."

Keen thought he had answered rather well. But now he felt like he'd walked right into a trap he didn't understand. He looked over at Kierra for some sense of comprehension.

Kierra was quiet, and she was still staring at the wagon floor. After a few long and awkwardly quiet moments had passed, all three males in the cart said simultaneously, "Kierra?"

"I'm waiting for all of you to shut up so I can sing." She said it somewhat defiantly, but her voice gravelly and strained and she wouldn't look up even to meet Keen's eyes and he was bending his neck to try to get his gaze up under hers. She waited until he stopped trying before she moved her hands into deliberate positions on his hip and heart and started to sing quietly but, Keen thought, a bit remorsefully.

Keen touched her hand over his heart and closed his eyes. Her touch and her voice were breathtaking. He could feel his body giving into the things he needed most: rest, relaxing tension, reducing inflammation, relieving pain, stopping internal bleeding, beginning to heal. It was all subtle. None of it was sudden or significant by itself, but all of it together was wonderful. By the end of her song Keen had gone from feeling fresh from that nightmarish tent to the way a person feels on the morning when you wake up and realize that you've finally started to heal. Everything still hurt tremendously, but it was more stiff than sharp, more achey than tense, more exhausted than fevered. He had no idea what the words she sang said, but if there were angels or gods in the world, he was sure they knew. As soon as the music drifted to a close, Keen was asleep.

Keen woke sometime later and thought he could faintly smell bread and hear voices. Keen wasn't sure how long he'd slept, but he could tell by the stiffness in every part of him that he was still in the hard wooden wagon, although it seemed to have stopped. He was facing the outer railing, but the voices were coming from behind him. They weren't above and behind his head, though, as if coming from the driver's seat; they were behind his back as if coming from outside the other side of the cart.

He could make out Kierra's voice speaking low and softly, "Because I was afraid of him. I didn't know what he'd do if I told him."

Afraid of who? Keen wondered. Surely she wouldn't tell Joran she was afraid of Keen?

"I suppose that makes sense," Joran responded seriously, "Still, he might have behaved better if he'd known."

Keen frowned at the railing in front of him.

"So now what?" asked the quiet one.

"Obviously I have to explain all of this to Keen," Kierra answered.

So, they *were* talking about him, but had Kierra really said she was afraid of him?

"What do you think he'll do?" Joran asked.

Nothing to hurt Kierra, Keen assured them all silently in his head. What was going on?

"I have no idea," Kierra admitted quietly, "But I'm prepared for whatever."

Keen closed his eyes again as he heard the trio approaching the wagon again. He felt Kierra check to make sure that he was still sleeping which he pretended to be. His mind was reeling. He could neither believe that Kierra could be afraid of him, nor could he believe that she could lie to her brother and say that she was. Keen trusted Kierra more than anything. Now what was he supposed to think?

As the light finally faded from the worst day of his life the wagon rolled to a stop.

"What is this place?" Kierra demanded.

"It's an abandoned prison camp," Joran told her.

Keen opened his eyes and tried to sit up. He was stiff and incredibly sore, but after most of a day of sleep and Kierra's song, he felt a little better. He was, at least, able to drag himself into a semi-sitting pose and able to realize that he was starving. He leaned his head against the driver's bench and looked around.

To his left were a series of strange cages. Each was man-sized but grown from strong ivy and dried hard, then covered with a thick weave of living vines. He wasn't sure how a man would be put into one, but he was sure that once inside, those vine enclosures would be as secure as six-inch hard wood poles and waterproof enough. They were suspended naturally off of the forest floor by about a foot or more with ditches underneath for basic sanitation. There were nearly twenty in total over there he guessed, although it was hard to tell in the forest's darkening shadows.

To his right were a smaller number of slightly larger and more habitable structures. These seemed to have been made by teasing the bark away from living trees as they grew without harming the trees so that the trees appeared to have strange, bulbous growths at their bases which were only identifiable as elf-made by the presence of doors, awning-covered windows, and small chimneys peeping out of them. They looked just large enough to hold maybe a small bed and the wood stove and probably not much more, but Keen imagined they were much more cozy than the cages. The wagon was stopped immediately in front of what looked to be the last in a line of about 10 of these.

"Why in the world are we here?" she asked indignantly.

Keen thought he could almost hear Joran roll his eyes.

"Because it was the closest place I could think of that I knew for a fact we could use," he answered her with clearly thinning patience.

"And what is that?" she asked, apparently indicating something behind him. Keen tried to turn around. He wished he hadn't. He knew what that was. Well, what it was was a dead tree with strong low and high branches. But that really didn't answer Kierra's question.

Joran sighed. "Do you really need me to answer that question, Kierra? Obviously we don't plan to hang Keen. We just need a place to spend the night where no one's going to try to tell us we can't have him. Will you just trust me, please?"

"Sorry," she stammered, "It's been a bad several days."

"I know. That's why I came..."

"We came," he quieter one reminded him.

"Sorry, we came. That's why we came, remember?"

"Yes, thank you. Really. Thank you both."

"Yes," agreed Keen, "Thank you both, more than I can ever say."

"You're both welcome. Keen, we saved you some food from our last stop if you're hungry."

"I am, thanks, but if you want me in one of those cages you're going to need to get the wagon closer. I still can't walk that far.

"What? No!" Joran still sounded exasperated as a general rule. Keen wondered if he had another emotion, "You can have a cabin. That's why the wagon's over here. Unless you *want* a cage, that is, but I never thought they looked very comfortable personally." He smirked at Keen who returned the sentiment.

"No, that's OK, I've had my share of bad accommodations for a while. Thanks, though."

"Don't mention it."

Joran and the other one moved to help Keen out of the wagon and into the cabin. It was, indeed, small and cozy. It had a polished wooden floor, a slightly wider bed than Keen had expected, a nightstand, a stool, a trunk and a potbelly stove similar to the one that had stood by his cot for the last two days except that this one was slightly smaller and had nothing ominous hanging out of it. It also had a heavy kettle of water sitting on top of it to keep the air moist. The mattress felt like it was stuffed with feathers or fur, which was softer than anything Keen had ever felt in his life and the quilted blanket was warm and comfortable. There was a welcoming lantern on the nightstand that gave the space the feel that someone's mother could well have prepared it for them. Keen was embarrassed to get into it as dirty as he was, which he must have conveyed to his hosts when he looked down at his clothes as they sat him on the bed.

"Do you want to try to get a bath tonight?"

Kierra was coming in behind them with a small loaf of bread that looked like it had slices of meat cut between it. Keen's stomach grumbled audibly at the sight.

"How much trouble would that be?" he asked.

The quieter one shook his head, "It's not," and he left.

Joran looked at Kierra with the expression of someone bracing himself for something unpleasant, "Are you staying in here, or do you want your own cabin?"

Keen was just taking the delicious-looking food from her, and he knew the shock must have registered on his face. He looked up at Kierra, who didn't meet his gaze, so he looked instead, wide-eyed and clearly shocked, loaf of meaty bread still in his hungry hands, over at Joran who was watching his sister.

"Why don't you leave me the cabin next door in case I want it?" she answered.

"Well, I can," he answered, "But if you want to know the truth, I've got too many guards for this place, so if you're not going to use it, which, frankly, I suspect you're not, there's no sense in it sitting empty. But if you want it, then I want you to have it."

Kierra looked at Keen who still had neither taken a bite of his food nor rested his eyebrows, "Do you care if I sleep in here?"

"Nope." What was he supposed to say?

"OK," she shrugged and looked at Joran, "I will then."

With that, Joran turned and left.

"Is that OK?" Keen asked carefully, still not sure it was safe to eat, or blink, or breathe.

"Why wouldn't it be OK?" Kierra asked him, a little prickly Keen thought.

He watched her for a moment weighing his answer very carefully and wishing he could just keep his mouth shut and get away with it. No, Keen, he thought. Your mother didn't raise an idiot. He sighed.

"Well, two things are bothering me, I guess," he started slowly, really wishing he could just eat and bathe and go to sleep. His idea of having the beautiful woman he was in love with alone with him in a private bedroom did not involve this much confusion. There is something wrong, he thought to himself, if I can have her here alone, in this room, all night, and all I want to do is eat, bathe and sleep. He sighed again and looked into her lovely eyes. He really did love her. He'd do anything she wanted him to do right now if she asked. Just as long as she asked really really clearly so that he understood exactly what it was she wanted.

"First, I don't think I understood a word of that conversation you were having with your brother, and I felt like I needed to defend myself, and maybe even defend you, but I didn't even know what was going on. So that's bothering me, and second..." And this was the part he didn't want to bring up, but he was an honest man. He prided himself on it, so he wasn't going to stop being honest now just because she was looking at him like that. He looked away from her. "I woke up today while the wagon was stopped, and I heard the very end of your conversation. I'm sure I heard you wrong or misunderstood or something, but I really didn't like what I heard, so...there's that."

He looked back at her. She had a quizzical look on her face, not a shocked or scared look like she'd been caught at something, so that was a good sign Keen thought.

"What did you hear?"

"It sounded like your brother was asking you why you hadn't told me something and you were saying you were afraid of how I was going to react. And I can't imagine why you'd be afraid of me for anything."

"Afraid of you?" Kierra looked shocked. That was good. Keep that going, thought Keen, "I'm not afraid of you. Are you sure you weren't dreaming?"

"Fairly certain."

A knock on the door brought them out of their conversation and they looked up. The door wasn't actually closed, but the quieter one had come by and didn't want to just walk in and interrupt.

"I filled a bath pan at the river and am heating it at the fire pit. You'll have to come out here to use it, though."

"Thanks," said Keen.

"Jerith?" asked Kierra, "What were we talking about when we stopped for supper?"

"Mostly Keen and how you bonded with him by accident and hadn't told him yet."

Keen took a bite of his bread. The meat inside was roasted and seasoned and was the best he'd eaten since before he'd left home, which he realized suddenly had been nearly a month ago now.

"Did I say anything about being afraid of him, though? He thought he overheard us talking."

The one called Jerith thought a moment and said finally, "No. You were afraid to tell Kethran about your bond to Keen because you were afraid of what he might do if he found out about it. Joran thought Kethran might not have been so hard on Keen if he'd have realized you could sense what he was doing, but you were afraid it would have made it worse not better."

Realization and memory dawned on Kierra and she nodded largely. "Yes. I did say I hadn't told *Kethran* about the bond because I was afraid of what *he* might do. Thanks, Jerith. I knew there had to be some explanation."

Jerith nodded, "This water'll probably be warm enough by the time he's done eating, but I suspect you'll need our help to get him over there."

"Thanks," she said again.

Keen was eating heartily now. He was a little embarrassed, but relieved. He had been sure they were talking about him, but he was going to let that go. Clearly he had just been wrong, and the other thing, this bond thing, that was what he really needed to get to the bottom of.

"Feel better?" Kierra asked.

Keen's mouth was full of meat and bread. He wasn't sure if she meant the food or the conversation, but the answer was the same, "Yes."

"How could you think..."

"I didn't. That's why I asked," he cut her off, "It made no sense. I knew what I was hearing, but it made no sense, so I asked. Kierra, what's going on? I feel awful. I know we need to talk. Today made that obvious, but I don't have much in me, so I'm really torn." He was starting to realize that just trying to sit up like this was making his body shake. Kierra seemed to be noticing it, too, "I want to understand what's going on, and why your brother thinks we...you know..." Kierra raised an eyebrow at his bashful expression, "And...just all of it. Are you OK? Can we start there? It's starting to sound like you're not OK. Are you?"

She looked down at her lap and then out the door at the night sky. "Sort of," she replied, "I will be."

Keen reached over and took her hand that was sitting in her lap, "Then I've got all night."

She chuckled, "You're a lot less alright than I am. You need to sleep. Let's get your bath, and get you to bed. We can talk any time..." Her voice trailed off like she wasn't sure that statement was true, and Keen wasn't either.

He picked her hand up and kissed it. He only meant it as the kind of gesture that she'd shown him twice before when she'd kissed him on the cheek, but the expression on her face changed so suddenly and so deeply, Keen wasn't sure what he'd done. It was like she'd glazed over and gone to a deeper place like the place that her songs seemed to come from. No sooner than he'd kissed her, it was like she was no longer in the room.

"Kierra?"

She snapped out of it with such a startle that it appeared to have frightened her. She looked at him, almost terrified and bit her lip to keep from crying again.

"My ordeal is over for now, thanks to you and your brother and whoever Jerith is..."

"Hmmmm..." Kierra still seemed to be a bit lost, "Oh, yeah, sorry, Jerith's my cousin. I should have introduced you."

"My point is, I think your ordeal, whatever it is, is still going on, and you need to explain to me what it is."

"It isn't an ordeal exactly," she looked down at her hands in her lap again which were now playing with his, "And it isn't going to be over. It's just a change is all. I'll get used to it. Don't worry..."

Keen finished the last few bites of his meal with his free hand while watching her absent-mindedly play with his other one. She had a look on her face that suggested she was worriedly trying to figure something out and wasn't really paying attention to what she was doing. A couple of times she reached up and wiped a tear from her face. But apparently she was paying enough attention that when Keen finished his bread, she looked up and suggested that they go and get his bath, which he agreed to.

Joran and Jerith offered to help Keen with his bath in an awkward moment between them and Kierra, which Keen let them resolve. He was torn. Clearly, he'd rather have Kierra bathing him, but only in an environment where they were alone. Here, Joran and Jerith had posted guards around the camp's perimeter and would know what was going on, even if they stayed out of sight themselves. And while Keen would admit that he had no idea what the elves' ideas about modesty and marriage were, he knew how he was raised, and you just didn't ask a girl you weren't married to to bathe you right in front of her brothers. Especially when her brothers had just saved you from torture and certain death, were armed military officers and had twelve armed guards working for them. The fact that the bath was taking place in the middle of a prison camp that sported its own gibbots just added to the warning bells going off in Keen's head. OK, maybe Jerith wasn't actually her brother. That hardly made the bath a good idea.

So, awkward as it was, Keen found himself receiving the compassionate and professional assistance of armed male elves who were definitely not Kierra. Still, the bath was warm and wonderful, and now that he felt his hip starting to heal following the enchanting song of earlier in the day, the warm water was as soothing as he might have imagined it. The only thing that could have made it more perfect would have been a tub large enough to stretch his bad leg out in. As it was, he'd only be able to sit here so long.

Kierra had offered to take his clothes to wash. He'd been reluctant to let her take his undergarments, especially since he feared he'd likely soiled them somewhat during his torments that morning, but there was no protesting the sad longing she seemed to have developed about her. He just hoped they weren't as bad as he feared they were.

Joran and Jerith sat with him while he soaked, though they politely made constant eye contact with the trees and the camp in general. They did, at least, until Keen spoke.

"Kierra still hasn't explained to me what's going on. I don't suppose since you two seem to think you understand humans a bit that you'd be willing to try?"

Joran sighed, looked down and then across Keen's bath over at Jerith. Keen looked from one to the other as they exchanged concerned expressions.

"She didn't say anything?" Joran asked at last.

"Well, she did explain to me what I overheard while we were stopped."

"Yeah, sorry about that," Jerith interrupted, "If we'd known you were awake, we'd have gotten you some food."

"You were awake?" Joran asked.

"Just for a few minutes. At the end of your conversation. It's not important. What *is important* is this other thing that no one seems to want to explain to me," he was starting to feel a bit sick again. He may have eaten too fast. And worry, movement and chill autumn air weren't helping. He tried to relax.

Joran paused, but then he finally gave in and tried to explain, "Elves mate for life, like wolves do, and, well, a lot of natural beings do..."

"And you don't think that humans do?" Keen asked.

Joran considered him for a while, which was unnerving since Joran was fully clothed and still wearing some of his armor, and Keen was wet and naked.

"Obviously, between you and me, I am not the expert on being human, but it's not been my understanding that humans have very much in the way of instincts at all," he paused again, waiting, maybe to see if he was offending Keen, maybe to just to find out if he was right, Keen couldn't be sure because, frankly, Keen didn't know what he was talking about. Keen thought of instincts as something animals had. Sure, he, Keen, knew when he needed to eat, sleep, relieve himself, and that sort of thing, and he certainly had ideas about beautiful women that he would have figured out on his own even if his father and grandfather, and eventually his older brother, hadn't been around to tell him certain things, but if pressed he'd probably agree with Joran that humans didn't spend a lot of time living by instincts. Wits maybe, but not instincts.

After getting little reaction from Keen, Joran pressed on unenthusiastically, "When humans mate it may be that they choose their first partner for life, or it may be that they choose to have many partners over the course of their lives, or they may make any arrangement that they want to based on their culture and their circumstances as I understand things...is that not correct?"

Keen considered this, and he considered his answer carefully, both in light of the fact that this was Kierra's brother and in light of the fact that he, Keen, had still never *touched* Kierra. "Yes, but that range of choices still includes the choice to mate for life," Keen decided to insist, which it does, he went on in his internal conversation, bringing many healthy and long-lived relationships in his own family firmly and wistfully to the forefront of his memory.

"But it's a choice," Joran countered, "Do you know anything about, say, wolves?"

"A little, I guess..."

"Wolves mate for life. Period. It's not a choice. There's no second or third or other option. When a wolf mates, that mate is their partner for life. If they lose their mate, they almost never mate again. They know instinctively their mate is gone. They mourn that loss the rest of their lives. It's not a choice they make; it's an instinct they have. Elves are like that. And I don't know if we can ever fully understand each other on this, because for you it's a choice. If you were to choose an elf partner and decide to commit to that partnership for the rest of your life it still wouldn't be the same thing. Because we develop a bond. It's an instinct that we have about our lovers, a connection we share, that humans just don't have.

Take me and my lover, for example. Before we chose each other, I had considered relationships with her and two other women," at this he glance at Jerith who seemed to grimace and look away, but Joran continued and Keen didn't ask what that was about, "and she had also considered at least one other relationship," with that Joran brought his eyes back to Keen's but Keen thought Joran may have revealed a painful past briefly there. "I can't speak for her, and I won't try..." Jerith shifted uncomfortably behind Keen who tried to pretend he wasn't noticing all of the discomfort, "but I struggled for a while with my choice. I was very attracted to all three of the women I knew and wanted. I had strong friendships and emotional ties to all of them and they were all just beautiful, but once Rana and I chose each other, that was it. Once we bonded, I lost all attraction to the other two. I still care about them. I still remember to an extent what I felt before, but it's not the same. At this point either of them could dance naked through the camp here, and it wouldn't do anything for me..."

"Seriously?" interjected Keen incredulously. He understood fidelity, but claiming to not even be attracted to other women seemed like a bit of a stretch to him.

Joran shrugged, "That's how it works. And if she dies," he swallowed and paled, as if he could think of nothing more tragic that could happen in the world, "I wouldn't get that back either. I will never lose my attraction to her. Age, time, tension, nothing will change how much I want her every time she's around, but I will never want anyone else again. My instinct for attraction changed the moment I was with her for the first time. That's what mating for life is, and humans just don't do that...unless I'm wrong..."

"Uh...no..." Keen, who if pressed would have to admit that he had already not mated for life more than once, finally had to concede. No he was quite capable of a night of simple passion and then moving on. No regrets there, thank you very much. In fact, he was starting to really want to put his clothes on. All of this talk of never being attracted to another woman again was creepy.

"The other thing about a bond is that we can tell when our mates are in mortal danger or in severe pain. Probably wolves and other creatures that mate for life can, too. We've seen evidence of that ourselves just watching the other beings of the forest. And that brings us back to Kierra, and you."

Keen looked up curiously. He was still quite sure that he had, in fact, not "mated" with Kierra. He didn't even like the term and liked it less now that it carried some serious weight with it. But he was here to find out what was going on with her. If she was just attracted to him, it sounded like she could move on from that. As much as he liked her, loved her even, maybe that was better. Although, no sooner than he had that thought, he was immediately attacked by the silent jealous rage that stalked the part of him that refused to imagine her with anyone else. Ever. For any reason. Without all of her clothes sewn on and up to her neck and down to her ankles. He shook that away. He didn't get to have it both ways.

"Elven bonds typically form when two elves make love for the first time. They are typically mutual, permanent, last beyond death and never fade in strength or attraction. There are rare exceptions, but they're really rare. Still, they happen. For example, sometimes, like in a rape, the bond doesn't form at all. Or sometimes, like if a lover is killed really young or really soon after taking a lover, the bond does break eventually and an elf has been known to be able to reform a new bond later with someone else. Like I said, these kinds of things are rare, but they do happen.

Another really rare thing that can happen is an accidental bond."

Keen perked up. The water in his bath was getting really chilly, but he knew in the pit of his stomach they were getting to the part he needed to hear.

"Sometimes when two people go through something really extraordinary together, especially something life-or-death, a bond can form between them without their becoming lovers first."

Jerith was starting to help Keen up for which he was grateful. He was starting to shiver and his teeth were chattering. But as he was drying off and trying clumsily to get into the clean elven tunic he was being offered for a nightshirt, he kept at the topic of conversation, "So, Kierra can sense when I'm in trouble?"

"Yes," Joran answered warily.

"And she could tell I was in pain when Kethran had me in that tent?"

"Yep,"

"But you know we didn't..." he trailed off modestly, and both elves looked at him strangely like his modesty was somehow odd to them.

"Yes," Joran replied, "We know."

"So, she can still mate with someone else, right? I mean she's not, like, stuck, is she?"

He seemed to have hit the nerve they had been avoiding. They glanced painfully at each other and Joran tightened his jaw. It was Jerith who answered, "No she can't. A bond's a bond, however you come by it."

"But, we, I mean I, well, we....what?" Keen stammered.

Joran was no longer meeting his gaze. He looked angry, but he continued to help Jerith get Keen into his shoes. Jerith continued the conversation.

"This is the point where you need to talk to Kierra. She didn't realize the bond had formed until you were arrested, but because it was Kethran's men, the danger you were in was real enough that she felt it strongly. She had no idea before that, and once you leave," and he and Joran once again exchanged pained glances, "It's going to be very painful for her."

"So, why hasn't she told me any of this..."

"I suspect," said Jerith simply, "That she's having a hard time figuring out what to say so that you don't feel guilty about leaving. She's having a hard time holding it together"

"I've noticed," Keen admitted quietly. There had been a lot of tears lately. Maybe now, he had an explanation for them.

Jerith nodded. Joran looked worried.

Kierra was waiting for them as they made their slow way back to the little cabin. She had Keen's clean clothes strung up in the tree branches to dry, and she eagerly helped him get under the covers and made sure he was comfortable. Keen looked back at Joran. Jerith had already left. Joran looked pained, but turned and followed Jerith out without a word.

"I wish you had told me yourself," Keen told her as soon as they were alone.

Kierra looked shocked, "They explained it to you?"

Keen nodded at her, his eyes never leaving hers, even as they began once again, and right on cue thought Keen, to fill with tears.

"I was working on what to say. I was going to tell you now. Oh, I wish they hadn't done that. Keen, this isn't your fault; I hope you know that. Please tell me they didn't make you feel bad about any of it, because you shouldn't."

"No, they didn't. They just explained."

She nodded and sat down on the edge of the bed and then jumped back up like it burned her, "Oh, I'm sorry! Do you mind if I sit here?"

Keen couldn't help but chuckle, "Kierra we've been sleeping together in caves for how long? Turning our backs while each other have bowel movements? I dropped my pants for you to sew my hip...No, I don't care if you sit next to me. Kierra, it's still just me. Same as I was before Kethran entered our lives, and I think if we're both honest, our feelings for each other haven't really changed, we've just figured out what they are is all. If a ghost army sped past outside right now, I think you'd find that we haven't changed all that much really."

Kierra sat back down, "Except for my bond."

"You don't think that was there before, and you just didn't know it? Because the way Joran explained it was you just didn't realize it until I was arrested. That made it sound like it had already been there for some amount of time."

"You're right. Honestly I think it may have happened as early as the day I almost didn't make it back from getting water, and you sat up all night watching over me."

Keen reached over and grabbed her hand in her lap. She closed her eyes and a tear rolled freely down her face.

"I can't leave you like this."

It was a simple statement, but Keen knew it was true. He hated to leave his family. He hated to never see them again. His heart wrenched at the thought. He especially hated never being able to let them know what had happened to him, but he couldn't leave her like this. If she could never fall in love again, never have another family, never have another chance at finding a partner: that was terrible. And how many human men ever had that chance: to have a beautiful elven woman who would never even look at another man? How could he leave her now?

She was staring at him. Her expression was frozen. She didn't want to question the statement. He could see it in her eyes. She was desperate to hear what he had just said, and yet they both knew that it would be nearly impossible to make happen. It didn't matter. He wasn't going anywhere.

He pulled her face down to his and cupped it in his hands. He felt the last of her tears fall onto his own cheeks, her lip quivered at the possibility that he might give her what she needed most in the world. Her large elf eyes stared deeply into his own as he whispered, "I won't leave you like this, Kierra. Your countrymen are just going to have to get used to me now." And just as her face broke into a silent sob, he pulled her face further onto his own and kissed her sweet-tasting lips deeply. He'd wanted her for so long anyway. There was no reason he could see now not to give in to that impulse. He let his hand run through the back of her soft, straight, brown hair as she gave in totally to his kiss. Her hands were on his shoulders, one elbow supporting her weight on the pillow behind his head when she finally pulled away and looked longingly into his face with an impish grin.

"Why don't you shut the door," Keen suggested. And as usual, she was startlingly fast.

The next morning there was no turning back any more. Keen had awoken with Kierra in his arms many times before now, but this was wholly different. He pulled her now-familiar naked body closer into his and wrapped his warmth around her again and she snuggled, still-sleeping into him. Last night could only have been more perfect if his hip had not relegated him to his back. Still, that hadn't stopped her passion or enthusiasm. He kissed the top of her head and smiled down at the brown mop it had become. Last night was perfect.

A knock at the door brought him out of his reverie and caused Kierra's head to shoot up so quickly that she knocked into Keen's chin making his eyes water.

"Oops, sorry!" she stammered, flying nude out of bed, "Hang on!" she yelled at the door as she pulled her green dress-like tunic and leggings on quickly. Keen reached to the floor for the large elven tunic he'd been wearing last night, briefly, and pulled it over his head, remaining otherwise under the covers. Kierra, checked his modesty with a shoulder-raising, chin-ducking chuckle as she opened the door to reveal Joran and Jerith bearing bowls of breakfast.

Two seconds in the room and the male elves knew more than they wanted to know. Joran's friendly eyes turned to fire and Keen became instantly glad that rumors of evil elven magic from back home had turned out not to be true. That elf would have engulfed him in flames from the doorway if he could have. Jerith seemed to eying Kierra with a pitying stare that actually did more to anger Keen than Joran's gaze was doing.

Keen's response was brilliant. "What?" he asked stupidly.

"Did you *have* to make it worse?" Joran spat, setting a bowl of bran and cream on the bedside table so hard it splashed its contents onto the bed.

Behind him, Jerith gently handed Kierra a bowl and offered to walk her out of the cabin. She refused.

"What are you talking about?"

"I'm not stupid," Joran insisted, "Do you think I can't smell sex?"

"I'm not leaving her," Keen informed him, sitting up, "How am I making anything worse? Do you think I'd just take advantage of her? I'm staying. I can't leave her like this, and I told her so. And I don't know how it's going to work, but if she's stuck with this bond, then I'm stuck with it, too." Keen shrugged, "So, you're stuck with me, too, I'm afraid. Think of me as an irritating rash that just won't go away if you want to, but I'm not leaving without Kierra."

Joran's face dropped. He and Jerith both looked back at Kierra whose face was as peaceful and as much like her own as it had been since they'd left the caves. She wasn't crying. She wasn't angry. She was just...whole again. She smiled at them matter-of-factly. They looked back at Keen who had sat up and helped himself to his slightly sloppy breakfast. Joran sat down on a stool by the bed cautiously, as if he didn't know how to respond.

Keen just watched the room. These were his in-laws now, at least in his mind, and he didn't need to upset them. He didn't know the rules of family dynamics here, and he was giving up his own home and family to do this for Kierra. He'd need her family in order to have any family at all. He just sat and ate his breakfast in silence. He wasn't wrong. He knew that. They'd figure that out, surely.

"But you can't bond," Joran struggled.

"No," Keen agreed, "But I can commit."

Joran just watched his face. He was clearly trying to understand.

"Do you remember what Jerith said to Kethran as we were leaving?" Keen asked, "About honor and decency? How do you think the two of you have managed to stay committed to those things despite the war, and Kethran hasn't?"

"Kethran's been through a lot..." Joran started.

"And you haven't?"

"Well, yes, but it's not the same."

"Do you think you'd stoop to those things if you'd been through the things he'd been through, then?"

"I like to think not."

"What do you think would make you able to resist? Obviously it's not instinct. You're both elves."

Joran considered Keen curiously. Jerith and Kierra were watching them intently, too. After several long moments, it was Kierra who spoke, "In ancient times all of the elves were sworn to guard the Sacred Trust: the forest. At one time, the ancient elven forests covered much of this continent. But with the splitting of the elven races, most of the old forests were lost. The willowelves are the only race of elves left still guarding the trees, and because of war, we are now dying out. It used to be believed that the same bonds we had for our mates connected us to our forests, but that proved not to be true. In droves, whole races of elves abandoned the Sacred Trust for other endeavors. It's the same thing. Some of us remain true to the virtues of our culture even still, but some of us continue to be tempted to fall away from those virtues citing necessity or vengence."

"So, that, then," said Keen, "That commitment that's not a bond. It's not an instinct. It's a choice. Right?"

All three elves slowly, frowning, begrudgingly, thoughtfully, agreed.

"That is what I can give Kierra. It's the same choice you make when you choose decency and honor over the kinds of choices Kethran makes. Humans live by the choices we make. Unfortunately, we too often choose fear instead of more noble things and we make bad choices, which is why you don't understand us. But we can make good choices, too, and we can make powerful commitments. In many ways I think, because it is a choice, it may be stronger, like an ancient commitment to trees. I may be wrong; I've never felt a bond. But either way, the fact is: I'm staying."

Joran nodded. His face had softened, though he wasn't yet smiling. "Welcome to the Willows, then," he said simply. Kierra ran up behind her brother and hugged his neck. That's when he smiled.

He patted her hands and said simply, "Rana and Nira are here."

Kierra looked excited, "When did they get here?"

"In the night," Joran looked tired, but Keen noticed, it was a good kind of tired, "They're really looking forward to seeing you. They were at your funeral, you know."

Kierra looked shocked from Joran to Jerith and back again.

"Oh."

Keen wondered silently and sadly if there had been one for him yet. Unfortunately, his family wouldn't get the same happy homecoming hers was getting. He set his jaw and didn't drop his gaze. Instead he bore it into Joran as the elf turned around. This is commitment, he thought. My family won't see me come home. Joran's saddened eyes understood. Kierra, not paying attention to the exchange, ran out of the door and Jerith closed it quietly behind her. Now what?

Jerith crossed the room carrying a small stool Keen hadn't realized he'd had with him. He moved to the far side of Keen's bed and sat down, effectively flanking Keen with his cousin. They didn't look aggressive, but they were clearly up to something. Keen set his breakfast bowl down and folded his hands across his lap, raising his eyebrows silently.

Joran spoke first, as usual, "Well, now we have even more reason to move you toward freedom quickly than we did before I guess."

"Ah, so I am still a prisoner?"

"Technically," Jerith admitted.

Keen nodded.

"We had to make something of a deal to get you out of Kethran's custody. If things had gotten violent, we'd have won, but he might've killed you. We agreed to keep you in custody and interrogate you. The actual agreement was 'until we got something out of you.' Kethran's choice of phrasing, you can imagine..."

"But I don't know anything," Keen protested.

"Oh, we know damn well you don't know anything about troop movements," Jerith countered.

"We've interrogated plenty of humans," Joran told him, "We know your lords keep you in the dark about everything except how to use your weapons, which is why we didn't agree to ask you for any particular information. But it is usually our experience that if we just let a person who wants to be cooperative talk, they usually think of something useful to say. We don't get very many cooperative humans, so probably anything you know could be useful to us. So, what *do* you know anything about?"

"See, we have every intention of reporting Kethran to Willowmark," Jerith went on to explain, "But we need to be able to say we did everything we were supposed to do when we do, and we can only claim to have held up our end of the agreement if we can produce information that came from you."

"But don't worry," said Joran with a wry grin, "we won't do anything worse to get it out of you than make you hang out with my sister. Although, the rest of my family is going to want to see her, and I guess meet you too, at some point."

"Boy you drive a hard bargain," Keen teased, "Okay, okay, I relent...I could tell you about how we were organized on the field? Or I could tell you about the ones who wanted to desert? You might could break our lines if another officer did the same thing again really...Or I could tell you about the cannons if you don't know much about those?"

"Any of that. All of that. And what are cannons?" answered Joran.

"They're the large metal tube-like weapons that shoot exploding projectiles."

"The magic exploding weapons???!!!" Joran and Jerith both sat forward excitedly, "Yes! Start with everything you know about those!"

Keen laughed. "Well, first of all they're not magic."

"Well, they sure as heck aren't natural," Jerith insisted.

Keen spent most of the day making himself useful to the elves. It turned out that he knew quite a bit that was extremely useful to them. He tried to imagine Kethran's face when he found out how much he could have gotten out of Keen. Even Keen hadn't realized how much he'd known that was important until he'd gotten going. He tried, also, to focus on how many innocent elven lives he was saving. He thought about a pregnant Kierra, living in a little village somewhere, being set upon by cannons and he just kept talking. What he tried not to think about was other humans like himself and his brothers who he was getting killed by the sentence.

Kierra was mildly perturbed when she realized that Keen was being interrogated, but it passed when she found out that Keen himself didn't really mind.

Over the course of the day he also met Rana and Nira. They were a pair of sisters that the three cousins had grown up nearby and were Joran and Jerith's mates repectively. They were slightly taller than Kierra, with Nira being the tallest by a small measure. Rana and Nira both dressed more like the males did: in shorter unembroidered tunis and pants rather than leggings. Both were lovely, but had a dangerous litheness about them that belied a muscular frame.

Late in the afternoon, after Keen had vomited up every detail he could think of, at least for the moment, and the elves' heads were swimming with the implications of some of it, they helped him to get up and move around the camp. Down by the fire he encountered the girls' bows which were larger, sleeker, and far more dangerous-looking than the small hunting bow that Kierra carried. In fact, the two new girls looked about as sleek and deadly as the bows they carried. No wonder Kierra laughed when Keen called her an archer.

By evening, Keen was officially declared a free man. The six of them had something of a celebration down by the firepit, and invited some of the other guards to join them. Keen hadn't paid any attention to the other twelve, but realized at this point that five of them were female. Keen wondered half-heartedly what it was really like to not be attracted to any of them any more, then prided himself on the choices he would make to not act on any but the one attraction he had. They drank mead and ate roasted boar and made plans to embark on Keen's new life among them first thing in the morning.

Keen felt welcome. Kierra was happy. These people were willing to treat him as one of them. But he wasn't. Faces were drifting through Keen's head wistfully as he tried to enjoy the evening: a mother, a grandmother, 2 brothers, 2 nieces, a nephew; people he was deciding to never see again. People who wouldn't understand this decision. He put his arm around Kierra. He couldn't love her any less. How could he love them less either? Inside, he knew that making Kierra whole had broken him. He just couldn't let her know how much.

Tollie

A flash of pre-dawn lightning illuminated the plaster ceiling above Tollie's widely-open sleepless eyes. Her room was dark, and nearly silent save for the gentle, barely-audible sound of Kyrt snoring his liquored stupor away into his pillow. Tollie's whole body ached. It ached so deeply it seeped into her soul. To say it had been a long two weeks would be to imply that time still had any meaning. So much of what had happened bruised more deeply than the time it had taken to happen.

But the one thing that HAD happened that mattered more to her than anything else possibly could was that today, finally, after years of anger, resentment, and more than a little jealousy, today she'd gotten her sister back. Tollie was home. Gone were the hated stone walls of the library and its endless books. Gone were the senseless scholars and their meaningless pouring over ancient stories in the hope of capturing some new insight. Her lonely bower with its pitiful view was mercifully relegated to the past. So, too, was that wretched, miserable existence she'd been wishing and willing away since her little family had pulled out of Brewhall all those years ago.

But gone, too, was half of that family. Her mother died not long after they'd left. Now her father, too, was just that: gone. She'd thought she'd lost her sister the day Tallie had walked out, but today, she'd gotten Tallie back. She still had a family.

Tallie had been a great listener, too. Unlike Ellerby, Tallie had listened intently to every word Tollie had said. She'd listened with her whole body. She'd oohed and ahed in all the right places and squealed with concern at each dangerous moment. And Tollie hadn't left anything out. Not anything. She glanced guiltily over in the direction of the nightstand where, in the dark, the faint noises of sleeping faeries originated.

Tollie rolled over and turned her back to the quiet sound. The trio that had fled the library really were lousy sneaks. They were leaving a trail of information for miles with everybody they encountered. Their only hope was that nobody would suspect that a halfling and two faeries could possibly be carrying anything significant. Or know anything. Or be anybody. That was a fading hope.

Tallie had changed. Tollie hadn't been as consciously aware of it until she'd finished talking. Tollie had always experienced her sister as having made everything about Tallie. Tollie had felt that she had spent her childhood making space for Tallie: for her rants, for her anger, for her feelings. Keeping Tallie, if not happy, then at least calm, was a nearly full time job for the family during the few years that Tallie stayed at the library. But today, Tallie had sat and really listened to Tollie. In the end, she'd given Tollie a brief glimpse of some of the hardships she herself had been dealing with, but she brushed it off as if it were mediocre compared to Tollie's concerns. Tollie wanted to accept it as a deep attempt on her sister's part to reconnect with her, but as she lay here in the dark now knowing how much she had revealed, she worried over her own new mistrust.

Tollie awoke the next morning after an unsettled night of tossing and turning and haunting dreams of running and being chased through her childhood garden. She could hear her sister's laughter ringing through her dreams, but it was never clear to her why she was laughing.

Kyrt was groggy, as he had been lately, but his mood had certainly seemed to have improved since they'd arrived yesterday. Jesp was being more attentive to him, which Tollie felt freed her somewhat from worrying over him. She felt a twinge of guilt over that thought, though, as a shudder of memory ran up her spine of how he got hurt in the first place.

Tollie received breakfast from the young wide-eyed servant who brought it to the door. Tollie acknowledged some pride in being the daughter of a former head of the school and the twin of the current one. But she also swallowed, once again, that knowledge that she simply didn't ever feel as smart as either of them, and if Tallie was going to choose to not be an ally right now, it would not be hard for her to outsmart Tollie. In fact, she may already have, just by giving Tollie what she wanted most, which was the close connection of a caring family member who just wanted to know what it was that Tollie was going through. No one since her mom had treated her like that, and Tallie certainly knew that.

"What's wrong?' asked Jesp, as Tollie absent-mindedly ladled out small dollops of honeyed oats and fresh fruits onto a shared plate for the faeries.

Tollie looked down at the eager faeries who had gathered over to the little table to eat, just as a tear fell from her nose onto the tablecloth. Tollie hadn't realized she was crying again. She stared into Jesp's small eyes and made a realization. She'd been too honest with her sister. She wasn't being honest enough with her friends. She needed to change that. Right now.

"Go ahead and eat. I need to go feed Harry and Fluffy. Then we'll talk. We need to talk."

Jesp and Kyrt exchanged concerned looks, but they returned their gaze earnestly to Tollie's with agreeable nods.

"OK," they assured her, "We'll be here."

Tollie made her way downstairs through the teeming halls of stirring, noisy students beginning their day. The noise and the chaos brought a smile back to her lips. She preferred this to the monotonous formality of the students at the library. She thought maybe if she had any enthusiasm left in her for book learning (which, she had to remind herself, she did not) this might be the kind of place that would tap that for her. She didn't see any staff or faculty out in the halls. She did notice, though, and it sent shivers down her spine, a small group of brooding well-dressed students standing in the stairwell watching her try to clumsily shuffle her way through the crowd. When she met their eyes, they didn't bother to look away. Clearly, they wanted her to know she had been seen and recognized.

Eventually, Tollie made her way out to the stable. The stable hands had already fed Harry, and, well, Fluffy had fed himself.

Tollie found Fluffy asleep and surrounded by bloody feathers. He opened one eye as Tollie approached, stretched broadly and began to purr. Tollie scratched the large, fat cat while shaking her head at him and sighing.

"I was so happy to see you, you know, you big goofy oaf of a cat, but if you're killing birds even after Jesp and Kyrt got to you yesterday, I guess I really can't keep you around, can I?"

"Tsk, tsk tsk," came a sinister voice from the shadows behind her, "How terribly touching. Tell me, my dear, what *is* it like to keep losing so much of your family?"

Tollie lifted Fluffy gently from the cart as she turned slowly around to face three tall, stocky halflings brandishing small clubs behind her and looking menacing. She began to answer, "Well, frankly..."

And just as quickly, she threw the cat in the face of the nearest thug and ran as fast as she could for the stable opening. Fluffy hissed and screeched and his target screamed and cussed. At least one other would-be attacker was caught off-guard by the sudden move, but the third nimbly cut off her escape by leaping between her and the exit with a grin.

"Cute and clever, but not as fast as you needed to be," he chided her as the other two regained their composure from the now-fleeing feline.

But it had been enough. The stable hand was returning from the main building and sensed trouble in the doorway.

"Hey!" he yelled as he hurried toward the shadowy figures he must have seen gathered there against the backdrop of the light, "What are you all doing there?"

"Tell your sister she can't win this," one of them said quietly behind her. Then someone poked her roughly in the small of the back with a club before all three turned and fled out the back. Tollie's knees buckled and she grabbed the door jam as she went down from the blow, but it wasn't as bad as it could have been.

The stable hand reached her quickly and helped her back up.

"You OK?"

Tollie looked up into his deep brown, concerned eyes. He was a young man, not much older than she, and had a strong but surprisingly soft grip on her hand.

"You're Tallie's sister, aren't you?" he asked her, clearly surprised to see her face.

Tollie nodded, the wind knocked out of her, either by the thug or the handsome rescuer, she wasn't sure which.

The young man helped her to a bench and held her hand until she sat down.

"Can I get you some water?"

Again Tollie nodded, speechless, and feeling more and more silly by the passing moment. She felt her face start to blush.

He left to get her the drink and Tollie found herself looking around and shivering, momentarily worried that her attackers would return. They didn't, but when her rescuer did, he had Tallie with him.

"Tollie!" she exclaimed, "What happened?" then turning to the young man that Tollie would really like to have been left alone with for at least a moment or two longer, she went on, "Thank you, Thomas, for rescuing her! OH! This is all my fault!"

And with that Tallie sank down on the bench beside Tollie and began to sob into her hands.

Tollie looked up at Thomas who was clutching a cup and looking helpless at the two of them. Tollie reached for the water and said, "Thanks, um, Thomas, is it?"

The handsome face blushed as he nodded.

"My sister could probably do with some water, too."

"Oh, to heck with water," Tallie gasped from her sobbing, "Would you bring me an ale...and nothing local."

"Sure thing, Tallie, you?" he asked Tollie. Tollie looked at her sister who had gone back to crying in earnest, "Sure. An ale would be perfect."

Thomas brought them ales as Tallie calmed down, confessing repeatedly to them both that she was no longer sure that she could keep going. She was, finally, giving in to all the pressure. And Tollie realized that she owed it to her sister to give her the same gift her sister had given. Tollie set her own problems aside, and just listened to Tallie this time: just gave her the space to speak. For once, it felt good to stop worrying about herself and her own dilemmas.

The school had operated for years on a combination of tuition and grant money. Much of that grant money had come from the brewers' guild and other pockets of wealth in the region. Slowly over the years, an expectation had grown that students with "certain" last names, or who bore letters of introductions from grant-bestowing families were not actually expected to do the work. Ellerby had, in fact, not allowed the practice, although most of the teachers who worked for him ignored his policy. The board had hired Tallie in no small part because the school's reputation was in decline since Ellerby left. In decline, Tallie knew, because these families had flooded the school with their good-for-nothing thug-like children the moment Ellerby was gone. Tallie had taken Ellerby's practice a step farther. She had even fired two professors for passing students who hadn't earned their marks. Since then they'd burned down her home, murdered her pet cat (she briefly stopped here to sob over the discovery of Fluffy who she thought had run away away after Fluffy's mother, the older cat, had been found dead), severely beaten two board members who had sided with her, threatened her life, sent her a box of poisoned candles, and set fire to at least one classroom. Now they'd attacked Tollie. Tallie was almost happy to hear that Tollie had gotten involved in something more important. She was ready for an excuse to leave and do something else.

"But the bottom line is," she finally summed up, wiping her eyes on her sleeve, and her nose on a handkerchief provided by Thomas just before finishing off her mug of ale, "You're not safe here. I wish you were. I wish you could just hide out here until we could figure something out, or until it blows over, or until...whatever you need...but it isn't safe. Once anyone realizes," and at this she glanced carefully around outside both in front of and behind the stables while Tollie glanced curiously at Thomas who she really didn't know at all, "once anyone realizes that you're trying to hide from something, they'll stop at nothing to try to figure out who and why."

Tallie looked at Tollie and must have realized that she was instead looking at Thomas.

"Oh sorry," she stammered, "This is Thomas. His dad's an alum and an old friend of our dad's. He was sent to come to school here, but well," Tallie glanced at Thomas and blushed. Thomas looked at his shoes, "Thomas is really good with animals," Tallie finished, "Really more so than with books."

Tollie felt a rush of deep connection toward Thomas. "Yeah," she said, "I'm no good with books either."

Thomas glanced up and smiled at her. He really was very handsome. Tallie looked from one to the other and smiled, "Yes, the two of you remind me of each other. Smart. But not bookish." She sighed, "I envy you both sometimes."

This statement shocked Tollie and her face must have said so. Tallie laughed and shook her head, "Find that hard to believe do you? Anyway, Thomas keeps the stables, but also the exotic animals for the magic classes, and he gathers supplies from the wilder places for the professors that need those things. And he gives me safe space when I need it. Sometimes my office just seems like a cage anymore."

Tollie thought back to her bower room in the library tower. And then she thought of the empty room next to it. How many cages had her sister spent her life in?

Tollie looked at Thomas who seemed to be trying to determine, rather sheepishly, whether or not Tollie was at all impressed with his job description, such as it was. Truthfully, she envied him. She shot him a shy look, which he returned, then she stood up.

Immediately her legs tried to buckle as the pain in her back shot down both of them. She really had been hit hard. Thomas reached out a hand to steady her, and Tollie was pretty certain that she blushed. She wasn't sure where life was going to lead her from here, but she was certainly hoping that it might involve less violence very soon.

She finished her ale and returned to her room. The faeries were nowhere in sight, although they both returned from the window boxes shortly after she came in the door, and they were giggling. Tollie decided she didn't want to know. She flopped herself down on her bed and sighed heavily. The two faeries made their awkward flying way over to her and perched on her stomach with concerned expressions.

"You OK?" Kyrt asked.

"You were gone a while," Jesp added.

Then somewhat facetiously, Kyrt asked "So, how was Fluffy?"

Jesp snorted and shot him a bemused grimace.

"You were right. I can't keep him," Tollie sighed again, "But I think Tallie will. I got attacked again."

Jesp sat up in alert and Kyrt took to his wings as if an intruder needed to be defended off in that moment, "What?!!" he exclaimed.

"By who? Where?" Jesp urged.

Tollie sighed again. It seemed to be her primary method of communication today, "Down in the stables, and no not by Fluffy, although he did manage a few birds while the two of you weren't around," she grimaced, "No, some of my sister's enemies came after me. Fortunately, there's a...an" Tollie grappled for a better title than 'stable hand' which she'd been mentally using for Thomas, now that she'd learned more about him, she went with "animal handler," and grimaced again: that didn't sound good either, "who arrived in time."

"Are you hurt?" asked Kyrt settling back down on the bed to stand next to Tollie.

"Yes, but not badly. Unfortunately, though, we're going to have to think of somewhere else to go. There are people here just itching for a reason to get back at my family, so they'll be looking for something to bother me about."

"Does your sister have any ideas?" asked Jesp.

"I don't know yet," Tollie thought about that question for a moment. She'd felt guilty earlier for revealing so much to her sister without asking the faeries what they thought, but it sounded like Jesp, at least, expected her to talk to Tallie. Time to confess she thought. This time she held in the sigh, "I told my sister. I told her everything. I really should have asked you guys first, but I guess I was just so relieved to see her; I didn't think."

The faeries looked at each other. "We assumed you were going to talk to her," Jesp said carefully. "What else were we going to do?"

If they were larger, Tollie would have hugged them both.

The three of them stayed put in the room for most of the day. None of them wanted to go out and invite more trouble in. They had been through so much just to get here. The reality that they now couldn't stay and had to figure out where to go next was heavy in the room between them. Tollie found her mind drifting back to the girl in the story her father had had her read. She was trapped. She had nowhere and no one to turn to. She'd trusted the faeries, but knew their limitations and only gave them so much. What she'd done was really very drastic; it was really foolish, in fact. But, foolish or not, it had ended a great evil. Whether it was in her bloodline or outside of it was not quite clear. It may have even been accidental, and she may even have been part of the evil she ended. She may or may not have caused a great war, or maybe ended one, or both. No one knew. She'd acted impulsively. She'd acted desperately. She may have acted hopelessly. She may have acted selfishly.

But what she did had worked. History had to conclude that. Andarraine ended with her sacrifice at the Gatewell, whatever that was. Or wherever it was. Perhaps it would be worthwhile to try to figure that out, but the only way Tollie knew how to do that would be be to go back to the Library. Research. That was her upbringing. Unfortunately she still wasn't any good at it. But her father had been. Tollie sat up abruptly.

"Did you think of something?" Jesp asked excitedly from the dresser where she and Kyrt were sharing the innards of a grape.

"My father gave me that book before he died," she was thinking fast now, "He knew something was going on. I'm not at all sure what exactly he was trying to figure out, but somehow he thought that book was relevant. It seems silly to me, but the crown is obviously mentioned in it, and that's what someone's looking for..."she trailed off. It could have been that he was just hiding the book under her slow-studying nose because it held the only real clues as to the location of the crown. Her study of it may have had more to do with hiding it in plain sight than with her needing to know anything from it. Her heart sank.

"Well, that makes sense," Jesp suggested after a few moments, "We can't just keep hiding it. Someone's going to figure out that it was us that took it. Then they're going to figure out where we went, because, let's face it, we don't blend in to any crowd anywhere, and they'll find wherever we hide it. Anywhere we go, it's just a matter of time. We need to figure out what it's for."

She said it so matter-of-factly, she made it sound easy, but she was right. Just hiding it was foolish. Whoever was after it would be relentless. It would just be a matter of time before it was found anywhere. They needed an idea that didn't involve just hiding it somewhere, and that involved knowing it's story.

As if reading her mind, Kyrt piped in, "Stories have power, you know. Look at what we did at the courthouse. We changed what happened because we changed the story."

"You didn't change what happened," Tollie insisted.

"Oh yeah? Prove it. Your memory of it is only your version of the story now. If you compared it to Ella's, it wouldn't match anyway just because people's memories are different. The way the story will play out in history, into the future, will be based on the way we told it, not the way you remember it. People change all kinds of things. Don't you ever wonder why history is only full of heroes and villains? It's because of the stories we tell..."

"That's why it's so dangerous to write them down," Jesp interrupted him, "It's like you're trying to say, 'it can only have happened this way and no one can remember anything else or figure anything else out.' Books are dangerous."

Tollie rolled her eyes, but she was thinking. How did the story help them at all? She slid off the bed and, ignoring her aching, bruised back, retrieved the book she'd been so glad to be finished with.

"What about the other books?" Kyrt asked her.

Tollie looked over at him curiously, her mind racing.

"Your dad wanted all of them hidden, too, right? What are they about?"

"Well, faeries, actually, and elves...long lineages of elves and the various races and how they came to be...."

"Were they really split apart by magic?" Jesp asked facetiously.

"Sort of, more by not agreeing how to handle it and what should be done with it, who should be taught how to wield it and that sort of thing, not like a big spell was cast and it split the elven races, but folklore tends to remember it more like that....that's why books ARE important. Because folk stories will say things like 'magic split apart the elven races' and over time people will believe that what happened is more like a magical event; when really you have to go back to written history to understand that, no, it was people's different beliefs and philosophies about magic that split the elven races. Basically it was politics, greed and arrogance, not really magic, that divided them, but I doubt even very many of them know that anymore."

"Why do you know?" asked Kyrt innocently.

Tollie paused, remembering a garden and summers spent sitting at her father's knee. "My Papa used to read me stories...." she started, "old stories...."

Tollie's mind drifted. What Ellerby did was read to his daughters from his work. He just read it in a way that was sing-songy and fun, with made-up voices and sound effects so that the stories of ages past that a historian would know became children's entertainment in that long-ago garden. Tollie and Tallie hadn't grown up on just children's tales. Tollie hadn't really thought about that until just now. Children can come to accept almost anything their parents do as normal.

"OK," Jesp prodded, "Is that everything in these books?"

"Well, let's see..." Tollie jumped back off of the bed again where she'd settled once more with the first book. She retrieved eleven volumes out from under her bed. One she tossed up onto the bed without another glance. It was a lineage of elves. She'd already looked at it some. Another talked about the first divisions among the elven races. She threw it onto the first. A smaller, more decorative one was simply titled "Faeries" and clearly depicted four fae on the cover, handsomely painted. Kyrt and Jesp regarded them with disturbed interest. Two were books of geography, one fairly old, one extremely ancient and very delicate. Three were books of children's stories, although Tollie stopped at the title of the second of these when she realized it was titled "Fairy Tales" and wondered if it was, in fact, a book of fae stories instead. One was a small history of the late reigns of Andarraine, but another was an even smaller work claiming to debunk the findings of the first. The last was a book called "Origins of Symbols" which had a couple of small bookmarks in it. Opening to the marked pages, Tollie found information about the meanings and designs of crowns, scepters and wells.

All of this Tollie went over aloud with the faeries who were especially perturbed by the "Fairy Tales" book. Tollie picked that volume up and flipped through it nervously. Her hands were trembling, and it didn't take her long to confirm her fears. Her heart sank and she felt herself pale instantly.

"What is it?" Kyrt pressed, horror in his voice.

Dutifully, Tollie read:

> "Hey ho with a mite and mo
> Hey diddle diddle and a pig's big toe.
> Lady fair with gold in your hair
> How did you make the ghosts go over there?
> Widdle widdle wee and ticky ticky tee
> It was long ago and you will never know.
> Faelings dance and faelings prance
> But lady dark had them all in a trance.
> Because...
> With this circle of gold I will late get old
> With a staff of silver I will rule for ever
> Gold on my head and a well lined of lead
> Staff of control with power so bold.
> But lady dark all happy as a lark
> You let the gold go without any mark
> You set away the silver with nary a shiver
> And into the well you did choose to dwell.

And we all ask why, because

Hey ho with a mite and mo

Hey diddle diddle and a pig's big toe

My dad had the gold and the silver old

But someone had him and me so cold

If I wore the crown I wouldn't frown

To die in the well it wouldn't let me fell

The ghosts they moan and the ghosts they groan

But when I joined the stone they were all set free!"

They all set in stunned silence for a moment, all of them staring at the book as if it had just betrayed them all, which, Tollie suspected, the faeries must have felt like it had.

"That's a bit different than we learned it," Kyrt said at last, still glowering at it and breathing stiffly through his nose like a very small bull.

"Is it?" Tollie asked, finally looking up, "In what way?"

"Well, for one thing, Gram was right about the 'never get old' thing," Jesp mused, "You said something different."

Tollie looked down, "You're right. It says, 'Late get old.' What else?"

They went back through the poem and picked out other differences: "'a well lined of lead and a staff of control with power so bold' that's not in our version either," Kyrt blurted out wide-eyed and still slightly horrified.

"And then at the end," Jesp went on, "The one that had her and her dad was 'cold' here not 'bold' like in ours, and when she set the ghosts free she 'joined the stone,' what does that mean?"

"I don't know," Tollie confessed, "Except that it means that my father knew a lot about what was going on."

"Ok, back up," said Kyrt, "We have the crown. Where are the scepter and the well? We know from our own stories that other faeries are guarding the scepter somewhere in the Willows, but I didn't know anything about a well, did you?" he asked Jesp who shook her head. "You?" he asked Tollie.

"The place where she set the murdered souls free, or whatever it was she did, was at a place called the Gatewell. I've seen it described as a well and also as a lead pit, but once as a thing that 'loomed on the horizon.' I don't know how a well or a pit 'looms on the horizon.' But that's the only reference to a well I've seen in the story so far."

"So, what's the deal with that? Because it sounds like she gave up the crown and scepter that were protecting her so that she could sacrifice herself just so she could do that. Why? To free lost souls?" Jesp seemed genuinely disturbed. Frankly, so was Tollie.

"That's the thing. People have struggled with the answer to that question for two millennia. She destroyed the entire Empire of Andarraine with her ghost army according to most scholars. She turned the only army that tried to stop her, an army of elves, into an undead forest. Why would you destroy your own people and yourself? Except that this one author that my Papa had me reading seemed to think that she wasn't trying to do that. He seemed to think that she was trying to stop some terrible evil that had taken control of the Empire and that it maybe backfired or something. Or maybe even that the people of the Empire had already been destroyed by a great evil and she even died to release them, except that there's no evidence of that. We know that there was a huge migration into the Barrow Hills after that, so there were survivors. I don't know. But the Kingdom of Andarraine essentially ended the day that the last ruler, who was a young teenage girl apparently, threw herself into the Gatewell and died. Intentionally. And now someone wants the crown."

"And probably the scepter," reasoned Jesp, "That's where we should go. We should find the scepter first. Before someone else does."

"Assuming they don't already have it," Kyrt pointed out.

"That would be bad," Tollie realized, "Because we haven't figured out yet what exactly it controls. Do you guys have any idea where it is?"

The faeries answered in unison, "Alderbrook."

"And where is that?"

Two little faces turned and looked at each other and shrugged.

"Somewhere in the Willows," Kyrt answered.

Tollie looked at the books of geography, "I bet it's written down."

Tollie searched the two geography books for the rest of the afternoon and evening while the faeries got them ready to leave with the help of Thomas. Tollie would have liked to have been doing something that Thomas could have helped with herself and tried really hard not to appear bookish after having presented herself as not, but she really needed to find out where Alderbrook was and was afraid to say the name of the place out loud for fear of being overheard by anyone. Tallie was dealing with the local authorities for the rest of the day. Refusing to be intimidated, she'd had Tollie's attackers arrested after Thomas had identified them.

Tollie woke up the next morning frustrated with her lack of success from the day before and anxious for a plan to get back on the road. As wonderful as her reunion with Tallie had been, her sense of urgency surrounding their situation had increased exponentially yesterday with both the attack in the stables and the discovery of the fae poem in the library book. She sat with the older geography book laid genially open next to her breakfast plate, its faded pages carefully arrayed so as not to receive further damage from her plate of sausage. Kyrt walked across the table to the maps and stared down at them with his hands on his hips.

"Any luck?" he asked her staring uncomprehendingly down at the faded diagrams.

Tollie didn't even look up, "Not a clue. The Willows' borders have changed so many times through the years, and place names keep changing, and apparently they're not very fond of maps themselves. And it doesn't help that they saw a lot of war with the shadowelves and incursions into their territory by various human tribes in the first thousand years after Andarraine. I might as well pin a map of the forest to a wall and throw a dart at it frankly."

"OK," Kyrt agreed, "If that would give us a place to start."

Tollie looked up at him annoyed. Jesp jumped into the air from where she'd been playing absentmindedly with the half-eaten end of a strawberry.

"We have a place to start?" she exclaimed, "Let's go!" and made to race out the door.

"No!" shouted Tollie exasperatedly, "I was joking!"

Both faeries looked disappointed.

"You know," said Kyrt, "We could just head into the Willows and find some fae and ask...." he let his voice trail off innocently.

Tollie glared at him, not least because she didn't want to risk the possibility that she'd wasted a bunch of time staring at books.

There was a knock at the door that turned out to be Thomas. He came in grinning at all the books surrounding Tollie and said, "Your things are ready to go whenever you are."

Both fae looked at Tollie. She shut the loose pages of the old book back between its ancient covers and looked up at Thomas' round, friendly face. Tallie trusts him, she thought.

"Do you happen to know where Alderbrook is?" she asked him.

"The faerie fountain?" he asked without missing a beat, "Yeah, but you don't wanna go there. That place got overrun by shadowelves almost six years ago now. Right before the first comet flew in fact. I used to barter for water with those fae sometimes for the alchemical department here. Been up there several times before..."

His nervously sad eyes betrayed what he didn't want to say. They darted back to the faeries and over to Tollie again a couple of times as he decided how much to divulge. Ultimately, he just let the silence hang. Whatever happened, it was bad, and Thomas had seen enough of it.

Tollie glance back at the fae, too. She knew that whatever had happened to Alderbrook could happen to the Garden, and she didn't want to spend too much time dwelling on that fact, but she needed more information. She couldn't just drop it there.

"There was more there than just faeries and alchemical water, Thomas. We really need to find out if they got everything..."

"Oh, I guarantee they did," he stopped trying to bounce his eyes around from target to target and settled, finally, on his own shoes, "They dug the whole place up. Nothing there now but a crater as deep as two men are tall, and human men at that. And as wide as a halfling's house in a decent part of town here. With the creek still running in, it'll be a lake one day. Right now, it's a big ole mud pit. There's nothing there, Tollie. You got a map?"

Tollie flipped open the set of maps of the Willows she had been using. They were almost as old as Andarraine itself.

"Oh I doubt it'd be labeled on something this old. The elves didn't really interact with the fae until more recently. But it'd be about here." He pointed to a bend in the end of a river where it was a little more than a creek at the edge of the

Willows themselves near the border of the Clearing where the Crags drop off into the Eastern Desert. On this particular map it was well within elvish territory, but Tollie knew that today it was much closer to the divided border between the two Elvish kingdoms of the Willows and the Darkwald, the kingdom of the shadowelves. Thomas was right. That was nowhere for them to be taking the crown. She looked at the faeries.

"Now what?"

"If it were me," Thomas went on, "And I know it's not, so tell me to be quiet if you want to, but if I wanted to know about anything that might be left of Alderbrook I'd go to Willowmark. The willowelves hadn't always paid much attention to the faeries, but for the last several generations they'd developed stronger ties. They'd even accepted the occasional diplomat to speak to the Treesingers' Court up there. Seems to me that if there were survivors, they might go there for safety. I don't honestly know where they'd go," and here he did look back at Jesp and Kyrt, "But then I'm not fae."

"What's Willowmark?" Jesp asked.

Tollie answered, "It's the capital of the Willows....sort of. It's more like a central settlement high in the trees. It's hard to find and full of elves, but if the fae knew they were welcome and knew how to find it, do you think they'd have gone there?"

Jesp and Kyrt both shrugged.

"It's worth a try," Jesp said simply.

"Better than a dart," Kyrt agreed.

"Do you know how to find it?" Jesp asked.

"Uh....no," Tollie answered.

Thomas was looking at his shoes again. "I do," he said.

Tollie felt her face blush. She was glad Thomas wasn't looking.

"Let me talk to Tallie," was all she answered. Then she shot the faeries a dirty look as she heard them start to giggle.

"Oh, right, Tallie, sorry," Thomas stammered, "That was the other thing I was supposed to tell you. Your maid and your father's manservant have arrived from the Library with yours and your father's personal effects that survived the fire. They're meeting with Tallie right now. She seemed to think maybe you should stay out of sight since people think you're dead."

"Papa's manservant? Harold? He was the gardener... And he wouldn't have come looking for us....he knows....." Tollie's mind raced. What was going on? She looked at the faeries who also looked concerned.

"How much do you trust your maid?" Jesp asked hurriedly.

Tollie shrugged, "I never thought about it."

"Where was she when your Dad died?"

"She...well, she..." Tollie's eyes widened....Maeve FOUND him....but why had Maeve been going to see him at that hour? And why hadn't she seen his attacker? "She was the one that sounded the alarm! Oh Alura!" Tollie looked at Thomas in alarm, "And Papa didn't have a manservant! Tallie!"

"Stay here!" Thomas yelled and he ran out of the door, but the faeries were fast behind him.

Tollie hated this. Her last family member in danger and she was left behind to do nothing, just to wait and hope that one more wouldn't be murdered. Of course, her mother hadn't been murdered, but still, it had always felt to Tollie that the library itself had killed her.

Her friends were only gone a few moments when they returned. Thomas looked grim, Kyrt pale and Jesp pissed.

"Is Tallie OK?"

Thomas nodded, "Yes, she figured out that those two weren't what they seemed and sent them to guest rooms with fake sobbing and promises of jobs here at the school. I think you're going to have more company to Willowmark. She's meeting us by the ponies."

"What about the school?"

"Oh, guess who the 'manservant' is? Come on. Guess! She even said he was her brother, the maid did!" Jesp fumed.

Tollie shook her head in futility.

Kyrt chimed in, "Let's just say the last time we saw him in Stable Glen we'd just had him and his cronies sentenced to hang for trying to murder you."

"What?!" Tollie's memories of that day were still fresh enough she could smell the oil.

"Tallie has a detailed will," Thomas assured her, "The school will be OK.

We need to go. Now."

They gathered the books and the cleaner satchel they now had the crown in. Thomas led them down servants' accesses and through a backdoor to the stables where a grim-faced Tallie stood ready with three packed ponies and no cart.

"What about Harry?" Tollie protested.

"Tollie, we need speed. I had Thomas repack you onto these ponies anyway. He said you were carrying some weird stuff, and I'm not asking. He just took it out of crates and put it in satchels. Now, can we go?"

Tollie nodded. She draped the sack containing the crown carefully around the saddle of the pony she was being offered and immediately both Jesp and Kyrt sat on it and grabbed a strap. Thomas tucked the books quickly and carefully into the edges of the already-packed saddlebags until he had them as evenly distributed as he could manage. And without any further ado, the three ponies were spurred onto the road and into as fast a trot as they would agree to under all the weight.

Tollie followed Thomas with Tallie behind her. The saddle was uncomfortable immediately. The saddlebags rubbed against her knees. She kept glancing at her littlest friends to make sure they were secure. As usual, they had manic looks about them but were clinging to their sack for dear life, their tiny, fragile wings folded tightly down behind them. Tollie wondered how easily they might tear.

The group rode for several hours before they stopped for food. Everyone was aching by that point and no one said very much except to verify that Thomas knew where they were going.

"If it's alright, I know a place where we can hide out tonight near the border," he answered. Everyone agreed, but he didn't elaborate. Tollie wondered why she trusted him. Was it because she liked him? Or because her sister trusted him? Then again, why did she trust her sister? The point had come where they had had to trust somebody, and so these two were it. She certainly liked trusting them. She looked at Jesp and Kyrt as they climbed back onto the ponies. She just hoped she didn't get them killed.

They rode well into the night, and Thomas seemed very nervous as they moved along the riverbank. Tollie came up next to him finally and asked him what was making him so jittery.

"The Darkwald is across that river," he answered, "You just can't be too careful around here."

His 'place to hide out' turned out to be an abandoned boat dock on the riverbank. It was damp and creepy, but was a place he had camped in before when he was out on the road, he'd said, and thought it to be safe. The faeries offered to watch while the others slept and then suggested that they climb into the bags during the ride the next day and sleep. This plan initially made Tallie nervous, but Thomas clearly had an idea of how useful faeries could be and talked her into it.

The next morning they got up, fished for breakfast, and moved on. It was becoming clear quickly that Thomas was very handy to have out in the wilderness which was a good thing, since he had no intention of traveling anymore on the road.

That day they moved at a more leisurely pace along the route of the river, but just far enough from the banks that they couldn't be seen easily by anyone traveling on it. The riverbank itself was overgrown with ivy, and the sparse trees were covered in draping canopies of the stuff making their ponies' footfalls more difficult but their presence harder to detect. By dusk they'd climbed up and out of the ivy-caked river bed and had reached the edge of the wood line where the larger trees dominated the ground and kept their own domain.

"We should stop here," Tallie suggested.

"Already?" Thomas asked, "Are you sure? We still have daylight left."

"We're reaching the border of the Meadows," she explained, "And I didn't get a chance to tell you what my unpleasant visitors told me. Of course, I don't know how much of what they said was truth, but according to them, the shadowelves overran the Library not long after the fire."

"WHAT???" Tollie exclaimed, horrified.

"What about the Garden?" Jesp asked, nearly falling out of her satchel.

"I don't know," Tallie admitted, shaking her head, "What I do know, though, is that the closer we get to the Morrowlands, the more we have to worry about it."

"I wish you had mentioned that before," said Thomas.

"Sorry," Tallie agreed, "I was trying not to think about it.

"Then we'll need to cross the river sooner rather than later."

"Is there anyway we can find out about the Garden?" Jesp asked desperately.

All three halflings looked sorrowfully at her.

"No," Tollie told her, "I wish there was."

They made their camp in the soft ivy at the edge of the tall trees, but Tollie suspected that it was a long and difficult watch for her two small friends.

Brody

The next day passed with little conversation. Although the rain let up mid-morning and the sun finally came out, making for a very pleasant day, the reality of what had been discovered in the cave was heavy on all of them. They'd buried the remains. Arisa said some beautiful words over the sad little gravesite about the freedom of the spirit and the beauty of the mountain where it could roam. But not only was their sadness deep and their sense of horror profound, they were also keenly aware that they were not alone on the mountain.

Brody knew that he and Finn needed the rest of the story, now more than ever, but he didn't feel like talking anymore than anybody else did. He comforted himself a little once Finn and Adrik had confirmed that the tracks were about six days old. He knew for sure where his own brothers had been 6 days ago. He was with them. He wished he was with them now, and wondered if he ever would be again.

That afternoon they reached the first campsite they had shared after the flood. He knew that the remnants of everything he'd ever known were just out of sight below him and he began to dread what they would find when they headed down there, but that would be tomorrow. For today, they agreed, they would set up camp and try to finish the conversations they needed to have, maybe coming up with an actual plan.

They sat in a somber little circle each apparently hoping another would start the conversation. Brody felt particularly bad for Adrik. The reality of his life so far was harsh and terrible, and Brody knew like Adrik did, that he'd never escape the stigma of it, and never be able to lead another man's life. He bore the very evidence of his past in his visage, and no one would ever trust him. Brody understood this better now that he had seen what Adrik's kin were capable of.

"OK," Brody began, taking the lead no one wanted, "I'd be happy to pick up the story and run with it, but I'd be making it up, and that's not going to be helpful."

"You're right," Arisa said quietly, looking down at her hands, "Where did we leave off?"

Adrik backed himself up against a tree and looked up at its branches high above, just beginning to turn to beautiful autumn colors. He seemed as distant as if he were in another world, and Brody suspected that leaving him there was best. What could he say? What would possibly comfort him right now?

As Brody was contemplating his pity for Adrik, Finn answered Arisa's question, "Let's see. I think Adrik's in the dungeon and you're suspicious of the scholars' intentions."

"Right, only Adrik's not in the dungeon yet. I've backed up to catch you up to where I was. Sorry, I guess that wasn't clear."

"It's fine," Brody prodded, "Just keep going."

"Well, I realized that in two thousand years of 'keeping' the prophecy and studying the runes that make it up, no one had ever written it out in a form that could be easily read, and no one even in living memory knew what the full thing said. I knew from my brief poking about that there was a rune for the comet listed in the prophecy tomes, so I knew I was right about it being related. What I *should have done* was study everything that was known about the Fire Titan from the collections of history and rune studies that had been done, but no, I was too irritated and stupid to be that sensible." She sighed heavily, looked at her feet and shook her head, clearly still at war with herself over whatever she'd done, "It's probably what the elder Librarians *were* doing," she admitted quietly.

Coming out of his reverie, Adrik came to her rescue again, "Well, you should have been irritated and if you were stupid you wouldn't have survived. Arisa, you've got to get over this idea that you screwed up! Your sacrifice may very well save this stinking, wretched world! You said yourself that people are often drawn to their destinies. Don't you think you were drawn to yours?"

She smiled sweetly at him but chided gently, "I happen to think the world smells quite lovely at the moment, thank you."

He grimaced at her and fell silent.

"Well, we *do* seem to keep using that word *drawn*. Your father even mentioned it, didn't he?"

Brody nodded.

"OK. I guess Adrik's right, *as usual*," she said loudly and slowly in his direction. He snorted.

"So, well, I stole the runic password combination from the Chancellor's office chamber, snuck down to the sub-basement after hours and, well, I read the prophecy," she was developing a glazed look about her and Adrik was already watching her at attention. She was staring off into the distance and swaying slightly and Adrik was looking increasingly worried.

"Arisa?" Brody tried.

"Arisa?" Adrik followed, but she was no longer responding to anyone.

Brody had an idea. It seemed foolish and he certainly felt foolish doing it, but maybe there was something to this idea of being *drawn* to certain actions.

He moved in front of her. Immediately he felt Adrik leap up from his position now behind Brody and move so that Arisa was still visible to him. Brody sat down cross legged and closed his eyes. For what he planned to do, he needed to pretend she was a spirit.

He called up the sense of stillness in the moment that accompanied his usually-panic-inspired ability to call his father. Only this time, he called Arisa. He breathed deeply. He could smell her damp clothes, her sharp, sweet musk, the soap she used in her hair. It was enough.

"Can you hear me, Arisa?" his voice was low and quiet, nearly a whisper. He felt cold. Aspects of this he hadn't noticed before because of the peril he had been in became more apparent. The shadows were coalescing around him. Of course, that's what others could see and sense. He'd ignored the odd breezy coldness before.

Arisa's voice was barely a whisper. Her eyes were closed. "Yes," she answered, "I can."

"Are you OK?"

"Yes, I think so. "

Adrik moved next to them. Brody could sense his presence, feel him just outside of the shadows that now enclosed he and Arisa. Adrik's form seemed to blend easily with those shadows, as if they knew their own.

"What do you see?" he asked her quietly.

"The Gatewell. The rune," she cringed, "It's dark and discomfiting. I don't like the way it *feels* when I look at it"

"Don't *read* it," Brody knew he was grasping now. He didn't understand these runes well enough to give her any good advice, but he and Finn needed to understand. Brody was developing the impression, in fact, that even Adrik's understanding of their situation was far from complete. He needed her to be able to finish explaining this to him, "What do you need to tell me about it?"

She hesitated a moment and then started speaking as if in a trance, "The Gatewell lost its lid, and the spirits destroyed Andarraine. I don't understand it but I know it's true. There was another spirit hidden inside. There was a trade: a life for a life," she almost cried the words, "Oh dear, I didn't realize, but it's right here in front of me. The hidden spirit isn't here anymore." She opened her eyes and tears spilled from them, "We may have wasted our time coming here. I'm so so sorry."

This last she directed at Adrik upon whom she fell sobbing, but no sooner had the statement made its impact than she began convulsing violently in Adrik's arms.

"Do something!" he yelled trying to hold her protectively so that she wouldn't be injured by the gyration of her body.

Brody was terrified he'd created this. He felt the shadows slip back into the earth just before she'd seized, "Has this ever happened before?"

"Yes," moaned Adrik, "Sometimes when she's been dreaming in the night. Never while she was conscious!"

Finn came over from where he'd been walking a protective perimeter around them. He got Arisa's bedding out and helped Adrik lay her down. She stopping seizing shortly and seemed to be breathing normally.

Brody watched the whole thing in horror. He hadn't meant to hurt her. He'd even thought that he might be giving her a safe way to talk to them. The truth was he didn't have the faintest clue how his own magic worked. He'd never forgive himself if he'd killed Arisa, especially experimenting like that. He promised himself silently at that moment, that he wouldn't try his powers again. Not on a person. Not unless it was himself.

Arisa's eyes began to flutter momentarily and her lips were moving. Brody didn't trust himself to get near her. "What is she saying?" he asked the other two.

Adrik leaned over her pale, unconscious form, gently lowering his good ear to her lips. Watching him, Brody couldn't help but be struck at the difference between this man before him, and the way he perceived others of Adrik's kind to be.

Adrik spoke clearly, slowly, but shakily, eyes widening as he intoned, "For without the strength of magic known...The gods of lore may again be shown...The way to take what once was theirs...And make the world their wretched lairs," His face went slightly ashen, "I think we just heard part of the Prophecy," he gasped. They all looked down at Arisa who was completely still.

They finished setting up camp and Brody began preparing a meal. He felt alien to the others, like he'd committed a crime or had a disease. His sense of guilt for what he felt he'd *done* to Arisa was overwhelming. He fried bacon and potatoes with onions for an early supper. Keeping his back to the others, he could hear them moving around behind him. Just as he was finishing up with the meal and about to set out plates, he heard Arisa moan behind him.

He turned. Adrik was still sitting with her, supporting her head on his own arm as she tried to sit up. Finn was nowhere in sight. Brody rushed to her with a cup of ale and a plate of food, but handed it to Adrik to feed her. Then he got more for Adrik. Brody himself waited to eat until Finn returned, grim faced, from wherever he'd been. He was relieved to see Arisa take in sustenance. She seemed to know where she was and who the others were, and Brody took those for good signs.

"That was awesome," she finally gasped after managing the last of her supper. Adrik was just getting started on his.

"I'm glad you liked it," Brody offered sheepishly, taking her plate.

"No, not the food," Arisa grinned broadly at him, "Although that was quite good, too. That thing you did! That's the closest I've come to that memory yet!" The excitement in her voice was rising, and Brody felt a little bubble of self-forgiveness rising in his belly.

She paused and looked around at them, Brody staring at her blankly, Adrik with his mouth gaping and Finn suppressing a grin as he continued to eat.

"For the first time, I can remember what the room looked like! I can even see the pedestal!"

"Well, don't think about it too hard!" Brody leaned forward in his urgency, "Please don't have another fit!"

She looked at him curiously for a moment, then looked at Adrik. She seemed only now to be taking in the fact that he was practically holding her and had been feeding her.

"I had a seizure?" she asked him sheepishly.

All three of them nodded at her.

"Oh dear, I'm so sorry. That must have alarmed you all terribly."

"*You're* sorry?" Brody couldn't help himself, such was his disbelief, "*I'm* sorry! I was terrified I'd killed you!"

Arisa was blushing slightly now and the effect was quite attractive. Brody felt his own cheeks get warm at the thought and he looked back down at his plate.

"You've done it twice before after particularly fitful nights," Adrik told her gently, his arm still around her shoulders.

"You never told me," she whimpered softly, "I'm so sorry."

"It's hardly your fault," Adrik insisted, "It's this damn prophecy, and all the ways its screwed you up!"

Arisa looked at him a moment as Brody looked up at them both. She had a tear running down the cheek facing him.

"No," she swallowed, "I've had seizures my whole life. At least, as a child anyway. It'd been years..." she looked away biting her lip and then looked straight at Brody, "Oh please don't blame yourself!" she begged, "What you did was amazing!"

"What!?" Adrik exclaimed, removing his arm from her. Brody didn't know what to feel. Finn shook his head and began collecting the other plates to wash.

"Oh, you all must be so furious with me!" Arisa exclaimed, fully sobbing now and dropping her face into her hands.

Adrik put his arm back around her. He looked disgusted and was shaking his head, but he didn't look angry. Brody tried not to laugh.

"So where have you been?" he asked Finn as a way of changing the subject.

Finn shot Brody a dark look and turned his gaze back to the empty plates.

"I went down to Luring," he answered without looking up. The look on his face was enough. Brody didn't want to know.

Arisa spent the rest of the evening weak, dizzy and depressed, although they'd all assured her that they weren't angry. It seemed ridiculous to think they would be. Finn was more quiet than usual, and even Adrik didn't push the subject or make a joke. Brody was sorely torn between his relief that Arisa was OK and his growing trepidation about their journey into Luring tomorrow.

Arisa went on with her story in bits and pieces as she could, remembering how she'd woken up a week after she read the Prophecy. Apparently she'd gotten herself out of the chamber, though she doesn't remember doing it. They'd found her in one of the lower libraries in a coma and assumed she'd had a seizure. She probably had. It was like a dream to her after that, and one she remembered very little of.

Adrik picked up the story after that. Arisa knew what she'd done, he told them, but the only details she could grasp were that the comet was indeed relevant and that the Gatewell rune had been featured. She'd researched the Gatewell and discovered that runic historians believed it to have been the origin of the magic that destroyed Andarraine. She'd also found out where it was. At some point she'd found out that a shadowelf had shown up claiming to know something about it, so she'd snuck down to the dungeon and met Adrik. Then they escaped together and agreed to find the Gatewell in the hopes of learning more about how Andarraine was destroyed. And that was it.

"So she hasn't remembered anything else?" Finn asked Adrik.

"Well, some," Arisa answered for herself, "I have dreams, but I only remember snippets of those. I meditate and can almost touch the memory, but it's gone again when I come out. The only other thing I've been able to remember is that there are four comets, they're called 'Titans' in the prophecy, and there's one for each element, but that's something a lot of people already suspect. That, and they herald this...whatever that's coming." She looked defeated, Brody thought. He felt bad for her.

"And ever since she did this," Adrik went on, "She's had random spurts of magic manifest at stressful times which have included," he was building up a huge grin and looking at her. Arisa was shaking her head in an embarrassed sort of fashion. "Raining just over the two of us no matter where we moved, spitting acid, shooting fireballs at the vine things that attacked us, firing lightning at wolves, and, my favorite, turning invisible in the middle of an argument with a prison guard!"

Adrik was laughing. Arisa was looking mortified and still shaking her head. Brody was feeling less alone, though he pointed out that the "vine things" were most likely bramblemen.

"What *are* bramblemen?" Arisa asked curiously.

"They're, well, they're vine-things," laughed Brody, "They come from the Unbreaking, but they're almost never spotted on this side of the lake. Finn said there was some legend..."

"Yeah," Finn agreed, "There's a legend that there's a tribe of them high on the Unbreaking that have a poison that can turn a person into something like themselves, and that there's a whole forest of them up there, like a frozen army. The day we found you, I suspected that's what had attacked you."

Arisa looked horrified and Adrik curious, but they didn't ask any more questions.

"OK, then," Finn brought them out of their personal spaces again, "So we're heading up onto the most evil mountain in the world trying to figure out how Andarraine was destroyed," it was matter of fact. Not at all a question, but it did seem like a terribly hopeless expedition, "And I'm assuming that we're doing it in the hopes that we can use the knowledge to stop the new Andarraine or whatever it is from coming back? Or destroy it when it gets here?"

"Or learn something of it or the Prophecy so we might know what to do next," Adrik stated lowly, "The truth is: as far as Arisa and I know or have been able to find out, we are the only two trying to stop this thing, and the Gatewell is the only real clue we have."

"You mean the four of us," Finn reminded him stubbornly.

"I thought you guys were just along until we found your fathers?" he smiled at them. It wasn't an accusation.

"Oh no," Brody said, "If I have magic now I'm part of this, and this new bit of the Prophecy we've now *heard* suggests that magic will be needed."

"What new bit?" asked Arisa anxiously.

"Don't you remember your little conversation with Brody?" Adrik asked her.

"What? No." she stammered.

"What do you remember of the way I used my magic for you then?" Brody worded the question carefully. He still wasn't sure that what he'd done or if it had been the best thing, but he didn't want to point that out now.

"I remember..."

"Careful," Adrik cut her off.

She nodded, "The room, the pedestal. I could almost see it again. I think I read it again!"

She looked at Adrik triumphantly.

"And I can talk about it!!" she exclaimed happily, then added more quietly, "But I still can't remember what I read."

"For without the strength of magic known...The gods of lore may again be shown...The way to take what once was theirs...And make the world their wretched lairs," Adrik recited.

She stared at him. "How did you know that?" she asked incredulously.

"Brody had you talking while you were...in your trance or whatever," Adrik answered her.

Her eyes widened as she looked at Brody. Brody swallowed hard. He wasn't sure if she was pleased or furious.

"Wow! How'd you do that?" Her face was breaking into a wide grin and Brody felt his own follow her cue. He started to explain, but Finn cut them off.

"Sshhh. Quiet." he was reaching for his axes. Adrik jumped nimbly to his feet and was just to his bow when what appeared to be thick balls of bramble dropped out of the trees.

"Bramblemen!" Finn yelled as chaos erupted around them in the twilight.

Adrik had his bow up and loaded in a flash. Arisa, who'd been caught almost completely by surprise didn't react in time and was hit squarely by two of them as they fell. Finn had his ax into the back of one before it had a chance to get itself upright and was already drawing the second ax. Nearly a dozen bramblemen still managed to right themselves and took no time in heading for Adrik.

Brody decided to be deliberate in his intentions this time and quieted himself as much as he could, drawing inward whether than focusing out. He could hear the fight around him. His friends were shouting. It sounded as if the whole forest were moving and thrashing around him. He tried to think of his father and became drenched suddenly in cold, icy water. Startled, he opened his eyes. Adrik was on his back on the ground, six bramblemen on top of him. Finn was littering the ground with broken vines and thorns as he hacked his way to try to reach the fallen elf. Arisa was standing nearby, up to her ankles in fresh mud and soaking wet.

She pointed her hands at the writhing pile, and water shot in a pillar straight through the trees with such force that she knocked two of the bramblemen off of Adrik. But two more piled on from the growing number that surrounded them all. The spray coming off of Arisa was drenching Brody.

And he was reminded, suddenly and clearly, as if time itself stood still for a breath or two, of a day not so long ago. Of standing on the edge of the world, balanced on slippery rock, a waterfall at his feet. Of a sense of belonging and of life that was good here *because* he belonged to it and it was beautiful. He'd been touched by the Water Titan. Water. He needed water, and even if water had nothing to do with it, the dead of his village was in that lake. He needed the lake.

Without another thought he ran forward. He dodged Arisa's water spray and Finn's ax. He knocked three bramblemen over as he slammed into them, realizing that they weren't really any heavier or more solid than dead vines. He ran until he reached the point where he could see the lake, just through the trees, lying serenely below him like an old friend. He could still see the battle waging above him, but only just.

"Brody!" Finn yelled, "Where the hell are you going?"

"For help!" he yelled back and closed his eyes.

They were eager. They were watching. All they needed was someone to pull them out. Brody reached for the familiar spirits, trying to stop himself from thinking of who each had been in life, but he'd known them all. Tears poured from his eyes as he felt their life's yearning race through him in a maddening tide. Sadness threatened to drown him, but he kept calling. The injustice of their deaths, the fear of their drowning, the sorrow of being ripped from life all flooded into him as the dead escaped the depths and rushed to the aid of their own. Brody couldn't see. He couldn't hear. All he could do was feel and scream until at last he could no longer do either of those.

They rushed up to him. They rushed through him. They were cold and wet and powerful, like a tidal wave of rushing nothingness threatening to knock him out of himself. He stood fast and kept calling.

They wanted to hear their names, but he resisted. The pain of a lifetime of memories welled up in him and threatened to drown him right where he stood on dry land. He felt himself reaching for air and relief, desperately clawing for his own identity away from the rush. He felt something snap as he broke free, like old boards breaking across his face. He could no longer stand up against the tide.

He felt something slam against his face, breaking his nose. He breathed in the wet earth. He heard nothing but the silence of a still forest around him. He had collapsed, and the world went dark around him.

He awoke sputtering and coughing, looking up into Finn's wet, grinning face. It took him a few moments to realize that Fletch was resting his head on his thigh and that he was laying up at the camp, his bed things laying over low branches to dry. He patted the dog in astonishment and looked back at Finn, who was laughing.

"That little guy would have been the hero of the hour if you hadn't trumped him," Finn finally said. Brody realized that he had so rarely seen Finn laugh over the years, that it almost made his face look unnatural.

Brody pushed himself up onto his elbows and looked around. The camp was drenched. The sun was peeking warily through the lower branches of the eastern trees. Arisa was bent over Adrik's slowly-moving body. All five of them were covered in mud and the detritus of soggy autumn leaves. Brody looked back at Finn, waited for the world to stop spinning, then tried to focus on the middle of the three grinning faces in front him. He blinked his eyes, and three Finns became one again.

"What happened?" he asked.

"Well, let's just say those things were taking Adrik down faster than we could get them off. It was like they had it out for him in particular. But then this flying muddy fuzzball came out of nowhere and bowled about three of them off him," Finn laughed more heartily and Fletch looked up at him wagging his tail, "Then he did this rolling land, scrambled back up and barked at the bramblemen until he caught one by the leg-end and started dragging him around knocking some others over."

Finn's laughter was so intense and so genuine, Brody started laughing, too. Even Arisa looked over and grinned, but Brody could see now that she had tears running down her cheeks.

"Adrik?" Brody asked the camp at large in alarm.

"He'll be fine," Arisa replied quietly, wiping the tears from her face. Finn's laughter died away.

"He got petrified again," Finn offered, "Arisa fixed him up with that potion-stuff of hers." He leaned in and whispered to Brody conspiratorially, "She's been crying since the fight. Says it's got something to do with having channeled so much water." Finn shrugged. He continued in a normal tone, "Adrik's gonna be fine, though. Wasn't even very wounded. And Fletch here," he reached over and patted the stinkiest muddiest dog in the history of the world, "apparently followed us down here."

Brody noticed that Finn was cradling his left arm again. He nodded toward it as a question.

"It's OK," Finn answered, "Just sore. It would have been much worse, if it hadn't been for you just now. The weird water you channeled up here seemed almost alive. It washed the bramblemen away, almost like it was chasing them..." he trailed off, apparently at a loss for words.

Brody looked over at Arisa who was helping Adrik sit up. Adrik looked dizzy and weak, but Finn was right: he didn't appear injured. Brody looked back at Finn and remembered his journey down to the village yesterday.

"So how bad is it....back home?"

The dark look came back into Finn's eyes and he shook his head. "We have a lot of funerals to give today," he answered, boring his gaze steadily into Brody's. "I hope you deal with the dead better than I do."

In truth, it was as awful as they could have imagined. The water had receded to below its normal levels and the shores around it looked buoyed on every side by gray sandbags. Only they weren't sandbags. Most of them were still recognizable, though barely, and many were heart-shatteringly small. None of their little group, not even Adrik, bothered to try to stem the flow of silent tears that accompanied the long two days of work. None spoke much, but instead spent endless back-breaking, arm-aching hours sending the dead all deeper into the waiting waters. Fletch was alternately strangely quiet, and howling a determined eulogy.

Brody could hardly bear the weight of it. Each was a soul he'd known in life. A soul that had come to his rescue when the bramblemen attacked. And each seemed to whisper "thank you" as they dropped with a plop and a splash to feed the fish that once fed them.

The four of them and Fletch camped two nights on the ruined floor of Brody's family home, staring up through the missing roof to the sparkling stars above. To Brody, it seemed that they were laughing at him and his pain, threatening future storms and more devastation. He thought again of his little family, and hoped through his bitter tears, that they were finally safe.

Having not found any salvageable lake craft, they decided to trek around the lake. Their options were to walk over the slick rocks at the top of the waterfall that fell into Graffling River Valley, or under the falls that supplied the flowing water of Luring Lake from above. They decided on the latter path. It was likely to be their safest route, but more importantly would take them more quickly to the area of the lake where the men had planned to fish on that fateful day 5 years ago.

So it was, then, that more than 2 full weeks after the great catch, after the finding of the elves, after the night of the storm that destroyed Luring village, that the five new friends, for Fletch was surely one of them now, set out with purpose toward the shadow of the Unbreaking. It was an average day, the autumn chill crisp under the weak mountain sun, and from up here, it seemed they were the only living beings left in the world.

Chapter 6:

12th Day of the 12th Month, 5th Day of the Week, Autumn
Arzenday, Shilirs 12

Kierra

The next morning they were leaving for home. It was hard to believe. It had been exactly 2 weeks since the day her unit had received orders that they would ambush the humans who were rolling into their positions that night. Two weeks tonight, thought Kierra, from when we were sneaking up on them and a tide of undeath was unleashed on us instead. Two weeks since I met Keen. In some ways it seemed like forever. It some ways it seemed like it had been no time at all.

She was returning home elated and triumphant. She'd survived against impossible odds. Keen had stayed with her. And now her brother really had great intelligence about the explosive magic the humans had been using AND another good shot at getting Kethran taken out of command. Kierra's mood was almost perfect: almost.

But there was the little voice nagging at the back of her mind as they rode through the forest paths toward home. Even though she knew she was taking Keen to a good place, she could never know how much he was leaving behind. And if Kierra was completely honest, she couldn't imagine leaving her home and family forever. What was she doing to him? Her happiness came with a price: guilt, selfish, selfish guilt.

She'd been willing to let him go. Preparing for it. She couldn't stop the tears. She'd tried. But she had never ever planned to ask him to stay. Joran and Jerith assured her, too, that they'd never asked him to stay either. Joran was shocked. Jerith had thought he might have had it in him, but still even he had expected that Kierra would have had to have asked. None of them thought that he would just drop everything and stay, and Kierra had already decided that she couldn't ask. No matter how much it was killing her to know that he was leaving and going to a place where she could never follow him, she could never have asked him to give up everything and everyone he'd ever loved for her. But here he was doing it anyway.

And it was wonderful. Wonderful right up to that point where Kierra knew that Keen was suffering a pain that even she couldn't feel with him, and that he wasn't sharing with her. The last two nights had been like a dream. His strong, solid body was so masculine and sexy; once she finally had let go with him, it was so easy to latch on and release all of her inhibitions.

She curled up against him as they rode along in the cart, and he put his arm tightly around her. She looked into his handsome face as she reviewed her longings for him, and he opened his eyes and smiled. He was holding her so close to him, she was practically on top of him again. She bit her bottom lip at him pointedly and he chuckled at her, glancing meaningfully up at Joran and Rana sitting on the driver's bench and back at her with a smile. And with that, they shared a lovers' laugh. It would all be so perfect if it weren't for that one evil feeling in her heart: guilt. Guilt. Guilt. Guilt. She wasn't sure if she'd ever be rid of it.

It must have shown on her face because Keen furrowed his brow as if to ask her what was wrong. But Kierra shook her head. Nothing, she mouthed the word. It wasn't exactly the truth, but the truth was that it was nothing she intended to bring up here.

She glanced ahead. Jerith and Nira were riding ahead of the cart and deep in conversation. Kierra wondered what they were being so serious about. She knew how difficult the love quadrangle between the four of them had once gotten, especially once Joran had very nearly not chosen either sister as his lover, but Kierra was glad it had turned out the way it had. Nira and Jerith were especially well suited. Their parents had tried too hard to push for the opposite pairing and it had nearly been disastrous. Joran and Rana were thought by many to be too mutually high-strung. But, in truth, they calmed each other down strangely, and Nira and Jerith gave each the space they each needed to be thoughtful. Kierra hoped she and Keen would prove to be as good together.

She looked back down at her wonderful, strong, supportive, committed lover. She thought they were just as good for each other. She was nervous about what her family and village were going to think, but if they'd already had a funeral for her, at least they'd start off with gratitude for the fact that he'd saved her. And that was a good place for them to start with him.

Kierra had continued to sing over Keen's wounded hip each night, and as they stopped to camp on the road home it was no different. Camping was a little more difficult for Keen than it was for the others, but it reminded Kierra of the way things had been for so long before Kethran and his men intervened. And Keen's hip really was improving finally. Healing was slow. The process was still natural, but already the infection was nearly gone and the swelling had almost entirely subsided. Kierra thought that with one more day of singing the original wound could finally start to heal.

Early the next morning, they packed back up from their campsite and headed toward the village where Kierra had grown up. She was excited to finally think of being home by nightfall, probably earlier, and sleeping in her own bed by that night, but she tried to quell her enthusiasm around Keen, settling instead for showering him in gratitude for making her homecoming possible.

Keen hadn't slept well, however, so after quietly reminding her that she'd saved him, too, and that he didn't feel he deserved all the praise, he fell back to sleep in the wagon. She was watching over him, wondering about him, his past, their future together, his hidden sadness. She'd lost track of how long they'd been riding, although they hadn't yet stopped for a midday meal, when a commotion ahead caught her attention and was clearly causing the wagon to slow down.

Up ahead there was frantic shouting and a plea for help. Kierra turned in her seat to see what was going on as Joran and Rana leaped out of the wagon to join Jerith and Nira running forward down the path. Up ahead, a tree was down across the narrow dirt lane. A young elven couple were frantically trying to wrestle with it and begging for help. Standing up in the cart for a better look, Kierra could see that the tree had landed on a small carriage and now she could hear the faint cry of an infant coming from the wreckage. The young man pulled his mate away bodily as the desperately sobbing and begging young female pleaded with first Jerith and Nira and then Joran and Rana. Briefly her eyes even strayed as far as Kierra. Surely, even from here, the golden embroidery on her green tunic identified her as a treesinger. Kierra jumped out of the wagon and ran ahead. How could she have stayed behind?

No sooner than she left, Keen jerked awake. "Where are you going?"

"It's OK," she stopped, and turned to assure him, "We're helping stranded travelers." And with that, she ran off.

Rana and Nira were trying to climb into the mangled carriage, but no matter what they did, the wreckage shifted and both baby and mother screamed. Joran and Jerith were trying to find a way to rig a rope system like a pulley to lift the tree off of the crash site. They were struggling but succeeding at looping a rope around the small but solidly heavy tree. Still, they were shifting some of the boards and no one could quite tell where the child precisely was.

Kierra felt useless. Once the child was out, she could sing to heal its wounds and calm its fears, whatever it needed, but she could not think of one song she knew that could move the tree or the babe safely. But the young parents kept looking to her for some sudden inspiration, especially after Joran realized how short the rope they had left was after hooking the tree, and how far from the road the stronger trees were. That's when Keen hobbled far enough down the path that he was noticed.

The parents shrieked. Kierra moved to calm them and assured them that the human was with her. Keen looked at the situation and his eyes met Joran's. Kierra just watched in a kind of silent horror along with everyone else as Keen hobbled over to the ruined carriage and squatted torturously down into his bad hip. It was all Kierra could do not to wince herself as that searing sensation of deep warning hit the pit of her stomach. He was in pain.

Then Joran and Jerith backed up, eyes wide in near-terror as Keen, wobbly as he was on a bad injury, lifted the tree up, his whole body shaking with the effort: grunting groaning, panting, until he had it beneath his chin, against his chest and somewhat up onto his shoulders. No one was breathing.

Then in a horribly strained voice into the collective silence, Keen moaned through gritted teeth, "Someone. Get. Damn. Baby."

Nira and Rana jumped, but Rana was a little closer. She squeezed just under the hole Keen had made and emerged moments later with a wiggling, crying blanket. As soon as she was free, Keen threw the tree onto the carriage remains with a deafening crash and keeled over forward onto his all fours.

Kierra resisted the urge to run to him first and stopped on her way to check the baby. Fighting with his swaddling was a beautiful but tiny little newborn boy. He had a few scratches that might even turn to bruises, but he wasn't really hurt, merely terrified. Rana confirmed that she'd found him in a protected pocket below the crumbled seat. Kierra sang him a short blessing and gave him to his delighted parents, and then she ran to Keen, who by this point had rolled over onto his right side against the storm-damaged tree and was still panting.

She shook her head at him in disbelief when she reached him, but wasted no time in singing him the Healer's Song which she was using on his hip:

Anna'shon na'la par tu

As kin'shando asha shail

Anna nan may tru

Shava thalla thruvin thilla kail

As shado ly ki nil ra'nay

As na'tu thilla tu lashay

Y'ail'tu morna la mornu

Anna na'shilya thilla tu

Anna tu'thilla lashay my

Y trath kin thruvin illa

Anna shilsa san shand tu dry

Y'na my tu shandi shilla

Lu leyen kin luan lan lu

Ashana, tu'alur mir su

Ashandi wy y'la tu wy

Lu luantai'y my[4]

---

[4] Pronunciation Guide:

    Ah-nah shohn nah-lah par too
    As kin shan doh ah-shoo shale (long a like ale)
    Ah-nah throo-vin nahn may troo
    Shah-vah thah-lah thee-lah kale
    As sh-doh lye kee neel rah nay
    As nah-too thee-lah too lah-shay
    Ee-ale too more-nah lah more-noo
    Ah-nah nah-sheel-yah theel-ah too

    Ah-nah too-thee-lah lah-shay mye
    Ee trahth kin throo-vin i-Lah
    Ah-nah sheel-sah sahn shahnd too drye
    Ee-nah mye too shahnd-ee shee-lah
    Loo leh-yehn kin loo-ahn lahn loo

(May it be always for you

That in darkness light will shine

May the future hold as true

Ills will seek never to find

That shadows stalk but lose their prey

That you will always find your way

And ever will your skies be blue

May hope be the path for you

May you find the way to heal

And be blessed in coming days

May love loose the pain you feel

And mend your broken heart always

Rest now, in peaceful dreaming sleep

The stars, your spirit safely keeps

Life will guard and be your shield

Slumber peacefully and heal.)[5]

    Ah-shah-nah, too-ah-loor meer soo
    Ah-shahn-dee wye, ee-lah too wye
    Loo loo-ahn-tah-ee ee mye.

[5] Literal Translation:
    May here always be for/on behalf of you
    That with/in darkness light shines
    May the future hold as true
    Ills seek finding never
    That shadows stalk but lose their prey
    That always you find your way/path/road
    And ever your skies be blue
    May always hope find you

    May you find a way/path/road to heal/fix/mend
    And blessed in/with future days
    May love loosen the pain you feel
    And always heal/fix/mend your darkened hearts
    Rest/sleep/peace now, in peace/rest-ful dream- rest/sleep/peace
    The Ashana (the sacred stars of the Kingdom of Elevar, believed to be where prophetic dreams came from) your spirit safe keeps

They arrived in the village late in the afternoon. Everyone was shocked and thrilled to see Kierra alive. Her homecoming was as momentous and wonderful as she could have hoped for. Joran and Jerith had sent one of their troops ahead with the news that Kierra had been rescued by a human defector and that they were the only two survivors to be found since the curse began. Apparently everyone already knew about the ghosts and the two decimated armies they'd left in their wake. A few elves from the back of their lines had gotten away, but after so much time had passed, hope for more survivors had been lost. The small family that Keen had helped rescue on the road had traveled with them, and brought tales of Keen's rescue of their infant to add to the tales of his rescue of Kierra, so all-in-all Keen received a hero's welcome, which he accepted bashfully.

Kierra's village was built similarly to the prison camp they had left two nights back, a fact that seemed to surprise Keen. The tendency of Willowelves to construct their homes and other buildings out of wood without harming the trees was strange to him. Her village, like most in the Willows, was specifically built around particularly old and huge trees so that more of the plant could be used without devastating it. Its limbs, vines and even bark were woven, living, into multi-room dwellings that were very comfortable, and were almost all Kierra had ever known. She had stayed in dead-wood constructions and tents in Willowmark, where deadfall from the forest was often hauled up into the canopy and used for construction, but that didn't have the feel of home to her. And, of course, she'd spent time in caves, but she suspected that wasn't what Keen was used to either.

It was nearing dark by the time the small village managed to put together the feast they insisted on throwing in hers and Keen's honor. Keen was very conscientious about trying to help prepare in any way that he could, which the elders in Kierra's family appreciated. In addition to the family members he'd already met, Keen was now trying unnecessarily, at least in Kierra's opinion, to impress her mother, aunt, two grandmothers, a grandfather and a great-grandfather who couldn't hear anything he said and pretended not to understand him anyway.

"Just tell him it's because he's got no teeth. He could understand you if he

---

Life (Darkened stardust, literally) guards/shields and is your guard/shield
Rest/sleep/peace rest/peace-fully and heal/fix/mend

had teeth," Kierra teased, "He hates that."

"I don't want to make him mad!" Keen insisted shocked.

Kierra laughed. "Ashan has been a pain ever since Asha died. Watch out. He'll be poking you with that cane every time you walk by next. At least, as soon as he figures out you won't throw him in the river for it."

"I thought he said his name was Cynner..."

"It is. Ashan means elder or great-grandfather. It's an old Elven word. It's short for ashandi which means life...and dark stardust for that matter, but I'm not sure what that's about..."

Keen raised an eyebrow. "OK. And who do we ask before I'm old enough to be called 'dark stardust' by anybody?"

Kierra chuckled. She really liked the idea that he planned to stay that long. He really planned to stay with her forever, didn't he? She felt slightly dizzy thinking about it...and guilty. There was that again.

"Some of the elder treesingers may know. If not," she shrugged and added, "only the hallowelves..."

"The who?"

Kierra shook her head, "It's just a saying. Hallowelves are a legendary fifth race of elves that may or may not have ever existed but are very unlikely to exist now if they ever did. But supposedly they knew all of the 'mystical secrets of elvenkind'," which Kierra added with a spooky mystical flare.

"Fifth race of elves? That implies there are three other races of elves besides you guys!"

"Oh, there are," Kierra answered, "We're not 'all the elves,' we're just the willoweleves."

"Willowelves?"

Some of the other villagers were starting to take an interest in the conversation. Keen was looking around nervously, like he thought he might offend someone. He added in a whisper, "I know you call your kingdom 'the Willows,' but most of these trees are oak, elm, cypress, and, um...not willow. I assume you know that."

Kierra and several others chuckled good-naturedly.

Jerith patted him on the back, "At least you know your trees."

"In old elvish," Kierra explained, "'Willa' means 'tree.' We're 'tree-elves.' We got that name when we defended the Sacred Trust of the forest and the other races abandoned it. Techinically we should be the 'willa-elves' and our kingdom 'the willa' or 'the forest' but over time it's gotten mistranslated into the common tongue. Although there are actual willows here in places. Not a lot, but there are some."

Many of the villagers were smiling at him. Kierra hoped it didn't seem patronizing. She wanted this to feel like home for him as soon as it could, even though she knew it would take a while. She didn't know anything about where he was from, but she could only imagine that it must be strange in comparison. Still, it produced Keen, so it obviously had some good things about it, and he must miss those things.

She wondered if he'd like to tell them all about it, but then she didn't want to ask him if it hurt to talk about. She didn't know what to do. If there was a song she could sing, she'd be right at home, but there wasn't one. She kept watching him for a sign of how he felt, but he seemed to be good at burying that information.

Her own mother and her Aunt Riella, who was Jerith's mother, spent most of their time with Keen asking him about foods he liked to eat and getting to him to explain games and activities he was fond of playing. They suggested he might teach some of them to the local kids, and they all laughed at the differences in challenges of stamina and speed. Her father's parents were mostly quiet and just watched everything that went on, although her grandfather engaged Jerith and Joran in conversation about military matters over to the side, and her grandmother stayed as close to Kierra all evening as she could get away with. Her mother's father chased the kids around as usual, teasing them and playing games and being far too energetic for his age, and eventually it was he who got his own father, Kierra's Ashan, to leave Keen alone.

Keen kept looking over at Kierra for some sign as to how well he was going over with her family. She smiled at him and tried to send him looks of loving kindness. At some point she found a quiet moment where she could just say to him, "With all the lives you've saved around here, you don't have to worry about being accepted. You really can just relax."

"At some point they're going to find out that you guys did more to save me than I did to save you."

"We're not keeping score in one of your sport-games," she countered.

"That's a good thing. I'm tired. I think I hurt my shoulders with that tree."

"I bet you did!"

And shortly thereafter Kierra managed to make an exit for Keen and take him off to her mother's cottage where she had been living before she left for war.

"We can build our own place, or take over an empty cottage if there is one. I just wanted to stay here for now because of my dad..." she let her voice trail off. She hadn't told him about that yet.

"I don't mind staying with your mom as long as we can have a private place to sleep," he said smiling impishly and pulling her close. She looked longingly up into his deep brown eyes, but he continued, "What about your dad, though? Where is he?"

"Could we maybe talk about that tomorrow?"

Keen frowned, but in a concerned way, "Sure."

Making love to Keen in her own bed was pure joy. He was tired, sore and stiff, but his relief in finally being somewhere safe and off of the road came out as a more loving, emotional and gentle passion in him. If they hadn't both been exhausted, Kierra could have enjoyed him like that all night. Afterward she sang for his hip again and rubbed his sore shoulder. Then, making sure that he was sleeping, she got up to check on her mom.

The floor of the cottage was uneven from room to room as each changed from natural vines to bark and then to a hall that followed the looping roots of the huge old tree itself, moving just underground, and re-emerging into another vine chamber. Kierra knew the house well. She'd grown up here and could navigate it in the dark of night with her eyes closed. The central room around the trunk was circular and large and contained a sitting area, a dining area and a kitchen, all somewhat open to each other. The rest of the house twisted and intersected off from there, including the front entrance, which was the shortest distance out.

Kierra and Joran each had rooms, although Joran had moved in with Rana and Rana's Aunt and Uncle two years ago. Kierra's mother had been teasing them that her grandchildren could stay in Joran's room when they visited her overnight. Kierra's dad had a room where he tinkered with woodmaking: mostly bows, but when Kierra was young he made them toys and things, too. And on the far side of the house, past the pantry and the laundry, Kierra's parents had their room.

Kierra slipped into the chamber. In daytime, it had a green cast from the leaves growing along the outside of its walls. In moonlight the hue was blue. In either cast, the viney pattern and the rustling leaves made for friendly shadows that danced over the large room playfully. Her parents' bed sat caddy-cornered in the middle of the room. It was a wooden piece made from a tangle of ancient dead vines someone had once found in the woods and brought back for that purpose. It had been in the family now for generations.

The floor of the room was smooth stones brought up from the river bed, like many of the rooms in the house. There was little other furniture besides a pair of small tables and a matching pair of large ornate trunks. Her mother's quilted blankets were white, and her curtains had been crocheted from white thread which blew gently in the breeze like spider's web.

But in the bed, Kierra could see that her mother was not well, as usual. She could hear her slow, deep struggling breath, gasping in the night air, and she could see her fists on top of the quilt, gripping the cloth for support. Kierra crept over to her and laid a gentle hand over her mother's tightened knuckles. Her mom opened her tear-strained eyes and looked at Kierra.

"Oh, you shouldn't be in here," she began to sit up, wiping her face, "You should be with Keen. He's in a strange place..."

"I came to sing for you. I haven't been able to in weeks..."

"It's not going to help that much, Kierra. I know you're trying..." and she broke out into tears. She reached for Kierra and hugged her daughter close, "I'm just glad you're alright.," she cried, "I don't think I can stand much more of this." She pulled away as if she'd been shocked, "But how can I say that? I'm hardly going through anything by comparison!" she cupped her hand over her mouth like she'd said something terrible.

Kierra didn't know what to say. She'd sat with her mom so many nights like this before she'd left. It was why she'd left Willowmark and come home. Sometimes she'd wondered if it wasn't also part of why she'd left, but she had to shake that out of her head. What she'd gone to do was a good thing: she'd gone to help the troops, men like her brother and father, women like Rana and Nira. She wasn't abandoning her mother, but knowing she'd left her like this was hard. Knowing she'd let her mother think she'd died was awful.

She helped her mother lay back down and she sang her the same healing song she sang for Keen. She knew it wouldn't help. There was nothing wrong with her. But the song was a soothing one, and it did help her drift into an uneasy sleep. She watched her mother breathe unsteadily as the nightmares crept into her dream world. Tears ran down Kierra's face. Kierra reached down lovingly and stroked her mother's hair thinking about how terrible an elven bond could be. Until the shadowelves finished torturing her father and let him die, her mother would never have peace.

The next morning, Kierra helped Keen move unsteadily through his new home. Between his bad hip and his unsteady human reflexes, the unfamiliar terrain of the elven house was a bad fall waiting to happen for him. Still, he accepted his gracelessness with good humor and Kierra, though exhausted from her long night, enjoyed having him there.

Her mother slept in, so Keen and Kierra cooked breakfast. Joran stopped in to check on their mother, and Kierra confirmed that it had been another bad night. Joran gave her a dark look, and headed to her bedroom to look in on her. Keen looked at Kierra quizzically as he stirred the dough mix Kierra had given him to help with.

She sighed, "Have I told you that the Willows is being invaded on two fronts?"

Keen frowned and shook his head.

Kierra nodded.

"The reason that so many of the officers you're meeting, like Joran and Jerith...even Kethran...are young, and why there are so few treesingers to go around is because the seasoned, experienced army is already engaged on the northern border where we've *already* been invaded...6 years ago in fact. *That* kingdom is another kingdom of elves and they're...well they're horrible."

"A kingdom of horrible elves? Not hallowelves then" he teased.

"No," she answered him darkly, "Shadowelves. Their kingdom is called the

Darkwald, and six years ago they invaded us, and although we've made their progress very costly and difficult, they've made slow and steady progress into the Willows over the course of that time. Initially, they pushed as far as a small river tributary that we call the Lalora and they stopped. Then they dug up this really old fountain that was sacred a long long time ago to a goddess that was venerated in the time of Andarraine and that had become a faerie community."

Keen shuddered. Kierra frowned.

"What is it?"

He frowned, "Bad idea to go meddling with old gods," he answered very seriously, and then he made a sign like a fist near his heart and then kissed it. Kierra frowned at him then continued her story.

"The surviving faeries, and there weren't many, made their way to Willowmark, our capital. It's the first time in millennia that the Treesinger's Court has allowed refugees into the city. We shored up defenses on the far bank while they tore up the fountain and basically turned it into a muddy lake."

Keen looked horrified and made his fist sign again.

"But then they started marching again, and now that you've invaded us, too, we can't prevent their forward progress. Anyway, my father's a shavanir,[6] the highest rank of officer. So is my uncle, although he'd just made shavanir before..." She paused.

"Before?"

Kierra hated talking about it. She just wanted her father and her Uncle Pellen to come home and for the whole nightmare to turn out to have been nothing but. She took a deep breath and plowed on.

"When they made their first really big push past the river, not quite two months ago, my dad and an older shavanir who had command of the whole thing set an ambush so it looked like they had fewer forces than they did, so they lured a big shadowelf army into an ambush. It worked, and the shadowelves didn't take any land that day, and the army managed to evacuate several villages in the area before the next advance, but when the battle was over, my dad and my uncle and 8 other men were missing from the battlefield and the older shavanir was dead. It's

---

[6] Pronounced "Shah-Vahn-eer:" Literally "Lead Warrior" or "Leader of War"

typical.."

Kierra was crying again now. She'd really given Keen a better impression of herself when they'd been alone in the woods together. She was afraid of what he must be starting to think of her now. She didn't want him to start to see her the way Joran did. She'd grown up with Nira and Rana as her good friends, and now even they treated her like she needed help all of the time. She hated it, but she was sobbing uncontrollably, and Keen's strong, comforting arms were wrapping around her.

She curled up against his impossibly firm chest and continued, "The shadowelves never leave a defeat empty-handed. They love to take prisoners. And...well...Kethran got all of his little toys from raiding a shadowelf camp early in his career. Joran says that's what made him snap: seeing all the prisoners and what...they'd...done to them..."

Now it was really flooding out. She was gripping Keen's tunic in her fist and sobbing into his neck. He held her tightly and began to rock. She wrapped her other arm around his shoulder and just cried. He was an officer to everyone else, but he was her daddy. He had made her toys when she was little because he liked to make things and he loved her. He'd try to sit her in his lap by the fire at night to tell her stories, but she'd climb all over him instead, and he'd just laugh. He'd tell her she'd never be a treesinger because she was too good at being a tree*climber*. And he just loved her, and she wanted him back. Whole. She didn't want a war and two invasions and all of this destruction. Why did it have to happen to her family? Why her daddy?

She was crying so hard and so loudly she hadn't heard Joran come in, but she felt his hand on her back, and she looked, startled up at him. His eyes were reddened. He knew why she was crying. It was in his heart, too. She reached up and hugged him, still sitting in Keen's lap where she'd ended up, and Joran returned the warmth, wordlessly.

It was Joran that spoke first, "That's something the humans often don't understand but the shadowelves understand perfectly well," he said gesturing with his head back toward the direction of their mother's room, "When the humans destroy elven lives, they don't have any grasp of the impact it has on the mate, but the shadowelves know damn well that when they torment one of us, they torment two."

Keen glanced back through the archway toward Kierra's mother's bedchamber, horror dawning on his face.

"Well, at least my family won't be going through anything like that," he said simply.

Keen hadn't meant it, but the statement hit Kierra in the gut like nothing else maybe could have. She knew what it was like to have a loved one have marched off to war, never to come home. She knew what it was like day after day to wonder, to hope, to pray, to wish and deep down to know you will never really know. If her father hadn't had a living mate, they'd have never known anything.

"Oh, Keen," Kierra cried, "You can't do that to your family," and she fell on him and balled. It felt like it would destroy her, but once again she knew in her heart that she would have to let him go.

Over the course of the rest of the day, Kierra's mother came out of the room and joined in what had become a growing conversation between Keen, Joran and Kierra about Keen's family, and what his leaving them with no word and no closure would mean to them. Her mom was glad they were having the conversation openly. She'd always said that "open talk heals open wounds," and she was right. All of Kierra's guilt was melting away. She hated where she feared the conversation was going, but she no longer felt like she was taking advantage of Keen.

She learned that he'd lost his own father as a small child to a freak accident while the man was making repairs on their home. Keen himself had few memories of him. He'd been raised by a mother and a maternal grandmother who'd moved in to help her own youngest child raise three very young fatherless boys. Kierra enjoyed listening to Keen talk about his family. It was clear that he loved them, if for no other reason than the fact that he said so much once he got going. Kierra had never heard him talk for so long.

He'd had a sister that died before he was born. He had an older brother who thought he was the head of the house because their father was dead, a term that Keen had to explain, and which he waffled about when she asked. Apparently, males and females had different family roles and obligations in his culture. It seemed strange to Kierra, but she let it go.

He had a younger brother that, as Keen put it, was into anything "odd."

When pressed he explained that his younger brother couldn't keep his nose out of anything different, unusual or exotic. He loved to hear about faraway places, and always wanted to know why the old gods were so feared. He was the child growing up that if one child said there was a monster in the old shed, would insist on going to see for himself and would be heartily disappointed to find a broken down cart and moldy hay.

He had two nieces and a nephew, all by his older brother, and another one on the way. And the shocking revelation of the whole conversation came when Keen announced that he had 139 first cousins!

"A hundred and thirty-nine?" Kierra's mother exclaimed, "You're making that up! How could you possibly know them all?"

"Well, I'm really only close to about 17 of them," Keen mused, "But I'm not making it up. My mom's the youngest of twelve children, and my father was one of ten. On my mom's side, there's seventy-nine in my generation including me and my brothers, and there's sixty-six on my dad's, also including us three. So if you take us out of one side or the other, there's 142 in my generation, or 139 other than the three of us. There's already over 300 in my nieces' and nephew's generation. I couldn't possibly tell you who even a quarter of them are, although I could probably name the ones that have children..." he said shutting one eye, and looking up with the other as if he were really going to start recalling all of those names right there for them. Uncharacteristically, Joran was speechless. Kierra and her mother just laughed.

"Anyway," Keen went on without bothering with the name count, "It's my mom I think about most I guess. And, too, I'm a bit of a buffer in the family between Krieg and Kaith, my brothers. Krieg wanted to be career military, but he got wounded. So between thinking he's responsible for all of us and then that, he can be pretty uptight. He's a really good guy, but sometimes...well...a bit humorless. And he's got a temper. He'd never hurt anybody, mind you, but he can yell a lot."

"It's hard for us to think of someone who got wounded in your military as never having hurt anyone," said Joran curtly, "I'm sure you understand."

"Oh, no, He got wounded before we invaded here," Keen corrected, "See our last king couldn't really care less about elves as long as you minded your own business and just stayed out of our country. But King Olgar came from the

Meadows near the Barrow Hills and married our last king's daughter..."

"The Meadows?" exclaimed Joran, "There are very few humans in that country! That's an odd place for a human king to come from!"

Keen shrugged, "That's where he's from, and hardly anybody ever sees him. Shortly after he married the king's daughter, the old king took really ill and died. Then, all of a sudden elves minding their own business wasn't good enough anymore. And last year, he finally got enough support, I guess, to march the army over the border."

"But why?" asked Kierra.

Keen was looking at her. His eyes seemed to be full of love and pity, but she couldn't really be sure what he was feeling, "I don't really know. He wants to destroy Willowmark."

That statement sat heavily in the room like the thick black smoke of coal fire. But, again, Joran broke the silence, "We knew that."

"We did??" Kierra whipped around on her brother in shock.

He shrugged, "I've interrogated other humans. I told you that."

Keen sat a moment longer looking between them like he was considering what to say, or maybe even whether or not to keep talking, but he wrapped up what he had been saying with, "Krieg was wounded six years ago when cannon fire collapsed a wall he was standing on and he was buried alive for two days. Broke his ankle. He's fine now, but he can't run on that leg, so he can't be in the military. That was five years before we invaded the Willows. And I was just mentioning it to say that his and Kaith's temperament are so different. Kaith's really curious and funny and a little emotional really. And I have to get in the middle between them a lot." Keen sighed and looked up at the ceiling, "I guess no family's ever really right if someone's missing from them."

Kierra thought about her dad again, and how much he *belonged* here.

"No," she agreed begrudgingly, wanting desperately for Keen to belong here, too, "They're not."

And without much more conversation, Kierra convinced Keen that he really had to go back. In the end, he refused to go back to stay. He really wasn't going to leave Kierra. She threw her arms around him and refused to cry, just especially for him. Her mother smiled, and shed a few of the tears that Kierra missed. Joran smiled and nodded.

Keen seemed happy, even excited about the decision. He would go back, and explain his choice to his family. He would get to say goodbye and give them closure. Maybe they could even work out a way for him or them to visit occasionally, especially if the war ever ended. The important thing was that they'd know he was alive, not suffering, living a life he'd chosen, even happy. Hopefully they could have peace with that. He seemed to stumble over his mother as he talked, and Kierra suspected that his mother, like hers, would never really have peace over goodbye, but she didn't say anything else. She'd offered him yet another chance to leave, and he was choosing to return. If he came back, she could not let herself harbor guilt over that. She would choose to accept the love he was offering her at that point. And she sincerely hoped that day would come. But she couldn't ask him for it.

That night they made love like they might never have the chance again. Kierra tried to pretend it was merely raw passion and insisted on putting out of her mind the idea that it was, in fact, the truth that they might never have the chance again. She lay in his arms willing herself awake for most of the night, just for the memory of lying in his arms naked. She finally fell asleep near dawn.

Keen left very early the next day. Joran and Rana agreed to escort him to the border, which Kierra was immensely grateful for. She held in her tears, packed him food and bandages, and kissed him heartily goodbye.

"I'll see you before you know it," he assured her.

"I know it already," she teased with a smile.

He smiled back at her, kissed her again, and they were off.

The rest of the day was difficult for Kierra. She tried to sleep some. She looked after her mother some. Occasionally she got a pang in the pit of her stomach that Keen was hurt, but she knew that was just him traveling on that bad hip. The day was a daze. Her family tried to keep her occupied, all of them knowing what being separated from a lover for the first time was like. It was terrible.

That night Kierra forgot to check on her mother. She awoke sometime in the middle of the night and realized that she'd left her mom to her own nightmares. Feeling that familiar pang of guilt, she crept out of bed again, and down the familiar passages to her mom's room.

Sneaking in, she realized that her mother was sleeping less tensely than she had in nearly two months. Kierra watched her for a moment, wondering if exhaustion had simply won out, but fearing the worst for her father.

Her mother stirred, then tensed.

"Mama?" she whispered.

Her mother opened her eyes.

"Kierra?"

"You tensed. You OK?"

Her mother breathed in deeply and looked around the room, seemingly confused, then looked over to the door where Kierra was standing bathed in moonlight.

"Something's changed..." she whispered.

Kierra took in a breath that caught in her throat. No. And yet, maybe it's best. She wanted to cry. She didn't want to lose her daddy...

"He...he feels different..."

Kierra didn't want to know the answer, but she knew she needed to know, "Different, how, mama?"

Her mother took in a deep breath and kept looking around the room as if she couldn't quite see it, "Before when I could sense his pain it was...terrorizing...it's been driving me insane..." she was gripping the covers again, the memory of her own torments flooding back to her, but then her hands relaxed, "But now...he's still hurting...I can feel him hurting," her voice cracked as tears started to flow at the thought of her lover's pain, "But it's not terrorizing me. It's just, like, tension...just a sense that he's there almost, but not all the insanity...I don't know. It's just....different...."

She drifted back to sleep and didn't seem to be having nightmares. Kierra watched her for a while longer. Her mother had probably not had really good sleep in six weeks. But she wondered what this change could mean.

The shadowelves were known for eventually leaving prisoners where they could be found: dead and mangled or half-dead and beyond saving. It wasn't enough that they destroyed lives in their path, they seemed intent on instilling terror in those that remained free. It was sick. Could they be moving him? Could they be preparing to leave him somewhere for a passing unit along the border to discover?

If so, his ordeal would at least be over soon, thought Kierra, fresh tears running down her face. She didn't dare hope. That was the part of the war they'd already won. They'd already conquered hope.

Two days later, there were still no answers. Kierra woke on her second morning without Keen and her second morning since her mother had been seemingly freed from her daily torment. Kierra's Aunt Riella had experienced the same change the same night. But both women could feel that their mates were still suffering and so were not dead.

So, two days later, Kierra began to make breakfast, focusing on the task at hand. There were too many things anymore that she had to try to keep her mind off of. She sliced fresh fruit and then sliced bread. She set the knife down and reached for the small crockery of butter when she doubled over, clutching her stomach.

Keen. Keen was in mortal danger. And he was far away. It felt like a knife to her gut and it was twisting. He was walking into a trap, and she might be too far away to stop it.

Joran and Rana weren't back yet. In fact, it was likely they were just walking away from the river now as he was crossing it. Jerith.

Blinded to everything that was not Keen, Kierra put down what she was working on and ran for her Aunt Riella's cottage across the little village green. Jerith. Nira. Please. Spirits of the forest, she prayed, please hear my prayer. I surround Keen in your Light. Protect him. I'm coming. I'm coming.

But at best, her coming was going to take days...

Jesp

Jesp and Kyrt snuggled into their saddle bags together after the longest night in the history of long nights. They'd tried to be very quiet and not wake the people who'd be responsible for getting them all around the shadowelves the next day, but they couldn't help spending their entire nightwatch talking themselves round and around in circles about the fate of the Garden and its occupants. Would they flee? No. Of course not. All of their family and friends would think the crown was still there and so would stay and fight: to the death if need be.

Maybe they would check. Maybe they would come up with the idea of taking the crown and fleeing. No. Once they realized the crown was gone, they'd stay and look for it.

What had they done?

What they'd done, Jesp and Kyrt had concluded over and over again all night long, was condemn every one of their loved ones to death at the hands of shadowelves. They'd meant to be doing the right thing. They thought they were doing what they were supposed to do by protecting the crown. But in truth, they'd let someone who was not fae talk them into making a rash decision without the advice of the others of their kind. And now those others will have paid for that.

Harold and Tollie had meant well, but the Garden Circle should have been told. Jesp and Kyrt had a responsibility to their own, and they'd failed them. They gotten caught up in the excitement of the moment and they hadn't taken responsibility, and now it was likely that people had died: a lot of people.

Tollie had offered them breakfast. They just shook their heads and climbed into their bumpy, itchy, hot beds. Tollie didn't say anything else and neither did they. It couldn't be fixed now. It was too late. That's the problem with rash decisions, Jesp thought as she shut her eyes and tried to drown out the sobbing in her brain, you can't take them back once you realize how bad they are.

She could hear Tollie in her head saying, "Heroes aren't perfect; they're just people." Yeah, thought Jesp, really dumb, stupid, thoughtless people who don't deserve to be called heroes at all. What was I thinking that I could ever have made a guard? She thought about her parents and swallowed. Or even a good daughter? And she started to cry again. She'd done so much of that all night long. Even Kyrt had. It really had been a long night.

Eventually Jesp fell asleep. She assumed Kyrt did, too. They didn't speak anymore after they went to bed, and although she knew that she was crying as quietly as she could into the lump of burlap that was passing for her pillow, she didn't hear another noise out of her lover. Her sleep was uneasy. She was vaguely aware of being sweaty and uncomfortable and of dreams plagued by the funerals of her parents and the scolding accusations of her tormented friends. She could see the Garden simultaneously burned to the ground, dug up and flooded, haunted and ghost-like and pristine and untouched like the day she left it. Nevertheless, she must have slept somewhat, because at some point she became vaguely aware that it was darker outside than it had been for most of the rest of her time of self-torment-in-a-bag.

Darker would mean that they were stopping soon, and that the faeries would be on yet another long night's watch. Jesp both dreaded it, and looked forward to at least not being alone in her misery any more. She realized that the pony was, in fact, still, but decided to wait until Tollie came to rouse her. She waited.

She wondered vaguely if Tollie thought any less of her now that she'd had a chance to realize, too, that Jesp and Kyrt shouldn't have run off with the crown like they had. Or if Tallie and Thomas would have advised the fae differently. Jesp turned over in her saddle bag listening for the sound of Tollie bringing supper. Funny. She didn't even smell food. She listened a little more intently. They must have only just stopped.

Everything seemed eerily quiet all around her. The pony moved again, like it was wandering over to some grass. Should it be free to be doing that? Jesp waited some more, then stuck her head out of her bag and looked around.

It was very dark, not just dusk as she would have expected as the time she would have been awoken, and the ponies seemed to be wandering riderless and gnawing on whatever undergrowth they found intriguing. Jesp climbed anxiously up and out onto the the...

The crown was gone!!

"Kyrt!" she whispered urgently to the lump on the other side of the missing crown bag. She shook at him desperately, "Kyrt!!!"

"Hmmmm?" he came around groggily, looking disheveled and poorly rested.

"The halflings and the crown are all missing!!!"

Kyrt shot out of the bag and onto his wings in a flash. Jesp was retrieving her weapons from the saddlebags as Kyrt exclaimed, "No, here's Tollie here!"

Jesp handed him his bow and raced down to where Tollie lay on the ground on Kyrt's side of the pony some distance back from where the pony had wandered. She had a lump on her head and was out cold. A quick search turned up an unconscious Thomas as well, but Tallie was nowhere to be found, and neither was the crown.

Tollie's head wound appeared large and awful to Jesp, but compared to the size of her head was hopefully minor. And it appeared to have come from her fall from the pony, rather than her having been struck. Kyrt went to find her bandages while Jesp investigated her injury and she discovered another disturbing clue: the faeries' own arrow poison they had just mixed up before the trip had been removed, and most of it was missing.

"Jesp, if she used this much on the two of them, they're lucky to be breathing!"

Searching Tollie again, Jesp found what looked like little more than a toothpick stuck in her shoulder and a similar projectile was found near Thomas. A wooden straw like a blow-dart gun had been left not far back behind them. Tallie had often ridden in the back, Jesp remembered, her heart sinking as she looked down at the face of her friend whose chest she was standing on. This news was going to crush Tollie.

And it cemented Jesp's sense of having failed the Garden, too. Now, they hadn't even saved the crown. She looked over at Kyrt who looked more furious than she'd ever seen him. Jesp, however, found that she lacked the tears to cry.

It was another long night. The faeries couldn't move the halflings. They were able to use bits of dried fruits they found in the saddlebags to lure the ponies over to trees where they could be tied up. It then took them hours to drag water in small containers up to where the ponies could reach it, but they managed to water them, more or less, enough at least to keep them from becoming unhealthy.

They managed, also, out of breath and exhausted though they were, to trickle water into both Tollie and Thomas using larger sturdier leaves and bravery. It had never occurred to either fae before now, that the halflings could bite their legs off, but they certainly could.

It was nearly dawn when Thomas finally started to stir, and the sun was up before he was awake enough to be useful at all. He went to Tollie first. He was much more able than the faeries had been at getting some water into her and then moving her gently into the shade of a tree. He checked the knot on her head and pronounced it to be "not that bad," but he looked worried.

He watered the ponies and fed them from the packed feed explaining that it was better for them than the scrub and grass they were eating. He seemed to be going through automatic motions without putting much thought into them, Jesp thought to herself, and she wondered if he could stand the idea that Tallie had betrayed them.

Several hours later, Tollie woke up. It was drizzling lightly by then and Thomas was sitting next to her with broth and with a pair of faeries in his lap eating the last good strawberry. Jesp let Thomas explain. It seemed kinder. Jesp was so angry, she knew she was going to say something she shouldn't, although if she was honest, she was mostly angry at herself. Kyrt was so busy fuming, he'd managed to smear strawberry all over his face and hadn't said a word since Thomas had woken up, except to thank him for getting the piece of fruit out. Jesp didn't have to try very hard to follow him to where he'd gone. She wasn't very far behind him on that path.

Tollie cried quietly for a while, and stammered something about just wanting to have a family again. Jesp would like that, too, she thought bitterly to herself, but she had sense enough, she thought, not to say so. Jesp hated not to be there for Tollie this time, but she really left that to Thomas and paid little attention to their conversations about Tallie. She and Kyrt destroyed their helpless strawberry, and Jesp tried to pretend she wasn't enjoying the bloody-looking mess they were creating out of it.

Eventually, Tollie stood up. She looked woosy and off-balance. Thomas, who had long since stopped paying attention to the messy faeries in his lap, stood up to catch her, knocking them into the air mere inches from the ground. The last of the strawberry rolled gratefully into the dirt and leaves.

"Oops, sorry," he apologized as he stepped on it, splashing the last of its juice onto Jesp's feet.

Jesp and Kyrt immediately rose higher into the air, not wanting to meet the same fate as the strawberry.

"So, do you guys remember anything?" Kyrt asked them both, a hint of accusation in his voice in Jesp's opinion. She shot him what she hoped was a quizzical look. His arms were folded over his chest, and he wasn't paying Jesp any attention.

Thomas looked down at the two fae guiltily. "I think I kind of remember maybe a bee sting? Then I got all drunk feeling and dizzy, so I got down off of Robin before I fell off...or threw up. The last thing I remember is looking up at Robin's four pony feet and wondering how I'd gotten all the way onto my back."

Tollie shook her head slowly, then held it with both hands as if she needed to steady it again. "I don't even remember that. I think I remember hearing you say something about a bee, and then feeling a sting, too. Maybe. But I might even be making that up. I don't even know. What I do know," and here she drew herself up as tall as she could, "is that we can't just sit here feeling sorry for ourselves. We're going after that crown. Tallie underestimated us if she thinks we're gonna just sit here and wish we hadn't trusted her. Does she not think we won't go all the way back to Brewhall for it?"

Jesp shot into the air and circled Tollie's head. It was the only way to express the explosion of gratitude she suddenly felt for her friend. Damn right, she thought. We're coming for you, Tallie. Traitor.

They set out immediately. Tollie was still shaky, but only in body, not in resolve. She leaned forward on Sally, her pony, and gripped the reins tightly with both fists. Jesp and Kyrt rode Molly, Tallie's pony, each taking a side of the reins where Tallie's hands would have gone, though the fact that Thomas had secured the pony to the back of his own probably had more to do with their success in steering. Thomas didn't ride; he led Robin forward as he tried to track Tallie through the underbrush.

At first, this seemed simple enough for him to do, but then he began to hesitate. Apparently, to Thomas, the tracks appeared to have been altered.

"What do you mean, altered?" asked Tollie.

"Well, it's kind of a sloppy job, so I'm not sure what she was trying to do exactly. It looks like she tried to make new tracks and hide old ones. One thing's for sure, though, she wasn't alone, but she wanted us to think she was. She had at least one and maybe two people with her. The good news is, this mess will have slowed them down. I think these are the real ones. They went that way," and he pointed off into thicker brush that nonetheless did lead in a straighter line back toward Brewhall.

Jesp flew low over the dirt. She'd often studied the ground in the garden, but never truly unkempt ground like out here. But she was impressed with Thomas. He reminded her of Harold back home. There was obviously disturbed plant life and easy-to-see footprints leading off in a direction that would have avoided more of the undergrowth. If none of them had been paying attention, they'd have followed that trail without question. Jesp didn't really see what Thomas saw, but something certainly was wrong with the bush he was looking at. It was a juniper, and although it hadn't exactly been trampled, it had been bent rather rudely and had snapped back poorly. Jesp didn't see how Thomas was getting the idea that there had been more than one person, but she was convinced that he knew what he was talking about.

They set off in that direction. Jesp couldn't imagine that they were being slowed down any less trying to follow the trail than Tallie was trying to conceal it, but after about an hour it paid off. Apparently, she and whoever was helping her assumed they'd done a good enough job by that point that they didn't need to keep trying. Very suddenly, the tracks became abrupt and clear. Now, Jesp had to concede, Tallie couldn't have been making this mess by herself.

Despite the fact that none of them had eaten since mid-morning, and all of them were hungry and tired, and two of them were beginning to feel ill from the effects of the poison, they continued to press on as the sun was struggling to be seen above the canopy of the forest. It was fortunate for them that the trail was no longer difficult to follow, because even Thomas was waning in his ability to focus by dusk.

But that was just when they heard something moving ahead of them.

Whatever it was, it was larger than a rabbit, slower than a deer, and moaning like a wounded boar. Thomas pulled a large dagger from his belt and the faeries raised their bows. Tollie got down off of Sally and crouched behind her.

Thomas nodded at Jesp and Kyrt who flew forward above the noise-maker. It lurched forward with a bloody moan through the ivy beneath them, its curly brown hair, matted with leaves, but its clothing unmistakable. It was Tallie.

She had a dagger protruding from her back, and with her head down in shear effort, trying desperately to keep struggling forward, she hadn't seen the faeries. She was headed, not away from them, but back toward them.

Kyrt and Jesp lowered their bows, looking at each other with concern and curiosity. Jesp cocked her head toward Thomas, trying to suggest to Kyrt that he fly back to the others. He got the message. Jesp flew down to Tallie.

Jesp landed on a soft, moss-covered holly bush by her head.

"Tallie?"

Tallie's head shot up. She had a near-crazed look in her eye that turned to relief as she recognized Jesp. Blood trickled from the side of her mouth and she fell over to her side as she whispered, "Thomas...he...betrayed us."

Jesp's head was still ringing from the accusation, as the other three reached the now-unconscious form of Tollie's sister. Jesp looked at Tollie's grief-stricken eyes, filled with shock and horror, and knew that she was only going to make it worse. Tollie already appeared torn between so many different emotions as she watched her probably-dying sister be treated, bandaged and carried back to her pony.

"Tollie," Jesp began gently after flying over to where just she and Kyrt could possibly hear her whisper, "You guys should know that before she passed out, Tallie insinuated that Thomas was to blame for this."

"What do you mean?" Tollie gasped looking back at the halfling fellow that, Jesp had to admit, she really liked as a match for Tollie.

"Tallie said it was Thomas that betrayed us."

"How could that possibly be right?" Kyrt asked, a befuddled expression across his handsome face. Jesp shook that last thought about his face out of her head and shrugged.

"I have a feeling there are more twists to this story yet. Thomas did seem to know that more people were involved when no one else could see any other tracks."

"I thought that was just because he was a good tracker," Tollie said dejectedly, and Kyrt nodded.

"Well, yes," Jesp agreed, "But where are they? And where is the crown?"

"And what happened to my sister?"

Thomas had joined them by this point and he immediately asked the question no one wanted to answer, "Did she say anything?"

All three looked guiltily from one to the other. Shockingly, in Jesp's opinion, Tollie went straight for honesty, "She said it was you, Thomas."

"Me?" he said incredulously, "How could she possibly expect anyone to believe that? I was with you guys!"

"I don't know," Jesp admitted, "It'll have to be one heck of a story."

But it wasn't. She told it over the meager rations that passed for that night's supper, and it was more mysterious than what they knew so far. Tallie came to about an hour later after some water and broth were fed into her. Thomas kept looking at her like she might explode. Jesp though she could kind of understand since they all expected her to accuse him of treachery as soon as she could speak, which she did.

According to Tallie, who was weak, and couldn't speak for long or give much detail, she'd been grabbed from behind by someone who'd dropped from the trees onto the pony behind her. They'd put a sack over her head before she could see them, but they'd told her that she'd be going back with them because "Thomas" had told them that she'd be worth money alive back in Brewhall. She also overheard a female telling "Thomas" to hurry up with hiding the tracks so he could "get back." Thomas, of course, vehemently denied that it was him, and was aghast that Tallie could accuse him of such a thing as long as she'd known him.

Of course, a teary argument ensued, as much as Tallie could participate anyway. She was heartbroken that any of them could have believed that she could have betrayed them, although Jesp thought that Thomas secretly wanted to find a way back to that version of the story. Tollie cared for Tallie as best she could, but by the middle of the night, everyone was exhausted beyond the point of rationality.

Tallie was fast asleep anyway. Thomas had lost everyone's trust, although not completely. Jesp hadn't exactly taken a poll around the small camp, but she was fairly certain that the other two, like herself, was having a hard time with Tallie's story. It had been hard to believe that Tallie would betray them, but somehow, Thomas was even more difficult to blame.

Jesp and Kyrt offered to keep watch for as long as they could so the halflings could sleep. They had, at least, had non-poisoned sleep most recently. They nearly made it until dawn, but they knew that each passing hour placed the crown farther and farther from their possession. That thought was the fire that kept them awake. They talked very little as the night wore on, except to remind each other that the halflings would be able to drive the ponies back toward Brewhall and the crown, the more sleep they got...the more sleep they got...

But the faeries couldn't quite make it to sunrise. They were nodding off into their own bows. Jesp's first instinct was to wake Thomas, but she stopped herself and looked sadly back at Kyrt, who breathed heavily and said, "You know, if we both go to sleep, we're leaving Tollie in the same situation she was in when this happened in the first place."

"What have we got left to steal?"

"The books? Tallie is apparently worth something. And, if we still have a traitor among us, they'll want to stop us from going back." Kyrt was being very matter-of-fact, despite being very drowsy, or perhaps because of it, but he was also being very right, and Jesp knew it.

"What should we do?"

"Well, for starters, we should have thought of this before now," he admitted, "But we didn't. Second, I don't think we have a choice but to do it anyway and maybe point it out to Tollie so she's on her guard, because I don't think either of us could stay up any longer if we wanted to."

Jesp shook her head, "I'll stay up. You get a couple of hours. I'll ride with Tollie and then trade places with you. We can't leave her alone right now. I may be dead tired but I'm also dead angry, and that'll get me a second wind here eventually."

"You sure?" he asked looking guilty, "I could stay up."

"Nope. I got it. Go to bed," and she kissed him. She hadn't gotten to in a couple of days, and it made him smile. She still had Kyrt, and gratitude for him washed over her like a refreshing wave. "There," she grinned, "That was all I needed."

Kyrt flew off to his saddle bag bed, and Jesp roused Tollie gently, "Hey," she shook her awake, "I'm going to stay up with you for awhile."

Tollie looked up at her gratefully and nodded. Her face looked tear-stained, her eyes were blood-shot. Tollie really needed a break, thought Jesp. She thought she remembered from her songs that Alura, the Goddess of all fragile life, the one that the faeries had once served, had taken in the halflings at her temples and that they still revered her for it, even though most of the races had turned away from the old gods. Alura, thought Jesp, this one needs a break.

Tollie and Jesp got Thomas and Tallie up for breakfast. Both of them eyed each other suspiciously but sadly. Strange, thought Jesp, they didn't even seem angry, just really sorry. They must have been close. Jesp sat up on Sally until they left. She didn't have any more energy than that.

It was while Thomas and Tollie were trying to help Tallie onto Molly that Jesp saw a very strange sight coming through the woods behind them. "Uh, guys?" was all she managed to say.

It looked like a black bag, maybe with straps, like a backpack, flying by itself on four pairs of butterfly wings. Jesp would have thought faery wings, but the colors were wrong. Each was a mix of the seasonal combinations that differentiated the varieties of fae back home. Although, she had seen those strange fae in the Meadows. They had wings like these: all mixed up and colorful.

"Guys?"

Thomas and Tollie joined Jesp fairly quickly. Thomas had his long dagger out again. Jesp felt simultaneously nervous and comforted by it. Tallie was struggling to get down off of her pony by herself, so Tollie told her just to stay where she was.

Kyrt heard the commotion and came out of his saddle bag with his bow ready. They had just assembled, when the strange flying creature reached them. It was, in fact, a backpack. A backpack being flown by faeries.

These were the same odd type of fae that they had seen at Tollie and Tallie's family home, the night that they had first met Fluffy. They had weapons flung over their backs, and even tucked into their belts, but struggling as they were with the weight of the bag, they didn't have any drawn. Therefore, Jesp, Kyrt and

Thomas lowered theirs.

They flew over to Sally and sat the bag down on top of her saddle. Then the four of them sat down on top of it, and Jesp realized that these weren't just *like* the four they had met before, they were, in fact, the same four. She tightened her grip on her bow and looked over at Kyrt. He glanced at her and nodded before looking back at them.

"Thought you'd want this back," one with yellow, purple, and pink wings said with a smile that showed at least one metallic tooth. His face, like the others was painted, maybe even tattooed, across one eye and down the side of his face in a swirled pattern that matched, as all of theirs did, at least two colors from his own wings, in his case the yellow and purple. To Jesp, this made him a strange mix of summer, spring and autumn like herself, with none of Kyrt's gorgeous winter. The others had similarly confusing combinations.

Kyrt flew over to the bag. The strange fae watched him, but they moved enough for him to investigate through the bag's opening.

"It's the crown," he confirmed breathlessly.

Jesp closed her eyes and breathed a sigh of relief. Then she opened them and smiled broadly at the new faeries. "How did you get it?"

"Oh we stole it from you," admitted a winter/spring mixed female brazenly and another one next to her giggled, "But we didn't realize what it was they'd had us steal until we'd gotten away. We don't steal faerie artifacts. That was their mistake. Stupid elves. They should have known better."

"Anyway," continued the first male, "They're going to know it was us that took it back, and you're not that far behind them, so you need to make fast tracks in the other direction like yesterday."

Jesp looked over at Tollie, standing sadly between her sister and her would-be-suitor.

"Who? Who did this?"

"Two elves. Morrowelves. They work for Lord Greening, the old Library Chancellor that got shafted by that halfling. Maeve and Thomas, I think their names are. Anyway, what difference does it make? You need to go."

"We'll leave in a minute," Jesp exclaimed, a little more angrily than she had intended, "They'd be fools to come up on us right now while we're armed and looking for them. I want a few more answers."

She locked eyes with the male that spoke first. She'd never met a fae like him, and she didn't trust him. As far as Jesp was concerned, Thomas and Tallie were cleared, but not these guys. Not yet.

And more importantly, they knew some things that Jesp wanted to know, and she'd risk another ambush they knew was coming from only two elves, one of whom they'd defeated before, to get those answers. Jesp was taking charge.

"First of all, Kyrt, check and make sure that's the real thing."

"How?"

"I don't know, but get it out and get a better look at it, please. Second, who are you? And did you say they work for Lord Greening? I thought he was just a lawyer thing...person...or whatever. I'm confused."

"No," said Tallie, "Lord Elmer Greening was the Library Chancellor when Preslor Remling was Lord Librarian. Remling had the post before Dad. Greening was the one everybody expected to get promoted, but the Library elders brought Dad in instead, mostly because they didn't trust Greening. He became the Chancellor at Ash Lake for a while after that, but yes, I had heard that he was working as an attorney along the border towns here recently. I don't know why."

"See, you don't need us," the winter/spring female mused, nudging another male, a summer/winter/autumn, to make to leave.

"Don't leave yet," Thomas said, and grabbed the female out of the air. This alarmed Jesp, and caused the three males with her, to draw their weapons. Thomas wasn't playing games, either, he drew his large dagger across her neck, "You can fill me full of poison darts, but she'll die as I fall, so I'd put those down if I were you."

The three males looked mutinous, but they lowered their weapons. They glowered back at Jesp, who felt totally in control. At first she wasn't sure what Thomas was doing, but more and more she was becoming convinced that he was, in fact, on the right side.

"I didn't remember Lord Greening's name," admitted Tollie quietly.

"Oh I doubt I learned his name until I was back in Brewhall. What does that matter?"

"It matters," answered Jesp, "Because we've met him before. But we'll talk about that later. Who are you, and how are you mixed up with Maeve and Thomas?

Why did they take Tallie...although we probably can guess that answer...and why did you bring the crown back, assuming that you did?" and at this she looked at Kyrt who was now struggling to pull the crown out of the backpack.

Tollie and Tallie both reached to help him and neither Jesp nor Kyrt refused their help. The tension was gone between the three of them, and that was such a relief it was momentarily replacing sleep for Jesp.

The male that had nearly been encouraged to leave with the now-captive and clearly terrified female spoke up, "We're members of one of the Meadows tribes. It won't matter to you which one, because we're not in any of your precious songs. We're a small tribe, and because the Brewer's Guild essentially owns all of our tribal lands, we have to work for them, like mercenaries, whether we like it or not."

"That's not right!" protested Tallie.

"Yes, well," he continued, rolling his eyes, "Anyway, we were supposed to help Maeve and Thomas steal a particular bag off of one of the ponies. In exchange for our help, the Brewhall bastards were supposed to get Tallie. But then after we got away, we realized what we stole, so we came back. Doesn't matter cuz Tallie here got away anyway, so they can't go back to Brewhall. Anything else? Can we have Kibeesy back?" He was beginning to look genuinely worried.

Thomas had one other thing to say, "So, was anyone else involved? Other than the two elves and the Brewer's Guild? Anyone?"

The three male fae shrugged, "Not that we know of."

And Thomas let the female named Kibeesy go. She flew back to her group and, just like they had done back in the Meadows, they flew off in a diagonal formation.

Jesp looked at Kyrt who was smiling.

"What?" Jesp asked curiously.

"When I was pulling the crown out of the ground I hit the bag pretty hard against a rock in the Garden. We'd never pulled it all the way out and really looked at it. But I scratched it. There's a ding in it right here, on the opposite side from the part we've always seen from the opening, which is the part opposite from where I would have been carrying it. It's right where I would have hit that rock."

Thomas looked at the crown he was helping Kyrt to hold aloft. It was a circlet of braided metals: three different metals in three different colors, braided together. They'd taken it out of its bag once, so they knew that the braids flattened out in the back into three straight lines that would sit low on someone's head, and that there were three gemstones set into the front: one a clear diamond, one an amber-colored diamond and in the middle, a large ruby. But they'd never really investigated it. It was really in pretty good shape, despite being quite dirty, and lightly scratched, but there was, just over what would be a wearer's left ear, a definite dent.

Looking up from the piece Thomas shook his head, "Unless they had a drawing or replica to go off of somewhere, this is too detailed to have copied that fast, even in a city, which we're nowhere near. Is there anyway they could have had a copy made ahead of time? Is there a picture anywhere?"

Jesp and Kyrt looked desperately at Tollie. Please say no, Jesp shouted in her head, and please don't be lying.

But Tollie only shrugged, "I don't think there's anyway to know for sure, except that there's not one in any of the books my father rescued, and he seemed to know what was going on. So, that makes me think not."

"I'd be inclined to doubt it, too," Tallie agreed, "I've never read any reference to a depiction of the crown of Andarraine. All the old statues of the royal family were smashed and the paintings were burned. I don't know where else you'd get a copy of the crown."

"Why?" asked Jesp.

"People thought they were evil," Tallie answered, "Them and their gods."

"Wow," said Thomas, "Just wow. So, Tallie, how did you end up with a knife in your back?"

"That doesn't matter. I feel like I put one in yours when I got back. I'm so sorry, Thomas. I'm just...I'm so sorry."

Thomas shook his head, "No, don't be. That wasn't any fun, but you heard what you heard and you had to tell it. That's what you should have done, I guess. But hopefully we all know now we can trust each other. But the knife? I'd still like the rest of the story."

"Well, I didn't realize they had the crown. I thought they'd just taken me. I fought and I fought and I fought, because I sure as heck did NOT want to be drug back to Brewhall like that. They eventually decided that it wasn't worth it and tried to kill me and leave me, so I tried to make it back to you. I guess I should have realized then that I wasn't what they were really after, but by then I had a knife in my back, and wasn't thinking about anything else."

"Oh, Tallie!" Tollie flung herself on her sister, who was still weak and laid against her pony's neck, but had more color at least in her lips and around her eyes than she had when she was found. Thomas smiled weakly at the two of them and looked at the two fae. He was still holding the crown really more than Kyrt was, so he began, with Kyrt's assistance, to put it back in its new bag.

Convinced that they had the crown back, Jesp excused herself to some well-deserved sleep. She'd been awake now for over 30 hours, and she could hardly fly over to Sally to collapse into a saddle bag. No one argued. She didn't even bother to find out how any other watch would be divided. She just passed out.

She was nudged gently awake by Tollie sometime after dark. Tollie had hot oatmeal and honey for her supper.

"We've split the watches. It was Kyrt's idea, although I think he regretted it as soon as he said it," she smiled, "We tied Tallie to her pony and pulled her along. I don't know how well she slept, but she's your partner for the night. Kyrt pointed out that the two of you are unexpected, and so having one on each watch is a benefit. I don't think either Tallie or Thomas was offended either, which was nice."

Jesp flew to the saddle where Kyrt was sleepily eating some oatmeal before climbing into bed. He hadn't had much sleep at all now in 2 days, and it showed.

"I'll miss you tonight."

He smiled, "Do you know how long I wanted to hear you say that?"

She kissed his cheek. He finished his supper and climbed into the warm spot in the bag she'd left behind. She watched him for a moment and realized how much she'd like to climb in there with him. She looked up and realized that 3 pairs of halfling eyes were watching her. They all looked away quickly, grinning and blushing. She glared at the tops of their heads, grinned back down at Kyrt, and then finished her meal.

She and Tallie sat up all night. Tallie was still weak and sore, but she was fairly alert. She was angry. They all were by this point, but Tallie was really starting to fume.

"Sooooo," Jesp ventured carefully, "You've left. Isn't that good enough for those bastards?"

"Oh, no," steamed Tallie, "No, I wouldn't have let my Dad down like that. See, I didn't just get appointed to the governing board of the school, my parents inherited over a third of the school between them, which they've left to me. Tollie's getting everything else, I don't know if she even knows anything about their will, but I got the school. I've been using my own wages over the last few years to buy out those few folks who were still clinging on solely because they were loyal to the school and its reputation, but who otherwise really wanted to move on. They wouldn't sell to the Guild at any price, but they sold to me for cheap, which has really angered the Guild like you would not believe. So, I now own just over half of the school by itself. The Brewer's Guild and their cronies have tried to buy as much of it as they could, but they've only gotten about a third. That's because Thomas' Dad owns the rest, and he won't sell. He's opened another private school in the Meadows that's starting to do really well, and he wants the reputation of Brewhall Academy to remain strong because he's built his new school's reputation on the affiliation.

Anyway, I've left my share to be managed in my absence by Thomas' three older brothers, and if I die, Tollie gets it, or it goes to Thomas' family. So, the only way the Brewer's Guild can get what they want is to get their hands on me alive and force me to sell, change my will or change my policies in writing. Otherwise, they can't get around me." She smiled broadly, "And now that they've driven me out, they've screwed themselves up even worse, because I suspect that Thomas' family will move the whole school's basic academic structure to Goldenrod Level where Level Means Boarding School is, which will be bad news for the town of Brewhall. That breaks my heart, but it's the Guild's fault, not mine." her voice had become quite staccato toward the end of that statement, and Jesp detected the remorse she was trying not to claim. Still, Jesp liked hearing that the bad guys weren't going to win. That sounded good.

But it also made it clear why Tallie naming Thomas as a traitor had been so hard for both of them. Clearly, Tallie trusted no one more than Thomas' family. That must have broken both of their hearts, like naming Kyrt a traitor would have done to Jesp. She knew Thomas wasn't a romantic interest of Tallie's, but still. Thomas was clearly a *fixture,* and nothing seemed more important than that right now in their lives.

The night passed. Tallie and Jesp were both on edge and several passing deer and who-knows-what-other animals that passed by in the dark had nearly been skewered as a result. When daylight broke, Jesp realized that they'd only made it back as far as they'd gotten before they'd been attacked. Although Thomas had obviously been careful enough not to put them in the same place twice, Jesp recognized a bend in the stream where she'd braced a leaf trying to get water for ponies when Thomas and Tollie were unconscious. She pointed this out to Tallie, and they woke everyone with a sense of urgency to get moving again.

Jesp had a lot of trouble sleeping the next day. The relative lack of motion after about mid-morning wasn't bad, but the sawing, hacking and crashing going on all around her was terrible. Several times she stuck her head out groggily and snarled for which she received apologies. By mid-afternoon, Jesp was moved onto Tallie's pony which was moved further away from where, evidently, Tollie and Thomas were attempting to build a raft. Kyrt stood guard over the two sleeping people, which was a better situation for Tallie, who elected to curl up instead in the ivy under a tree. As a result, Kyrt invited himself into Jesp's saddle bag for a while, which resulted in Jesp losing even more sleep, but she hardly minded.

That night a very sleepy Jesp and a slightly better-rested Tallie watched over the riverside camp and half-finished raft-making site. The far bank of the river was eerily quiet and the shadows were unnaturally deep. Jesp found herself wishing dearly that the others hadn't drawn nearly so much attention to themselves during the day. Nonetheless, dawn broke with a light drizzle, and just as quiet as the night had been.

Despite the rain, Jesp slept better the next day. She expected the continued work on the raft, and she'd started her day's sleep farther away from it. She also got her romp with Kyrt out of the way before falling asleep, rather than in the middle of the day.

When Kyrt woke her for her night watch, he warned her that they'd seen movement across the water on the shores of the Darkwald, a fact that had made Thomas especially nervous. They'd moved their camp and their now-finished raft up and away from the river bank.

But despite the risk, Jesp and Tallie took turns sneaking down to the riverbank for a quick bath. Despite all of the risk-taking and noise during the day, the night was fine, and Jesp was starting, once again to get her hopes up that they might successfully get the crown safely to Willowmark.

Jesp had a little more trouble sleeping through the raft being dragged, carried, hoisted, cussed at and whatever else was going on out there as they tried to get the thing up the river bank to wherever it was that they intended to cross. Apparently, the trees they needed didn't have the decency to grow closer to the shoreline they required. But eventually she drifted off to sleep. Drifted, being an appropriate term for the sensation she had, once the pony stopped walking for just long enough for her to float off to sleep.

When Jesp awoke after dusk for supper, they were across the river and just inside the Willows, but they had a problem. Although they'd crossed back into the Morrowlands before crossing the river, thus ensuring that they'd cross into the Willows and not into the Darkwald, they had, in fact verified that a shadowelf army was encamped on the banks right in their path. If they crossed back over the river, they ran the risk of coming too close to the Library with the very items the Library was being scoured for. But, Thomas assured them, they were no match for shadowelf scouts if there were any in this part of the forest, and as the Darkwald was already invading the Willows, the presence of that small camp meant that there would be.

The group decided instead for another route. They decided to try to go straight down the middle of the river at night. It probably wasn't much less risky, but they couldn't think of a particularly good option that they had left.

They piled their bags and gear on top of their raft with the faeries, trying to lay it all as flat as they could. Then the halflings tied the ponies to the front of the raft. Tollie and Tallie each took hold of one side of the raft and Thomas led the ponies as together they dragged, and the faeries rode, the raft back out into the water.

The halflings all tried to keep their heads just barely out of the water. Each of the sisters was holding onto one side of the raft, and Thomas was leading the ponies as they swam, pulling the raft upstream. The faeries had their bows out and stood in the midst of their packs watching for trouble.

And that's the thing about faeries: no one expects them. And that's what killed both shadowelves that dropped down onto the raft from their lofty hiding places in the leafy canopy that draped over the river. Bows drawn, they'd spotted the halflings in the water, and were seconds from piercing both Tollie and Tallie through the head. But that was seconds too late. The faeries with poisoned arrows hidden in the baggage where the ambush landed were slightly faster. The elves dropped to the raft, then dropped in the water where they drowned.

After that, Thomas pulled the ponies closer to the Morrowlands side of the river, but as the narrow ford that once joined routes from the Willows to the Library loomed nearer, it became clear that they were headed straight into trouble. Campfires could be seen on both sides of the river, and in the distance, there was smoke visible on the horizon. It appeared that the Library truly had fallen.

As they approached closer, Jesp could just make out ropes that had been strung across the two banks to make a simpler ferry system connecting the camps on both sides to one another. That meant that both were shadowelf camps. And if they held both sides of the river, then they had the river itself and would be watching.

Jesp thought about flying low over the water and asking Thomas what he thought they should do, but leaving her hiding place among the bags risked revealing their secret weapon to the enemy, and that put them all in greater danger. She was helpless. Whatever Thomas decided to do now would be their fate. And if he really was a traitor, he could hand them over to the shadowelves, literally on a rope, and they could do nothing about it. After all, if it was the shadowelves that overran Alderbrook and the Library, then most likely, they were somehow behind the whole thing to get the crown.

Jesp swallowed hard. Please, Thomas. Please don't be swimming us right into the hands of the enemy. At least not on purpose. Please.

Jesp felt the raft hesitate. They were still far enough away from the shadowelf ferry that they hadn't been seen. Thomas began swimming the ponies over to the Willows side of the bank. He wasn't foolish enough to try to swim down the middle of that. And he wasn't a traitor either. Thank goodness, thought Jesp. Thank you, Thomas.

They climbed out of the water quietly and Thomas explained that after seeing that two-bank encampment, he wanted to try to go deep into the Willows and around that camp. It was still dangerous. There was no way to know now how far into the Willows the shadowelves had marched, and, at this point, they may well be in the Darkwald for all they could know. They were going to have to sleep in shorter shifts and move at night, he suggested. No one argued. In fact, the only person who spoke up other than to nod in agreement to Thomas' plan was Tallie, who wanted to thank the faeries for taking out two shadowelves. Apparently, she had still been harboring doubts about their ability to act as guards, to which Thomas replied, "I told you so." Jesp really did like him.

They spent the next night moving as far into the depth of the Willows as they dared and then going wide around the military encampment they'd seen. Knowing that it had been the invasion force to take the Library and therefore the Garden, Jesp was losing more and more appetite and starting to feel ill. She was beginning to spend time thinking about Harold, too, and wondering what ever became of her old friend. She'd cry quietly when she thought no one could hear or see her, but everything was so deathly quiet around them, she doubted she really had that privacy.

During the following day they all took turns getting a couple of hours of sleep and each was included in at least two naps. It wasn't great, but if it kept them alive it was worth it. Jesp didn't get the sleep she was offered, not all of it anyway. She was drowning in her own despair. Every time she closed her eyes, she saw those two camps on either side of the river, and all of those shadowelves headed straight for the Garden. Then she'd open her eyes and smell the lingering smoke. By the time the next day ended and they gotten moving again, Jesp was starting to feel feverish.

Adrik

Adrik supposed it made sense that in the wake of the Water Titan he would have so much trouble staying dry, but it did nothing to improve his mood. Their first morning's walk had not been too bad, around the rocky shoreline of Luring Lake. The lake itself was rather large to be nestled so high in the mountains and they expected it to take at least a full day's walk to reach the far side.

At first the company was largely brooding and silent. This suited Adrik fine. He was deeply uncomfortable with some of the emotions that had been stirred up in him over the last 3 or 4 days and could do without recounting any of them. Fletch ran about happily jumping in and out of the water and chasing everything that would run from him including squirrels, rabbits, frogs, fish and leaves. Adrik found it comforting, stupid little dog, but it had the right idea: they'd buried the dead; move on.

But another sense was troubling Adrik, and it was one he could not shake so easily. It was the growing and deepening knowledge that he had never buried anyone he gave a damn about seeing gone. Before now, he didn't see that as a problem. Now it was irritating him. He wondered about the one of his sisters that he cared about, silently hoping she was still OK, and that her new lover was able to do more for her now than Adrik would probably ever be able to do again. He had to shake that thought out of his head. It hurt, and he was getting genuinely tired of all of these emotions bothering him.

Just before high noon they reached the falls. Adrik would have been grateful for pristine trickles of mountain falls over gently sloping rocks. The humans had described these falls as "smaller." They were, by contrast, a quarter of a mile wide and raging like a small army. They were certainly shorter in height than the others would have been, but they were definitely longer. The spray reached them 10 minutes before they made it to the falls proper and they were drenched in under five. The noise was deafening by the time he realized they would need a plan to cross this monster.

"WHAT NOW?" he yelled

Arisa, who was walking in front of him, turned and made an indistinct noise while mouthing the word, "WHAT?"

"WHAT'S THE PLAN?"

She shook her head while cupping her ear. Finn and Brody up ahead of them realized the pair had stopped and doubled back to see what the problem was. But the problem was, to Adrik's annoyance, that they couldn't properly discuss the problem. A lot of pointing and gesturing ensued which seemed to mean "we're just gonna walk through it," but which Adrik assumed must mean something more reasonable like, "We have a plan," or better yet, "Screw this. Why are we here?" He and Arisa exchanged nervous glances and shrugged at one another. After all, Adrik grumbled to himself, this is what peasant guides were for, right?

As it turned out there was something of a pathway behind the falls. It wasn't wide enough to serve as anything useful like, say, a spot to have lunch, but it meant only getting soaked without the pain and risk of drowning that going under the falls would have provided. The thought of lunch brought up a new bad mood, as he was hungry and knew full well that his rations were as drenched as he was.

Two hours later they weren't any drier. Though they had left the incessant spray behind a mile and a half back, the bank on this side was steep and slick with mud, and every one of them had slipped into the lake multiple times. It was Adrik's good fortune, Arisa's too really, that both fishermen could swim, as the lake was quite deep on this side.

In addition to being miserably wet and hungry, they also began finding more bodies over here that had to be dealt with as they were found. As these were waterlogged corpses of more than 2 weeks, Adrik was much less hungry by the time they stopped.

In one day they'd made it to a point directly across from the old Clorr household. The village did not extend to this side of the lake past the falls, possibly due to superstition, but more likely because there was no decent footing to be had. As dusk settled in over them, they were standing on a steep embankment of mud that caked the foot of the Gatewell mountain for 20 feet up its base. They were standing precariously at an angle, and no more level ground was visible.

At least this time, Adrik could be heard when he asked, "Now what?"

The air had turned quite chilly and all of them were shivering in their wet clothes. Arisa even looked a little blue. Their packs and bedrolls were wet. Their feet squelched in their boots, Their weapons would need drying and care. Even Fletch looked like a slick ball of mud shivering on four soaked scrawny legs.

Brody and Finn had a silent conversation between them that looked to Adrik like "Do you know what to do?" "Nope. You?" when Finn, ever the more practical of the two answered.

"We had hoped to make it further obviously, but dusk is getting earlier as winter approaches. We really only have two choices honestly. We can press on with lanterns: there's a small flat area about a mile or two ahead that was used as an emergency boat dock. It's not big, but it's flat. Or we can backtrack the last two hours and head up the path to the top of the falls where the village men would sometimes camp in the spring when the river fishing was so good."

"Two or three hours either way?" Adrik confirmed, irritation growing and stomach growling, "Arisa?" he knew there was an edge to his voice he didn't try to conceal, "What do you want to do?"

Her hair resembled a waterfall flowing angrily over her head and face and it was dripping into the lake. Her blue eyes shone dimly out from underneath it as she shivered from head to toe. Teeth chattering she responded, "I-i-i-i-f-f-f-f w-w-w-ee l-l-l-ight-t-t t-t-t-orches in-st-st-stead, w-w-eeee m-m-m-i-i-ight dr-dr-dry out-t-t-t."

"Yeah in five years," Adrik answered angrily, "onward it is then."

Torches were an improvement, and Adrik mused that if they were seen by anyone across the lake or out on it, they'd be mistaken for spirits because of the amount of steam wafting off of them. Only a moment's observation would prove that assumption false, though, as after 3 more trips into the lake, Adrik felt he hadn't the grace of an elf, let alone a spirit.

He was feeling feverish and Arisa was sneezing by the time they reached the gently sloping "flat spot" promised by their guides. It was barely large enough for all four to sit around a torch, much less camp, and it slid its muddy way into the water without perch. It was indeed hollowed out of the mud for the purpose of docking a small row boat in an emergency. Adrik and Arisa looked at each other and then back at the humans.

The hour was late, the day had been miserable, the world around them was freezing cold and pitch black dark, they were hungry and exhausted, and Adrik's temper was so close to the surface now he felt that if he opened his mouth to sneeze, he'd explode. Nonetheless, Finn pulled out the pieces of leather he was working on and offered them to be sat upon. Having a dry perch for his rear end quieted Adrik's mood slightly, at least for the moment.

Finn propped their four torches up like a teepee and started laying wet twigs underneath it to dry. They looked strange to Adrik.

"Where did those come from?" he asked, then realized the answer as he asked it.

"The bramblemen. It's decent campfire wood."

Brody was spearing sausages and smoked meats on more bramblemen twigs and was holding them over the torches to dry out. Adrik felt a little disturbed, but couldn't decide why, so he shook it off as the smell of the meat began to fill the air.

That night they slept uncomfortably in tight balls too close together. All three men had waited without a word until Arisa laid down, not wanting to impose themselves on her somehow. She slept near the edge of the "flat" space and Adrik immediately took up the space nearest her. They had soaked traveling gear for bedclothes, mud for a bed and the rock of the mountain for a pillow, but what made the night least comfortable for Adrik was that a sleeping and cold Arisa unconsciously snuggled up to him for warmth. He spent most of the night trying to be warm for her without prodding her with unbidden parts of his anatomy.

Adrik was grateful for the morning, there being little worse than being exhausted and unable to sleep. They were still damp and sticky when they woke, but there were enough dry bramble twigs for a small fire and a hot breakfast. Adrik cringed at the thought of pulling his soaked and muddy boots back onto his feet, but there was nothing for it.

The four of them dried as best they could before setting off for what would hopefully be better fortune. Fletch on the other hand, gleefully leapt into the water after a particularly fearsome-looking lily pad, splashing the breakfasters and earning choice swear words and shrieks for his trouble. Remorseful he jumped right back out, and shook his excess water all over the campsite.

They were finally all packed up and resigned to the day's march when it happened.

Adrik was looking out toward the west where they were headed, trying to pretend he didn't feel illness setting in behind his eyes and in his throat, when a sigh and a splash brought his attention back around. Finn and Brody were locked in conversation against the mountain's edge and had also looked up startled. Fletch was barking so hard at some bubbles in the water that he was bouncing. Arisa was nowhere.

It took a second for her absence to register with the three men. Then all at once, they all three jumped into the water. Adrik considered his folly a second too late. In his desperation to reach Arisa, he'd jumped straight in, feet first, at the bubbles. He'd forgotten he couldn't swim.

He opened his eyes into the murky darkness. There were mud and bubbles rising up in clouds all around him and his eyes burned like he'd opened them in acid. He saw with horror that Arisa was convulsing violently as Finn and Brody fought with her ever deeper in the water. In her seizure, she kicked Brody square in the jaw, and head butted Finn's bad arm. They kept trying to grab her more securely, and as Adrik watched in terror, he realized that he was sinking like a stone. Finally, Finn managed to hook her around the waist from behind and head to the surface with her. Brody began swimming down for Adrik.

The mud was clearing as Arisa's tremor-ridden body was hoisted from the lake. As Brody reached Adrik and began dragging him up toward the surface now desperately far over head, Adrik saw something else that disturbed him even more. His eyes grew wide as he was jerked away from the visage, but a growing need to breathe drew his focus away.

His lungs were screaming at him to open his mouth. His eyes were growing dark and the water began to seem comforting, reminding him of how tired he was. He just wanted to sleep and breathe. He ached for air until he felt he would vomit. Then suddenly the light burst open above him and air rushed unbidden and burning into his desperate lungs. Brody was trying violently to keep Adrik's head above water, but the latter was throwing up water and breakfast and trying not to drown in it as he was yanked to the shore. He turned on hands and knees and retched the water up out of his toenails, gasping for air between heaves.

Arisa was sputtering in the mud while Finn struck her back. Water was coming up, but words were, too. Her body shivered like it had in the night, but Adrik knew by the look on Finn's face that she was still seizing. As he came more to his senses he heard pieces of what she was reciting.

"That must be treasssjj, guarded sure, ah ...se succuh to evil's lo. Deep <gasp> under <gasp, cough> riv-riv-riv fortress built. Of r-r-rock a br-brick a r-r-rune a silt," she was coming around a bit and flopped onto her back with a sigh, "Like sepeker entemed within <gasp gasp gasp> " Arisa opened her eyes and finished quite clearly, "The mighty idols sing their din." Silence fell on the group.

They glanced around at each other and then at Arisa. She had fallen asleep in Adrik's vomit. The men moved her and cleaned her off in the lake as best they could, and Adrik made a silent mental note to remember the image of Arisa laying in his puke the next time she snuggled up to him in the night so that he could get more sleep.

They were stuck until Arisa woke up. Between Finn's bad arm and Adrik's exhaustion from nearly drowning, no one could help Brody carry Arisa and he couldn't do it himself in the sloping, slick mud. Finn filled them in on what they'd missed, and Adrik was impressed with his memory, and his translation of drowned-woman-speak.

"She started off incoherent, then got coherent, then started coughing and stuff again as she woke up. But it sounded like she said:

Then Earth shall crumble through the sky

Revealing fortress left to lie

Wherein an ancient secret kept

Of power unconquered has but slept

That must be treasured, guarded sure

Or else succumb to evil's lure.

Deep under river fortress built

Of rock and brick and rune and silt

Like sepulcher entombed within

The mighty idols sing their din."

Finn finished in his usual matter-of-fact tone and looked squarely at Adrik like he should know what that meant. Adrik shook his head and turned to look at

Brody, "You?"

"I hope it means 'don't jump in the lake if you can't swim, dummy.' But if not, I don't have a clue."

Adrik grimaced at him and they both laughed. It was good to lighten the mood.

Finn, however, was steadfast in his desire to be serious about the message, "Well, it's another part of the prophecy, right? Has she said anything else when she's had a seizure before?"

Again Adrik shook his head. "No, either she's getting closer to actual memories of it, or Brody broke something last time."

He grinned back at Brody thinking to share a joke again, but Brody looked shocked and hurt.

"Kidding," Adrik added with quiet annoyance.

"OK...so what was the part before?" asked Finn refusing to be deterred.

Adrik was ready with this answer. He'd recited the damned thing over and over to himself despite what it might do to him in order to make sure he would remember.

"For without the strength of magic known...The gods of lore may again be shown...The way to take what once was theirs...And make the world their wretched lairs,"

"And now we add 'Then Earth shall crumble through the sky...Revealing fortress left to lie...Wherein an ancient secret kept...Of power unconquered has but slept...That must be treasured, guarded sure...Or else succumb to evil's lure...Deep under river fortress built...Of rock and brick and rune and silt...Like sepulcher entombed within...The mighty idols sing their din.' Does that make any sense to anyone?" asked Finn without much hope in his voice.

Adrik and Brody shook their heads, then Adrik added, "No, and there's something else. I saw something I wish I hadn't seen while I was in the lake. There's a skeleton down there with a sword through it. A *shadowelf* sword through it. It's skeletal which means....it's been there a few years."

Arisa remained unconscious for most of the day. Although she was breathing and could be made to take liquids, it was still worrying Adrik more than he cared to admit. Finn scouted ahead to see exactly how far they had to make it to reach a better campsite. Fletch went with him, though he had to be carried away from Arisa's limp body. Adrik was mildly sorry to see him go, even if he did growl at Adrik every time he got close to her. Once Brody was confident that Adrik was stable enough to look after Arisa, and Fletch was gone and so couldn't prevent Adrik from doing it, he offered to jump back into the lake and see if he could find the skeleton Adrik mentioned.

Adrik himself felt useless. He couldn't scout, which was something he was normally very good at, because he kept slipping into the water and couldn't swim. He couldn't help Arisa; he could only hope that wherever she was now, she could get herself back. He certainly couldn't assist Brody in his quest, and he was quite apprehensive of what Brody might find down there. He had to keep reminding himself that any shadowelf that might be down there will certainly have drowned after 5 years, whatever magic they may have.

Brody dove and resurfaced 3 times without success. It was impossible now, an hour or more after the event, to tell exactly where those bubbles had been or how steep an angle they had swam up from. Adrik decided on Brody's fourth submerging to start getting lunch together. He remembered that Arisa was carrying the harder salted meats, and these were less likely to be soaked, Adrik reasoned. He pulled her slimy soft-leather pack toward him as he lay in the mud, still exhausted from his own ordeal. It still pissed him off, he thought to himself, pursing his lips and flopping Arisa's pack open with more force than was technically necessary, that these humans had managed to save their lives now so many times he was going to have to concede that they could not have managed this journey without them. Damn it.

He pulled out the carefully wrapped, waterlogged jerky and heard the tinkle of glass. He was caught by surprise for a moment and then remembered that Arisa had specifically visited an alchemist on their way out of the Felwater Valley. He laughed sarcastically to himself as he remembered her saying, "And he talked me into several vials of anti-petrification potions. Honestly. I can't say no to anybody!"

Adrik found the leather pouch the alchemist had given her and unwrapped the little bottles carefully. Anti-petrification potion. That would be this blue one, like she tried to give me on the mountain ledge 5 years ago. He remembered briefly an image of the bottle coming toward him before he blacked out. He hadn't been aware of it before, but now he could see it in his memory as he was holding one. It felt strangely light, like it and its contents were nearly weightless. But there was only one like it in here, and Adrik suddenly realized with a start that the bramblemen were even more dangerous to them without this stuff. Arisa had gone for healing potions but had come back with more. Adrik wasn't even sure entirely what she had bought. By the time Arisa had gone to the alchemist, he was already in a huff about all of her "pre-fleeing-for-their-lives-shopping" she had decided to do. He smiled down at the little bottle in his hand. Her shopping had saved their lives, and it made him feel strangely warm rather than annoyed.

Adrik was fairly certain that the clear, watery vials contained the healing potions, only because he'd seen some similar ones before. They were pleasantly warm to the touch and slightly larger than the others. He was just beginning to wonder to himself what the other potions were when a loud splash erupted behind him.

"Found it!" Brody yelled from about 30 feet out. "Hey! Adrik! Throw me the rope!"

Adrik tucked the vials back into their pouch and placed the pouch careully back on top of all of Arisa's neatly folded things, briefly deciding to be disgusted with himself for thinking of her neatness as "cute." He dragged himself up, cracking his mud-caked clothing and squelching his butt out of the puddle his weight had made. He retrieved a length of solid hemp rope from his own pack, then tightly wrapped and knotted the last ten feet of it so as to make a weighty end to toss. Still, it took about 6 tosses to get the end to Brody, who was trying not to move much for fear of losing his find.

Brody made two more dives looking for the thing again, during which time Finn returned. On his third trip down, he succeeded in getting the rope tied to it. It took hours to bring it all up because the skeleton came up in pieces. It still had some hair and most of a pair of leather pants, but all of it nondescript. The skeleton was too stocky to be elven and too brunette to be shadowelf in particular. It looked to be a large human man and that brought a mingled sense of grim relief and excitement. Finn went down for the sword when Brody dove for the last of the skeleton: its right foot which was stuck in a boot in the mud-caked lake bottom. As

Adrik watched the lake for them to resurface, the world behind him was rent with an ear-splitting scream and mad barking.

Adrik jumped to his feet, pulling his falchion in one swift action. There lying on the bank in front of him was a screaming Arisa, who had awoken to find herself staring at a skull.

Adrik stifled a laugh, so deep was his relief, and knelt to move the skull and comfort her. Fletch, too, had realized the issue, and quickly moved to lick Arisa's ear until she sat herself up to get away from him. Adrik caught her, and held her for a full minute or two before they broke away from each other. He didn't want to let go.

Finn and Brody emerged grim-faced. Both men were quite sure that the boot had belonged to Brody's father, and suddenly the little camp took on a deeper reverence. Here lying in pieces around them was the man Brody had nearly died waiting for five years ago: the father that had never come home. Adrik had heard the story by now, having been tactless enough, as Arisa told him, to have asked about the scar. Arisa's face contorted with shared pain and she immediately grabbed Brody and pulled him into tight lingering hug. Adrik wanted to throw the man back into the lake, but he composed himself and stared down at the corpse and sword.

One thing was sure in Adrik's mind, besides the fact that he wanted Arisa to let go of Brody. Brody's father was killed by a shadowelf. Kajiri's minions had, in fact, been up here five years ago. He remembered the party climbing down the mountain on the opposite side of the river from he and Arisa on the day the bramblemen attacked. Five years later, he was sure of who they were. But where had they gone and what had they done?

Brody sobbed quietly for a while, sitting in the mud, dripping from the lake. He rested his arms on his knees and hid his face in them. Arisa sat with him on one side and Finn on the other, each trying to comfort him. Fletch assumed himself between the man's legs, so as to reach his interior. From Adrik's point of view, it was a bizarre visage: the little dog's tail sticking out between Brody's shins and wagging.

Adrik knew he was no good at these sorts of moments and was just trying to keep himself busy as it passed. He had no idea what had happened to his own father who had also disappeared when he was a child. The difference being that Adrik didn't care and believed strongly that his mother had killed him. He'd been cruel and indifferent and Adrik would not find himself weeping over a pile of his old bones. For the second time in an hour, Adrik felt a rush of jealousy toward Brody.

Adrik mused over his own childhood as he carefully reassembled the skeleton in front of him. He was doing it absentmindedly, anatomy having been a study of his youth for unkind reasons. His mother demanded strict obedience, not even mistakes were forgiven. Punishment was cruel. His parents both believed that a scar kept you from forgetting your failure. Perhaps that's why Brody's scar intrigued Adrik so much. Adrik, himslef, always hid all of his. To him each was a failure on some level. He was ashamed of them.

"That's amazing!" broke him out of his private moment of self-loathing. It was Brody's tear-choked voice and Adrik looked up. Brody was staring at the puzzle Adrik was putting together. It had taken him more than an hour, so many of the smaller bones having come loose, but he already had over half of the skeleton reassembled. He had no way to hold it together, of course, and Adrik wasn't sure that the exercise had served any purpose, but it had been busywork while he avoided the emotional work going on nearby.

Brody got up and came closer, awe and gratitude on his face. Adrik saw that behind Brody, both Finn and Arisa were beaming at him. He didn't understand, but he was glad to know he hadn't screwed up. Brody reached down and touched his father's shoulder, then his hand. Adrik assumed he was imagining the man laying there, maybe asleep. Then the shadows rose.

The air turned terribly cold like it did in the night now, and the world around their little muddy landing grew dark as dusk. Brody's eyes were unfocused, far away, and Adrik watched in fascinated horror as Brody began to speak to his father. There was a whisper on the wind, faint and chilling, but Adrik made out words like "sea" and "above" and "flood." Brody was whispering too faintly for Adrik to hear him, but there was no doubt that a conversation was going on. When it ended, the sun with its much needed warmth failed to join them again. Twilight had fallen, and Brody raised his head and looked directly at Adrik.

"Thank you," he said, a tear still lingering at his chin, "I have some answers now, and some questions. But first," and here he wiped his eyes and cleared the last tear before it fell, "We need to find a way to let him rest."

In the end it was decided that the bones would be placed in Brody's own new leather pack he had bought in Kipping. All of Brody's belongings were split up between his bedroll and the other men's packs. Arisa wrote the rune for "Father" on the outside of the pack with some ink she had brought, and there was a sense of what that concept meant to her that hung in the air for several moments after she wrote it. Brody and Finn said their goodbyes, then Brody swam the bag back down to the bottom of the lake and placed it, Adrik could only guess where. The night was inky black by the time he resurfaced. Adrik had retrieved the rest of the bones out of the boot and seen to it that the man was reassembled one last time before he was laid to rest. He assured Brody that all of the pieces were indeed there, which was a lie that he thought Brody of all people would be able to call him on, but which went unchallenged. The sword remained in Adrik's possession. Brody seemed unable to look at it.

They ate their meager supper, dreading the prospect of another night in the mud, but it was too dark to do anything else. They discussed the problem before turning in, but the obstacles remained difficult to overcome. Finn finally had the chance to fill them in on his day's progress, for what little it was worth at that moment.

"OK, I went ahead to find a better campsite. The bad news is I walked fairly swiftly for almost two hours and didn't find one," Adrik's heart sank at this news, "The good news is I think I found the remnants of some of our fathers' fishing boats up on a ledge on the mountain not far from here. If we can get up there, it looked a little bigger and a lot drier than this is. Problem is, I don't know how we'd get up there."

"How did *they* get up there?" Brody asked incredulously.

Finn shrugged, "Flood," he answered simply.

Indeed, the next morning, after walking about 30 minutes west then turning around and backtracking, the party could just see the butt end of a lake-style fishing boat projecting out from a ledge at least 25 feet above the water line. Backing up and looking harder, it appeared that another one was in front of it, turned up on its nose as if the two had collided up against the mountain. It wasn't easy to tell, but it did look like the ledge itself was at least as big as what they had so far, and maybe slightly larger. But Finn had pegged the real difficulty succinctly: even with elven climbing skills, Adrik wasn't sure how to get up there.

Another problem was presenting itself quickly. Although Adrik had been mildly aware of a soreness in the back of his throat and a fullness behind his eyes for two nights now, Arisa was actually feverish, pale, and beginning to look really very ill. Adrik sneezed loudly looking up at their hope for dry sleep and nearly fell back into the water. The humans were very concerned, and Arisa tried to explain to them, hoarsely, that while elves were far more agile, perceptive and quick than humans, humans by far had the better strength, stature and stamina. She and Adrik simply could not tolerate this constant wet environment as long as the two humans could.

It was getting quite late in the afternoon when the decision was made to give up on the ledge and to keep heading west. It was a setback they knew. The answers they were looking for were right here, but the elves had to recuperate their constitutions or they would be of no use to anyone.

Adrik hated having to admit weakness, but as darkness approached, even he had to concede that he was barely able to keep going. Arisa was being carried at this point, a job being alternated between the two humans, and Adrik wasn't even jealous about it. He couldn't have helped her right now. He knew the fever was settling into his body with every passing hour and as the chill of the night took root in his very bones, his whole body was aching.

That's when something small and loud fell onto his back from above. Fletch who had been trudging along in an unusual morose silence, began barking at once as something else landed on Finn at the head of the line. Adrik manage to throw the thing off and pull his sword, but nearly threw it into Brody carrying Arisa in front of him and making Brody stumble. Adrik looked down in startled panic at the frightened eyes of a human child brandishing a scaling knife at him. Adrik lowered his sword.

Finn had been equally successful at overcoming and disarming the little girl that had attacked him. He, in fact, had to fish her back out of the lake where'd he knocked her in his instinct to defend himself. Holding her up by the back of her filthy dress Finn recognized her and the mood changed.

That night they slept in a hollow in the mountain less than five feet above the water line. It was a large but very open cave and offered little real protection, but it was dry. It was home, they learned, to a small group of children from Luring. 6 of them in total, 4 of them siblings and two neighbors, had clung to flotsam in the storm and had washed up miraculously here almost 3 weeks ago. They'd lived off of rain water and what rotting debris from the village they could fish out of the lake. The floor of their "camp" was littered with soggy bread, rotten apples, and even the skeletal remains of frogs that had been cooked and picked clean. The oldest of these children, the one who'd landed on Finn, was a 14-year-old girl named Lore who took great pride in explaining to them that it was *she* who'd figured out how to start a fire. Lore, it was explained, was a friend of Rista's and a child that Finn's sister had babysat years ago. The rest of her family had been among those that they had sent back to the lake during their time in Luring a few days back, but that fact was recounted outside of Lore's earshot.

The rest of the 5 children included four siblings, Bran, who at age 11 had taken it upon himself to attack Adrik, ten-year-old brother Lee and twin girls Ann and Fran who at age 6 were the youngest, and also a neighbor of the siblings and cousin to Lore, 8-year-old Timmy. They were scrawny, dirty, hungry and scared, but also quite proud of having survived. They had believed they were the only ones left, believing that if any had survived, someone would have come looking for them. They had given up hope and resigned themselves to this bleak future.

Brody and Finn explained to them that they *had* looked for survivors, but that so many were still missing it was impossible to know *who* might still be alive. They, too, had given up hope.

The next morning, the children's plight turned into another delay, which worried Adrik. If indeed the shadowelves were behind the return of *both* Titans so far, then they would already be looking to release the next one, and there were only four in total. Meanwhile, Adrik and his small band, were still nowhere closer to understanding how his compatriots had done what they'd *already* done, much less to figuring out how to thwart them. Adrik had already lived in a world dominated by shadowelf culture. He did not want to live in a world *enslaved* by it, and, he admitted bitterly to himself, his own fate in such a world would be worse even than what these children would get. Queen Kajiri would make an example out of a traitor, and there was no turning back from being named that now. They simply could not fail. It wasn't even worth contemplating the possibility. Adrik couldn't face even in his mind what would be in store for him if they did.

Still, he couldn't deny the fact that he and Arisa were too ill to go on right away, and the children's hideaway was the best place they had for recovery. And so it was that Adrik ended up babysitting a group of human kids for two days. Arisa had another seizure while Finn and Brody were gone looking for help. Adrik tried to pretend that he wasn't amused at how much this freaked the kids out. The result of it was, though, that he got another piece of the Prophecy but lost any help he would have had in caring for the little brood.

He fed them by shooting birds out of the sky and roasting them, which they delighted at watching. Both Bran and Lore wanted to learn how to do it, and both were pretty good for beginners once they got to try. He washed their clothes along with his and Arisa's and all the bedding including what Finn and Brody left behind. He strung his rope up for a laundry line and marveled at himself as a sniffling and sneezing house mother. He taught the two older ones to fight dirty with their little knives and even conceded to a bedtime story one night which turned into more of a ghost story since Adrik really didn't know any good children's tales.

Shaking his head as he retrieved more laundry on the second day, he decided that he'd fallen a long way from the palatial estate where he'd grown up and was educated. As he remembered fondly the servants, the food and the luxury of his upbringing, he remembered, too, the lashings and the required obedience, the constant stress of never being allowed to falter, even for a moment. In some ways, these kids still had it better.

He looked out across the lake. It was a perfect sapphire blue. The mountain air was crisp and clean and cool. Birds soared overhead, and the smell of late-blooming blossoms falling across the wind was pervasive. Suddenly Adrik understood what Brody had meant on a day two weeks ago when, speaking to a small group of peasants huddled together on a ridge trying to decide where to go with what little remained of their lives, Brody had said, and Adrik had thought it was ridiculous, that he'd always felt free on the lake.

Freedom was not something Adrik had understood, he realized. To him, having not been enslaved meant that he was free. He was wealthy, aristocratic even, and spoiled in some sense. It couldn't have been said that he was not free. But as he spotted Finn and Brody making their careful way back around the foot of the mountain heading east he realized that he had a sense now of control over his own destiny, of infinite choices laid out before him and of the world being open and inviting around him. Brody, a simple, illiterate, uneducated peasant with almost nothing to call his own, had just taught Adrik the meaning of freedom. Now Adrik had to decide if it was what he wanted. He looked back out at the lake and breathed it in and knew that it was.

Brody and Finn had found merchants traveling up to Kipping, trying to make a last trip with their wares before winter hit hard and made mountain travel impossible. They'd agreed to take the children with them, for a price. Adrik grumbled about it, of course, but Arisa gladly gave up the money so they could go. Adrik had the thought, though he kept it to himself, that these "merchants" could just as easily sell the children elsewhere for a profit, but, he reasoned, if they were up this far, they probably were really going to Kipping and people there would recognize the kids. He hoped.

Two more days and Finn and Brody were back. Adrik had been over his fever for a day now and Arisa was stronger and able to help out more. Adrik had taken the last day to go back to the boats up on their ledge and had found a solution, hopefully, to that obstacle. All in all, they had a lot to discuss that night, now nearly three weeks into their journey.

Finn and Brody had purchased more supplies while they were gone, at Arisa's request, including a new backpack for Brody. They were stuck with what supplies the merchants had to sell, but there were carrots and radishes, hard cheese and bread and two small kegs of good ale to brighten their supper meal and their mood. They had also, however, brought back news. King Olgar, the ruler of this little human kingdom, had invaded the elven territories to the northeast of his capital, due north of the mountain.

"The willowelves," Arisa said, concern written all over her face. Finn and Brody looked relieved.

"The merchants said they are taking news of higher taxes up to Kipping with them. It'll be a hard winter if they've been raised by much," Finn told them grimly, "But word is that King Olgar has declared elves to be 'the problem,' whatever that means, and has insisted all elves be exterminated." He looked dour-faced at Adrik and Arisa. Brody was looking down at his half-eaten dinner. Arisa look horrified.

"Anyway, we reminded the children that the two of you helped save them and that they shouldn't repay you by telling anyone that they've seen you."

Adrik nodded. There would be soldiers after them soon.

"Anything new up here?" Brody asked weakly, looking up from his plate at last.

"Well, two things," Adrik answered, determinedly not looking concerned about their news, "One is that Arisa's had another seizure, so there's more prophecy. And two is that I think I've figured out how to get up to where the boats are."

"And three, I think I've figured out how Queen Kajiri is locating the Titans," Arisa added.

Adrik couldn't contain his shock at that declaration, "How??"

"Who?" asked Brody.

"What?" asked Finn.

Arisa sat back and smiled.

Chapter 7:

18th Day of the 12th Month, 4th Day of the Week, Autumn
Kylarsday, Shilirs 18

Keen

Keen sat on the edge of a cot. His hands were in his lap as he stared at the filthy floor. His brother's tirade was still going on, but he'd stopped listening. There was no explaining away the damage he had done. Not now. He couldn't make his brother understand. He couldn't, because the cost was far too high.

A lull in the beratement meant that he should pay attention again. He closed his eyes, steadied his breathing and looked up.

They were all staring at him. Krieg, his older brother was standing over him, red-faced and furious, his arms crossed and breathing heavily through his nose. Beyond him to Keen's left, Krieg's pregnant wife and three children were sitting, wide-eyed and terrified, on a cot near the bars of their prison cell. To Keen's right, and still behind Krieg, their mother and grandmother sat on another dirty cot, watching the scene with tears rolling down their cheeks, holding each other. Keen's younger brother, Kaith, was to his immediate right, standing next to a fourth cot and leaning up against the wall under the small barred window that looked out onto the walled Gallows Courtyard. Keen couldn't read his expression. It was as if Kaith was trying to read Keen's.

Keen had told them most of the story before the city guard had shown up. How the guard had been alerted to his presence, he didn't know, although it never really occurred to him that he needed to sneak around once he got safely over the border. He'd assumed that he'd be treated like a missing, wounded soldier who'd made it back.

But they'd arrested him and his whole family. He'd been labeled a traitor, and the punishment was to be that he and his entire family would be hanged at dawn. He looked into the scared eyes of his young nieces and nephew. What could he possibly say to them?

"Well?" Krieg demanded. Keen understood his anger. Keen's actions were going to cost him his life, and worse, the lives of his wife and children. What could

Keen say?

Keen's wet eyes met his brother's furious ones.

"Well, what, Krieg? I told you I didn't mean for any of this to happen. Do you really think I would have come back if I'd had any idea that it would hurt any of you? I just wanted you to know the truth..."

"Well, the truth just got us killed, Keen. And that's on you."

Keen wanted to find a way to fix this, but he was out of ideas. Kaith had spent the last several hours trying to pry the bars out of the little window, but gave up when, lacking for any success whatsoever, their mother had pointed out that all that window would be good for would be shoving the two littlest children out onto the Gallows Court. Krieg had tried to break, and then with his wife's hairpin to pick, the lock on the outside of their cell. But the lock was too strong for even Krieg to break, and it being on the outside of the bars, he had no real hope of picking it either. Now his tactic seemed to be to make Keen feel as guilty and horrible as possible, as if Keen admitting that he was entirely responsible would save anyone. Keen would do it, if he thought that were true.

Krieg was a big man, bigger than Keen who was himself larger than the average man. Krieg had planned on a military career, but had been injured while guarding a dam against attacks from desert nomadic fighters who wanted the water. Those nomads had invented the cannons, and Krieg had been lucky to survive that attack, when a cannon tore down the wall he was standing on and he'd been buried alive for nearly two days. But Krieg was tenacious and he was trapped near the river the dam had been built over, so he'd been able to reach water. Still, his ankle was broken and, although it was hardly noticeable now, Krieg would limp when carrying any weight or when running. That injury had all but destroyed his military career.

He'd learned about cannons during those few years, and he was one of the people that had brought that knowledge back home. For a while he had remained employed teaching the military about cannon and black powder technology. That's how Keen had learned so much about them. Eventually, he'd given them as much as he could and so they let him go. It was devastating to Krieg, but his father-in-law had hired him on at the sawmill he operated. Cannons and dead trees: Krieg was the opposite of the willowelves.

Keen hadn't told his family about his interrogations. He hadn't mentioned Kethran except to say that he was arrested and that Kierra and her family had gotten him out of it. He hadn't because he was trying to impress upon his family the basic decency of the elves, and Kethran wasn't a good example of that.

But he hadn't mentioned his interrogation by Joran and Jerith, either. He knew that Krieg, at least, would certainly consider him a traitor for that. Maybe he was, he thought bitterly to himself. *My own country is murdering elves senselessly and is now going to murder my family to cover that fact up. So, maybe I am willing to betray it.*

He looked up. Krieg's eyes were still boring into him as the man continued to fume. Keen suspected that for Krieg, it had to be easier to glare at Keen than to turn around and look at his little family, huddled together terrified behind him.

His family had reacted the way he'd expected. Surely, they'd reasoned, he was under some kind of spell. Elves were evil, monstrous even, and wielded terrible magic. Obviously, Keen had been a victim of some cruel magic while he was captured. They tried to convince him that he was being controlled or manipulated. They were horrified at the idea that he'd slept with one. They were sure she had exerted some strange elf power over him, and that if he'd just stay home long enough for it to wear off, he'd see it.

And Keen had made it worse by admitting to the singing. He'd wanted them to imagine the beauty of it and how the elves understood it as natural, not magical. But all he'd managed to do was to prove to them that Kierra had used mystic powers which had clearly affected his mind. Now Kierra's name was synonymous with "sorceress" in their minds.

Keen understood. He'd grown up on those same ideas of elves, too. The military even had paintings of elves with large inhuman eyes, huge pointed ears that made them look like their heads had wings, a feral posture and a hungry look in their big eyes. They were made to look demonic so that people wouldn't question the need to eradicate them. Wanted posters depicting cruel-looking inhuman elves hung all over the kingdom with dire warnings about the elves' ability to control minds and attack with dangerous magic.

"So, that's it?" Krieg continued, "You still can't see the truth about them?"

Keen looked sadly into his older brother's face. He'd told him about the cave, about Kierra saving him over and over again. He'd told them all. He'd explained the bond and his decision to stay. He'd even described the innocent little village full of very normal people. All a facade, they'd assured him: just an elaborate ruse to gain his trust for some nefarious purpose.

"I've seen the truth, Krieg. I wish you'd trust me instead of the people who are willing to kill your children to cover up their lies. I'm your brother. Credit me with more sense than that."

"MORE SENSE??? YOU HAVEN'T SHOWN ANY SENSE AT ALL!!"

"That's enough," their grandmother broke in, "You two yelling at each other isn't helping anything."

"I wasn't yelling," Keen answered her defensively, still looking hurt at his brother.

"Well, quit your arguing then," she insisted, "We only have a few hours left together and this isn't how I want to spend them!"

Krieg turned toward her gently, "Yes, Granny."

He sat down next to his wife without looking at her and buried his face in his hands. His youngest child, his son, tried to climb onto his knee and a lump formed in Keen's very dry throat.

"Keen."

Keen heard his name whispered barely audibly over the conversation Krieg was now trying to have with his small boy. Keen looked up. Standing just beyond the bars was a tall, thin person completely covered in a cloak. He was leaning up against the wall opposite Keen's position and just inside Keen's view so that he couldn't be seen by anyone else in the cell. Keen furrowed his eyebrows and approached the bars.

The hooded figure turned to look into the cell discreetly as Keen approached, but turned his face back to Keen when Keen reached him.

It was Joran.

"What in the world?" he whispered barely louder than breath. Behind him, Keen could sense Krieg tense and turn his attention to whatever Keen was doing.

"What are you doing here?" Keen asked elatedly.

"Trying to help. Kierra sensed you were in trouble. What's going on?"

Relief washed over Keen like he thought he'd never feel again, "They're going to hang my whole family! Can you get us out of here?"

"What?" Joran reacted in shock and looked back into the cell just behind Keen, "Even the children?"

Keen nodded desperately as a second hooded figure approached. It was Jerith.

Joran pulled a human longsword out of the depths of his cloak. It was still attached to a belt. He handed it through the bars to Keen as Jerith produced a set of iron keys. Behind Keen, Krieg nearly jumped at the sight of a sword and the obvious arrival of a rescue.

Keen ignored his brother. Cloaked as they were, Joran and Jerith looked like tall, thin humans. Their barely-larger-than average eyes didn't look inhuman at all, much less with their somewhat-larger-than human ears covered by a hood. He knew Krieg would assume these were humans, and he wasn't going to say anything. The last thing he needed was for Krieg to show his prejudice right now.

As the barred door swung quietly open, Keen turned and motioned to his anxious family, all of whom were watching him, to come through. Krieg got his wife and children up in no time. Kaith helped Granny. Keen and Krieg waited for everyone to get through before exiting themselves, at which point Keen gestured for his brother to head out ahead of him. Krieg's eyes met Keen's and they were softer.

Keen knew that Krieg was a devoted family man who had worked hard to support those that counted on him. Their father had died when they were all young, and Krieg had taken up the mantle of man-of-the-house as soon as he could work. Krieg was angry, Keen reasoned to himself as the group crept up the short hallway toward the open gateway that led out to the Gallows Courtyard, because he'd been helpless, and Krieg didn't handle helplessness well at all.

Keen remembered visiting his brother in the hospital tent when his brother had been carried back wounded. He laid on a cot with his broken ankle, angry. Keen thought at first that it was the pain, but had realized many times since then that it had been the helplessness and the sense of being broken that had rallied his temper.

When they got to the open archway, they flanked it as stealthily as the awkward group could manage. There were two dead guards lying on either side of it.

"That one still has a sword," Jerith stated simply, nodding down at the one at his feet and speaking to Krieg and Kaith. Krieg went for it immediately and looked much happier once he'd secured the thing to his waist.

"There's a guard that patrols out there," Joran explained in his quiet whisper. "Once he passes by and is completely out of sight we'll run straight across to the wall."

The courtyard was large and open with a gallows large enough to hang ten people at once sitting just beyond its center toward the far wall. A large locked gate stood just out of sight to their left to allow gawkers in for public executions, but that gate would be guarded.

"The wall?" Krieg whispered back, not quite as quietly as Joran had been, "Then what?"

"There will be a ladder when we get there," Joran answered simply as the patrolling guard came into sight. Joran was watching the guard and not Krieg.

"You're not alone?" Krieg tried to whisper more quietly.

Although Keen was standing behind Joran he could tell by the way the man jerked his head toward Krieg before shaking it that he'd sent an unimistakable "Shut up" signal with his expression. Krieg turned to look out to the courtyard from behind Jerith without another word.

Krieg still had not realized that their rescuers were elves. Keen could tell by his comfortable demeanor. Keen guessed that Krieg just assumed they were men Keen knew from the army. He looked around at the scared faces surrounding him. A few moments ago, none of them had trusted him anymore. Now they were looking at him with eyes that said clearly that trust had been restored. Still, none of them knew they were being assisted by elves and Keen was no more going to point it out than he was going to warn their rescuers that his family hated the elven race. Keen was developing even more tension now that his family had less.

The lone patrolman passed out of sight and Joran whispered, "Run!"

Jerith and Joran reached for Krieg's very pregnant wife to help her run. Krieg picked up Granny. Kaith already had Krieg's son in his arms. Keen lifted his younger niece and his mother took the older one by the hand. They all ran for the gallows and beyond to the wall, Krieg and Keen both limping as they did.

The gallows looming into large and horrible view brought a lump to Keen's throat. It already had nooses ready for tomorrow morning's executions: nine in total, just enough for Keen's whole family. They'd even made smaller ones on longer ropes for the three children. The sight nearly stopped his heart.

They skirted to the right around the horror of the gallows platform, away from the direction where the guard had gone, and straight for the wall behind. Keen could just make out two long, dark lumps along the top of the wall. As they approached, the lumps revealed themselves to be two more cloaked figures lying on their bellies along the wall. They immediately dropped a rope ladder between them as they saw the group coming.

As Keen reached the ladder he lifted his niece up to the top of it and looked gratefully into the eyes of Rana and Nira who reached down to help her up. Keen turned to help the rest of his family.

After the children, their pregnant mother, Keen's mother and then Granny had been sent up the ladder, Keen's brothers and the elves beckoned for him to go up next, indicating his still-injured hip as the reason, and all watching terrified behind them. The guard would be coming back around soon.

Keen hoisted himself up the ladder, as much with his arms as anything, and reached the top in time to see Granny being helped over to a nearby tree where a fifth cloaked figure was waiting to receive her. Keen looked over at this last figure and Kierra's face broke into a wide and relieved smile as she took Granny's hand.

Keen made it up onto the wall and looked down. Ten feet below him, the most vulnerable members of his family were looking up at him, waiting. Keen looked at Kierra who was bracing herself to try to help him over to the tree, but Keen shook his head at her. He positioned himself quickly onto his rear-end and slid off down to the ground. He bent his bad leg up as he fell, so as not to land on it. He landed hard on his good leg which gave out under him allowing him to fall onto all fours. He knew he'd twisted that good ankle, but he righted himself up onto it anyway as his six-year-old niece made to climb back into his arms. He hoped he could still carry her.

Kaith came over next, and accepted the tree-route, although he was too slow about it. Then Krieg's head was visible at the top of the ladder at the same time that Joran and Jerith both appeared on either side of him, apparently having scaled the wall without the ladder. Rana and Nira had leaped gracefully over to the tree without help to get out of their lovers' way.

Krieg looked around at the four of them, clearly impressed, but still apparently unaware that they were anything other than human. He slid off the wall as Keen had, grimacing when his weight hit his bad ankle. Rana, Nira and Kierra came down out of the tree as Joran and Jerith pulled up the ladder and let it drop to the ground at Keen's feet. They quickly crossed to the tree and came down as everyone else began lifting children and preparing for the next run.

Rana took Lynnie, the niece Keen had been holding, and Nira took little Max from Kaith. Kaith then got under Keen's arm on his bad side. Krieg lifted Granny once more and Rana said, "Head for the river!"

Krieg paused, "The river?"

"Yes, we have boats," an exasperated Joran answered, "Now, run!"

The prison was on the outskirts of the city and not far from the river so that it could get supplies more easily. A large woodland, one of the few left in the Southern Highlands, separated the imposing structure from the water. The group avoided the single road that led down to the water's edge and made, instead, for the trees.

Keen hobbled as quickly as he could, grateful for his younger brother's help. Kierra stayed with them, one hand on Keen's free arm, glancing nervously back behind them frequently. The group was no good at speed or stealth, and It wasn't long before they heard alarm bells ringing behind them.

Keen's family members had all noticed the way Kierra was clinging to him as they ran, and several of them, including both of his brothers, had raised their eyebrows at him as if to suggest that he needed to snap out of his elf fascination and pay attention to the girl that was risking her life to save them. Great, thought Keen in a bemused sort of way, here we are running for our lives and my family are trying to play matchmaker.

The trek through the brief woods was arduous and took longer than it should have. They could hear horns and horses rallying behind them, but they reached sight of the quiet, welcoming river's edge before they could see their pursuers. Floating easily with the gentle sway of the current were two small dug-out style canoes. Keen made a quick mental count and realized they would have to fit 14 between two boats that looked designed to fit about 5 people each.

Rana and Nira had gotten there first and deposited Lynnie and Max into the nearest canoe, leaping in themselves and beginning to untie it. Joran and Jerith headed for the second boat and helped Lara, Krieg's wife, who they had been practically carrying between them, into that one. Krieg deposited Granny next to Lara before turning to help Emma, his oldest. Keen's mother, having handed Emma off to Krieg, climbed into the first boat with her two youngest grandchildren. Jerith headed to the back of the second canoe walking lithely across its edge which caused Krieg who had nearly overturned the skiff just by climbing into it, do a double take. Joran stood in the small space left at the bank's end and began untying their vessel. Kaith and Kierra were trying to help Keen into the first boat, and once he was himself deposited, he crawled carefully across the laps of his waiting family members to reach the far end where he could prop his back against the outer shell and offer his lap to someone. Much to the amusement of the eyebrow-raisers around him Kierra had followed him deftly back there and taken the seat on the open lap. Keen looked back and Kaith had barely found the room at the bow to crouch down with his knees at his nose.

Joran had produced a large branch from somewhere near the boat and began to push the small, heavily-laden vessel away from the bank. Keen now realized that Rana had tied the two boats together, so that the one Keen was sitting in was moving out into the open river waters, too.

Keen wrapped his arms around Kierra in his lap. She was still bundled in her dark cloak, but the shape of her body felt comforting and familiar. He breathed in the familiar clean, woodsy scent of her hair just under her hood and he kissed the top of her head.

"Thank you for coming for me," he said quietly into the back of her head.

Kierra turned to face him, her eyes watery, her face set in a soft, but determined expression, "I will always come for you, Keen," she answered him, "Always. Don't ever doubt that."

Keen could feel the eyes of his family on him, but he didn't care. They would find out soon enough that the young woman they were hoping would spur him out of his fascination with Kierra, was in fact Kierra.

Jerith was passing the large, dangerous-looking bows that had been stashed along the walls of the other canoe over to Nira and Rana. The girls, taking their bows, were assuming protective positions over the rest of the group by standing on the boats' edges. Nira was standing aft with one foot on the side of each skiff. Rana, near the prow, was balancing gracefully on one side. They both stood straight backed with bows drawn at the shore, waiting.

Kierra found the oars that had been stashed next to where Keen was sitting. He hadn't even noticed them, and she began passing them out to Jerith, Krieg and Kaith. Joran crouched watchfully at the prow of his boat, waiting for the now-silent shore to erupt into something else.

It did.

Rana caught the first arrow aimed at them in the loop at the end of her bow just in front of Lynnie's nose. She spun it around in time to catch another flying toward Keen and Kierra with the opposite bow-end. Both Nira and Rana were spinning their bows with blurring speed plucking arrows out of the air and letting them drop harmlessly into the water.

"Elves!" came a cry from the shore. Krieg jerked forcing Nira off balance for a moment and an arrow got past her barely missing Jerith who dodged it quickly.

Rana shook the hood off of her head and yelled back, "You're damn right, elves, you child-murdering monsters!"

Keen glanced at Krieg and saw his eyes widen at Rana.

With that rallying cry, both archers let loose a barrage of arrows into the trees that were too fast for Keen to count. Humans fell from their branches like dead flies, half a dozen each within a few short seconds.

"Kierra!" cried Joran, diving toward Krieg to get Krieg's oar out of the water as Jerith pulled his in, "Sing us out of here!"

Keen watched Krieg's slow, shocked expression as the rescuers burst into elves before his eyes all around him. Keen smiled weakly at him.

Kierra struggled out of her own cloak and reached down to touch the water. Despite the arrows flying and the dancing of the two archers back and forth as they caught and shot arrows with equal alacrity, Keen laid back and closed his eyes. He wanted to let Kierra's voice wash over him.

She began to sing. It was faster song than she'd sung to him before, but it flowed like water. In his arms he could feel her drawing each breath and swaying gently. The boats picked up speed.

A whoosh and a thud startled him out of his reverie. An arrow had narrowly missed his ear and embedded into the hull of the canoe beside his face.

"Sorry, Keen!" Nira barked at him then returned quickly to the work of not missing another. She knocked two arrows at once, and Keen watched as both hit their disparate targets on the shore.

The boats were speeding along now, but the elven women had stopped firing. Rana reached to catch another arrow headed for Max's head and it splintered her bow, falling off into the water after impact. Nira leaped in front of her and began catching the arrows from the few archers left on the shore.

"Shoot them!" Krieg insisted, but Rana who was drawing a short sword and almost immediately knocking another arrow our of the air replied calmly, "We're out of bow range. Human bows are slow as dirt, but they have better range than ours." She knocked another arrow from the air.

The sun was rising. Keen barely had time to think about the fact that at this moment, their kinsmen had intended to be opening the trap doors at their feet that would have ended their lives. The longest night of Keen's life had come to an end, and so far, they weren't dead.

"We should be heading out of bow range now," Nira pointed out, her bow still raised defensively. The last two arrows fell just short of their craft and into the water.

"We may have another problem, though," Krieg informed them, fear etched in his steady voice.

Along the bank the trees had thinned and were giving way to open grass. A large stone wall sat just at the top of the embankment. In the gathering light of dawn, men were wheeling heavy carts slowly down to the rivers edge, and with them...cannons.

Joran perched defensively on his feet, squatted in the front of his skiff. He looked wide-eyed back at Keen who was busy glancing around at all of them for answers.

"The barrels, right?" Joran asked trepidatiously, "Just get them wet?"

Keen nodded slowly, uncertain of how Joran could be planning to do such a thing, "Once they're open anyway."

"Unless you're planning to soak them," Krieg cut in, "In which case they could be closed."

Kierra changed her song. The water grew choppier. Max and Lynnine reached for their grandmother as the ride became especially rough.

"Can you do it?" Joran asked nervously.

Keen was afraid Joran was talking to him. Terror rose in his chest. How could Joran think that he would pull such a thing off?

But it was Kierra still in his lap that nodded her head at her brother. Kierra was staring fixedly and determinedly at the three small cannons now being aimed in their direction.

"I take it they can reach us from there?" Nira asked quietly, her voice trembling.

Krieg answered her, "Yep. No problem."

The barrels of black powder were wrenched open. Kierra's song reached an odd crescendo and a wave leapt out of the river and nearly missed the barrels, soaking the feet of the men loading them.

She shook her head as she kept singing. The humans in the two boats were holding on as the wavy water now threatened to toss them out. Krieg had his wife and daughter pulled close in his strong arms, but he was watching Kierra and glancing back to the shore with a fear Keen had never seen from his brother before. Even the elves were crouched low in the rocking canoes.

Kierra built her song up again and the second wave knocked over the nearest barrel, spilling its now-wet contents across the bank. The men were shouting, but two cannons were still being loaded.

The first fired. Keen and Kaith dove over their mother, grandmother, niece and nephew, leaving Kierra to wriggle out from under Keen to keep singing. In the other boat, Joran and Jerith flipped the skiff, dumping them all in the water as the well-placed cannonball burst the end of the canoe where Joran had been moments before.

Rana jumped to the other boat, landing on its bottom, and quickly fished

Emma from the water as Jerith and Krieg emerged, panting, holding Lara up. Joran's head appeared through the hole in their boat, and Nira made it the few feet to the far bank and was climbing out.

Kierra called up another wave and splashed it down right on top of the powder wagon, but the last cannon was already loaded.

"Please backfire," Keen heard his younger brother muttering, "Please be wet and backfire..."

Rana jumped back over as the last cannon prepared to fire. They were quickly approaching the bend in the river that would take them away from the encroaching rapids into the more serene Shill'Arin River that led into the Willows.

Rana began wrapping a cloth from her belt around the arrow she had pulled.

"How bad would it be if that thing went up over there?" she asked Keen.

Keen looked terrified at his brother, who was frowning.

"Quick!" she yelled, as Nira leapt back onto their boat behind Keen's head from a tree branch overhead, "How bad?"

"For them? Or for us?" Keen stammered.

Rana shot him an incredulous look.

"Bad," Krieg answered, trying to hold on to his family as the boat was being flipped back over by Joran and Jerith, "But worse for them."

Keen heard metal strike metal behind him. Rana knocked her cloth-covered arrow as the men on the shore lit their fuse. Nira reached across Keen and Kierra and lit Rana's arrow. Keen looked desperately toward the bend in the river. It wasn't nearly close enough.

Rana fired. Her flaming arrow reached the wagon before the cannon blew its contents toward them. The explosion was immediate.

A deafening noise and a gargantuan ball of flame engulfed the bank. The force of the explosion flipped both boats and flung them and their occupants through the air, down the river and back into the water along with dirt, wood and several tree branches. Keen couldn't see. He felt the boat knock hard into his back as he came down face-first and went under. Trying to come back up, he hit his head on the underside of a canoe but had found an air pocket. A soft body plunged into him under the water. He lifted it, and found himself holding Max, gasping for air.

They bumped into something hard and stationary under the water. Keen followed it up under the lip of the boat, holding tightly to Max as he moved. He was right. It had been a tree root and by climbing along it, he emerged next to the river bank, still clinging to the roots of an old tree as they spilled over the side of the bank into the water. Keen hoisted Max up onto the twisted knot of roots and looked around.

Their boat was hung on the roots. Nira came around from the far side carrying Lynnie in her arms. Granny emerged over the top of the overturned canoe, being hoisted from behind by someone, and once she was holding on by herself, Keen's mother received the same assistance. They had made it to the bend and could easily turn here onto the Elvish Shill'Arin River, although the water tried desperately to drag them past and into the rapids.

The other boat was heading quickly into the rougher, faster waters. Across the open mouth of the Shill'Arin, Keen saw Krieg's head pop out of the water along with Emma's as she clung to his neck. He held her toward the bank so she could grab on while he raised Lara up and out, gasping for air, with his other arm. He looked around desperately.

"We've got Lynnie and Max!" Keen shouted and watched the relief wash over his brother.

Joran and Jerith were helping a bleeding Kaith out of the water just beyond Krieg. Keen looked around in horror.

"KIERRA!?"

Then he saw it: a dark, soft figure, muddy and green, floating helplessly face down nearer to the middle of the river, headed for the rapids.

"Krieg!!" Keen yelled desperately pointing. She'd already passed his bank and any hope Keen had of reaching her himself.

Krieg nodded. He threw the ropes still attached to the boat over to Joran and Jertith and said something Keen couldn't hear. Then Krieg waded out along the edge of the unsecured craft. Keen could see his brother struggling against the strength of the water's current. He reached the end of the boat and extended himself as far out into the water as he could without letting go. It was enough.

Krieg snared Kierra by the back of her tunic and pulled her toward the boat Joran and Jerith were desperately tying to the nearest tree. On the shore Lara clung to Emma who was screaming "Daddy!" above the roar of the angry water.

A tall figure out of the corner of his eye cause Keen to look back for a moment. Rana had climbed onto his own boat behind his mother and grandmother, and had stood up on it trying to get help from him in getting them to safety.

Keen glanced again back at Krieg. He wished he had an elven bond. Then he'd know...

Krieg had strong armed her out of the water and practically tossed her to her waiting cousin. Joran and Lara were moving to help him out of the water.

Keen climbed up onto the bank and reached for Granny who was clinging for dear life to the underside of the canoe, lying on her stomach. What had he gotten his family into?

He slid Granny across the boat while Rana helped his mother crawl gently to shore. Granny's blouse was bloody, but she seemed to be only scratched up. She hugged him. He wasn't sure he deserved it, but pulled her in tightly anyway.

Keen looked back across at the far bank and saw Kierra's hand reach up and touch Jerith's face. Joran was standing over him panting and looked relieved. Keen's eyes caught Krieg's behind Joran. Keen nodded a thank you to his brother who smiled and nodded back.

Kaith's voice came from behind Krieg and was shouted across to the other side, "What now?"

Jerith was lifting Kierra clumsily in his arms as he tried to stand. Krieg stood and came over to them, taking Kierra gently from her cousin. In Krieg's broad arms, she looked like little more than a rag doll. Lara was helping Emma up and along the slippery bank. Even from here, Keen could see that Kaith was bleeding from his brow and was stumbling more than he should as he tried to walk. Joran saw it, too, and reached to help him.

Keen still had Granny in his arms. She looked a mess. Little Max was still sitting at his feet, clinging to ancient tree roots. Keen lifted him up. Nira still had Lynnie, so Rana moved to help Keen's mother who was clutching an injured arm. They were alive. Keen knew they didn't have him to thank for that, but he was grateful for it. He hoped they'd all forgive him some day, especially now that they had the days ahead of them again to do that.

Rana responded to Kaith's question, "Head up the bank. We'll find a way to cross!"

"We seem to have ended up with your boat!" Joran called, "Not sure how." He shook his head, "It may still be usable if we can get into calmer water again."

Joran left Kaith leaning against a tree away from the waters edge and clambered over to where Jerith was untying their surprisingly intact canoe. Then they turned it over and pulled it into the waters of the Shill'Arin.

The boat by Keen was splintered along one side and still had the hole in the bow where Joran had once been sitting. It had a crack along one side that was threatening to tear it in two. So, they turned away from it, and headed into the Willows.

As they moved along the banks in the shadow of the familiar trees, two things became immediately obvious. The elves were nervously watching the canopy as if they didn't trust the trees themselves, and they were clearly exhausted beyond hope of traveling much further.

Eventually Rana, who was using the trees to keep herself going by pushing off each with her hand as she passed, answered Keen's questioning look, "We've spotted scouts from both armies in this area recently. The humans aren't so much a worry; they make too much noise in the woods for elf ears to miss. But the shadowelves…"

And with that her voice trailed off as an uneasy shadow of fear and exhaustion drew her back into her own thoughts. The little ones were cold, wet and scared, and the adults weren't doing too much better. Keen glanced across to the far bank and saw that Krieg had a hand on his sword hilt. He kept following the elves' eyes up into the trees and glancing nervously back at Keen who didn't have a comforting look to respond with.

When they reached a narrow spot in the river, Joran signaled silently for Keen's group to wait for them to cross. He was clearly keeping everyone as silent as they could manage, but they were still audible all the way across the small river. Joran's nervousness, coupled with the extra noise Keen's family couldn't seem to help but make, tightened the dread in his chest with each minute as time kept passing more quietly than it should, if not as silently as it may have needed.

Kierra was being carried. When the small canoe had limped its way across the river one final time, Keen was glad to be the one carrying her at last, even if it was arguably a bad idea for him to be doing it. The other elves had reached a point that they could barely walk and Joran reminded Keen that their journey had been far and quick to reach the humans in the first place, and they had frailer stamina than the humans.

"Where can we rest then?" asked Keen leaning against a tree to support Kierra's limp weight. She had smiled at him when he lifted her, but now she barely had her eyes open. He comforted himself that he could feel her breathing easily against him, and that was all he needed from the universe right now, "Is there anything safe nearby?"

The four still-standing elves looked at each other before Joran's blood-shot eyes met Keen's, "Yes," he answered, "But your family may not like it."

Keen didn't wait for Krieg to react to this pronouncement, "Will we just be uncomfortable, or is it not really safe?"

"Oh it's safe. Elves don't harm children, pregnant women and families, and the officer in charge is a friend of my father's…"

"Officer in charge?" Krieg boke in nervously.

It looked to Keen as if simply moving his gaze from Keen to Krieg was taking all of Joran's remaining effort. But the elf met the large man's eyes and nodded stoically. "River base camp. I'm surprised we haven't seen a patrol yet really," Joran went on and looked back at Keen, "It's safe. I wouldn't take you there if it wasn't. You know that…"

Keen answered with an obvious nod.

Joran closed his tired eyes and nodded back, "I'm sure it'll make you all nervous, and they'll probably take those swords from you. But no one will hurt you, and it's the safest option we have for miles…"

Keen glanced down at Kierra who was watching him, and then he looked around, first at the other elves, then his family, ending on Krieg who looked almost as nervous as he did facing the cannons, but he was clearly resigned. No one had a thought of asking these elves to go on any further, and the human group was lost without them.

Keen looked back at Joran and nodded.

One glance back at Krieg told him that his older brother had never hoped he'd been so wrong in his life, but Keen knew he wouldn't be convinced until they made it out of the military encampment.

It clearly bothered both Rana and Nira that they were able to get so close to the camp without being stopped. Both appeared more and more agitated as they walked, as if the continued silence of the trees was a personal affront. Nira's agitation was making Jerith more brooding than Keen had ever seen him. He kept watching her with weary but perceptive eyes and following her erratic gaze up into the trees. She'd walk backwards for a while, tensely, and Jerith would watch the ground.

Joran stayed near Keen. It was clear that the silence in the trees was on his mind, too, but he was watching Kierra more worriedly than anything else. The sun was fully up by the time they heard the unmistakable sounds of a large group of people up ahead some distance. The sounds seemed normal for a large encampment and not like the sounds of fighting or agitation, so Keen's elven friends began to relax, their demeanors betraying their utter and complete exhaustion.

They were stopped soon after. A group of three elves with the same sleek, dangerous bows that Rana and Nira normally carried approached them cautiously. Their bows were in their hands, but not drawn, and their eyes wandered quickly over the whole group but lingered especially between Joran and Jerith.

"We were wondering when we'd see somebody," Joran admitted to them wearily.

The middle elf, a fairly short female, answered, "You were seen by scouts earlier, but they recognized the two of you," she indicated, of course, Joran and Jerith, the two officers, "and saw that you were carrying a wounded treesinger. They failed to mention that two of the humans with you are armed, though," she said peering distastefully at the swords on both Keen's and Krieg's waists, "I don't suppose it matters. The Forest Elder knows you're coming."

She glanced again at the two human swords, and Keen would have offered to hand his over if his hands weren't full of Kierra, but he decided to stay silent and let his in-laws handle it.

"Do you want them disarmed?" Joran asked almost agitatedly, but then that was Joran's go-to tone Keen thought, "Because that's not a problem."

"The Forest Elder will let you know," she answered back with an air that clearly said 'yes, but it's not up to me and I don't tend to agree with the person who gets that happy power.'

They turned and clearly expected to be followed.

Keen whispered quietly to Joran, while aware instinctively of Krieg trying to hear the conversation, "Who is the Forest Elder?"

"It's the command title for this base camp. I don't know who came up with that frankly, but like I said earlier, she's a friend of my Dad's. And my uncle's"

Keen nodded and glanced at Krieg who looked unmistakably like a man trying hard to trust because he had no other good option. But judging by the look on his face, trust must have a sour taste for Krieg, thought Keen.

The forest base camp sat along the banks of the river, much wider here again than at the point where they had crossed. It was clearly a permanent encampment. Most of the buildings were wooden, although there were tents scattered about as well. The place was full of wagons, fires, the smells of food and the oil of sharpening wheels. It was straw-strewn to cover the mud, and everywhere, everywhere, were well-armed and armored elves. Keen guessed the camp must have housed 300 or more regularly, and didn't bother to glance at Krieg. He figured he had a pretty good idea of how his brother felt about it.

The woman who approached them was clearly the age of Kierra's mother. She was wearing very shiny, very strange, but clearly formidable silver armor, and she was armed to the teeth. Her face was hard and set, but her eyes were friendly and concerned. So, Keen tried to focus on those eyes. Everything else made him feel like a lamb who just realized what the slaughterhouse might be for.

Joran and Jerith both went forward and had a quick conversation with the woman, who looked to be very motherly toward them. Her eyes kept rising to meet Keen's and to see Kierra, and she certainly took in the full strangeness of their group. At one point her gaze snapped back to Joran's, a look of horror on her face. Keen sincerely hoped that was the 'they were going to kill them all' part of the story and not the 'so we were hoping you'd help us save them and let them live in the Willows' part.

Eventually Keen was summoned forward and a younger scout was asked to take Kierra up to the Healers' hut. She informed him kindly, but firmly that he and Krieg would have to surrender their weapons, either to her or to one of Joran or Jerith.

Keen handed Kierra relunctantly over to the scout and unhooked his belt.

"What would make you more comfortable, ma'am?" he asked the woman.

She looked deeply into his eyes for a moment as if she were reading something written there and then shook her head, "It doesn't matter to me as long as it's an officer."

Keen handed the belt and sword directly to her and she nodded at him. Krieg approached cautiously from behind, unbuckling his belt, too. Wordlessly he handed his to the woman as well. He didn't meet Keen's eyes at all, and Keen feared that another tirade was on the horizon.

They were shown to a large three-room supply shed that held mostly food, herbs, bandages and oil from what Keen could tell. Certainly this was no armory, but it was also not a prison. The back room, which seemed to be mostly medical supplies and hard tack also had 4 bunk-style beds along its walls.

"Sometimes we get weary travelers, or too many wounded for the healer's cabin. Anyway, you're welcome to this space while you need it, but we haven't the supplies to support you ourselves more than a day or two, and I don't recommend hunting in the area on your own." With that the woman turned and left, leaving their bedraggled array of refugees alone with each other.

Joran turned to the group at large and said, "Thanks for being willing to come here. I don't think any of us could have made it much further. Kierra sung speed and stamina into us so we could get to you in time, but now that it's worn off, we've got nothing left."

Rana was climbing up into a top bed and turning to wait for Joran to join her. Jerith and Nira had also selected a top bunk for themselves, and were removing the belts and remnants of weapons they still carried as they climbed in. Joran looked back at them and then again at the humans and added, "If you all aren't tired, would you mind just hanging out in here for us so we can sleep?"

It was Lara who spoke first, "I'm exhausted. We didn't sleep at all last night. Will they mind if we sleep in these beds, too?"

Joran looked curiously at her a moment and responded, "Of course not. Please get some rest if you need it."

"I'm hungry," whined Max.

"Me, too," agreed Lynnie and Emma was nodding. Lara looked to Krieg who tried to shush them.

Joran's shoulders dropped like a man who almost got to go to bed but didn't.

"Can I go?" Keen asked. I'm tired but not like you are. Will they let me get some food from somewhere?"

Joran looked relieved and nodded.

"You, yes. I told Almara that you're Kierra's lover. They'll accept that… they have to, in fact."

"Is Almara the woman we were talking to? The Elder or whatever?"

"The Forest Elder, yes. She and our fathers served together years ago when they were young and all city guards in WIllowmark. Her name is Almara. If she's not busy, you could ask her where to find food for your family. If she is busy…" he trailed off thoughtfully for a moment, "I guess ask anyone. I can't imagine they don't all already know you're here."

"I'll figure it out." Keen looked down at Max and Lynnie and then over at Emma and Lara who were climbing into a bottom bunk away from the elves, "I'll find you all something."

Keen wandered out into the camp. What he really wanted to find, was wherever they'd taken Kierra, but he started with food. He asked the first elf he saw, whom he startled, and was directed to a central fire where a large cauldron bubbled with something that smelled heavily of herbs and potatoes. The cook stirring the pot was clearly trying to stay on the opposite side of the large stew from Keen, and was wide eyed and wary the whole time, but he provided Keen with several bowls of hot, tasty-smelling food and a tray.

As Keen was walking away with his steaming treasure, a male elf came running up behind him yelling, "Excuse me!"

Keen turned. The elf was dressed strangely. More accurately, he was dressed just like Kierra, except that Keen had only ever seen her wearing that look. His green tunic was shorter and his leggings a little more pant-like, but the gold embroidery across the front was exactly the same as what Kierra wore. Keen had always just assumed that as a civilian, she just wore what she liked. Now he realized it meant something else.

"You're a Treesinger," Keen told him, although he realized he sounded stupid immediately.

The man smirked bemusedly, looked down at his garments and back up at Keen.

"I wanted to tell you that Kierra's OK," he said still smiling, "We're talking to her a bit more about everything that's happened, but we'll bring her back here shortly to get some rest."

"Good. She needs it. She needs to eat, too," Keen insisted, the smells coming from his tray making his stomach grumble loudly.

The man nodded. "But there's something I wanted to tell you, as her lover," he started looking more awkward and glancing down at his shoes for a moment before continuing, "When I sang for her healing…well…there were two." He looked into Keen's eyes to see if he understood. He didn't.

"Two what?" Keen was far too tired for riddles, he thought. Get to the point. Is Kierra OK or isn't she?

"Two lives. Inside of her. Hers and….well…another."

Keen pondered the man's face for what felt like an age. Was this some other kind of elven magic that Kierra hadn't explained to him yet?

The man in front of him sighed, "She's conceived. Very recently. The life in her has only just begun, but, she says it's yours. I thought you'd want to know."

Keens' brain, which clearly hadn't been working anyway, dropped clear down to his stomach like a brick. He was no longer hungry. In fact, he needed to get to a private tree, right away, or his brain was going to come flying out of his back end with the contents of his intestines. He stopped breathing. He knew he was staring at the man, but he didn't care. He was remembering her fragile form draped in his arms, not thirty minutes ago. She seemed too delicate to handle this, too breakable. He swallowed hard. Had he in fact broken her? What if she couldn't… what if he'd…

And with that his brain shut off completely. He looked helplessly down at the food in his hands and suddenly it didn't seem like nearly enough to sustain a Kierra that was growing another life, HIS child, inside of her. He felt goose bumps rising all over and he realized he was sweating.

When he looked back up at the elf, the man looked concerned and unsure. "Um…can I help you get that back to where you're going?"

Keen shook his head, found his voice, and said, "No. Thank you. For telling me. And for helping. And… Just help Kierra. Whatever she needs…"

The treesinger smiled weakly, "Well, it'll be you she needs overall, but right now, we'll bring her back for food and sleep." He nodded uncertainly at Keen and turned to go back in the direction he came from.

Keen delivered the food in a trance. Several people asked him what was wrong, especially Krieg who seemed to take his demeanor as a paranoid sign.

"Nothing," he kept lying over and over, "It's nothing."

He left and got more food for himself and Kierra. His reappearance did nothing to improve the mood of the cook, but he clearly wasn't going to try to refuse Keen anything.

He was nearing the shed when he saw Kierra coming. She was walking on her own again, which was good at least, but had two Treesingers with her. Both were male, and one was the elf who had brought him the news.

She smiled sleepily at Keen as she approached and he held up the final two bowls of stew he was carrying. She breathed in the steam and smell and laid her head against his upper arm. He wanted to put the arm around her, but he had hot stew in his hands. He looked to the other Treesingers, but they were walking away.

But Kierra was fine walking in by herself. His family had left them a lower bunk nearest the door with Kaith on the top. Kierra sat down and accepted her food gladly. She looked up at Krieg, who was eating with his family over by their bed and thanked him for rescuing her from the water.

He looked at her for a moment, then at Keen and back again before answering, "Least I could do. You saved us all."

"Oh I had help," she mused as she blew on a hot spoonful of needed nourishment.

"Yes, but, they came because of you, right?"

She looked over at him, shrugged her shoulders and smiled. Then she began to eat.

Keen stood in the doorway holding his uneaten soup in his hands, watching Kierra like she might explode.

"What's gotten into you Keen?" Krieg finally asked him.

Kierra looked up worriedly, but when her eyes met his, they widened in shock.

"They TOLD you?"

He nodded weekly.

Kierra looked mutinous, but was too hungry and tired to say any more. She just shook her head angrily and finished her meal.

Krieg, however, was still waiting for an answer. It appeared, as Keen glanced around the room, that only Jerith, Nira and Rana were asleep. Everyone else seemed to be more or less watching him.

"It seems I'm going to be a father," he said weakly to no one in particular. And he sat down next to Kierra to eat and to see her off to some good rest. He was content to ignore the rest of the room for now. He was reminded viscerally of the night he sat vigil over her while willing her not to die. Strange, how similar he felt right now.

As he laid down beside her sleeping form several minutes later, curling up around her, he decided that all he could do was be strong for her. And hope.

Eventually he drifted off to sleep.

Tollie

Tollie was really starting to worry about Jesp. Her wings looked droopy; she said very little, and she'd stopped talking much or even smiling. They were all struggling with the reality of the things that were going on around them, but Jesp was starting to really look ill.

Tollie discussed her concerns with Tallie during their shared watch that night, but it wasn't very helpful. Tallie pointed out, not unreasonably, that whatever the truth might be about Jesp's condition, there was nothing they could do about it. If Tollie was honest with herself, Tallie didn't really look any better. It hadn't been long enough for her stab wound to have healed, but plenty of time for it to have become infected. Tollie worried that she'd sounded insensitive, worrying over Jesp when she should have asked about Tallie.

She sighed. Again. That, at least, was something she was good at.

The few hours they stayed up, leading the beleaguered ponies along, seemed like all night. It didn't help that they had to guess at how much time had really passed, and tempers were growing closer to the surface. Time passed faster for those that were being asked to awaken and too slowly for those carrying on.

Just as Tollie and Tallie were beginning to have that tired discussion of how much time had passed and how much longer their turn would continue, Kyrt woke up in Tollie's saddlebag and stuck his head out.

"What is that noise?" he asked sleepily.

"Just us talking," Tallie answered with an edge of annoyance in her voice.

"No," he whispered, a look of concentration on his small, weary face, "It's not that."

They stopped the ponies and listened for a moment. Sure enough, Tollie and Tallie had been so engrossed in their own exhaustion and conversation they had missed the unmistakable noises of someone nearby, trying to be quiet.

"…not leaving you," the first voice whispered.

"I don't have anyone waiting for me. It doesn't matter."

And a third voice, "It does. We're your family. It matters to us."

"I just can't. Please. Just leave me."

"Shhhh you three," said yet another, "I thought I heard something. Up there in the trees…"

Tollie glanced at Tallie's fearful expression and then down at Kyrt's very serious one.

"I'll wake Jesp," he whispered so quietly that Tallie frowned uncomprehendingly at Tollie, "We'll go check it out."

It took a few minutes, and all Tollie could hear was the ruffling of the saddle bags and the munching sounds the ponies had begun to make.

Shortly, the faeries emerged. Tollie took a worried look at Jesp as she flew off clumsily. Then she glanced at Tallie who was watching them nervously herself. Tallie nudged her pony over to Thomas' and procded his sleeping form near where he was tied to the saddle.

"Wha? Already?" he drooled into his hair, "Can't be…"

"Shhhh," she responded kindly, "Something's going on."

He quickly untied himself and sat up suddenly alert. He looked hard at Tallie, silently asking for what information she could give him.

It was unnecessary. The sounds of a fight broke out not far from the trees.

"There they are!" someone shouted.

There was a male scream, some furious rustling, then the sounds of very small bows letting loose.

"What the?" someone exclaimed.

"Run!"

"I told you we're not leaving you!"

More rustling, more shouting.

Thomas grabbed his dagger that he kept in his belt and got down off of Robin. Tallie grabbed one out of her bag, too, and Tollie realized with jolt of disgust that it was the one that Thomas had removed from Tallie's back. It had been cleaned, fortunately, but it was unmistakably the same.

Tollie didn't have a weapon, and really, she wouldn't know what to do with one if she did. Nonetheless, she climbed down off of Sally and crouched low, moving as quietly as she could behind her sister and her friend.

"Duck!" came the voices again.

"There's too many of them! Go!"

"No!"

"Where are those arrows coming from?"

"Those are faerie darts. Find the damn little wretches!"

"Here faerie faerie faerie. Come out and play. We have a wonderful bath for you back at camp. It dissolves faerie wings. Slowly. A little skin, too. You just wait!"

"Faeries?"

"Don't let them get the faeries!"

"Come on, Brenn, up you get."

"No down, down down!"

Then a cackling of laughter and a long painful groan.

The trio crept into a small clearing. Several badly wounded Willowelves were huddling together on the ground, but the trees opposite the halflings were full of shadowelves. A familiar small male voice called down, "Get the Willowelves out of there!"

"OOOOO…the faeries brought more playmates," laughed a shadowy tree in the distance, but a pptht noise that ended with a soft thud near it, caused a Shadowelf to lurch from a branch, nearly falling.

"Nice try, you little flying rodents, but I'm immune to sleeping poison!"

There was laughter coming from the other trees while Jesp's quiet voice said, "Uh oh," from somewhere above them.

Tollie wasn't thinking, and she was trying not to start. She just moved forward and forced her body to do what she had been told. 'Just get them out of here,' she repeated to her tired brain, not daring to look around, 'Just do it.'

She had started to run forward when a thought she didn't want to push aside leapt into her terrified mind, and Tollie turned and bolted.

"Tollie!" yelled Tallie.

"Hahahaha. At least one of the little ones has some sense. Don't worry, Little One! We won't forget you!" a snarling voice called after her, "We'll hunt you down later! It'll be lovely sport! Just ask the wretched fools here who thought they could escape."

Tollie heard Tallie behind her give a long yell of resolve, and Tollie knew with a lump in her throat that Tallie had rushed one of them.

Tollie reached the ponies and spurred them forward. She gathered all three reins into her hands and pulled them toward the sound of battle, a direction that none of them wished to be led into.

It took several long minutes, it seemed, but Tollie got to the clearing with Robin, Sally and Molly in tow.

There was one shadowelf on the ground and one in the trees being harassed by tiny arrows. Two were on their feet on the ground, but one of these was hopping up and down grabbing his foot and spitting curses Tollie had never heard. Thomas was on the ground nearby with a bloody dagger in his hand, lunging for the other foot. Tollie didn't see Tallie, but the last visible elf was being slowed by something as he advanced menacingly on the helpless Willowelves lying on the ground.

Tollie reached these elves with the ponies. There were ten of them in all, and they weren't just wounded. They were in worse shape than Tollie had ever seen living beings. One was missing an eye. Many were missing fingers. All were covered in shallow wounds, burns and huge bruises. They were all wearing ragged, filthy pants with no other clothing, not even shoes, and most of them were so swollen in so many places, that it was almost a wonder to Tollie that the faeries had realized they were Willowelves. Two of them could have passed for small ogres, and Tollie could not have selected the gender of more than a few.

"Here, these ponies aren't large enough to carry you, but you can lean on them for support," Tollie told them gently, indicating the scared animals in her possession.

Two of the men struggled onto their feet and lifted a third man between them. They thanked Tollie as a Shadowelf arrow barely missed the top of one of their heads. Tollie jumped, but tried to stay calm so the ponies wouldn't bolt. They leaned the wounded man against Molly who stomped her feet nervously. An arrow hit one her saddlebags, but didn't apparently penetrate through to the beast beneath.

An apparently female elf was helped up and leaned on Molly's other side. Then Tollie let go of one rein and said, "Go on, Molly! Go!"

All three ponies tried to follow, but Tollie managed to cling to the tethers of the last two.

When two more badly wounded elves were leaned against Robin, that pony gratefully joined Molly in waddling free of the clearing.

The harassed Shadowelf fell from the tree as Jesp and Kyrt could be overheard cheering above, but the slowed elf had reached Tollie.

Tollie dodged the first downward thrust of his large sword that would otherwise have cut her in half. One of the Willowelves who was helping his comrades plowed sideways into him, knocking him to the ground.

Three elves tried to cling to Sally as the pony tried to bolt. One fell to the ground as the other two barely stumbled along behind her. The one-eyed elf crawled to the fallen one and helped him up, limping his way off into the direction the ponies had gone.

The remaining two Willoweves were on top of the Shadowelf that had reached them and were pommeling every inch of him that they could reach. There was a thud nearby that drew Tollie's attention. Thomas was standing over a shadowelf panting and looking around, "Tallie?" he shouted into the trees.

Tollie reached down and grabbed the fallen elf's large sword that he was desperately reaching for and drug it over to where Thomas had fallen on his knees sobbing, "Oh, Tallie!"

The fae had followed her, too. Tallie was laying in the tall underbrush, eyes barely open, with a blood-soaked gash across her midsection. Her unseeing eyes stared blankly up at her sister. Next to her, a dying shadowelf sputtered laughter. Tallie's dagger was lodged in his throat, but he still held on to one of his own. It was coated in fresh blood. Tollie dodged the elf's weakened attempt to jab at her and stomped Tallie's dagger through his neck.

The sounds of struggle eventually stopped behind them, but Tollie didn't care. She stood helplessly staring down at her lifeless sister. The last of her family was gone. She hadn't felt this alone even when her father had died, because at least then, Tallie was still somewhere in the world, even if Tollie didn't think she cared. Now they were all gone.

Her grip loosened, and the heavy Shadowelf sword fell from her hands. Her foot, which she hadn't given a second thought, caught the huge thing by the blade. Tollie screamed.

Everyone around her jumped, and as quickly as they could limp and hobble, the last two Willowelves even made it over to help.

Tollie was sure her foot was cut in two. The pain seared like burning fire all the way up her short leg.

Thomas was desperately trying to pull it out when a friendly, if shaky, voice behind him said, "Here. Let me."

Tollie was still standing. Her left hand on a nearby tree for support. She was staring down at the ground, but not at her sword-split foot. She saw the feet of her rescuer. He was standing on the sides of them. The bottoms were thick, black and swollen from burns.

She felt the sword loosen and pull free. She screamed again and hit the leaf-strewn forest floor hands and nose first, staring helplessly at the elf's ruined feet.

"Oh my. Oh my I'm so sorry!" sobbed a nearby female voice, "She gave her life for us. She didn't have to....to do...to do that."

"We'll help you get her back to her family," the male elf said quietly.

Then there was Jesp's voice, "She's her only family. They were all each other had."

Tollie felt someone wrap her mangled foot in something soft, then Thomas' gentle hands offered to help her up to walk. "We can't stay here," he told her gently, his own tears choking his words.

"We can't leave her," Tollie insisted.

"The elves are getting her," Thomas replied.

Tollie risked a glance up. The two elves, one male and one female, both struggling to walk themselves, were cradling Tallie between them like parents mourning a stricken child. Tollie felt her tears begin to run freely, her sorrow choking her breath.

"Over here!" came a nasty shout.

The elves' faces shown with abject panic.

"We have to go!" Kyrt insisted, "Now! We'll cover you! Run!"

It was all Tollie could do to accept Thomas' help onto her good foot. She wrapped her left arm around him, and hobbled as quickly as she could manage back toward where the ponies had gone, hoping that the elves still had Tallie with them. Hoping, too, that she wouldn't lose Kyrt and Jesp in this.

They met up with the one-eyed elf who was using Sally to come back to look for them. He took Tollie from Thomas as angry voices and shouts filled the woods behind them. He placed her bad foot, which Tollie now realized was wrapped in Thomas' outer shirt, her purple toes peaking out from the thick knotted end, on top of one of his own upturned feet, and wrapped a surprisingly strong arm around her. He was still leaning on the startled pony for support with his other arm. Tollie could now see that his own left foot was not just burned, but badly mangled, too.

The other two elves laid Tallie's limp form on top of Sally and Tollie nearly fell into her new elf support as a new wave of horror and sadness hit her at the sight of Tallie's limp form.

Tollie wasn't sure how far they'd hobbled, or even in what direction they had gone. She was vaguely aware of her elf companion and others trying to make sure that no one was being left behind. Even the faeries had made a reappearance at some point. Tollie knew something was wrong with them, because they were caught out of the air by concerned voices and placed on a pony offered by some other stranger's voice. Tollie didn't look up. She realized that she was terrified stiff of raising her gaze and seeing Tallie draped lifelessly over Sally. So, she just kept moving forward in the direction the kind elf steered her.

She could hear Jesp and Kyrt talking. She couldn't tell what they were saying, but she knew their voices well, so they had made it back alive. That was what mattered. Tollie couldn't lose anyone else. She just couldn't. One more, she thought to herself, one more and I will come completely apart at the seams and float off into blissful nothingness. I will just cease to be. I cannot lose anyone else. She felt as though her own soul was bleeding out into the universe.

Eventually they stopped. Tollie could hear panting all around her. Then Jesp spoke.

"Any idea how much further Willowmark is?"

An elf answered, "Probably much too far away. We were only trying to reach our own front lines for help."

Then Thomas' voice replied, "Then maybe I should go on ahead and see if I can bring help back."

Tollie looked up in the direction of the voice. She tried to shoot Thomas a desperate look to say, no, please don't go. I can't lose you. His eyes met hers and he smiled sadly at her.

Jesp was somewhere behind him when she piped in with, "I'll go with you. I'm okay."

Thomas was still looking at Tollie, but he nodded at Jesp's words. He approached and told Tollie sweetly, "I'll come back. We're not leaving you. Or Tallie or Kyrt either." His eyes strayed to the pony where Tallie was laying dead. Tollie didn't follow his watery glance. She closed her eyes.

She knew she was in better shape than the elf that was helping her, but she couldn't seem to do any more than cling to him and put one badly damaged aching foot in front of the perfectly good one as he pulled her along. She was feeling guilty, but she couldn't make herself snap out of it.

Her elf spoke, "We'll look out for them. And thank you…for everything. We almost didn't make it."

Tollie opened her eyes and looked at Thomas who was nodding. Jesp flew over to him. She looked OK to Tollie. She flew over to Tollie with eyes full of concern, "We'll be right back with help. And Kyrt's here," she choked on her words, "If you need him."

"Is he OK?"

"He will be. Got his wing clipped by an arrow. I just hope it can be fixed…" her voice trailed off and Tollie followed her easily back to the memory of a time when she, Jesp, had a damaged wing and couldn't fly and where Kyrt had cared for her, "Other than that he's OK." Tollie had been with the pair long enough to know that not being able to fly was really not OK.

"I'll look after him," Tollie offered. She found that the offer filled her with some missing strength. She straightened up a little, but she still couldn't look at Sally's load.

"You sure?" the elf asked, "That foot's really bad."

Tollie looked down at the elf's feet guiltily and then up at the elf with her eyebrows raised. His ruined face broke into a friendly smile that was missing some teeth, "Don't worry about me," he said, and then he hesitated, "I have a family I'm trying to get back to. It's easier," he admitted, his smile fading and the guilt Tollie felt entering his eyes, "It's easier to have your body hurt than your family."

Tollie stared at him long and hard, the tears welling up all over again. He was right. She'd rather that her own body were as mangled as his, even if it could never be fixed, if it would bring back her family. Her lip quivered and she nodded curtly at him. He knew, she realized, that her need of his support had had very little to do with her foot, and he was right.

Tollie moved carefully and clumsily over to Robin and looked down at a miserable Kyrt. His right wing was torn from his back almost a third of its length and was bent at an angle that made even Tollie, who had no idea what it felt like to have wings, cringe. Tollie leaned over Robin's back and pulled Kyrt into a nest-like embrace. He laid his head on her arm. Neither had anything they needed to say out loud.

The sun had risen, but only shown dimly through the thick trees and the gathering forest mist. It looked to Tollie like the breaking dawn had about as much emotional energy as she, herself had. The waiting elves gathered around the three ponies and sat or laid down in the thickest underbrush. All of their fates, even Tallie's body's thought Tollie, now rested with Thomas and Jesp finding them help soon enough. Tollie let go of Kyrt, slid down the side of the pony so that she was sitting down gratefully on the soft leaves. Then she just let go of it all and sobbed into her own hands for what felt like hours.

By the time help arrived, it was already late at night. Fear had replaced sadness, and the elves had set up watches around the thick growth of bushes where they were hiding. Tollie had spent some time with Tallie finally. She cried the hardest while apologizing to her sister for having gotten her into this mess. Turned out that Tollie's problems had cost Tallie more than her own problems had. Kyrt gave her the space to say what she needed to say for a while. Then he climbed carefully out of the saddlebag that had been placed on the ground for him and walked trepidatiously toward her.

Watching Kyrt walking in the dark through the leaves with large feet all around him, his eyes wide with fear in light of the full moon, brought Tollie out of her reverie. She reached down and lifted him gently into her lap, which he thanked her for.

They were sitting there quietly, Tallie's hand in Tollie's, her body covered in a blanket from her own packs, Kyrt's head leaned against Tollie's chest, when the sounds of approaching men, horses and wagons became audible heading toward them.

At first, the noise brought palpable tension to the group, but someone whispered, "They're coming from the direction of home!" and tensions turned to hope and even a little excitement.

Sure enough, Thomas and Jesp had found the willowelves' own front lines, and the army set up there had come in force. These were elves prepared to fight the shadowelf armies that lurked out there in the darkness somewhere in order to bring their own home. Their armor shown in the moonlight; their weapons bristled with fury. Their faces were full of resolve and tenacity.

"We're saved," Tollie whispered to Tallie, "Thanks for watching over us."

She didn't know if she believed in anything like that, but it made her feel better to think that her sister was still somehow there.

Their rescuers had brought more than arms and numbers of men, they'd brought food, water, medical supplies and wagons. A decision was made to gather everyone up, assist them on the way, and to fall back to their last secure positions. This suited Tollie and Kyrt fine. It meant getting out of here.

The journey took a few hours, but Tollie didn't sleep. She lay in the back of a wagon, watching the treetops go by overhead. Once they reached the army's previous camp, a young man in a stunningly green tunic with elaborate gold embroidery down the front came to see Tollie about her foot. He unwrapped it, and Tollie finally took a good look at what she'd done to herself. She threw up and passed out.

The next day she was riding along in the back of a wagon with Thomas sitting beside her, Kyrt laying in his lap, and Jesp sitting on the railing behind his head. She'd woken up for a brief breakfast before being loaded into the wagon, but no one wanted to disturb her any further. The elf had sung her to sleep over and over again in the night, but she'd lost the foot, half of it at least. She was grateful that the elves were able to keep her out for most of it, but now she felt as though her foot were ten times the usual size and being smashed by giant bricks bathed in lava. No one could do much about that, though, since the painful part of the foot wasn't really there anymore.

Kyrt's wing had been strapped down with spider webbing, a trick Harold had used on Jesp and that the faeries themselves had suggested. The elves weren't sure what else to do for him, but assured him that there were faeries in Willowmark that could be consulted.

"Where's Tallie?" Tollie suddenly roused enough to ask.

"She got her own wagon," Thomas answered her kindly.

"She shouldn't be alone," Tollie choked.

"She's not. A treesinger rode with her as an honor guard."

It seemed to Tollie that they rode all day and all night. They stopped occasionally for food and other necessaries. Tollie didn't care to try and figure out how they were splitting the shifts or even where they were going. She just rode along, trying to ignore the hole where her foot had been, and the hole where her family had been.

Sometime in the night Tollie awoke to the most strangely beautiful sounds she'd ever heard. Somewhere in the distance, people were singing. The treesinger's song to her while her foot was amputated was soothing and beautiful on its own, as much as she had been able to focus on it, but this was beyond even the magic of that. It sounded to Tollie as if the angelic avatar of all the old gods had joined together in one ethereal chorus designed solely to beckon her toward them. She felt as though she would have had all the strength in the world to protest if the wagon failed to steer her in that direction. The music haunted her, and fluttered in and out of her dreams for the rest of the night.

And then sometime after dawn the next day, they were, at last, within view of Willowmark.

From Tollie's point of view, turning around and peering over the back of the wagon-driver's seat, it appeared as if one mighty river just out of view must have been split into three by the most enormous oak tree Tollie could ever have imagined. In fact, as they drew nearer, it appeared to be about six giant oaks grown so close together as to be indiscernible from each other. High up in the canopy, its bottom layers barely visible beneath the forest's other trees, was the underside of what had to be a fairly immense city, connected even from its multitude of top trunks to still more trees by bridges as high up as the tallest branches Tollie had seen elsewhere in the forest.

Then there was the music. The music that had been teasing her all night with peace and home and ethereal beauty beyond the world was coming from the city itself. It filled the surrounding forest. It called to the very trees and reverberated with the life of the woodlands. The birds, the forest animals on the ground, large and small, the insects in the air and below the ground, all were sung alive by its enchanting rhapsody. That music seemed to heal Tollie in ways she thought she could never be whole again.

She looked around at her friends. They were all shining with the same inner light she felt radiating from herself as they watched the mesmerizing city weave its seduction across what surely must have been the center of the world. As they traveled even closer, it seemed to Tollie that the distance between themselves and the enthralling haven before them was getting closer than their speed would have suggested. It was as if the city itself was trying to meet them halfway.

At the base of its immense arbors, long boats glided effortlessly in and out of the city's river harbors, each painted grayish white and golden like sunrise and each manned by one standing treesinger at the tall aftside end. Other smaller vessels dotted the spaces in between: fishing vessels, merchant craft, even canoes that appeared to be personal vehicles of travel, followed the endless journey of the rivers to and from the great alluring capital.

Tollie gasped.

The driver turned and smiled to her, "Beautiful, isn't she? The last of the great elven cities that existed before Andarraine."

All around her, Tollie saw the heads of tortured Willowelves peeking out of the other wagons, smiles spreading relentlessly across their swollen faces. Home, safety and family waited for them in those trees, things they'd almost never had again. Tollie swallowed hard. She wondered what waited for her up there in that canopy. But one thing was for sure, she finally felt that the crown might be safe.

She glanced at the faeries. They looked excited and eager, and Tollie smiled a rare smile down at the pair of them.

"Shanis!" cried the one-eyed elf from the back of his wagon, soliciting the attention of an officer riding alongside the wagon train, "Are they already sending out the Silent Boats?"

"Absolutely!" the man called Shanis replied, "We sent word of your escape ahead!"

The injured elf turned back toward a wagon rolling along behind him and shouted, "Brenn! Brenn!"

A sorrowful-looking wounded elf replied with a moan.

"Who were your closest friends in the unit?"

The answering elf looked thoughtfully at him and said, "Jayna and Dalven, why?"

The elf with only one good eye nodded and said, "I thought that's what I remembered. Shanis, would you send Silent Boats out for Jayna and Dalven from my old unit, too? They're the closest thing Brenn has for family right now."

"Sure thing," Shanis replied, "I'll do that first thing when we stop."

"Thanks, Shavanir," sighed the one called Brenn, "It'd be good to see them."

"We'll make sure you get to," Shanis told him.

They crossed an ornate wooden bridge near the base of the nearest immense trunk, the oaks of Willowmark so enormous above them that they could no longer discern their width or any separation between them, and then they began a slow spiral up and around the entirety of the collective trunks. As they ascended, the pathway was lined with flowering bushes, an occasional fountain and frequent ornate benches. But as they climbed they followed, and were followed by, more and more people flooding into the city. All were willowelves as far as Tollie could see, and most seemed to be carrying all of their worldly possessions in with them. On the other side, the only elves who seemed to be leaving were soldiers.

But at least there were faeries. All along the great spiraling pathway leading up and into the city, faeries flitted and fluttered in and out of the bushes and laughed and played around the fountains. Tollie noticed that Jesp's wings were fluttering excitedly as she watched them, and Kyrt was sitting up straighter watching them.

They spiraled so far up into the trees that clouds occasionally passed across their path, but eventually they evened out onto the first flat expanse that clearly sat beneath and across from many many more. And the view hit them all with an esoteric force that knocked the wind from their lungs.

From up here, Tollie thought she could see the whole forest. They were still under the canopy of the tallest trees, but higher, too, than many, and so they enjoyed the breathtaking view of shaded, living forest expanse, tree tops hosting multitudes of birds and insects, and vast clear blue skies. Tollie thought she could just make out mountains in the distance, but was so turned around from the upward spiral she wasn't sure if she was facing the Breaking or the Barrow Hills. Either way, it was lovely. She wished that Tallie could have seen it.

They were met by a middle-aged elven woman wearing a treesinger's outfit. She was flanked by four other treesingers. She held her arms wide in welcome and immediately approached the wagon containing the one-eyed elf and the male elf who had rescued Tollie from the sword-wielding shadowelf that nearly cleaved her in two.

"Shavanira!"[7] she exclaimed, "I can't tell you how relieved we all are!"

"Thank you, Elanra," one of them replied.

"We'll have you to the Healer's Village here directly. It is so good to see you both!"

"Elanra, is my daughter still in the city? I'd love to see her."

"No. She finished her training and went off into the world. She's become something of a war hero herself I've heard. I'm sure you'll find that you're very proud of what she's accomplished."

"A war hero?" the man exclaimed. Tollie strained over the edge of her wagon and saw that the voice belonged to the man who had lost his eye. "You're kidding!" he insisted, "My Kierra?"

---

[7] Shavanir plural

Brody

Brody could not remember a time when his heart was more heavy. Though the last five years had been tough, the last 3 weeks had been tougher. He had answers now, a sense of purpose, a part to play in the events of the wider world. He felt more like a man now than he ever had before, but still he felt like a sinking boat in a storm, out of control and lost. He also felt that he had held things up too many times. He was the one who had had to go back to his family in Kipping and see them settled while the elves sat and waited. He had been determined to lay the dead to rest at Luring even though it took two days. They'd wasted a day hauling his father's body up piece by piece and laying him to rest, and he had been unwilling to leave the children of his village alone and had therefore cost them 4 more days. 23 days it had been now since the elves had awoken and restarted their journey. And by Brody's calculation, they could have been to this point in 2 days if they had not been slowed down by him.

Now the king had ordered the execution of the elves. What he and Finn hadn't said and probably should have said was that news was traveling to Kipping even as they sat here that the king was both raising taxes *and* offering a large bounty for the capture of any elves in the kingdom. Brody wanted to believe in the integrity of his own people, but the truth was that he didn't. They were simple, superstitious, and poor, and it was only a matter of time, a short time probably, before they were being hunted by the very soldiers whose ranks Finn had once hoped to join.

Now he wanted to get on with it. He was glad to hear that there was so much news to be shared. Maybe now they could get somewhere. Maybe, miraculously, it will not have been too late.

Arisa's pronouncement had brought him out of his reverie. Finn, Adrik and he had all bombarded her with questions when she spoke, and it felt good to be caught up in it again. He was just fine with the focus remaining off of him for the moment.

"OK, for clarification," Arisa pronounced grandly, clearly enjoying the center stage, "Queen Kajiri is currently the queen of the Shadowelf Kingdom of Darkwald. She is bent on awakening the ancient evil that she, like most people, believe is heralded by the Prophecy. She *claims*," and here she glanced poignantly at Adrik, "To be responsible for releasing the two Titans so far."

"Well, we don't know what she's claiming about this second one," Adrik cut in. "We know that five years ago, well almost 6 actually, when we started this journey, she was claiming to have unleashed the Fire Titan and was looking to unleash Water next. I think it's obvious that your fathers," and here he gestured clearly to Finn and Brody, "somehow stumbled across her agents, possibly even thwarted them. We don't know what precisely unleashed the Titan this time."

"Except," Brody cut in, allowing yet another terrible visage of the last 3 weeks cross into his mind again, "We know there have been shadowelves up here recently, at least hiding in caves and eating children."

Adrik held his gaze for a moment and Brody feared he'd said too much, then Adrik glanced down again and said, "Yeah. That's true."

"Well, I've had a thought," Arisa continued excitedly, "And really I don't know why it didn't occur to me before, but it kinda came to me while I was sick. Most of the Runes that were studied at Felwater, the Rune Keep where I was apprenticed, came from the Prophecy. All of them come from the time period of Andarraine. There really aren't too many *places* that have corresponding runes. See, I said before that I had started to question the integrity of some of the lead Librarians. It would not be difficult to convince an unwitting scholar to *sell* a piece of information as seemingly harmless as 'which runes refer to *places?*' I bet there are only 4."

"But then how do you figure out which element belongs to each, without knowing the prophecy that is?" Brody asked, deeply intrigued.

"Well, every rune has been studied for 2 thousand years. Everything that's ever been known about each is contained in that library. If a librarian has sold information about just 4 seemingly innocuous runes, he or she may have sold all the information about those runes, or at least enough for someone who knew what they were looking for to get that clue. All she would have needed was a corresponding element. That information was probably right there."

"But how does she know what order they go in?" Adrik asked, clearly considering this possibility.

Arisa looked at him thoughtfully. "That I don't know," she admitted.

"The point is," Brody picked up and ran with the thread, "She had to be getting help from inside the Library. If you were only an apprentice, you don't really know how much the scholars or librarians, or whatever they were called, knew about the Prophecy, or how much they'd have been willing to sell. It sounds like there's a traitor in that Rune Keep that may have some answers we need."

"But that's a long way from here," Adrik pointed out, "And we always suspected something treacherous was going on there. How does this help us now?"

Arisa looked crestfallen. "I guess it doesn't," she conceded.

"I don't know that that's true," Finn offered chiming in, "How many place runes can you think of? If we can figure out which two places are left It's fifty-fifty which one's next. We may still be able to head this off."

Both elves considered him intently before Arisa answered, "There's a rune for an ancient graveyard in the desert beyond the Darkwald, one for this mountain, and one for an ancient coastal fortress far to the southwest of my own homeland." She looked at Adrik as if the answer might be written on his face, "But I can only think of those three."

"The rumor in the Darkwald before the Fire Titan came was that Kajiri had sent an expedition into the desert...No one knew why. There was a crater there or something she supposedly thought had magic potential. That was quite some time before the Fire Titan that I heard that, though, maybe 2 years."

"Well, it took two expeditions five years apart to get the Water Titan, right?" Brody offered, desperately wanting to say something useful here, "Maybe that first one didn't go right on the first try either?"

Adrik nodded, "Possible. But it's also possible that they got there and realized they had it out of order. If that's the case, then getting to that one now will be easier for her than it will be for us."

"Well, then let's hope that's not the case," Arisa was biting her lip now. "If we assume that the desert tombs...."

"Wait a minute!" Finn exclaimed, "Like sepulcher entombed within...The mighty idols sing their din!"

"But doesn't that passage refer to earth....tumbling out of the sky or something?" asked Brody, sincerely wishing he had Finn's memory.

"Yeah it does," he answered, "But several lines earlier."

"What's the new part?" Brody asked Adrik, remembering that he'd said there had been more.

"It's short, but I know where it goes. 'For when at last the Wind shall ride...And threaten desert, plain and tide,...By then all fate may be written...By those who've had the ear to listen.' She recited the part you just mentioned ending with 'The mighty idols sing their din' and then went straight into this new bit, like a continuation. So unlike the first two bits we got, we know how this bit fits into at least one other part."

"So what does that tell us?" Brody asked, feeling more and more stupid by the minute.

Adrik shrugged, "I doubt we'll know until we have the whole thing." He sighed, "Hopefully Arisa will remember."

He glanced at Arisa and she hung her head. Brody knew Adrik didn't mean to be accusing her. At least, he didn't believe that about Adrik, but it was clear that Arisa's failure to remember what she read was weighing on her. Then Brody himself had a rush of insight.

"Wait a minute! Yes it does tell us something!" he exclaimed, flush with a sense of revelation, "It tells us that Wind comes last! That means that earth, wherever that one is, is the next one!"

They all looked at Brody, smiles crossing their faces, all nodding. Brody couldn't believe his moment of inspiration. It washed away some of the lingering doubt he had been feeling. Then Finn spoke up and put more of the puzzle together, but in a way that was foreboding rather than exhilarating.

"Arisa? Is there a rune for the Rune Keep itself?" he asked quietly.

Arisa met Finn's eyes, and a look of fear crossed her face. "Yes..."

"And does 'Felwater' suggest there's water nearby? Maybe a river?"

She frowned, clearly not liking where this was heading. "Yes..."

"But we already know where water is," Adrik interjected.

"But, Arisa," Finn continued, his tone ever steady, "Would you describe it as a river fortress built of rock and brick and rune and silt?"

The blood ran out of Arisa's face immediately. Not since the worst of her fever had she looked so pale.

"Arisa?" Brody pressed.

"Yes." she swallowed, "Yes I would."

"That's where earth tumbles out of the sky. Whoever the traitor there is, let's hope he's not prepared to just fling the doors open and welcome this queen of yours in," Finn finished grimly.

Arisa looked shocked. Adrik was watching her intently like she might fall apart if he wasn't ready catch her. Brody had a new sense come over him as he watched her process what Finn just said.

He'd wanted to know what happened to his father. He wanted to know why the Unbreaking was cursed. He'd wanted to help save his family and what was left of the Luring survivors. He'd wanted to do something more with his life than had ever been available to him before. But watching Arisa, as the shock wore off and the tears started to flow, as she collapsed sobbing against Adrik's shoulder, Brody for the first time had a sense of other people's villages and families. For the first time, he realized that what they were up against would destroy more lives than he'd ever considered the existence of. He glanced out over the lake, his father's final resting place, and remembered the odd little funeral the four of them and one tail-wagging dog had put together for him. Arisa had drawn a symbol, a *rune*, on the bag that will forever serve as his coffin. It intensified his sense that his father was there and that he was close. Everything he thought of when he thought of him: his look, his smell, the feel of his shirt, the sound of his voice, were so tangible right at that moment.

But there was something else, too. Standing behind his own father, or possibly shining through him, was another man: an aging elf with a cane and a pronounced limp, reading a book and watching Arisa inscribe with a twinkle in his eye. His affection for her and hers for him had hung in the air just out of Brody's reach while he mourned his own father. Was this father in danger, too? Were all fathers and their children counting on him and his friends to save them, whether they knew it or not?

Arisa straightened up. Finn was apologizing for his bluntness. Adrik was still watching her like she might break. Brody was feeling very small and very very under-prepared.

Arisa wiped her eyes, assured Finn and Adrik that she was fine and looked at Brody, tears still wet on her face, "So, what did your father say?"

He felt the same knife wrenched from her gut thrust into his. He knew they must have seen that he spoke to his father. He'd even said that he'd gotten answers. He couldn't say why he hadn't expected them to bring it up. Foolish maybe, but he was caught by surprise.

Brody swallowed and went on as if it didn't bother him.

"Mostly he said he was proud of me and Finn and had messages for the rest of my family. He said it was us he was thinking of when they attacked the shadowelves. He knew he would die. They all did, but they thought they were saving the village." Brody glanced at Finn who looked down at his hands. "He said he was the only one thrown into the lake, that the others weren't down there and he wasn't entirely sure what had happened to them, but he knew they were dead."

Brody was watching Finn now, aware of how painful this had to be to hear, having no family left and still no real answers.

"He told me to listen to the spirits up here because they had the answers. He also said, and this is the part I don't entirely get yet, that the Gatewell is water magic and that I would be needed for that reason. Any thoughts on what that meant?"

He looked away from Finn who was still resolutely not meeting his gaze, though Brody saw him wipe at his eyes. He glanced instead at the elves.

"Does that mean the whole mountain is magic?" Arisa gulped at looked up at the dark mass hanging over their heads.

Adrik followed her gaze, then looked back at them and shook his head, "It's cursed. Brody told me that the first night we met," Adrik's eyes locked with Brody's as if he wanted to say something more, but Brody couldn't make out his expression. Adrik turned back to Arisa, "Maybe the curse is water magic."

"Well, whatever it means, we'll need more information to figure it and everything else out," Brody replied, "So, Adrik, tell us how we're going to get up to the fishing boats."

"Well, that's where we should start tomorrow, I think," Adrik concluded, the last drops of the open keg of ale and every crumb of their supper now gone. Fletch was sniffing around in the dirt for any final remaining scrap of jerky, but was finding none.

"I've left a rope up for us to climb, but the bottom line is that those two boats that we can see are so caked over in the mud, that they'll support my weight from a rope and grappling hook."

"So did you go up there?" Arisa asked him.

"No, it was already too late when I figured that much out."

It was beginning to drizzle. The clouds overhead did not look like storm clouds for a change, but the travelers were wary of any weather up here after all they'd been through. They slept all the way back in the cave up against the mountain, half-sitting, but they were dry and they slept well.

By the next day the rain was steady and unrelenting, and none of them was looking forward to having to go out in it; too recent were the memories of being soaked to the bone. With this rain, also, came a deeper chill and that morning felt closer to the onset of winter than any had yet. Bundled in cloaks, hoods and hats, they set off back toward the ledge of the mountain where the fishing boats had come to rest.

Adrik had explained over breakfast that the day before he had made his careful way back down here, keenly aware that if he fell in he was alone. He'd looked for any possible solution for hours. He'd tried climbing the slick muddy wall of the mountain. He'd looked for sturdy scrub to offer perch. He'd gone back and forth a good distance in either direction looking for a way up and a way across. As the afternoon was wearing on, he'd decided to throw his grappling hook up there, just to see if it might find an anchor out of sight. He had been trying to avoid hitting the boats, though, for fear of bringing one down on his head and knocking him into the water. But his last throw had accidentally landed in the nearest one, and in trying to get the grapple back down, Adrik had realized that his hook had finally found the foothold he'd been looking for in the boat itself.

Adrik and Arisa climbed up first, Arisa carrying Fletch in her pack. Then they hoisted the gear up and sent the rope back down for Brody and Finn, neither of whom had ever done any climbing of this type. Indeed it took two bruising falls and all of Adrik and Arisa's combined pulling strength to manage Brody up to the ledge. As he pulled himself up and over the edge, his jaw dropped. There were not just two boats up here, but six. They were lodged in the mud caking the outside of the mountain like they had been thrown there and stuck. The ledge they were standing on was as large as Brody's boyhood home had been, though there was no shelter up here from the rain.

Finn's ascension went more smoothly because Brody was able to help pull him up. He may have been smaller and thinner than Finn, but when he got on the rope to pull, it was clear that he was stronger than either elf. Finn arrived sputtering in the pouring rain, grinning that they had made some progress.

There was nothing in or around the boats that had belonged to the missing villagers. The boats were sturdy in their construction and were largely intact, but they had clearly collided with each other into this location. The question was, were the men still in them when they hit the mountain? Had they tried to make it to the dock in the storm only to find that the water had risen too high too quickly? Had they managed to dock at the emergency location that was so close by and rode the rising lake all the way up? Or had they left the boats down there and sought out higher ground, the boats later becoming dislodged and carried up here? It was only possible to tell that these boats had not ended up here on purpose, which was not really useful information.

Finn pulled over one of the boats that was standing on its end causing it to crash loudly at his feet and exclaimed, "Hey! Come look at this!"

A bridge had been built into the side of the mountain. It headed south from the ledge where they were standing. It's marble flooring was mud-caked and cracked, its former luster only wondered at. It had a marble railing that ran chest-high on the humans and was still very solid. The mud along the outside of the mountain had encrusted around it, obscuring the view of it and of the bridge completely from below.

Arisa and Adrik stared at it in wonder, then Arisa went back to the boat landing. "You know," she said, "The landing is kind-of balcony-shaped."

Despite the pouring rain, the four of them tried to clean mud away and look for clues in the floor of the ledge. They did, in fact, discover crumbling bits of marble and post settings for a railing along the edge. But despite elf eyes and hours of determined searching, they did not find an entrance to the mountain to access the balcony.

The rain showed no interest in letting up. The air was cold enough that it could well have snowed by nightfall, and Arisa began sneezing again. The company decided to try the bridge. They were 25 feet up directly over the frigid lake. The bridge appeared sturdy, but was so old, none of them was crazy about trusting it with their weight, but they had no choice. They'd come for answers and this was where the clues were leading.

Brody wondered if his father had come this way. If, with a terrible storm raging overhead, the lake rising beneath them, lightning striking all around, if a band of scared fishermen had crashed their boats into the mountain and dared this treacherous trek across its face in the hopes of finding shelter. What they found at some point, he knew, were shadowelves.

Adrik had told him sometime since the day they had found his father, that the sword had gone through his ribcage, through a lung and had nearly severed his spine in one thrust. While Brody hated to think of his father dying that way, then being tossed like trash into the lake, he was relieved to know that his death had been swift. He was very worried, however, about what they would find when and if they found Finn's father. With shadowelves, the other mens' fate could have been much worse.

Brody glanced at his friend, huddling under his own cloak, carrying little Fletch in his arms just behind Brody. Finn had suffered so much loss. Brody couldn't bear for his friend to have to see that his father had suffered for death. Brody shivered.

Adrik was carefully checking the wall of stone that rose out of sight to their left. Several times he came across unusual features and was quite certain that the face of the mountain here had been carved with intricate images at one time, now eroded almost imperceptibly away. Arisa was in front, carefully checking the integrity of the bridge floor as she went on since hers were the lightest feet in the party.

Brody tried to imagine what might have been here and how long ago. He had seen marble fresh from quarries being brought down the mountain by merchants stopping to trade. He had heard of its uses in building palaces and monuments and temples far below his world. But he had never seen anything with a marble balcony, intricate carvings or its own bridge. That a mountain could be a building or that a building could have become a mountain: he could hardly wrap his brain around it. He wanted to imagine it as beautiful, a temple to something benevolent or the home of someone generous, but this was from the period of the Andarraine Empire, which meant that, like it or not, its purpose was most likely sinister.

Then they saw it. There was a heavy stone door set into the side of the mountain. It too was so caked in mud that its original appearance could only be guessed at. It had been pried open, barely wide enough for a grown man to squeeze through. And the crowbar, one much like the ones the fishermen would have carried in their emergency kits, was lying on the bridge in front of it. Brody gulped. They had reached the end of the bridge.

Finn was looking over the side. "Hey guess where we are!" he exclaimed as Adrik was drawing his bow and looking apprehensively at the opening before them.

Brody and Arisa glanced down. They were almost directly over the muddy little emergency dock landing where they had spent those two miserable nights. Adrik, guarding the door heard what they had seen and concluded ominously, "Then, Brody, most likely your father was thrown into the lake from up here."

Brody stared down at the restless waters below him. Was his father already dead? Or was he impaled, in pain, and screaming as he fell? He watched the bitter rain fall into that same water, so cold and so far below. Adrik had assured him that death would have been quick from that wound. Brody just had to try harder to make himself believe it.

Adrik came up behind him and followed his stoic gaze down to the lake. As if reading his mind he answered, "He was already dead, you know. That wound he took would have killed him almost instantly."

Brody nodded at his friend gratefully. He had needed to hear that again.

Finn had taken up Adrik's position at the door, both axes drawn, so that the elf could have a chance to look. Brody could tell by the way his eyes darted about, not focused on anything that it was terribly dark in there. Brody fumbled with his pack, pulled out their lantern and lit it, protecting it from the rain. Fletch sat up excitedly from his perch at Finn's heals. He sniffed at the door and as Brody reached it, and slipped in ahead of him.

The darkness smelled like stagnant water. The air was still and bitterly cold. Somewhere in the distance Brody could hear a faint dripping noise, but the cavernous space into which he had stepped was as dry as a desert cave. Even with the lantern, his eyes took a moment to adjust to the gloom.

He made a few steps carefully forward so that the others could come out of the rain behind him. He felt the end of Adrik's bow brush his left elbow as Finn came around his right side, axes still drawn and ready. Arisa stepped in directly behind him with her own smaller brighter lantern. Fletch sat dutifully at his feet, sniffing the air and growling.

The room they'd entered was larger than any Brody had ever been in before. He imagined his father and the other village men standing here, a terrible storm threatening to tear the mountain down from outside. Had they stood here in the dark, or had they had light to see the peeling paint, the broken furniture, the cracked glass-like dark tiled floor?

The ceiling was 12 feet from the floor, Brody guessed, and the far wall at least 75 feet from where he stood. The chamber was roughly square and offered another exit on the left wall. The paint was eerie in its faded patterns in blue and gray and seemed to depict a howling storm, one much like the one his father had sought to escape. The large piece of furniture in the far corner was broken in half. It had four large posts on each corner held together by a low frame. A bed? The smaller stone-topped wood piece sitting next to it was a pile of rubble and what looked to be an old stone chest lay lidless and cracked on the ground next to Finn. There were bluish fibers littering the strange floor that Brody guessed were all that was left of an ancient rug.

Adrik nudged Brody and, receiving his attention, glanced to the floor. Where Brody was standing, the floor was stained with what was unmistakably a large pool of blood. Brody closed his eyes and tightened his lips, more angry now as the story he was reviewing in his head continued to play out. He looked to his right and immediately locked eyes with Finn, cold, furious determination written all over Finn's face. Brody nodded. He felt the same.

He tried to replay history in his own mind. His father had led the group into the room, very much as he, Brody, had done. An elven watchman or scout had been by the left door. The shadowelf panicked and killed his father in one blow. But there were too many of the humans, so he fled the chamber to alert others. Brody could see it so clearly...

"Brody?" Arisa whispered behind him, "Are there spirits here? You're doing it again aren't you?"

Brody came out of his trance and looked around. They were all watching him. But this had been new. He'd seen something that had happened, not spoken to someone still lingering here. How had he done it? And who, then, had thrown his father into the lake?

But that answer came to him, too. He didn't see any vision and he entered no trance state. He just knew because he knew the people who had been here. They'd wanted to chase down the killer. They were shocked and scared. They were trapped between an unknown enemy and the worst storm any of them had ever seen. But in their moment of fear and indecision, Brody knew that none of them would have left his father laying there like that, dead in a pool of his own blood. The superstitious villagers would never have stepped over a murdered corpse. His father's friends wouldn't have abandoned his body.

The lake was not so far below them that day. Judging by where their boats had come to rest, the water may have been just below the railing. It made more sense now that Brody thought about it, because the shadowelf would not have sent his sword down to the depths with the corpse, but the villagers would have feared to touch it.

"Brody?" Arisa asked again. He turned completely around and looked at her. She was terrified.

"I'm OK," he said, and he realized it was true, "I know what happened here."

"The shadowelves had a lookout positioned here," Brody began walking to the new door. Adrik raised his bow and aimed it at the opening, "My father came in first and startled him. The elf reacted and...and killed him," he swallowed having found that phrase difficult to say, "But then the other men rushed in and the shadowelf fled. It was my father's friends who put him in the lake. They did something decent for him before chasing down the elf. It probably got them killed," and at this he looked at Finn, feeling slightly guilty, "Because then the shadowelf had time to find his friends."

"But how did they know they needed to go and stop them?" Arisa asked.

"They probably didn't" Finn guessed. "They found a scary-looking black elf, no offense, Adrik," he glanced at Adrik who shrugged, "hiding in a cursed mountain during a cursed storm. They probably assumed they were up to some kind of magic that was going to hurt the village. And one of them had just killed Benn. Really they probably didn't know any more than that."

Brody nodded in agreement. That was exactly what happened, he was sure of it.

"But why did your father tell you he knew he was going to die?" Arisa asked suddenly.

Brody thought back to his conversation with his father, "I was thinking of you. You and your mom and Rista and Rann, and the little one I never knew. I want you to know that. When I knew I was about to die, you were all I cared about. I am proud of you, Brody."

So, he wasn't surprised then. Brody *saw* him walk into this very room, startle the shadowelf standing guard, and get killed for his trouble. But his father's own account sounded like he knew the elf was there. He closed his eyes, but he couldn't sense anymore of the past from here.

"I don't know," Brody answered her, "I guess we still don't really know what happened."

Adrik peered out of the next doorway. "Curses," he said bluntly, "this is going to be a nightmare."

Outside the chamber they had entered was a landing, similar in size and construction to the bridge that they had used to enter from. It lined the inside wall of the mountain in a huge circle some 200 feet or more across. It was gold-flecked marble with an intricately carved marble railing made up of interlocking waves petrified in their moment of peak. The walls all around were carved, seemingly from floor to ceiling, in odd disturbing images of ghosts and corpses, water demons and cruel-looking nymphs, of weeping women and scenes of betrayal.

The cylindrical chamber ringed by this walkway rose at least 60 feet above them and sank farther than they could see in the dark gloom. From light wells high above beams of light crisscrossed into the space mimicking the paths of stairways that latticed between other walkways and landings interspersed about every 12 feet all the way up, and as far as they could tell, all the way down.

But somehow, the light from the promise of the outside world somewhere far above them that had been teased into the dark place in proscribed patterns, could not penetrate whatever it was that lay below them. There was a dripping sound that came from overhead and landed in something wet somewhere far below. Glancing over the railing was dizzying, but dwelling on the friezes along the walls was horrifying.

As they stood there, slack-jawed and silent, save for the growling of the dog, a whispering voice seemed to reach up from the depths of the very mountain. It was a female voice that sounded young and human to Brody. It echoed as if emanating from a deep place.

"Whooooo is there?" it asked of the empty spaces between them, "Why now have you come back?"

Brody jumped back from the railing like he had been burned, so startled had he been by the girl's voice. "Wh-wha? What was that?" he asked the others.

Fletch had begun barking his fiercest bark. He wanted to let that young lady know that he would tear her apart or annoy her to death, one. But the other three stared blankly at Brody having not been startled at all. Then they looked at each other before turning back to him.

"What was what?" Finn asked over the dog's incessant din.

Arisa reached to calm the dog, but Fletch jumped out of her reach and bit her hand before continuing his tirade at the ghostly voice.

"Ouch! Fletch!"

"FLETCH!" Brody reprimanded at once and the little dog whimpered, tucked his tail and hung his head, silent. Brody turned to Arisa, "You OK?"

Arisa nodded but still looked alarmed at Brody and at Fletch. Brody felt a rush of gratitude for the little fuzz ball, even if he had bit Arisa. He found himself once again the only one besides the dog that could hear the voices.

Adrik rushed to Arisa's side. He looked as if he wanted to punt Fletch over the railing. Brody thought he had scooped him up just in time.

Arisa's hand was barely scratched, but Adrik's temper was seething.

"What the heck is the problem NOW?" he demanded of Brody. Adrik looked at him too often as if he was a weepy little kid who lost his daddy and couldn't just get over it. Brody felt his own temper rising. At least, right now, he thought, he was ready to stand up for himself.

Brody stared back at Adrik in silence. Adrik, for his part was carefully keeping his dark face inscrutable. Adrik's temper seemed to be building with heaving breaths in his chest but Brody was determined for once not to back down. He could feel the heat rising from under the collar of his tunic like a volcano. Finn and Arisa exchanged nervous glances and jumped between the two at once.

"So, what is he seeing or hearing NOW that no one else does? Huh?" Adrik spat angrily at Arisa. Brody moved to defend Arisa, but Finn grabbed his sleeve.

"I-I'm OK, Adrik," she stammered helplessly, showing him her hand again.

"I KNOW YOU ARE," he was yelling now, "That stupid little dog couldn't hurt a damn RAT! But SERIOUSLY! How do we know Brody doesn't get possessed by evil spirits? How do we know it's his dad he's talking to? Huh? Something is very very wrong about this place, and it seems to LIKE *HIM*! DOESN'T THAT BOTHER ANYBODY ELSE?"

From behind the two people that had jumped between them, Brody was squaring his shoulders, drawing himself up to his full height which was quite a bit taller than it usually looked, thought Brody to himself, since he rarely stood up very straight. Still, what did he think he was going to do? Fight Adrik? Adrik who had an education and military training? Who had endured pain, sadistic parents and cruel taskmasters? Adrik had led a small army not that long ago, at least according to him. Brody was still Mister I-Suck-With-A-Fishing-Pole and he knew he was in for some injury if he thought he could get in Adrik's face. Strangely, though, he found he didn't care.

Finn was removing Brody from the landing, pushing him and Fletch back into the bed chamber. Adrik watched them go, though Arisa remained between him and the door. Brody tried to break his eye contact with Adrik as Brody backed away which was made easier when Arisa slapped Adrik.

The moment hung in the air and Brody momentarily thought it had been he himself who had been slapped, so sudden was the shock. Adrik deflated completely and looked at her, seemingly confused. Brody thought about the things he'd just thought and said and suddenly couldn't understand why either of them was angry. He allowed Finn to finish guiding him into the room. What had just happened?

"Better?" he heard Arisa ask Adrik sweetly.

Brody was embarrassed. He slid down the wall and sat on the floor looking up at Finn who, Brody just realized, looked as angry as Brody had felt a moment earlier.

"Whatever that was," they heard Arisa saying outside, "It was getting to me, too. Sorry I took it out on you, but what is going on here?" She just rambled these words out as if they were figuring out what to have for dinner. Brody didn't look out to see how Adrik was reacting. He was taking stock of his own emotions. Now that he was back off of the landing, he seemed to feel better immediately.

He looked back up at Finn, who was beginning to seat himself on the floor and was patting Fletch absent-mindedly.

So what *had* happened?

"I don't know," Adrik admitted lamely.

Arisa answered, "That's what I thought."

She left him on the landing and came back into the first chamber.

She'd just entered the room when they all heard Adrik mumbling outside, "I remembered being a small child locked in my chamber waiting for my father to come back with his whip. I remembered the lingering armies of shadow that sometimes crept around the Darkwald at night that I'd had to face as part of my early training. I remembered....No,"

The three of them in the bedchamber looked out at Adrik. He was crouched against the railing like a small child, his knuckles light gray from the tight grip he had on the marble. Arisa stepped out.

"Did you say something?" she asked him, then looked at him curiously, cowering as he was on the floor.

Adrik leapt to his feet at once. "No," he assured her, "But something's definitely wrong out here."

Brody tried to stand and step back out, too, but immediately he was washed over completely by wave upon wave of emotion. It was welling up in him as a heavy pain lodging somewhere around his diaphragm. It must have shown on his face as he couldn't take his eyes off of the far wall. Arisa paled and became concerned again.

"Adrik? Brody? Come on in here. This isn't good."

Brody followed her and sat back down on the floor, his back against the peeling wall next to the balcony-bridge exit he didn't have a word for. He bent his long legs and rested his arms on his knees. He kept his hands busy picking at his finger nails. He looked up at Adrik as the latter walked in several long seconds later. Brody tried to keep his face stony, but he said nothing. Fearlessly, he locked eyes with Adrik.

Finn was standing watching Brody, arms crossed, casually protective. Fletch came back in off of the bridge and climbed under Brody's knees. Brody moved his hand to pat the dog, keeping him out of Adrik's sight. Adrik just stared into Brody's unflinching face.

Arisa grabbed his shoulder and shook him. He blinked hard and turned to look at her. She was still watching him nervously. They all were. What were they afraid that he'd do, Brody asked himself? But Brody knew the answer to that question. Arisa had said it herself that the decision to keep going down the "right" path was one he made every moment, not one that came naturally to him. And they all knew it. At any moment, on any day, he could change his mind.

Arisa was carefully explaining the rush of fear that she had felt when she went back out for Adrik and that the look on Adrik's face had told her that his emotions, too, were beyond his control. Adrik was staring at the floor. Finn and Brody nodded agreement. They had been caught off guard, too. What to do next?

Brody wasn't saying much. Arisa and Finn were having a discussion about where they all should go, what specifically they were looking for, so they could spend as little time as possible out on that landing. Problem was, as Arisa was explaining patiently, they really had no idea what they were looking for. Clues. It suddenly sounded even more stupid than it ever had before. They were looking for clues.

Arisa and Finn went on discussing. They rehashed what of the prophecy was known to them. They discussed the likeliest set of floorplans for this...building if that's what it was, based on the fact that it appeared to have a bedroom. They seemed to have agreed that this level was likely to be useless, so the question they kept raising was up or down?

"Down," Brody interrupted Finn as he was asking Arisa if other buildings like this existed anywhere else, "We need to go way down. All the way down."

Adrik looked up from his own private thoughts. Arisa and Finn stopped talking at once and looked at Brody as if a very ill person had just awoken from sickbed.

"Down is reasonable," Arisa answered cautiously, "If we assume the main entrance was on the ground level there could be public rooms down there that might at least tell us what this place was used for." She looked over at Finn. They had been leaning toward going up.

Brody shook his head, "No, farther down than that." Brody was sweating and seemed almost like he really was just awaking from a disease, but that voice: it was the only thing that had happened on the landing that *didn't* scare him. It didn't cause him to feel lonely or lost or afraid, and certainly he hadn't felt angry. In fact, if he was honest with himself, he wanted to hear it again. And it had sounded like it came from down. It echoed slightly like it was in...

"The rune for this mountain..." he blurted out.

"The Gatewell rune," Arisa interjected promptly.

"I...We...need to find a well."

Brody silently hoped to himself that he wasn't leading his friends in the very worst possible direction.

The room seemed to darken with this pronouncement, but glancing around Brody realized that the sun was setting. More than needing another clue, right now they needed a plan for the night. They needed a safe place to sleep.

Reluctantly, they spent the night right where they were. They divided into two shifts to stand watch: Adrik and Arisa on one, Brody and Finn on the other. The night was dark, cold and creepy, but nothing other than their dreams came to disturb them.

The sun penetrated the dusty air the following morning heralding clearer skies outside than they had seen for a while. But despite every desire in his being to go out into the sunlight, Brody braced himself for the journey deeper into the cursed mountain. He glanced at Adrik who was pulling his boots back on, a piece of jerky still hanging out of his mouth from his unfinished breakfast, and looked away before the Shadowelf could look up and catch his eye. Brody had watched him sleep in the night, too, and had come to a conclusion: he trusted Adrik.

Whatever strange spell this fortress had cast on them yesterday didn't change who either of them *were,* and what they were unconditionally, Brody thought, were friends.

No sooner than they stepped back out on the landing, Brody felt the tension rising in him again. He tried to ignore it. He realized he was bitter. He'd carried a terrible bitterness inside of him over the way he'd been treated since the day his father died. He was bitter about having had to grow up so soon. Bitter at the merchants who were bringing news of the bounty on elves up to the people he bitterly knew would want to collect it.

He shook his head. As they reached the first landing and began down the stairs he kept reminding himself that these weren't his feelings, not really. Not amplified like this this. But as he led the group stoically onto the next landing down and trudged across it to the next stairwell, he found that he was arguing with himself about what was and wasn't his own heart.

"The shadowelf...." it was *her* voice again, and Brody stopped dead in his tracks, "This place is poison for him..."

Finn walked into Brody because of his abrupt halt, but when Brody turned he looked back at Adrik. Adrik hadn't left the bottom of the stairs. He was sitting there like a statue with his face in his hands.

"A-ar-risa?" Brody stammered.

Arisa looked back in alarm, "I could have sworn he was right behind me!" She raced back over to him.

Finn tried a crooked door just at the top of the next flight of stairs. It ground its way open, scraping the ancient floor and groaning loudly on the rusted remains of hinges. Finn stuck his torch inside. Fletch slipped in and Finn stuck his head back out.

"Arisa. Bring him in here."

Brody watched as Arisa helped Adrik shakily to his feet. He was glaring at the floor as if each tile had deserved the worst vengeance Adrik could conjure, and Brody imagined that Adrik could imagine quite a lot of vengeance. Brody had never seen such hatred on his friend's face.

"Why is he here?" asked the voice in Brody's head.

"Who?" Brody stopped, but he spoke the question in his head. He was past wondering if anyone else could hear it.

"The shadowelf."

Brody thought about the question. There were many answers, really. Looking for answers. Because he's our friend. Trying to help us save the world. He'd just about settled on 'Why do you care and who are you anyway?' when she responded,

"I see."

"You see what? Are you reading my mind?"

There was a pause before she said, somewhat ruefully Brody thought, "How did you think we were having this conversation?"

"Brody?" This voice was male and familiar, but Brody couldn't quite place it. His heart quickened excitedly and he tried to answer in his head, "Yes?"

"Brody?" It was the same voice. It hadn't seemed to have heard him. He searched his mind to place it. It felt like he was swimming on the lake.

"Brody!" Now it was adamant, almost scared, and he felt something grab his shoulders and start to shake him.

Instinctively he pushed the thing away with both hands and opened his eyes.

Finn was sprawled on the floor in front of him looking shocked. Brody looked at his own hands as if he didn't recognize them. The voice: it was Finn's. That's what he hadn't recognized. Why not?

He looked around. Fletch was growling lowly at Brody. He'd never done that before. Finn looked too startled, maybe even *scared*, to get up. Arisa was peering out of the doorway of the room they were about to enter. He couldn't see Adrik anywhere.

Brody reached a shaking hand down to Finn. Fletch stopped growling and trotted over to lick Brody's filthy boot. Finn accepted the hand and got to his feet, although he was still staring wide-eyed at Brody. Arisa looked worried.

Slowly Finn spoke, as if he wasn't sure he wanted to hear the answer, "What was that?"

Brody twisted his face into an unspoken apology. "The girl's voice. I...I...guess we were having a conversation."

Arisa looked curious. Finn still looked scared, so she spoke, "Why don't you come in here and talk to us about it?"

Brody headed forward, but he thought loudly and clearly in his head, "Can you hear us...or me...everywhere we go in here?"

There was silence in his head as he concentrated on moving forward into the room beyond the door, keeping his eyes open and refusing to lose his connection on reality if he could. He must have looked strange concentrating as hard as he was on the simple act of moving a few feet forward, because the others were still watching him with a mix of caution and concern. Even Adrik, who Brody could now see sitting on the floor of ruined, grime-covered tile, his back against the wall and Arisa's lantern at his feet, even his expression had softened as he watched Brody curiously.

As he crossed the threshold he heard it,

"Yes."

"Then, tell me. Poison how? I want to warn him."

Finn helped him sit and Brody tried steadfastly to pay attention to both possible conversations at once. The effort made his head hurt. Everyone was watching him fearfully, even Adrik to a degree, but Brody wanted the answer to his question, so he sat and leaned his head back against the wall and closed his eyes.

It took a long moment before any answer came, and when it did, it certainly wasn't reassuring.

"The shadowelves were created here. The ruling elves...they were furious. The shadow leaking from my well...it, it got to them. It poisoned their souls. The light here is dangerous, too; full of lost hope and betrayal. This...isn't a good place."

"And you?"

"I'm still here," the voice whispered sadly, "I always will be."

"Brody?" came the timid voice of Arisa. She sounded as if she were on the verge of tears, "Brody?"

Brody opened his eyes; everyone was watching him. He looked at Adrik and realized that Adrik looked more tired and scared than Brody had ever seen him. He owed them the truth, but he worried about how they would take it; how they would react to him. Was it possible that he was truly losing his mind?

"There's one spirit here that's talking to me," he admitted cautiously. He looked from Adrik's nervous, curious face up to Finn's worried one standing above him. He continued, "Everything here seems to...to...*feel* a certain way: angry, terrifying, even maddening...everything except this one voice. I...I'm trying to talk to her."

"What does she say?" asked Finn matter-of-factly.

"Well, most importantly," Brody answered, getting excited despite himself, "Is that the shadowelves were created here." He paused to watch that register. Adrik, especially, looked stunned. "She says that when the what she calls 'ruling elves' came here that the shadow from the well poisoned their souls. She called it 'her' well, so that has me concerned, of course, but she said this place is particularly poisonous to Adrik because of that. She said even the light here is dangerous: full of hopelessness or something." He paused, "what do you think? Should I stop talking to her or keep trying?"

Brody knew he wanted to keep talking to her, but since he couldn't explain why exactly, he realized that he needed to consider, whether he wanted to or not, that he may be suffering the effects of an even more sinister magic.

They all looked around. Adrik looked resigned.

"Can she tell us where the well is and why it's so important?" Finn asked.

"Should I ask her?" Brody looked around hopefully at his friends.

Adrik nodded with a sigh and Arisa crouched next to him trying to comfort, well Brody wasn't sure if she was comforting him or herself.

"OK then," Brody responded, "Give me a moment." He closed his eyes again.

"I really have no idea why it would be important to you," came the girl's voice immediately. Brody thought she sounded like she would be pretty, beautiful even. He tried to shake that thought, but it was too late, he could hear her giggle in his head.

"I might have been once, but there's nothing left of me now."

"There's something left. You have a voice."

There was a pause before she admitted, "Actually, you're the first that could hear my my voice. I didn't know I had that anymore."

Brody heard the sadness and the loneliness in her voice. He wanted to help her desperately, but how could he? If only he could hear her, he was pretty sure he knew what that meant, and he'd never really been able to do anything for the dead except to lay them to rest.

"You've got a kindness about you I've never encountered before," she told him, then asked, "Do you really trust the shadowelf?"

"Adrik? Yes." Brody hadn't even hesitated. The answer came out instantly, but he knew it was true. He *did* trust Adrik.

"What are you looking for?" she asked him.

"Oh, you know, what every kind person wants I guess: a way to save the world," he smirked at himself for sounding so naïve, but that was what they were looking for ultimately, wasn't it?

"I doubt you'll find it here anymore."

"Anymore? What do you mean?"

"Let's just say you don't want to do what I did. The price has been *way* too high."

"Did it save the world?"

"At the time. Yes."

"Then I do. I'm a small price to pay really."

Did he really think that? He thought about his mother and what she would say, but he shook it out of his head. If he had to pay a high price for the rest of the world to go on, he at least wanted to believe that he could do it.

The voice was quiet for a while. Brody opened his eyes and looked up at his friends gathered around watching him.

"Well?" Adrik asked, his familiar impatience returning.

Brody was blank. He hadn't learned anything yet.

"If you're here," the voice began again. Brody shut his eyes. "Then the prophecy? Is it really happening?"

"Yes," Brody answered although as soon as he did, he wished he hadn't. He wasn't as sure of the disembodied voice as he was of Adrik.

She paused a while again. This time Brody waited with his eyes shut.

"I don't know what I can tell you that will help, but there seem to be anxious spirits near me waiting for you. Be careful coming down. The further you come down the well, the worse it gets."

"What spirits?" Brody sensed a trap.

"I don't know. They're new, relatively speaking. Men, all of them, and human. Simple men if I had to guess. I can sense them. I can't see them."

Brody's heart raced. Could it be them?

"What about shadowelves?" he asked cautiously.

"No. Shadowelf spirits don't linger here. They get syphoned out."

Instinctively, Brody opened his eyes and looked at Adrik.

"What?" Adrik asked again.

Brody explained over some quick food what little he'd learned. He admitted to his fears and his hopes. Finn became visibly anxious and Adrik visibly reticent, but they agreed that down was where they needed to head, for better or for worse.

They made a slow journey down into the darkness. Whenever they became overwhelmed, they darted into a side room to calm down. Before long, Adrik was having trouble even walking, and Finn was taking more and more of his weight as he helped Adrik to keep going. By the time the vestiges of light petered out overhead, Adrik's eyes had rolled up inside of his head and he began clawing at the walls.

"He can't go any farther," Arisa insisted as they helped Adrik into a strange, small round chamber with what looked to Brody like an ancient blood-soaked stone altar off to one side. All of them were bruised and scratched from having had to fight Adrik out of his head and into the room.

Finn nodded and looked at Brody, "Brody and I can take the two watches," he looked back to Arisa, "You stay with him. In the morning, Brody and I can go down alone. It doesn't sound like there's anything good down there for Adrik, and we can bring up anything worthwhile we find."

"Okay," Arisa agreed

The next morning Adrik was covered in sweat. He had tossed and turned with nightmares through both watches. Brody hadn't gotten much sleep. Nonetheless, he was anxious for the day's journey, for answers, and for the chance to put the mountain behind them. Arisa wished them luck, and then turned to tend Adrik as the latter started waking at last.

Fletch led the way like he knew where he was going. He sniffed the ground eagerly, wagged his tail often and barked once or twice here and there. The noise startled the two old friends each time, but Brody couldn't help sharing the dog's strange excitement. They'd wanted answers for years, and Brody thought today might finally be that day.

After what felt like hours, they reached the bottom of the gloom. The final six or seven floors had been bathed in a thick darkness their lantern couldn't penetrate, and now they found they had descended onto a final landing that glowed with a watery blue light.

There were no doors off of this landing. A ladder protruded from a large hole in the center of the floor, but that held no interest for either young man. Instead they both had their eyes tearing up uncontrollably at the sight of more than twenty grinning familiar ghosts. They had found the missing fishermen at last.

Chapter 8:

21st Day of the 12th Month, 7th Day of the Week, Autumn
Anupday, Shilirs 21

Kierra

Kierra stumbled a bit through the woods, which she found mortifying. None of Keen's family seemed to notice, but Keen certainly did. She smiled at him, trying to ignore the haunting worry etched deeply into his gaze. There was still so much she didn't understand about him. She was tired, still, it was true. But being tired didn't jeopardize her health. Surely, they were all still tired to some degree. Why wouldn't they be?

But Keen seemed to have taken the news of their unborn child as some daunting obstacle, which worried Kierra. Surely Keen had known that by becoming lovers, an eventual child was probable. Admittedly it had happened faster than she could have imagined, but then humans were much more fertile than elves, so why did it surprise Keen so much? And more importantly, why did the idea seem to fill him with dread rather than joy?

She didn't want to believe that Keen would not love their child. How could he claim to love Kierra herself and not love the child they'd created together? But something had certainly changed between them. It was as if Keen were now treating her as a duty, a responsibility, rather than as a companion. She shuddered at the thought.

"What is it?" Keen asked automatically, "Are you cold?"

Kierra looked up into his soft brown eyes, searching for the passion and affection she'd always found there. But all she saw was worry. She shook her head, and tried to put the distracting thoughts out of her mind.

They walked along the river bank flanked by five of Almara's archers. There was a general tension among all of them. It wasn't just Keen, she reasoned. No one liked the thought of nearby shadowelves. She wondered briefly if her father had been scared before...

She had to shake that thought from her mind. As deeply and dearly as she missed him, she couldn't afford the energy of mourning his fate right now. They had to make it back to a safe path and then home. She and Keen could spend the rest of their lives lost in worry if they had to, but not until they were all safe.

The wide river flowed gently along, splashing merrily past them as they headed upstream. She could hear the undercurrent of song in its playful murmuring and in the occasional languid rustle of the trees. If she wasn't careful, the quiet welcoming of their combined lullaby would surely make her sleepy. It was difficult to imagine the terror of the shadowelves under the peace of the trees, and yet the tension of the soldiers around her told her the risk was very real.

And yet in her mind and heart, the song seemed to grow. It tugged at her in a way she hadn't felt since leaving her training behind in Willowmark. It was the song that moved the waters and drew everything that was life-giving and good toward the inexorable life-heart of the forest itself, which was its capital and central refuge. She missed those peaceful times, times before her family's lives were shattered by the awful news that her father had been captured. She felt the pull so strongly, and heard the song so loudly, it was almost as if...

"Wait," she stopped suddenly.

The others stopped, concern and confusion a palpable reaction as Kierra made her way gingerly to the water's edge and peered along its length upriver, cautiously. The river clearly bent north now. She was sure it had been ever so slightly straighter just a few moments ago. That, and the tug she knew for sure she felt now, meant only one thing.

"A Silent Boat is coming this way."

The other elves joined her at the river's edge. The humans reluctantly followed, likely not wanting to be left behind on a dangerous trail.

Elves loved the Silent Boats. They were always a beautiful reminder of the life blood of the forest, and the fact that they were all connected to it as it changed, ebbed and flowed. They were deep enough into the protected sanctuary of the Willows, that the living forest was no longer a fixed thing, but a changing and breathing one, its pathways always leading to their mark, its river always leading to its center, but their routes never remaining quite the same. It was how she had discovered her gift all those years ago: young elves knew better than to stray from the trails they knew if they were away from home. Her family had been traveling to see relatives, and she'd heard the song of a jay and gone to chase it. Her family had been worried sick and a search party had been mounted as soon as she was out of sight, but Kierra always knew where she was in the forest, no matter how much it moved and altered its course. She could hear its song in her heart long before she could hear it with her ears. She wandered back to their camp a few hours later, blissfully unaware that there had been any reason to worry.

And she heard it now as plain as any music made by hand or mouth. The river was singing its call and response to the Mother Tree that guided the treesingers to their destinations and then home again.

"I don't see it," one of the guards responded.

"You will," Kierra assured her, "It's headed straight for us."

And then she knew what she had said was true. The Silent Boat, messenger and summoner of the Treesinger Council, was not just headed in their direction. It was headed to them in particular. And that meant there was news, or a summons, intended for one or all of them. A lump formed in her throat. She'd always welcomed the sight and even the beckoning of the Silent Boats, but just now, she couldn't think of any good that their presence might mean. She turned to the group.

"It's still at least 20 minutes out, but it's coming straight for us: for one or more of us in particular."

She looked at Joran, trying to ask him silently for his opinion without alarming Keen and his family any further. His gaze held questioning concern in response.

"So…are we allowed to ask…?" Kaith had spoken rarely since they'd met, but he seemed less fearful than the rest. Even now as he asked his question, his eyes twinkled with what Kierra could only assume was exasperated amusement.

"The Silent Boats," one of the archers began, "Are the means by which the ruling council of treesingers communicate with the rest of us. They are probably just bringing new orders, or news from other camps on the front lines."

Kaith nodded, and Kierra relaxed. Of course, the Boat was likely trying to reach their escort, not them. She glanced toward Joran, but he had already turned away and begun heading back up to the path.

Nira addressed his retreating back, "Shouldn't we wait for it?"

Joran reached the path and turned, some unnamed disappointment crossing his features, "No need. If it's still 20 minutes out, then we're wasting time. It'll find us if we're the ones it needs. They always do, and we need to get farther into the forest before dark."

Nodding and murmuring assent, the group tore themselves from the excitement of a glimpse of a Silent Boat and back toward their arduous journey.

They walked farther than Kierra anticipated before the singing of the waters became loud enough for the others to hear. Nervousness had begun to take its hold again. The sun was getting low above the canopy and the shadows longer under the trees. But they still needed to traverse another 2 or 3 miles before their escort could safely leave them, and twice that if they were going to find a safe place to camp. They remained at least 10 miles, she guessed, from the nearest settled village, and a day's walk at least farther before they were home. Kierra had never minded camping out under the trees. Even as a child the darkness of the forest at night had never frightened her, but things were different under the Willows now, and peace anywhere seemed so much harder to come by.

But they stopped anyway. That they could hear the song was a well-known indication among Willowelves that the Boat's message was for them, and their trail had veered a little farther away from the water so that its rushing was audible, but its water no longer visible. Quietly, and as a single unit, they all turned toward the trees that separated them from the vital artery of flowing water, and began to make their way back down to the river's edge.

They could see the Boat clearly as they stepped out from the trees. The Silent Boat was roughly 8 feet long and slender, with a high, pointed bow that terminated in a golden spiral from which a single lantern hung. It was painted in white paint that with moisture and age had thinned in places revealing patches of brown and gray wood beneath which gave it an air of ancient authority and a beauty that suggested nature at work. All around, the trim was painted in gold, which never seemed to fade or tarnish. The stern rose high into an alcove in which a single treesinger stood upright as she guided the craft.

The treesinger that approached along the river was slender, female, and had long, straight dark brown hair. Over her green and gold robes of office she wore the plain, hooded white cloak of the Silent Boat messengers. She maintained the standard pleasant but blank expression that the messengers were taught to convey.

As her craft drew closer, her eyes betrayed a compassionate sadness as they met Kierra's own gaze.

The audible song gently faded out until Kierra knew that only she and the new arrival could still hear the music that persisted all around them. The river water splashed up onto its bank noisily as the Silent Boat ran its prow aground, as if in protest of the end of the song. The messenger smiled kindly at them all, and Kierra thought that they must have looked haggard and worn standing there waiting for her. She dropped the small anchor that rested at her feet and climbed out into the shallow water to come ashore.

"I have come for Wythira[8] Jerith and Joran, and the treesinger, Kierra," she stated softly, meeting Kierra's eyes as she said her name, "The Council has summoned you to Willowmark."

"Why?" asked Joran, almost defiantly.

"That isn't for me to know or say," she answered simply.

Kierra turned to him in annoyance, "You know she can't tell you, even if she happens to know, which she probably doesn't."

"But we can't leave now," Joran insisted.

"We are traveling with human refugees," Kierra explained patiently to the messenger, "We can't just leave them here. The archers escorting us can only take them as far as the edge of the current areas of fighting. Our human friends won't know their way beyond that. And, really, they shouldn't travel in the Willows unescorted in any case. What do you recommend?"

"I passed a stranded fishing boat just 50 yards or so upriver, probably abandoned by someone fleeing the violence. It looked old, but travel-worthy. I can wait while you retrieve it. If these refugees plan to stay in the Willows, the Council will want know. You might as well bring them along."

Exasperated, Joran took Rana and Nira to fetch the extra craft. Keen pulled Kierra aside.

"Willowmark? I know that not everything we've been told about your kingdom is true," he whispered to her, "But that place has a reputation that's going to make my family uncomfortable."

---

[8] Wythir plural

"Like what?" Kierra reacted, trying not to sound offended.

Keen sighed. It sounded a bit like embarrassment to Kierra. Then he answered, "We've been taught that Willowmark is a city built inside a magical tree that moves around and is never in the same place twice. I know that sounds ridiculous, but…"

"No, it doesn't. Willowmark is a city built up in the canopy of the Heart of the Forest, which is mostly three giant trees growing together, although the city stretches into the tops of a few others now," she drew a breath and went on, no longer whispering, "It isn't magic. It's alive. The whole forest is one large, living entity. And being alive, it changes, as all living things do. And, yes, that means it moves. It's not like it gets up and walks around or anything: but the forest is constantly shifting, and Willowmark shifts with it. But it's perfectly safe. I told you: no one here is going to harm your family. And the messenger is right; eventually it will be up to the Treesingers Council to decide whether or not your family can stay. You're different. Because of our relationship, no one would think to make you leave, except maybe Kethran," she added darkly. Keen grimaced and nodded, "But that same assumption doesn't extend to the rest of your family. The Council will take your plight seriously. They're typically a pretty fair and compassionate lot…mostly, but it's their decision ultimately, and, anyway, if we're being summoned, we have no choice but to go. That's the law."

"Do you know why you're being summoned?"

Kierra bit her lip. It was unlikely that word of Keen's family had reached Willowmark yet, although it was certainly possible that Kethran had made good on his promise to take his complaint about Keen's presence to them. Still, she knew word had already spread through the Willows that she had chosen him as a mate. Could Joran and Jerith still be reprimanded? She didn't want to jump to conclusions, but more importantly, she didn't want Keen and his family to see how nervous she really was. They were already so scared.

She shook her head, "No. I have no idea."

"That isn't very comforting," Keen frowned.

"I know, but…" she searched for something helpful to say, "I trust the Council. Trust me that whatever it is, it's at least safe."

Keen nodded silently and blew out a breath. He turned to look at his family and Kierra followed his gaze. Terror reflected on every face, but resignation did, too. Kierra wished she could think of something more comforting to say. She couldn't imagine what they were going through.

"It'll be alright," she added to no one in particular, "It will be."

The fishing craft came into view. It was, indeed, old and well-worn, but it appeared sturdy and well-built, also. When it reached the bank, Nira jumped out and roped the new craft to the Silent Boat. Then, once again, they all piled into two small boats. Krieg took his wife and children, and loaded them all into the fishing craft. Kierra couldn't help but smirk; she was pretty sure he didn't trust that Silent Boat any more than she trusted cannons. She had no intention of bringing it up, though. Keen and Kaith helped their grandmother in after Krieg's family. The rest then piled into the Silent Boat.

Kierra felt unwarranted exhilaration. She hadn't been on a Silent Boat since before she'd joined the war. It brought back to her a younger version of herself: one more naïve, more self-assured, more…hopeful. She stopped herself. The wars were both going badly. Her father and uncle were….she couldn't even allow herself to dwell on that thought. And Keen and his entire family were nearly executed and were now refugees and Kierra's responsibility. In addition, they'd left their mother and aunt alone, and neither was really well. The momentary thrill she had felt vanished like mist.

"Are you ok?" Keen asked, yet again, as he climbed in behind her.

She forced a smile at him and nodded. The lump forming in her throat was too powerful for her to dare try to speak.

She cuddled up against him and relaxed.

Sometime later she woke with a start. The vessel had hit a small swell and jumped. She heard several groans around her telling her that she was not the only one who had fallen to sleep, nor the only one jolted awake. She had no idea how much time may have passed, but the night was pitch black all around them and the air had turned much colder. Keen was behind her, with an arm draped protectively around her, snoring lightly into the crook at the fore of the boat. She was curled tightly into him, and his form was warm and inviting.

She looked to the aft of the craft. Silhouetted against the dark shadows of trees, the treesinger stood tall and straight, her whole being fixated on the song in the forest. There were several dark, stirring lumps in front of her. The rear-most two were emerging into Jerith- and Nira-shaped shadows, stretching and looking around. Closest to her, Kaith's open eyes stared up at her. He was laying on his back with his knees up across the boat. He had his mother's shivering form held tightly against him. Kierra couldn't make out much about his eyes, except for the motion of the occasional blink, but she sensed that if she could, she would see nervous questions in their depths.

Kierra pried herself off of Keen, shivering as she abandoned his warmth for the cold night air. He rolled over slightly, and went back to sleep. Kierra looked around. They were deep into the forest now, and the treesingers' song was pulling them up river against an increasingly strong flow of water. Despite the fact that most landmarks along the Shil'Arinn couldn't be relied upon to remain the same, much less be visible in the dark, Kierra knew exactly where they were. The Shil'Arinn was a larger river before sprouting three tributaries. The smaller body of water they had been traveling was little more than a tributary in its own right, though it carried the Shil'Arinn name forward. Judging by the swirling dance of the water, Kierra thought they must have just passed the junction where the last two branches separated. That meant they would soon come to the first branch, and the way that would take them home again…eventually.

Kierra watched the darkness expectantly. She wasn't entirely sure what she hoped to see, but something about just eyeing the way home after the journey they'd all had filled her with a small euphoria. From this juncture, home felt so close, and she was so tired that the idea of her own bed in her own village was the sweetest thing she could think of. She strained her eyes against the blackness, searching for the brief break in the trees that would indicate the Willa tributary of the Shil'Arinn: the path home.

She heard Ella's voice off to her right, "Look! There's another quiet ship!"

Kierra stifled a chuckle, but she leaned back and looked through the trees to her right, and, sure enough, another Silent Boat was approaching down what had to be the Willa. Her heart leapt. Much of the forest lay in that direction, not just her own village, but she felt a kinship at that moment with whoever might have been coming from that direction. She missed home terribly.

Others in the two crafts began to stir again. She felt Keen sit up behind her and wrap his arm around her middle.

"Is something going on?" he whispered.

"Not really," she whispered back, "There's another Silent Boat coming up the tributary on its way to Willowmark, too."

"Do you think it's related?"

"Related to what?"

"Do you think they've been summoned for the same reason as us?"

Kierra thought about it. She didn't know why they were being summoned, so it was hard to guess who else might be gathered for the same purpose. A pit formed in her stomach to replace the brief joy she had experienced before. A sense of dread overcame her. She sincerely hoped that Silent Boat did not contain Kethran.

They watched apprehensively as the other Boat approached the merging of the Willa with the Shil'Arinn. Kierra was up on her knees, trying to make herself as tall as she could, straining to see in the dark. The Boat and its passengers were little more than deep shadows against the night, but Kierra was certain that, in addition to the treesinger at the prow, there were 3 or 4 passengers huddled together in the cold. That didn't seem like something Kethran and his cronies would do. As they got even closer it became apparent that at least 2 of the passengers were women with longer hair billowing in the river breeze unkempt. Those were not soldiers.

Then a voice cut through the night, "Kierra? Is that you?" It was her mother's voice.

"Mom?" Joran answered back. Kierra could see him whip around in the second skiff to try to identify the shadow that had spoken.

"Yes, it's us. Oh, I'm so glad they were able to find you!" she replied tearfully.

"Mom, what are you doing here?" Kierra called out to her. The other Silent Boat had just maneuvered into the water ahead of their fishing vessel.

"Well, we're all here," she answered, "The whole family. How's Keen?"

Keen stiffened behind her and squeezed her a little tighter, but he answered, "I'm ok. Thanks for asking," then his voice became shakier as he asked, "Why would they call for your...whole...family?"

Kierra understood then. His own family had been gathered up by their government, hadn't it? She could just imagine the ashen pallor Krieg's face must have developed.

Kierra's aunt sighed loudly and answered, "Sweetheart, we think it has to do with our missing mates."

Kierra's blood ran cold. Suddenly she wished it had been Kethran in the other Boat. Had they finally found her father and uncle…or whatever was left of them?

Keen must have sensed her tension, because he began to rub his hand along her arm.

"Any chance it could be good news?" Keen asked. Kierra dropped her face into her hands as wracking sobs shook her shoulders. How much more could she handle?

Jerith answered stoically, "Not likely," as his own mother said, "It's over. Whatever it is, it'll be the end of it." Her voice cracked on the word "end."

Kaith raised up onto his elbows. His mother had sat up already. As Kierra lifted her teary face again, she caught his quizzical expression in the lantern light.

"My father and uncle were captured," she whispered as quietly as she could. She didn't even want to hear the words herself, "By shadowelves, who are… merciless," she finished somewhat lamely.

"I'm sorry," Kaith responded.

The travelers were silent for a while. In her heart, Kierra could hear the tune of the water and the song on the air being sung out into the night by the treesingers of Willowmark. Looking around she could see the upright forms of her companions, sitting in uneasy silence all around her. It felt somber but companionable. Kierra laid her head on Keen's shoulder and he wrapped both his arms tightly around her. She wished her dad could have met him. Would he have liked him? Or would so much war have made him wary of an outsider? Kierra gulped back more tears as the reality that she'd never know the answer washed over her with the forest's song.

Sometime later, the singing voices drifting down from Willowmark became audible to the ears. The Silent Boats picked up speed slightly as the pull of Willowmark became instantly stronger. The trees began to thin as the river grew ever wider around them. In the gathering dawn, more Silent Boats became visible coming and going, ahead and behind them. Just as the sky began to transition from the deep navy blue of the clinging night to the dark pink of impending dawn, the silhouette of one gigantic tree sprawling across the river ahead of them became visible through the mist. The cluster of smaller giant oaks that surrounded it, stretching along and out from the banks of the Shil'Arinn slowly appeared from the clutches of darkness. This was the Heart of the Forest. Emerging out from under the left and right of the Mother Tree, two other major rivers began their existence, separated from the deluge of melting water flowing down the from the mountains by the enormous root systems of the Heart of the Forest.

As they approached, the ramp-like bridges connecting the central tree to the canopies around it became visible like ragged moss draping between them. The song was becoming louder: its words and the individual voices that carried them becoming more and more discernible over the cacophony of nature. Morning birds, river insects, even wind, added to, rather than competed with, the growing chorus. The ramps and decks that wound around the Mother Tree providing perch for the city itself and its swelling number of citizens and refugees came into view just as the UnderTree docks of the Silent Boats, their nighttime lanterns still blazing, did also. Despite her overwhelming sense of foreboding and grief, Kierra also felt a sense of peace. Some part of her would always be at home here.

The crafts slid silently under the arching structure of ancient roots. Small docks on either side of the river sat patiently waiting in the dampness. Most of the Silent Boats were either absent, or in motion heading in or out. Kierra had seen the fleet this busy before, but rarely. It signaled turmoil and news pulsing in and out through the vasculature of the forest. She glanced across the water to a dock second in from the river: her old dock. She saw that its current treesinger was out on her craft at the moment. She felt a momentary pang of jealousy.

Operating a Silent Boat had never been Kierra's favorite duty; she preferred to sing, and the long hours of intense focus wore on her quickly, but she had enjoyed seeing the whole of the Willa: visiting its inhabitants wherever they'd made their homes, bringing them news both good and bad, sharing in the lives of all willowelves in some small way. It was in this duty that she learned to connect with the overall organism of the forest. She'd seen how interconnected everything was, and how crucial the Heart and its rivers were to its survival.

She broke away from her reverie. Other families were being helped ashore from the first few berths they passed. Still more were being led in from the smaller arrays of Silent Boat docks that perched alongside the two smaller rivers a small distance away where the rivers became wide enough to support them. Still others were unloading themselves from any number of a vast array of personal crafts that were docking along the banks of the Shil'Arinn itself, where the public docks were located. The crush of people seemed to make up one large, breathing animal approaching and climbing the great tree. Hope and fear, sadness, longing and excitement were all palpable within the anxious crowds.

Their own crafts were pulled into a wide, welcoming slot on the left bank, barely halfway through the natural cave. Each of the two Silent Boats docked stoically adjacent each other, while the small fishing vessel they'd been towing alongside of themselves was detached and brought into safe harbor behind them. Everyone began the process of disentangling themselves, stretching, working feeling back into sleeping limbs, and reluctantly, climbing out onto the two waiting piers that would lead them to whatever news awaited them above.

Kierra shivered at the thought of the words she might soon hear: words that would tear her world apart forever. She leaned against Keen's solid, warm frame. His arms slid around her, bringing with them the comfort she needed to keep going.

The Treesingers that had brought them this far motioned for them to follow closely behind. Taking quick stock that everyone was gathered and had what support they needed, they joined the living throng and headed up into the vast city of Willowmark.

Jesp

Jesp sat on a soft clump of oakmoss watching the maelstrom of activity go by. The Healers Village of Willowmark was a bustling hive: a city within a city. Mostly dominated by billowing white tents and narrow thoroughfares, Jesp could still make out the older permanent structures that once looked out over wide, attractive lanes and made up the original face of the city's hospital district. Most of these were huge natural knolls in the trunks of two of the largest oaks in the complex, but also included simple wooden structures dotted between them. Now one had to have a high vantage over the wave-strewn sea of cloth canopies that had engulfed the large street expanse in order to see them at all.

Jesp had that vantage. In addition to the tidal wave of tents that flooded the district, accommodations for the city's growing faerie population had been made in all shapes and sizes. Jesp sat along the small, remaining alley thoroughfare on the nub of a branch culled from a smaller trunk-like growth that had grown up through the street. It was as large as a young adult oak in its own right, but its branches on this level had been cut back in several places to prevent encroachment on the healers' work. Now, each of the nubs had bowl-shaped beds lined with moss and feathers for wounded fae to convalesce in. There was just enough space for one visitor to sit alongside each, and Jesp was watching over Kyrt's recovery from hers.

A small, knotty alcove in the bark allowed Kyrt's bed to sit out of the direct elements, and a leafy awning of carefully sculpted ivy protected them both from the occasional rain and provided tent-like privacy. Smaller knobs not large enough for fae beds were used by the treesingers to climb up to assist in the recovery of their smaller guests, but most of the work was being done by trained faeries who flitted between the small patient lodgings with greater ease. It was a lovely place to sit in the midst of such a sad and overwhelming reminder of war.

Gone from here were the romance and pageantry of well-armed elven guards as Jesp had known them, but gone, too, was the separation between the plights of elves and of fae. Willowmark had become a city of desperation and refugees: a city under siege.

Jesp had to allow Tollie and Thomas to take everything with them to wherever they had gone. There was no place to hide the crown in the small faery sick wards. That bothered Jesp less, though, than not knowing where her friends had gone or how they were doing.

Kyrt stirred in his sleep, jerking Jesp's attention back to her charge. They had managed to set his wing, and the treesingers' songs did seem to be allowing it heal back together. It would be slow, but ultimately Kyrt would be one of the lucky ones. Judging by the tears and wailing that surrounded them, Jesp knew that the lucky ones were few indeed.

Kyrt opened his eyes groggily and gazed up at her. Jesp could see the pain reflected in them.

"Do you need me to find a treesinger for you?" she asked him, inwardly cursing herself for sounding so much like her mother all of sudden.

He smiled weakly at her, a small hint of his usual twinkle reflecting in his strained expression.

"Jesp, where's our charge?"

"Excuse me?"

"You know, the whole reason we left in the first place? The one thing we're supposed to be doing here?"

Jesp looked down at her hands in her lap.

"With Tollie and Thomas..." she glanced out over the tent city beneath them, "Somewhere."

"Jesp." His voice was hoarse, but firm, "I'll be fine."

She nodded at him glumly and took a deep breath.

"You're right."

She stood up and bent over him, planting a lingering kiss on his lips that brought unmistakable heat to his eyes. She smiled.

"I'll be back for you."

"I know," he whispered, "I'll be right here."

Jesp stepped to the edge of their perch and leapt off, soaring over the tents without looking back. She couldn't look back. Guilt threatened to consume her. So much pain. So much loss. So much death. She had to fight her own overwhelming desire to give into despair and hide from all of it. She was terrified that she didn't have the strength to win that battle, but she had to. Now, more than ever, Jesp had to find the soldier she always wanted to be. She came with a mission, and whether she had to finish it alone or not, the mission had to come first.

She flew around for several minutes before she spotted Thomas coming out of a tent below her. He set off at such a brisk pace, she didn't have time to descend to him before she had to about face and flap her wings furiously just to keep up. He walked with swiftness, glancing around at his surroundings nervously as he went. As the edge of the tent encampment came into view, Jesp saw a small area along the very edge of the overlook where many carts and horses had been tied. She dove toward it, ignoring Thomas beneath her, and made a beeline for the three ponies tied together she recognized. Someone had given them each a basket of feed and there was a wide trough of water running the length of the overlook's edge. Jesp was grateful for that. She hadn't even thought about the poor ponies.

She landed on Robin's backside just as Thomas turned the corner out of the Healers District and began to make his way toward her. She waved at him enthusiastically.

Thomas smiled and picked up his pace to a jog to reach her.

"How's Kyrt?" He asked as soon as he was in earshot.

"Healing," she replied, "How's Tollie?"

Thomas frowned, "She's not doing so well. It's like she's just given up."

Jesp swallowed down the lump forming in her throat.

"And Tallie?" she asked.

Pain reflected deeply in his features.

"They took her to be cremated. Tollie didn't like it, but there's no other way for her to take her sister home, and Tollie really wants to lay her to rest with their mother. She keeps lamenting the fact that she couldn't do the same for her father, but after what happened to him, I really don't think that committing Tallie to fire made her feel any better."

Jesp felt the unbidden tear slide down her cheek, but chose to ignore it.

"You should stay with her, Thomas."

"I couldn't leave the ponies unattended," he answered defensively, "Not with everything that's at stake."

"I've got it," Jesp assured him, "Kyrt's ok, and the main item here is our responsibility anyway."

"What are you going to do with it?"

Jesp considered for a moment. She really had come to trust Tollie and Thomas. She and Kyrt had shared things with them that they never would have shared with anyone else, and both had proved willing to risk their lives for all of it. But, the Crown was a faery's charge and, selfish as it made her feel right then, its final destiny wasn't something she could share.

"I'll stay here and guard them for now. Tollie's books are here, too. I can stay in a saddle bag and keep watch until we figure it all out. Don't worry; just take care of Tollie."

Thomas looked like he wanted to argue, but instead he just frowned and nodded.

"Okay. If you're sure, but I'll come by periodically to check on you. I don't think there's anything more important either of us has to do right now other than this. And, Jesp," he paused and allowed remorse to twist his features, "Tollie would like to see you, too, you know."

Jesp felt her lip tremble. No, she told herself firmly, you're not going to break down now.

"Maybe we can switch off tomorrow morning," she conceded.

Thomas smiled weakly at her and nodded. Then he turned and walked solemnly away.

Jesp moved to the saddle bag that contained her charge and checked to make sure it was still there. Relieved to see it right where she'd left it, she curled up on top of it to take a nap.

Darkness had enveloped the city by the time she awoke. She poked her head out of her saddlebag and confirmed that no one was in sight. Now she had to do what she'd come here to do all along: she had to find a safe place to hide the crown. It had been removed from the backpack the strange "tribal" faeries had brought it to them in. The bag was potentially recognizable by outsiders. Instead, it now lay carefully wrapped in the dress Ella had made for Tollie.

Jesp considered her options. The dress was bright and colorful, but also elven. Rewrapping it in something else would be challenging and might draw more attention to her. It wouldn't weather the elements well, though. Then again, it wouldn't likely have to survive long in its new home. She could always go back sometime later and put it in another heavy bag.

So, decision made, Jesp grabbed hold of the carefully folded package. It wasn't physically heavy, but it weighed on Jesp like it contained all of the ancient stones of the Rune Keep. Jesp wrapped her arms and legs around it. She couldn't risk dropping it now. Then she flew off over the edge of the overlook.

Jesp had given a lot of thought to what kind of hiding place she wanted during the night, mostly through her dreams. Nightmare after nightmare had found and stolen the crown from many types of places. She needed somewhere out of sight, out of the elements, poorly trafficked, but not untrafficked, and away from the obvious choices of the faerie settlement, the treesingers' haunts, or the central parts of the city. And it needed to be high. If Willowmark were successfully infiltrated, or invaded, it would be accessed from the bottom up. Even the fae came into the city that way.

Jesp flew out to one of the satellite trees that made up part of the city. She chose a large one, close to the main three, that had multiple stories of city built into it, too. This one was only accessible by one bridge, if flight was ignored as a possibility. The bridge connected to the city's main shopping district on the middle trees, but led to three stories of residential space on the slightly smaller tree. The elves who lived here seemed to be mostly craftsmen and merchants with a few soldiers' families in the mix. Jesp could tell by the laundry they left out to dry, the crafts and activities left out overnight on porches, and the contents of wagons loaded for their morning commute into the city.

The bridge connected to the middle tier on the tree. This tier had the smaller houses on the tree, plus grocers' stalls and a school. The school was a complex of four buildings sitting along both sides of the main thoroughfare. Between 1 of the buildings and the trunk of the tree, Jesp found what appeared to be a large kitchen building. She looked up.

Above the kitchen, one of the many support beams that held the upper deck of the neighborhood aloft was fastened deeply into the large tree at an angle. Some enterprising bird or another had made a nest on it. She didn't like the size of the nest and thought its normal occupant might even now be out hunting for something roughly Jesp-sized for its dinner. The bark behind the nest was broken and open, revealing a hole where an earlier support beam might have been. It wasn't large, but it might be enough.

Looking around nervously for the nest's owner, Jesp flew up to the old hole. The bark and some of the interior wood had rotted, widening the hole from what had originally been intended. It took some wriggling, back muscles, dress-tearing and choice curse words, but Jesp managed to force her burden into the small space sideways. Then she broke off a piece of bark just below the upper deck and covered it. She was just flying around from the level of the kitchen roof to admire her work when the unmistakable screeching of large hawk drew her attention away. She looked and saw the beast flying straight for her from its forest hunt.

Jesp dove for the safety of the connecting bridge and its lone guard patrol. She flew silently just behind his back, warily watching the now-perched predator eying her hungrily from an upper branch. Once she made it across with the oblivious soldier, she soared low into the morass of closed market stalls and kept herself out of sight until she could rejoin throngs of bigger people elsewhere in city.

The bird flew through the open street of the market, but eventually gave up and flew back in the direction of the nest. Jesp was relieved to have gotten away, and concerned about ever retrieving the crown on her own, but she also felt that the thing was safe again. For a while at least.

Returning to the ponies, she dutifully made a count of all of Tollie's books hidden around the various saddle bags. There were 11. Jesp had to hope that Tollie had one with her. Otherwise, she'd just screwed up on her watch. Her heart sank, but she was too exhausted to do anything more than to curl up and sleep and wait for Thomas in the morning. One way or another, though, she and Kyrt had completed their mission. There was no way the crown's location was written down anywhere now.

Dropping off into sleep. A last dreamy thought crossed into Jesp's consciousness. She woke with a start and asked out loud to the rest of the contents of her saddlebag,

"How did those four fae know what the crown was?"

Adrik

Adrik had never felt so stupid, hopeless, helpless and tormented by his own memories in his life. He'd finally woken up from the endless sea of nightmares, but he had no memory of falling asleep. It was as if the waking nightmares of the trip down into the mountain had just continued all night without pause. He wasn't sure he'd even really slept, so much as just drawn deeper and deeper into himself. His head was pounding, his body ached relentlessly. Even the small amount of light in whatever chamber they were in was excruciating to his eyes, and Arisa's quiet voice felt like cymbals crashing in his brain.

But of course, he was the shadowelf, so he was the one the creepy evil magic affected the worst. Gods how he hated himself. He probably always had, but now the worst nightmare of them all was just reality: he was and always would be a shadowelf. Darkness was drawn to him. Evil penetrated his being easily. And it would never make any difference what he did in the world, he would never get to be anything but what he was: a shadow-darkened soul born to the descendants of people corrupted by black magic. Nothing, not even Arisa, was good enough to save him.

He was on his knees resting his aching forehead on the cool, albeit filthy, stone floor. The cold of the tile was all that felt comforting to him in that moment. All he wanted was for all of it to end.

He could keep going if he had to. As long as Arisa needed him, he would find the strength. For her. He'd do anything for her. But if he was going to be this much of a burden to her now, he thought, the best thing he could probably do for her would be to leave her with the humans and stop being such a burden. He just couldn't stand the thought.

More than anything, he'd come to realize that he needed her. In fact, more than that, he needed for her to need him. He needed one good and decent purpose for his miserable life to go on.

That and he really needed for the room to stop spinning.

"Adrik?"

He could hear the fear in her voice, and it made him hate himself that much more. How could she fear him? He would never under any circumstances hurt her. She was his one light, the one good thing he'd ever known.

"Adrik?"

He turned his aching head sideways and tried to focus his blurry vision on her without picking his head up from the comforting cold.

"What are you doing?"

Damn. She really was afraid. If he'd lost her trust, then he really had lost it all.

"Nothing," he choked out, "Just indulging in a little therapeutic self-loathing. Why?" He wasn't good at lightening the mood, but he had tried.

"Because it looks like you're worshipping that bloody altar...thing,"

"What bloody altar..." he lifted his throbbing head and looked up. Sure enough, he had just happened to angle himself toward something that looked exactly like a bloody altar, and one that had been used far too recently for his comfort. "Oh," was his best answer, and he peeled himself up off of the floor, spun slowly on his sore knees, and laid down on his stomach facing her instead. If he was going to worship something...

"Better?" he asked without looking back up at her.

He felt her hand smooth his hair and she began to rub his shoulders. Her touch was everything. She was a salve for his soul.

Then he realized they were alone. His eyes were closed, but he heard no movement in the room save for hers, not even the loud breathing of Brody's mutt. He raised his head again and opened his eyes.

"Where are the humans?"

"They went down by themselves."

That drew Adrik out of his self-pity. He sat up. Unfortunately, that ended the shoulder rub he was getting. He was sorry for that.

"What? Alone?"

Arisa looked at him, eyes full of pity. Damn it. He didn't want her pity. There were a great number of things he might want from her privately, but not her pity.

"The magic here is affecting you horribly," she admitted. He closed his eyes and laid back down. That's because I'm worthless, he thought. Then he added, again just to himself, I just don't want you to realize it.

Arisa kept talking, and he opened his eyes again, even though he couldn't really focus on anything, "And it scares me. I don't know how your ancestors got corrupted here, or even if that's true, but if they were some other kind of elf when they got here and were…changed. What will happen to me?"

Adrik sat up again and tried to focus on her. He hadn't even considered that possibility. He suddenly wanted to wrap her protectively in his arms, but he didn't dare try. He didn't want to alarm her, and he certainly couldn't handle her rejection. Instead he tried to screw his face up into a concerned frown.

"I know," she went on, looking away, "I'm being totally selfish."

"Selfish? You? Do you even know how to be selfish?" he asked incredulously.

Even through his blurry vision, he couldn't mistake the sardonic grimace she was shooting him. He grinned despite himself.

"I'm being serious," she insisted in what was almost her 'wounded' voice. Adrik continued to smirk at her.

"As badly as it's affecting you, the last thing I should be worried about is what *might* happen to me!" she confessed almost tearfully.

Adrik shook his head, then stopped when it made the pounding worse.

"You realize that statement alone is the very definition of unselfish?" he teased, "Selfish would be: Look how bad it is for you! That just proves that I have to worry about myself."

"Well, that's not far from how I feel…"

"No, Arisa. A selfish person, and trust me: I'm an expert on this, wouldn't feel guilty and selfish for having those thoughts. A truly selfish person would insist the rest of us think about their wellbeing first, too. Besides, you're not wrong. You could be in greater danger than the humans."

"They have names, you know."

"Fine, than Finn and Brody, happy? Anyway, I guess your insisting we let them come along turned out to be the right call."

She smiled at him.

"Harumph," he answered her and laid back down on the cold floor. Then, raising his head briefly again, added, "*Are* you ok?"

"In here I am. I think. Out there..." she glanced toward the door, "I don't think anyone's ok. What do you think this place is, Adrik?"

"It's a well of evil. It's a tower that has been built to contain...something: water magic, I guess. Whatever once lived here is clearly gone. Anything that would have thrived in this place is beyond even the unnatural darkness of my homeland. We could not have hoped to have made it even this far if such an evil being still lingered here. But the evil it crafted is still stuck in the well. I fear it will corrupt us all in short order, the more of it we breathe in."

Arisa looked at him aghast. "How did you figure that out?"

"I suspect that what Brody said was probably true. Somehow, I think my soul knows this place. And I hate it. I hate it because I hate myself, and that's what it keeps bringing out in me, Arisa: everything I hate about my life, my past, my bloodline." Adrik was pulling himself up to standing. He felt taller somehow, and Arisa looked fearful, "Everything I keep thinking that I can leave behind. Everything I am trying to overcome. Everything...that I can't really escape. That is the poison of this place. That's why it's so dangerous to me. I don't have the will to keep fighting it."

Arisa took a step back from him, stammering, "Wh-what do you mean?"

"For all the love of Light, Arisa! I wouldn't hurt you!"

"But you sound like you want to go back. Adrik, you can't! You just can't! Losing you would hurt me more than anything else you could possibly do!"

"I assure you that's not true."

She ran up to him and threw her arms around his middle.

"We'll get out of here! And then it'll be like it was before! You'll be better again! You'll see!" She was crying into his chest. He placed an arm around her while still bracing himself against the wall with the other.

"Arisa, I never intend to return to the Darkwald. All that awaits me there is an unendurably long stay in the Walden, the queen's impenetrable prison. I couldn't face that. Even I am not strong enough to face that. That's not what I meant. I just meant...this place keeps revealing to me the endless pain and futility of my existence. It makes me want," he hesitated. Could he say it out loud? Could he say it where she could hear it? "It makes me feel desperate...to end this existence…"

He pulled himself off of the wall and wrapped his other arm around her sobbing form. How long had he wanted to hold her? But even as he got his chance, he was only making her cry. He couldn't give her happiness. He had none to give, except for what she had given him.

"You are the only good thing I have ever known, Arisa. For you, I will keep going."

She looked up at him. Her tear-streaked face catching what little light graced this room even in the daylight. She nodded at him, her lip trembling as she searched his eyes. He wondered what she was hoping to find there.

"It will get better, Adrik. Somewhere in this world there is a place where we can both be free. I promise you…I will never stop looking for it until we find it. Never."

The resolve on her face was startlingly beautiful. Was she saying what he thought she was saying? It was too much even to wish for. He couldn't start fooling himself now, but if she were… If she were seriously suggesting a life…together… with her. He knew he could bring this whole mountain down with his bare hands for her.

Suddenly, his pain was clearing. And as it did, another memory returned: a day on a lake by a simple laundry line, when Adrik first felt the possibility of freedom and wondered what he'd do with it. Now, he knew exactly what he'd choose, if the choice were ever his. He'd choose Arisa. He'd choose her each and every day for as long as she wanted him by her side. She was his sunlight, his hope, his angel.

The darkness cleared. His fear, his self-loathing, it all lifted away from his soul as he looked into her soft blues eyes and decided that there in front of him truly was the color of hope. Hope and freedom: two things he'd never had before, but two things he understood now.

He wiped his own eyes roughly with his sleeve, and then found a clean soft spot on his tunic and gently dried hers. He smiled at her.

"I'm ok, Arisa. I feel better now."

"Are you sure?"

His smile widened at her, "Positive."

"I can't keep going without you, Adrik. I don't want to. You've become my whole world. Please. Please don't ever give up on me."

"Give up on you? It was me I was fighting the urge to give up on. I'm only still standing here precisely because I cannot give up on you."

She tightened her embrace around him, and he his around her. He lifted one hand to the back of her head and held her closer to his chest. He could have stood like that forever. He could have, except…

"Wait, did you say Finn and Brody went all the way down? Alone?'

She pulled away and nodded.

"Damn!" he exclaimed, and gathering his gear, he made for the stairwell and the landing.

Adrik focused all of his mind on the feel of Arisa in his arms just then. He even held onto the spot on his tunic where he'd just been holding her head. He held on to that one memory, that one feeling, and he ran. He ran for all he was worth across, down, across, down…he'd betrayed his sister…nope, holding Arisa…his own mother despised him…not going there, Arisa wants us to have a future…his father's furious face loomed way above him like it did when he was small…don't care, he thought, if I hadn't had reason to leave, there wouldn't be Arisa…just keep remembering…

He could hear her behind him, trying to keep up. As long as he could hear her coming, he didn't need to slow down, stop, or even turn around. If he could have gotten to where he needed to go with his eyes shut, he would have done it. He was sweating with the effort of keeping out everything that wasn't her, but it was working. His life may have been horrid, but it was getting better, and he had hope and a chance at freedom, and that was enough.

On the last level he didn't even bother with the stairs; he leapt over the railing to land behind Brody and Finn. He caught himself in a low crouch with one hand on…

OK. That was gross. He'd put his fist through the chest of a desiccated corpse. The floor was literally *covered* in corpses of many races. The ones on top were probably years old. The crunching of bones underneath suggested purely skeletal remains at the bottom. Adrik looked up at Finn and Brody. They had turned around when he landed and were standing there smiling widely at him like he'd just arrived at a party, and they were already drunk. They were both standing up to their hips in bodies and seemed utterly unconcerned. In fact, they looked happy. Adrik raised one very disturbed eyebrow at them.

"What? Oh my goodness!!!" came Arisa's exclamation.

Adrik looked over to his far left where Arisa was coming down the last flight of stairs, staring in horror at the creep show around them, and clinging to the ancient railing with both hands.

"Stay there!" Adrk yelled, "You don' need to come down here!"

"No!" answered Brody, "We want to introduce you guys!"

Adrik looked at the man in sheer alarm. He'd seen a lot of bad stuff, but this: this disturbed even him. Slowly, he responded to Brody.

"Introduce us? To what?"

Brody and Finn both turned and gestured happily to the empty air behind them. They were still smiling. Adrik looked back at Arisa. She looked just as horrified.

Adrik decided he just didn't need to know. He wanted to get or to do or to find whatever would let them leave most swiftly, and then he wanted to do just that: leave swiftly. So, he answered:

"Great…Nice to meet you." He was nodding slowly, eyebrows raised, like he was talking to the criminally insane. Without taking his eyes off of the space of absolutely nothing not 18 inches above the sea of corpses they were standing in, he asked Brody, "So, what…who," he corrected himself carefully, "Am I talking to?"

"Well this," Brody indicated a space right next to Finn, is Carren Kip, Finn's father," Finn smiled broadly at Adrik while Brody continued to indicate other empty spaces of air and name about a dozen and a half other names. Adrik cocked a questioning eyebrow at Finn. Finn looked back at the imaginary space where his father was supposed to be, so Adrik looked back to Arisa. She was looking back at Adrik with a fearful alarm that plainly asked whether or not their friends had completely lost their minds. Adrik shrugged at her to mean: maybe…just run with it?

Arisa glanced at the area where Brody was gesturing and said tentatively, "Hello?"

Adrik looked down. There were definitely human and shadowelf corpses here. There was enough left of gear, clothing and weaponry to discern that much. It struck him in that peculiar and intensely discomfiting moment how similar they all were in death. Skin tone, hair color, body shape: none of those was as discernible in the morass as the accoutrements of culture were. He caught himself wondering vaguely if, even though his bloodline had been tainted by dark soulless magic eons ago, he could have been different had he only grown up elsewhere. It hardly mattered, he told himself. He could change none of it.

He began to fish around beneath the freshest bodies. Doing so seemed to free some of the stench that had been kept somewhat in check by…something. He wondered how old the oldest bodies were, and what maybe they could tell him.

"Can you not see them?" Finn asked suddenly.

Adrik looked up at him. "Can you?"

Finn nodded, "They're like mist, but it would be impossible for me not to recognize them." He was shooting a fearful glance at Brody who was watching Adrik curiously.

"So are *they*," Adrik pointed to the space beyond his friends where *apparently* there were ghosts and then gestured down to the pile of mummified horror he was digging through, "*here?*"

Both men frowned and looked back at Arisa.

She was watching the humans back. Hopefully, thought Adrik, she was waiting for their answer, too. He didn't want to find out that the ghosts were plainly visible but that he, Adrik, was hallucinating piles of humanoid remains.

Everyone seemed to be locked in a game of passing confused frowns around. Adrik sighed dramatically.

"OK. Let's try something new. Arisa, what do you see?"

"A room full of corpses piled waist high," she replied looking very disturbed.

"What?" exclaimed Finn as Brody also interjected, "Corpses? Where?"

Adrik closed hs eyes so he could roll them in relative peace. He counted to five; he knew he was too impatient to make it to ten.

"Thank you, Arisa. Finn, what do you see?"

Finn looked between the two elves with a horrified expression, then looked down around at the mass burial surrounding him.

"Dirt, some rocks, a pit, a ladder, and…" he turned at looked to the space where the ghosts apparently stood, "And the fishermen."

"Wait, what?" Adrik asked, wondering what pit and ladder he was missing, but Brody also responded, "Dirt? You don't see the tile?"

"Tile?" asked Finn.

"What tile?" asked Adrik

"What do *you* see, Brody?" asked Arisa worriedly.

Brody looked around him, but unlike Arisa and Finn, he didn't just take in the floor. He gazed up and around as if the whole space were a wonder to behold. It wasn't. Not in Adrik's opinion.

"Everything's covered in tile: it's all shades of blue and gray and patterned like a stormy sea. It's really beautiful. I've never been anywhere like it."

"I'm pretty sure none of us has ever been anywhere like this," Adrik mused aloud.

"Do you see the pit?" Finn asked worriedly. He was gazing at a spot in the floor in the middle of the room, which, Adrik had to guess, would put it behind the invisible ghosts.

Brody turned and immediately looked to the same spot of floor, "I assumed that was the well. It's the darkest blue tile, and the ladder looks like it's made of silver."

"Looks like it's made of mud to me," Finn mentioned quietly.

"Adrik?" asked Arisa still standing on her stairwell perch and gripping the railing as if sanity could only be achieved through grasping something solid, "What about you? What does it look like to you?" She looked and sounded desperate. Adrik suspected he knew why.

"I see what you see, Arisa, don't worry. This room's a mass grave, although now that Brody's mentioned it, I can kind of tell that the mud-caked walls used to be tile. I couldn't have told you they were blue, though."

Arisa closed her eyes and nodded. Adrik couldn't help but chuckle.

Brody and Finn looked at each other, and then back to the ghosts.

"What's going on?" Brody asked nothing.

There was a long pause. Both Finn and Brody were nodding and looking around as if the air was responding to Brody's question, but Adrik became aware of another sound: the distant sound of combat.

He scrambled quickly to his feet and started, "Hey, guys! We may have company!"

Adrik began to wade through the sea of death back toward the staircase and Arisa. Brody and Finn were still listening to the sounds of their shared hallucination.

"Do you hear something?" Arisa asked him as he made his slow, sickening way over to her. He stopped.

To Adrik, the sounds were getting louder, like an army was advancing on them. He could even hear a storm thundering overhead. He looked up. As far as he could possibly tell, it was still daylight up there beyond the gloom. He stopped and looked back at Arisa frowning.

"You don't hear that?"

"Apparently," said Brody who was walking toward him easily, his legs passing straight through stacks of corpses while he looked around the upper parts of the chamber with casual interest, "There are a *lot* of spirits here."

Adrik gave his friend a bemused look, "Well there are a *lot* of bodies."

Brody gave Adrik a horrified and fearful expression, then turned his gaze downward and looked around the room.

"That's so weird. But, seriously, there are whole armies in here. If there were *that* many bodies, the whole mountain would full of them."

Adrik gave Brody a look of alarm. He wanted to go for terror, but he was determined not to let the contents of his bladder go.

"Anyway, Carren told us that he thought Finn was seeing what they saw: the fishermen. They said they don't see the bodies either. The girl...the spirit I had been talking to before: she said what I described sounded like what she remembered. I don't know what the two of you are seeing." He had concern in his gaze as if he thought that maybe Adrik and Arisa were ill. Adrik had some bad news for him.

"I'm pretty sure that Arisa and I are seeing is what's really here," he assured Brody, "Because I don't just see it. I can smell it, and feel it under my feet and around my legs."

Brody frowned and looked toward Arisa whose eyes shown with mingled horror and terror and whose face looked like her stomach and Adrik's bladder had gotten up to similar content-relieving ideas. She said nothing.

Brody turned slowly toward Finn and the ghosts. Finn was watching him.

"Well, we got our answers, I think, but if their bodies are here…"

"There's nothing we can reasonably do about it," Finn finished for him. Adrik was glad, and he tried to say so silently.

"OK," Brody answered quietly, "Then there's just one more thing I have to do."

They all turned to Brody. Adrik felt cold dread filling him.

"What's that?"

"I need to go to the bottom." Brody was looking at the center of the room again.

Finn looked over there, too. "Are you sure?"

Brody thought for a moment.

"No, but…I think I'll always wonder if I don't."

"Yeah," Finn reasoned, "But you'll be alive to wonder."

Adrik raised his eyebrows and nodded to the room at large. He did basically like Brody, and he certainly had shown impressive courage in trying to stand up to Adrik the day before. Very few people could stare him down without flinching. But he really did worry that Brody was maybe not all there all the time.

Brody sighed and looked Adrik straight in the eyes. Adrik felt his eyebrows trying to reach his hairline.

"She's down there," Brody admitted.

"You need a girlfriend," Adrik told him humorlessly, "One that the rest of us can see."

Brody narrowed his eyes at Adrik, and Adrik smirked back.

"I just feel like there's more to learn. We came here for a reason."

"And I thought you said you'd gotten the answers we needed already."

"Oh," and here Brody blushed, "I meant the answers that Finn and I needed. We still don't have a clue about the Prophecy."

Adrik whole body sent the message of his exasperation to the powers that be.

"I'll go check the well," Brody assured him calmly, "Hopefully we'll have more information then."

"You realize this whole thing's a well," Adrk pointed out, "And you're talking about traveling down into an invisible pit in the middle of the bottom of it."

"I thought it was a building."

"It is. But it's also a well for water magic, dark water magic: death magic and dark emotions."

"OK. But you've got my back, right?"

He didn't ask it like he was questioning Adrik, the elf realized. He said it more like he was reminding him. It felt strange to Adrik to be trusted like that, especially after yesterday, but he also realized he was nodding at the man in front of him. Of course he had his back.

Brody nodded at him solemnly, and turned to head toward the middle of the room. He stopped briefly as his and Finn's heads both jerked toward the spot where Finn's father apparently stood. Finn nodded and Brody was watching him.

"That's a good point, Finn. I've got Adrik here already. You look after Arisa."

"I'm fine," Arisa insisted.

"What's going on now?" Adrik asked as nonchalantly as he could muster.

"My dad thinks I may see what you see once he leaves, which he's about to do," Finn stated simply then glanced back toward his invisible father, "He thinks I should be away from whatever's here first."

"What about you?" Adrik asked Brody.

"If I'm seeing an even older vision of the room, then that probably won't change as long as the girl is here."

"Does 'the girl' have a name?" Adrik asked him as Finn walked just as easily as Brody through the corpses to reach Arisa and the stairwell.

Brody paused for a moment and then said, "Loriaz? No? Sorry, what? Lor-lee-ayze. Ok. Lor-li-aze. Nice to meet you, I'm Brody. This is Adrik."

Adrik waved stupidly at the center of the corpse pile.

"Lorliaze?" Arisa mused, "Why does that name sound familiar to me?"

"It does me, too," Adrik admitted, "But I can't think where from."

Arisa bit her lip. It was ridiculously adorable, "Me either," she admitted.

Brody walked easily to the center of the room. Adrik tried to just pretend he couldn't see all of the cadavers and to walk through them like Brody was doing. It was a mistake. He immediately tripped and fell face first into the first pile of remains. His hands hit the floor and his feet slipped up and onto a higher body in another stack. He briefly amused himself at the thought that he must look like he was trying to do a hand stand to Brody, and maybe Finn, if they couldn't see the bodies holding his weight. He tried not think about what he looked, or smelled, like fom Arisa's point of view. Then he heard Finn exclaim,

"Holy love of Light!!!"

Adrik tried to scramble back up and across the refuse of carcasses. Gods, this was gross. He heard conversation going on overhead, but he was too busy concentrating on not throwing up. He tried to use his hands to prop himself up and across the top of the mass of death, which worked, but also brought another boon. He realized that the pit Brody mentioned wasn't invisible; it was there under the bodies and so full of its own skeletons that it overflowed into the rest of morass.

Brody came and awkwardly helped Adrik back to his feet, looking bemusedly at him as he did.

"Is Finn ok?" Adrik asked.

"Yeah. The fishermen left," Brody paused and let his grief wash through him briefly, "And I think he can now see what you guys do. Honestly, I'm glad I can't."

Adrik stood up and wiped something blackish green off of his hands onto his trousers, "Yeah," he told Brody, "Be glad. At least I found your pit."

Brody chuckled, "I know. For a minute I thought you were going down it face first."

Adrik looked at him grimly, "I couldn't have. The skeletons overflowing from it would have held me up. You sure you want to go down there?"

"No. But I'm sure I need to."

"Oooo-kay. Then I'll hold the ladder. In fact, let's tie some rope around you first. I have a feeling we'll both be better off if I have to pull you up than if I have to go down after you."

Brody nodded. "Hopefully I won't need either, but a rope's a great idea."

It ended up being an easy journey. Adrik had the harder job trying to force his stomach to ignore the putred stench and his head the growing cacophony of an unseen spirit army all around him. For his part, Brody climbed down, picked up a rock, declared there was nothing there, and climbed right back out. The mud-caked ladder Adrik held for him, did indeed appear to have been silver. It was tarnished beyond the hope of repair, but was once stunning, Adrik thought. He gave the chilling room no other thought or backward glance as they reached the staircase and their companions.

Adrik had just begun to feel relieved at having made it out of the stinking pit of rotten flesh when all of the emotions that had plagued him before slammed back into his psyche with nearly physical force. He called out…something unintelligible probably, and grabbed his head. He tried to remember his moment with Arisa. He just couldn't recall it.

Strong hands grabbed him. He thought they were his father's at first and he tried to recoil, but he heard Finn's voice behind him, "It's me, Adrik. I'm just going to get you out of here."

A couple of agonizing landings later, and Finn put him down on the ground somewhere less disturbing. Adrik tried to uncurl his tightly wound body. It all ached again, but his eyes met Arisa's and the inner turmoil eased, at least.

They'd found a room that was especially large. It had once been a very grand hall of some sort. Adrik didn't care for the openness of it, but he had no desire to suggest going back out onto the landing.

They ate a quick and cold meal and passed around an aleskin. Both did a good bit toward easing Adrik's latest discomfort.

"Well, if you're feeling better," Arisa began, "Then maybe we can hear what Brody and Finn discovered. And may I just say," and here she beamed at the humans, "that today has proven that we couldn't have gotten anything accomplished here without the two of you. We're really lucky you two decided to join us."

Adrik sighed his favorite martyred sigh, "I guess we are." He grinned at Brody and Finn.

"Well, we owe you our thanks, too," Finn replied in his characteristic deadpan, "We never would have known what really happened if you hadn't brought us along."

Brody nodded and sat down against the wall. Fletch had reappeared at some point and was now in Brody's lap. Adrik vaguely wondered where the dog had been, but decided not to waste time on it.

Brody began, "The simple answers, that are of less concern to you, basically amount to the fact that our fathers had seen the shadowelves come up here and thought the village was in danger. They'd followed them from a distance. That's why my dad said he knew he was going to die. He didn't know he'd surprise a lookout as soon as he walked in, but none of them expected to survive the storm, the mountain and the elves. In fact, they went out on the landing and found the shadowelves writhing around in agony out there. It scared them, and that fear is the emotion that overtook them. In the end, it drove them all mad and they jumped over the rail to their deaths." Brody stopped and became quiet for a moment. Then he glanced at the ever-steady gaze of Finn and continued, "As for the well, or the pit, or whatever: I didn't find anything down there except a rock," and here he pulled a palm-sized chunk of black river rock out of his pocket. It looked like average stone from more than one riverbed in his and Arisa's parts of the world, but as he considered it, he couldn't remember seeing any like it up in the Highlands.

Brody went on, "I finally saw what you saw down there after we reached the first landing," he shook his head with disgust, "Glad I couldn't see it before. I figure the rock must've come off of one of the bodies, but it's oddly warm and seems a harmless souvenir."

"Because who doesn't want to bring back a souvenir from the most evil place they've ever been," Adrik teased.

"Yeah, well, it's the only place I've ever been."

"So, you learned nothing else?" Arisa asked, desperation lacing her voice.

Brody gave her a sincerely apologetic look, "No. All I saw down there was a tiled pit with this one loose rock."

"Wait," Adrik cut in, "You couldn't see anything else? Most of those corpses had gear and weapons on them. Why would you see a river rock from one and nothing else?"

Brody shrugged, "I don't know, but I didn't. I *did* however get a sense of the magic of the place. The pit had a broken lid-looking thing lying next to it, and there were soooo many ghosts, most of which were armed to the teeth and even had horses. Somehow, and I think it has something to do with the lid, the place collected souls and could turn them loose if desired. But I don't know how…or why. Still, it reminded me of how you said Andarraine was destroyed: the lid, and the angry spirits? The thing is: the only thing new I learned about it was that it was literal…and the spirits seem to still be there."

"Well that's something," Finn chimed in stoically, "If the spirits are still there and the evil comes back, we just have to figure out how to release them again."

"There was a life for a life trade," Arisa reminded him.

"And," Brody added, "Lorliaze said that it was too high a price to pay. She's still trapped here."

"Wait!" exclaimed Adrik getting to his feet, "The spirit you've been talking to is the same one that released the ghost army two thousand years ago?"

Brody shrugged, "Maybe. She seems to be quiet now."

"Can I see that rock?" Arisa asked him. Brody handed it to her.

She turned it over and over in her hands.

"What are you thinking?" Adrik asked her softly.

"I don't know. I…"

And then Arisa's eyes rolled back in her head. Her body began convulsing more violently than they'd ever seen it. Adrik dove for her head, wanting to keep it off of the stone floor, but Arisa's jerking, seizing frame rose suddenly and quickly into the air above their heads. She spun slowly out of their reach, clinging to the little rock, her shaking, writhing form entirely incoherent.

"ARISA!!!" Adrik was jumping desperately trying to knock the rock from her grasp, "DO SOMETHING!!!!" he yelled at the two humans who were, apparently, frozen with shock. They both got to their feet, but Arisa had risen even higher and had slowly spun to an odd standing position in the air. Her shaking stopped. She lifted her hands to hold the black stone in front of her. Her head straightened, but her eyes remained rolled so far back into her head that they were solid, ghostly white. Then, in a voice strong and clear, she spoke to the room:

> *"When twice the world has made as mark*
> *A thousand years through light and dark,*
> *The great Sky Titans then shall fly*

As once they did in time gone by.
Then magic lost shall flow once more
From mountain high to distant shore,
And challenged shall be men again
By greed and lust and need to mend.
By Fire shall the sword and shield
Be tested on each battlefield:
The world rent sunder and apart
Then ruled by greed or by great heart.
The Titan's maw holds clenched inside
The runes that shattered will collide
To bring the Fire Titan hence
And harken all to wartime's chance.
Before those tested have endured,
The Water Titan's ride has lured
The Great Storm Gods from whence they hid
When Gatewell's Fortress lost its lid.
The spirit once that herein lain
Whose death destroyed that evil reign
Has now no presence such to halt
The storms brought forth at water's fault.
Then Earth shall crumble through the sky
Revealing fortress left to lie
Wherein an ancient secret kept
Of power unconquered has but slept
That must be treasured, guarded sure
Or else succumb to evil's lure.
Deep under river fortress built
Of rock and brick and rune and silt
Like sepulchre entombed within
The mighty idols sing their din.
For when at last the Wind shall ride
And threaten desert, plain and tide,

The fate of all may have be written
By those who've had the ear to listen.
On coastal shores where stars burn bright
The Titan's fortress shines at night.
And e'er by men of noble heart
Or terrible wretched gathering dark,
That fate of worlds will hence be laid
Till once again this price is paid.
Beware the two that rode before!
Beware the treasure left unsure
That in their fortresses now lie
And offer secrets time passed by!
Without the strength of magic known
These gods of lore may again be shown
The way to take what once was theirs
And make the world their wretched lairs.
For once again, two royal lines
That ruled all men in ancient times
Shall take up crown and scepter each
Or leave each throne to loathesome litch."

Arisa's eyes rolled forward again, but still appeared to be blind to the room, "And there's a signature at the bottom. It says, 'Queen Lorliaze Andarraine'"

Arisa's body floated gently to the floor, the rock slipping from her hand and rolling across the ancient tiles, it came to a seemingly innocent stop right at Brody's feet.

Chapter 9:

22nd Day of the 12th Month, 1st Day of the Week, Autumn
Wocatsday, Shilirs 22

Keen

Keen was exhausted. The only times he could remember feeling worse were times of war: the caves with Kierra, and the hospitality of Kethran. Now he and his entire family along with that of his in-laws, were trudging slowly but determinedly up, up and around and around toward whatever awaited them in the bowers of Willowmark. He had his head down as he marched, one hand still protectively at Kierra's back. She seemed to be getting stronger, and he was glad for that. He wanted his amazing little elf back: the one who had kept them alive for so long when death rode so freely through the forest.

He didn't know what to hope for when they reached the apex of their climb. He couldn't admit to anyone: not Kierra and her family, and not to his own, that he was terrified of being marched up into the tree city at the call of an unknown summons. He wished he could say he hadn't been utterly and completely relieved when Kierra's Aunt Riella had suggested that the summons might be about Kierra's father instead of about Keen. Everything terrible that had happened recently seemed to be about Keen. He'd be very happy to let someone else take the leading role for a while.

But he felt terrible now for having had those thoughts. Kierra might be about to learn the fate of her father, and from what he'd heard of the possibilities there, he was consumed with dread for her. How much would they tell her and her family? Would they just announce his death? Or would they detail the condition they found him in? Somehow that latter information had to be getting out, because they all seemed to know what to expect. Would there be a body? Would she have to see it?

They continued their climb a bit farther before the lower levels of the city began to open up around them. Then Keen saw something he'd never seen before: flying in and out of the bushes along the ramp up were...

"Faeries!" Emma exclaimed, and she and her siblings broke from the group and ran straight to the bushes in glee. The group of them stopped in their tracks. A few of them were bumped into from behind. Keen smiled broadly. He thought faeries were a myth. They had all been told that.

Other elf children joined them happily giggling and reaching for the flying fae. Most of the faeries dove quickly out of sight from the children, but 3 remained and circled their heads before dancing on their wings just out of reach of the jumping youngsters' outstretched hands.

Kierra began to giggle. Keen laughed out loud. Soon the brooding group were all smiles and laughter and were part of a larger group of refugee families all sharing this one moment of joyful normalcy. The faeries flew off toward a fountain along the next rise, joining many other faeries splashing around there. Lara had to call out for her offspring to stay with the family; many other adults were reigning theirs in, too, lest they all get mixed up and lost in the crowd.

"I didn't know there were faeries here!" Keen chuckled.

"There didn't used to be," Kierra answered smiling at him, "But the war has affected more than just humans and elves. For over a thousand years the borders of the Willows were closed to everyone but our own. There are a few fae lands that are inside what we consider to be our country, but they don't see it that way, so for most of that time, they've been the only non-willowelves allowed in the forest. And only the rare fae diplomat came into the actual city. This has long been a city of elves, and willowelves at that, but the shadowelves and the humans both have been displacing faeries. Especially bad was the faerie fountain at Alderbrook which the shadowelves attacked directly. The fae have no fortresses, no cities with walls or other defenses. They had nowhere to go, so they came here. The Treesinger Council let them stay. We may not want things to change, but we are connected enough to nature to understand that they do. So, the faeries became the first race to be allowed to live in the city in at least a millennium."

Keen looked back at the beautiful, playful little creatures sadly, "So, they're refugees?"

"Yes. I doubt most of them will ever be able to go home," Kierra sighed.

"Can we take them home with us?" Lynnie asked excitedly.

Kierra's mother smiled one of the few, genuine smiles Keen had ever seen grace her face and answered, "'Fraid not, sweetheart. They may seem like toys but those are people with friends and families, just like you have."

"Really?" asked Emma in surprise. Max was still jumping around trying to catch one. Fortunately, the faeries were laughing.

"What other races have been allowed in?" asked Kaith. Keen saw that familiar twinkle in Kaith's eye. Curiosity had come back to its natural home. Keen was glad to see it. Kaith had been the one member of his family who had been willing to hear him out about the elves. But that had been shut down by the arrest. Kaith was adventurous at heart, but not as courageous as that trait sometimes required. It was the source of more than a little stress between he and Krieg. Krieg had bravery without imagination; Kaith was all curiosity without grit. In Keen's mind, that meant he lacked real recklessness, which was a good thing, but Krieg thought of him as soft.

Keen felt Krieg tense behind him. Keen turned and saw that Krieg was shooting Kaith an exasperated look that threatened the coming storm of anger. But Joran answered before Krieg could tell Kaith to be quiet.

"None so far. If they let you stay, you'll be the only other ones."

"As far as we know, anyway," Rana cut in, "We've been away from the city for a while and a lot has happened."

"That's true," Joran conceded, and they each wrapped an arm around the other.

Keen turned and looked all around them at the crush of people heading up the ramps with them. Many were shooting fearful glances at them. All of them were elves. Keen wasn't sure what other races existed. Apparently, there were multiple races of elves, though he doubted he'd be able to tell the difference between them. He'd heard of halflings. They weren't allowed in the Southern Highlands anymore, but there had at one time been many living in their cities, even some in his home city of River Port. If there were faeries, too, what else might exist in this wide, strange world?

"So no other kinds of elves are here either?" Keen asked, keeping up the conversation so Kaith and Krieg wouldn't end up butting heads.

"No," answered Kierra conversationally, "We don't have great relationships with the others. Honestly, humans, halflings, faeries, and elflings sometimes seem more like us than other elves."

"The morrowelves are very decent people, too," Joran interjected, "The old prejudices are just ridiculous."

Kaith was watching Joran with interest, probably trying to decide how much he could ask. Keen went on for him.

"Morrowelves?"

"They live in the hilly grasslands to the north of your country's border," Joran answered.

"I thought that was part of *this* country," Krieg interrupted.

"No," said every elf in earshot, which included a few around them that were not in the family. Apparently, a few people were as curious about them as they were about the elves.

Joran chuckled looking around at the eavesdroppers, "The morrowelves abandoned the Sacred Trust for books and knowledge. Books and knowledge are fine, in general, but the morrowelves draw the line nowhere. They'll study anything, even if it's dangerous. And, of course, from our point of view, nothing is worth abandoning the forest. It's been an ongoing feud for centuries now. It's even come to blows more than once."

"But you feel differently?" asked Kaith and, right on cue, Krieg shot him a silencing glare.

Joran sighed. He turned and waited, then joined back into the march between Keen and Kaith, "My first assignment as an officer was to lead a small group of soldiers who were guarding a pair of diplomats heading into the Morrowlands. It was disastrous, at least the diplomatic part was. The captain of the guard with their emissaries and I got tired of staring each other down, so he and I with all of our men went drinking. We agreed that if none of the armed guards was in the way, it would be less tense. We were all very aware of the fact that if the ambassadors decided to make things ugly it would be us, not them, killing each other, and it almost came to that, but with Captain Marik of the morrowelves' help, I managed to get our envoy back over the border without anyone getting hurt."

"That doesn't sound like a disaster," Krieg replied.

Joran glanced back at Krieg who was walking behind Joran while helping Granny and Lara keep going and answered, "It was a diplomatic disaster, not a military one. We only avoided the military engagement because Marik and I got along and worked together to avoid it. Personally, I think when the soldiers are engaged in diplomacy and the diplomats are threatening war, it's a disaster."

At that Krieg actually laughed. It was a sound that brought laughter to most of the rest of their group. Joran did have a point.

"So what was going…" Kaith started, but they were interrupted by the treesinger who had been leading them.

"This is where we get off," she announced pleasantly, indicating what appeared to Keen to be the next to the top level of the center of the city. Kierra frowned. Keen tried to shoot her a questioning look, but she was too focused on their guide. Keen did not want any surprises now. They had just been relaxing somewhat.

"Elanra herself is meeting you just outside of the Myandei Mar."[9]

Kierra's face turned pale and her mother grabbed her arm for support. Both Joran and Jerith reached for their mothers. Fear rose up swiftly in Keen.

Kierra stumbled over her words, but forced her voice out clear and strong, "Then I can lead us from here," She informed the other treesinger simply. Keen didn't like the look on Kierra's face. It was terror.

The treesinger's face shown regret, but she nodded respectfully at Kierra, and began to work her way back down the great ramp. Kierra closed her eyes briefly, then she met Joran's. His face was unreadable. None of them were moving. Joran put his arm around his mother's shoulders. Riella was crying softly into Jerith's chest. Kierra hugged each of her grandparents, who were leaning on each other for support.

Keen couldn't take the tension anymore. "Is there something we should know?" he asked carefully, trying not to sound as scared as he was.

Kierra turned to him with damp eyes, full of the determined strength he'd seen in them so often during the first days that they'd known each other.

"The Elder of the Treesinger's Council is meeting us outside the hospital district," she stated simply, "It's likely they have my father's and uncle's bodies there."

Keen glanced around at the miserable faces of the kind elves he'd grown to

---

[9] Pronounced "MYE-en-day MAR" Literally Healers Village (plural) not Healers' Village (possessive)

care for. He felt like an outsider. He wished he could take his own family away somewhere and give Kierra's the space to grieve in private. He answered simply, "I am so sorry. What do you need from me?"

"From us," Keen's mother corrected sternly, "I remember having to see my husband after…"

Keen spun around. His mother had a single tear gracing her cheek. He hadn't thought of how this might remind her of Keen's own father.

"If you show us somewhere where we won't disturb anyone, we can lay low and give you privacy," she went on, "Or we can cook or whatever would be helpful."

The mothers and grandmothers all locked eyes and a solemn understanding passed between them all. This was women's work, this grief, and it wasn't unique to elves or humans. It was part of the greater life cycle that women understood so much more intrinsically than men, Keen thought. And they all six knew it.

Krieg looked around at them in bewilderment. Max asked, "What's going on?" so Kaith picked him up to keep him out of the way. Kierra's mother nodded at Keen's, "Thank you," then she added, extending her hand, "I'm Lillin. I'm Kierra's mother. In all of this craziness, we haven't been introduced."

They had all stopped and moved off to the side, the wide teeming city sprawling out around them. The sudden change from two families to one had left many of them, mostly the men, Keen mused, speechless.

"Morwen," Keen's mother responded, "And this is my mother, Hansela, my sons, well you know Keen, this is Krieg, and his wife Lara, and Kaith."

Keen felt bad, He should have thought to introduce them. But Lillin was unfazed, "Joran and Kierra are my children; their father is…was…Ranic. Rana is Joran's mate. This is Riella, she's Jerith's mother and the mate of Pellen, Ranic's brother. And these are Ranic's and Pellen's parents, Selena and Ranir, Nira here is both my nephew's mate and Rana's sister." Then Lilin looked at Lara and asked, "And your little ones?"

Lara smiled and introduced Lynnie, Emma and Max, who were all very shy in response. Handshakes were passed all around. Then the slow march of dread into the city resumed.

They walked quietly along through a bustling street. Many people were stopping for, and being given, directions. Large, proud, intricately decorated buildings rose on both sides of the street and were intermingled with trader's carts, food stalls, several stables, floral gardens bright with color, soldiers and civilians. It was all they could do to keep together through the press of bodies.

Eventually they veered left and accessed a street that ran along the city's edge rather than through its center. Keen stopped in his tracks. He felt the rest of his family pause with him. The view was the most incredible he'd ever seen. The forest stretched almost as far as the eye could see except for the unmistakable shadow of the Breaking on the far horizon to their left. Birds and butterflies flitted through the trees. Deciduous autumn leaves floated in the damp- and soil-scented breeze. The sky above the red and gold carpet of treetops beneath them was a clear and pale autumn blue. It looked to Keen like paradise.

Along the edge ran a high wooden rail carved to look like ivy. A long trough with water running through it from somewhere hung below it. Archers dotted the edge, all facing out, bows at the ready, and between them, every manner of land conveyance Keen could imagine had been tied along its length. Many were heavy laden with the worldly possessions of other unseen travelers. Occasionally, small family groups of children were playing in and around horses, ponies, mules and wagons, usually tended by an older elf teen or adult, but sometimes not. They even passed a person who initially looked like a human child, but instead was apparently an adult halfling male. He seemed to be having a conversation with the saddlebag attached to one of a group of three ponies secured together, but Lynnie's sharp child eyes spotted the truth.

"Look! That short person is talking to a faerie! See?"

Sure enough, a very beleaguered looking female faerie was poking her head out of the conversational saddlebag.

Jerith quietly mentioned, "I guess there are halflings here now, too." And they kept walking.

A large crowd of people were gathered ahead of them, away from the edge and just past an ornate wooden archway whose twisting ornamentation appeared to spell something out in an alphabet Keen couldn't read. They all looked anxious, and three treesingers wearing their green robes of office but with additional gold embroidery that trailed all the way down their long, flowing sleeves, seemed to be waiting with them. The crowd was morosely silent.

Kierra detoured off toward the treesingers who turned and seemed to recognize her. The treesingers all nodded stoically to her. Another group of civilian elves who had been traveling behind them, also joined the growing company. One of the waiting treesingers marked something down on a parchment he was holding and asked Kierra to move her group over to the side with the existing cluster. The treesinger leading the group behind them then approached, said something quietly to the elf with the parchment who made a similarly brief mark on his paper, and then took her leave of the family who had been following her. The growing swarm of elves was tense, but what was bothering Keen more was that many of the people coming and going through the nearby archway were looking at his family with shock, alarm, fear, and even ire. The three treesingers who were clearly in charge were watching the reactions intently.

Toward the back of the group there was a large open shed-like structure built up against what seemed to Keen like a large tree trunk growing through the street there, but which he realized was probably just a huge branch from one of the three enormous oaks that held up this part of the city. Near the ground the three had seemed to be grown so tightly together as to possibly be only one tree, but up here they were widely distinct allowing the city to twist and turn around them and through their many gigantic branches.

Kierra indicated the shed-like structure. It was about 8 feet deep, but almost twice as long and connected to another similar structure behind the waiting cluster of people as a smaller alleyway seemed to branch off there between the large branch and the next gargantuan trunk that dominated the edge of the area beyond the arch. The rest of that area appeared to be a morass of tents and activity for as far as Keen could see.

"Let's slip in here to wait," Kierra suggested gently, and they all ducked into the shack. There were a few tools leaned up against one side that looked to Keen like some kind of gardening implements, though not ones he could name. Otherwise, the stall was empty and appeared to have been recently swept out.

Keen noticed that Joran, Jerith, Rana, Nira and Kierra all stood with their backs toward the main street, facing their small cluster of families. It was casual and friendly, but clearly was also intended to shield them from view. Keen looked over at his own frightened family and suggested that they all sit up against the trunk-like branch that made up the back wall. He assumed that it wasn't their own family members that that his friends were trying to hide, and as his family settled down low, the elves visibly relaxed.

Kaith had obviously become a little more comfortable around their hosts, because his inquisitive side was coming out again.

"So all of these elves are your kind of elves?" he asked.

Kierra and her family looked around them outside as if confused by the question. Then they frowned at each other before Kierra answered, "Yes."

"How can you tell?" Kaith pressed.

Kierra looked at him curiously; Joran and Rana looked horrified; Nira had one eyebrow cocked, but Jerith looked like he wanted to laugh.

"You all really don't know anything about elves, do you?" Jerith teased, and Kierra shot him an accusatory stare.

"I thought I'd already made that pretty clear," Keen mused.

Kierra shook her head grinning and abandoned her post by the opening to sit on the ground in front of Keen.

"We look very different. The longer the elven races have remained separated, the more different we've become in appearance. Trust me, if you saw a member of one of the other elven races, you'd know."

"We'll have to take your word for it, I guess," Keen smiled at her.

Kierra opened her mouth to speak when a woman's voice called out from the waiting group to declare that everyone was gathered at last. Kierra's face turned instantly from amusement to dread. Keen reached forward and squeezed her hand as she made to stand back up.

The woman's voice floated over all of the assembled crowd as she addressed them. Lilin was clinging to Joran. Keen stood up behind Kierra and put his hands on her shoulders. She grabbed one of his hands in hers and leaned back against him. Outside, Keen could see that the woman who was speaking was an attractive middle-aged elf who was wearing, in addition to the overly embroidered long treesinger's tunic, a cape-like cloak that was similarly adorned. She glanced at Keen when he took Kierra's shoulders and smiled briefly at them. Her smile, even fleeting as it was, had the effect of putting Keen immediately at ease. He also noticed that several soldiers had joined the host.

"I'm so sorry to have kept you all waiting," the woman went on, "Most of you know who I am, of course, but for those of you who don't," and here she shot another passing glance at Keen, "I am Elanra, Elder Treesinger. For those of you who have never been to the city before, welcome.

"I have asked that you all assemble here, because we have *truly historic* good news to share."

At this pronouncement, there were confused frowns and rumbling murmurs throughout the assemblage. Kierra looked bewildered up at Keen who could only answer her with his own bewilderment.

Elanra went on, "You are all family and friends of the ten brave soldiers who were captured nearly 2 months ago now on the northern front while serving under one of the three officers who led that large offense." Then she glanced back at Kierra and her family and added, "Or who are 2 of those three officers. I am truly ecstatic to inform you all that 6 days ago, they escaped captivity!"

Gasps, cheers and weeping erupted immediately. Even Keen felt moisture well up in his eyes. Kierra gave a small shout and covered her face with both hands as her knees buckled. Keen had her in his arms immediately. She clung to his shoulders in loud wracking sobs.

"Escaped?!" came the voices from the crowd.

"Alive?"

"They're alive?"

"Where are they?"

"Did they make it back?"

"Can we see them?"

"They escaped!!!"

All around them elves were hugging, crying and grasping each other for support. Keen looked around. Lilin and Riella had fallen into the arms of Selena and Ranir, both of whom were sobbing uncontrollably. Jerith had his hand on his mother's back with tears streaming down his broadly smiling face. Nira had flung her arms around his neck. To his other side Joran and Rana were embracing, weeping and jumping up and down together. Keen felt one of his tears roll down to his chin. He didn't even try to stop it.

Crying was turning to cheering as Elanra tried to restore calm so she could go on speaking. Eventually, she could make herself heard again.

"They did escape, and surprisingly, with the aid of two shadowelves. They met some additional trouble trying to make their way back, but found aid again from some traveling halflings and fae who came across their path. Unfortunately, one of the halflings didn't make it. We are planning a city-wide funeral for her, and we especially hope that you all will attend.

"I do need to prepare you all, of course. They are all expected to survive, but unfortunately, they were in a shadowelf prison camp for weeks. Here shortly, we will take you to see them, but I need to prepare you. They are all in terrible shape," and here Elanra's own emotions got the best of her, and she choked on the word 'terrible.' The gathering grew immediately silent with cold dread.

Elanra went on, "Their spirits are high and they have all been cleaned, bandaged and sung on toward rapid healing, but you must understand that the shadowelves do not toy around with their treatment of prisoners. Each injury inflicted on these men was designed as much for the shock it would instill in us to see it, as it was for any other purpose. And while our treesingers are giving them every attention and every healing balm we have, none of them will be unscarred."

Elanra took a deep and steadying breath as she faced a crowd who had been run from sorrow through joy and back to dread and horror. Then she smiled broadly at them and finished, "I know we would all like to have them back as they were, but we do have them back, and that is what we need to dwell on. Although their bodies are not what they might have been before, their spirits are every bit as they were, and they are each overjoyed to be home and excited to see you. I encourage you to gather your own strength before we enter the Mar. Do not bring their spirits down with your own sense of horror at what they've been through. Our healers have counseled me to impress upon you that this is one important thing each of us can do to help them come back fully from what has been a terrible ordeal for them and for all of us. For today, and for the next couple of days, I encourage you to see them as they were, and dwell on the fact that they are home, and that it is a *miracle*.

"With wars on two fronts, the Myandei Mar is overcrowded at the moment. I need to ask that no more than 3 visit each patient at a time…for now. So, if the first 3 from each group would like to come up here, we'll show you where your loved ones are resting."

As soon as Enlanra finished speaking, there was immediate explosion of noise and action among those gathered. Kierra looked up into Keen's face with a confused mix of emotions and then looked around at her family. Joran stepped up.

"Mom, you and Kierra go with one of Nana and Papa. The other can go with Jerith and Aunt Riella. I'll wait here."

"What? No," Kierra protested, albeit insincerely Keen thought, "I'm responsible for Keen and his family. I should get them settled somewhere first…"

"Kierra," Keen insisted, "We can stay out of people's way while you go and see your dad…"

"Ki," Joran went on, "He'll want you to sing for him. I know the others already have, but, it's you…"

"He's right," Keen joined in, "If it was me, I'd be waiting for your voice most of all."

Kierra looked torn. It was clear to Keen that she wanted to rush right to her father's side, but she was hesitating, why? For his sake? For Joran's? Joran looked just as torn. They had to both want to go. If Keen's own father were suddenly found miraculously alive, he'd want to think of any excuse he could to get to be in the first group to see him.

Nira spoke up then, "Kierra, Rana and I will be out here. We can stay with Keen and his family. Besides, as a treesinger, don't you have unfettered access to the Myandei Mar anyway? You and Joran could both go."

Kierra and Joran studied each other briefly; then Kierra looked back up at Keen. The others who would be going were looking anxious to get moving. Keen tried to look as calm and supportive as he could. He couldn't let her see his nervousness. Not right now.

"We'll stay with Rana and Nira," he assured her, "Go on and see your dad."

And with that, she smiled up at him, kissed him gratefully, and headed off with her family through the archway.

The rest of the day was long and, from Keen's perspective, confusing. Rana and Nira managed, somehow, to requisition the two storage buildings where they were waiting, along with a third small one across the alley. Housing was, he supposed unsurprisingly, at a premium in a city filled with refugees. Tent space was running out and, it was explained, so were tents. So they all set about turning the crude little open buildings into a temporary living space. Blankets were found somewhere and hung across the wide openings to form a fourth "wall" of sorts, and a pair of small potbelly stoves of the type Keen had seen in the two military camps in which he had been housed, were procured from an archers' barracks by Rana and Nira and brought down for warmth.

The humans stayed put. Too many of the patients within the Myandei Mar were casualties of the Human War, and their loved ones did not want to be reminded of humanity. Keen's family felt safer, too. Hidden away in their own space, they had a small sense of security and togetherness.

Need was everywhere in the city. Rana and Nira spent their time flitting in and out, securing supplies and information, and allowing Keen's family to unwind and establish their own space. It was small and cramped, but it was warm and comforting, and despite the great dirth of basic items that they had arrived with, the small double shack was soon filled with bedding, a few toys for the children, sewing implements and cloth, and by the time a gentle afternoon rain began to chill the city outside, the smell of food cooking in donated iron cooking pots on the two small stoves. Keen and his family were all very much looking forward to food cooked according to their own custom, and as the beckoning aroma grew, Rana and Nira became increasingly interested in sampling "human" food.

They were lucky in so many ways. Late arrivals to the city were crammed two and three families to a tent, but most of the willowelves had managed to flee with basic supplies from home. Food was scarce, but still available, mostly because the forest itself was teeming with edible life and many refugees had added their labor to the number of hunters and gatherers bringing back these provisions.

Keen missed Kierra. She and her family had stayed within the Mar all day, but he understood. He knew there was nowhere she'd rather be right then than by her ailing father's side, and he didn't begrudge her that. She and her family deserved this good news more than anyone Keen could think of.

Krieg had been anxious each time the elven archers reappeared to learn of work that might be available to him in the city and how long it might be until the Council decided their fate. But the fact was, unsurprisingly, that the plight of one unarmed, unique family within such an overcrowded city was low on the list of immediate interest for its ruling body.

The flap was pushed aside again, and, predictably, Krieg tensed. But it was Kierra who emerged from the street. Her eyes were puffy and red and her cheeks were wet. Her restless eyes fell on Keen as he lept up from helping his mother remove a small pan of bread rolls from the belly of the stove. He moved directly for her, and she crumbled, sobbing into his arms again. Keen rocked her gently while holding tightly to her seemingly diminished frame as Joran entered the shack with his own eyes suspiciously red.

Joran wiped the moisture from his cheek as Keen asked, "That bad?"

Joran closed his eyes briefly and responded, "Where is Rana?"

Krieg stood and answered, somewhat apologetically, "She and Nira were trying to help me find work in the city. They've been gone about an hour."

"There's some food now," Keen's mother offered, ladling some freshly made stew over a piece of bread on a small wooden plate.

Joran shook his head and stepped back outside. Kierra took the proferred meal and sat down on the floor near their erstwhile entrance. Keen plopped down next to her and waited as patiently as he could for her to speak. She took a few half-hearted bites of her food.

"This is good. Thank you," she said sheepishly.

"It's simple," Keen's mother responded, "But it's a little bit of our home. I'm glad you like it."

Kaith helped put the next couple of rolls into the fiery belly of the stove while Keen's mother put plates together for the children. Joran returned looking forlorn and sat down on the other side of Kierra.

"It is and it isn't," he stated simply.

Keen looked at him, confused, and frowned.

"That bad," he explained.

"They burned out his eye!" Kierra exclaimed into her plate, "It's awful!"

Keen cringed, but he couldn't for the life of him think of anything comforting to say.

"His eye?" Kaith responded incredulously, looking up from the now-shut stove.

"Kaith," Krieg chastised, and shook his head at him.

"His eye, some of his fingers…" Joran swallowed hard, "He's covered in wounds right down to the bottoms of his feet. It's worse than I had even imagined."

Keen noticed that Kierra had stopped eating and was staring into her food. Keen reached up and brushed her hair away from her face. She smiled at him, and resumed eating.

Kaith, undeterred, asked, "So, how is it not bad, then?"

Kierra swallowed and sighed.

"He's just so happy," she answered him, "So grateful to be alive, and home. It's like his body's broken, but his spirit is just…rejeuvenated."

Keen found his voice and quietly asked, "How's Jerith?"

Kierra shrugged, "The same. His dad still has both of his eyes, but otherwise, he's in the same shape. He's still awake, though. Our dad finally managed to go to sleep, so we slipped out to check on you guys, and on Nira and Rana."

"Well, we made a fairly large pot of stew. The rolls don't really need to be heated," Keen's mother started as she pulled more rolls out of the small oven, "Does the rest of your family have food?"

"They will," Joran answered, "The treesingers will make sure."

"Well," Kierra contradicted him, "They'll feed everyone who doesn't have their own, but it'll help them out if we can feed ourselves."

"Then please let that be our job. There's plenty here."

Kierra smiled at her new mother-in-law, "Thank you."

"He wants to meet you, you know," Joran said, addressing Keen, then added with a mischievous smile, "Our dad. He's terribly curious about you."

Keen could feel the eyes of his family on him. Out of the corner of his eye, he noticed Krieg cock an amused eyebrow. He refused to look at them. Despite the beads of sweat that had inextricably formed on his brow, he schooled his face into pleasant curiosity, at least he hoped he had. He feared he was, instead, portraying goofy bewilderment.

"Should I help bring some food back then?" he asked simply.

Rana and Nira returned as they were gathering food for the family waiting in the Myandei Mar. Joran stepped outside for a private conversation with his mate. Nira listened tensely to Kierra's description of her father and uncle's conditions. Then Keen, Joran, Kierra, Rana and Nira left with a pot of stew, plates, utensils, unheated elvish bread and a large pitcher of fruit-infused water that the kids had made with their mother. Kierra explained that the initial visitor limit was simply meant to avoid clogging the already crowded avenues between the tents. Once inside her father's and uncle's private tent, they could have whatever family the patients wanted.

The avenues between the tents were narrow and crowded with treesingers, families, the sick and the wounded. Making it through the maze of the healing village with a pot of stew was quickly proving to Keen that he could have benefitted greatly from elven reflexes and grace. He was not looking forward to meeting his new father-in-law covered as he was in any number of small stew stains as he trudged along trying to preserve as much food through the journey as humanly possible.

Joran, who was carrying a basket of bread, seemed more stoic than Keen had ever seen him. He seemed almost unaware of the bodies he instinctively avoided, but failed to acknowledge. Keen glanced over at Kierra, cradling a jug of fruity water against her breast, and raised his eyebrows at her while throwing a questioning nod at Joran. Kierra grimaced concernedly and shrugged. Rana and Nira, carrying dishes and a second jug of water respectively, were flanking him, almost protectively Keen thought, and his own protective instincts began to kick in.

"Is there anything else you need, Joran?" he asked cautiously. "You seem a bit…lost, if you'll forgive me for noticing."

Joran glanced thoughtfully back at Keen and answered as he kept weaving his way forward, "You know, it's odd. I'm finding I have some sympathy for Kethran now, of all people."

Keen felt another dribble of stew splash onto his tunic.

"Um…why?" he stammered.

Joran glanced back a him again and grinned, "No, I don't mean you, it's just…I guess I'm finding that I'm grateful to him is all. If he hadn't already taught me to guard against becoming what he has become, I think seeing my dad and my uncle…I'm just so angry…And knowing what happened to Kethran's father and his brother…I get it now. I think I've reached a point where I just have to admit that if it wasn't for Kethran having become what he became, I might have instead…"

At that they fell silent, and it wasn't long enough before they reached their destination for Keen to think of anything else he could possibly say to that. Mostly, Keen understood. He had no idea what might have happened to Kethran's family, but it really wasn't all too difficult for Keen to imagine events that would drive himself over that precipitous edge.

"Well, here we are," Joran announced, stopping in front of a tent so similar in place and appearance to countless others they had passed, that Keen doubted he could find his way back to it specifically.

Jerith, having apparently heard Joran's announcement, opened the tent flap and grinned, first at Nira, then at the food, then at the rest of them.

"Wow! That smells good! How did you get it together so quickly?"

This he had addressed to Kierra, but Keen answered him anyway, "My family and I had been cooking most of the afternoon by the time Joran and Kierra got back." Then feeling sheepish about leaving them out, he added, "Rana and Nira have been running themselves ragged gathering the supplies we all needed."

They entered a warm, fairly roomy tent, with an ornate rug covering the ground that was flanked by two cots, each containing a severely injured elf, both of whom were sleeping. Kierra's mother, aunt, and grandparents filled the center of the space in chairs, of which there were two empty. Small potbelly stoves at the front corners, and along the back wall provided light and heat, and small tables sat by each stove, and at the head of each cot, supporting concoctions of herbs and oils, rolls of bandages, rags, towels and jugs of fresh water.

Kierra's mom got up and took the pot from Keen, smiling amusedly down at the stains on his tunic, which he self-conciously tried to wipe away. She shook her head at him, grinning, letting him know that his messy appearance mattered not at all to them. He smiled gently back at her.

The group ate in near silence, watching the two patients sleep. Kierra sat next to her father, who had a patch placed over a bandage covering one eye, and held his hand, humming softly to him as he slept. Their faces were bruised and their hands were heavily bandaged, but both men were clean and sleeping peacefully.

Keen wondered about the horrors that lay under those bandages, beneath those blankets and in the tormented memories of the men he watched sleep, but he voiced nothing. He sat on the ground next to Kierra's chair until there was enough evidence that everyone had eaten their fill that he felt it might not be rude to get up and gather their plates.

He felt like an outsider. These men were total strangers to him. Rana and Nira had shed a few silent tears when they had entered and had kissed the foreheads of the men lying in slumber, but Keen had only acknowledged everyone with a nod and began passing out food. He felt like a woman in attending to these chores, but he also felt useful doing them, so he kept going. He'd been around the elves long enough to know that their ideas about men and women were at least different from his own, so maybe, he reasoned, they wouldn't notice how strange he felt.

Eventually, Kierra's father spoke. Without opening his remaining eye, he asked softly, "Do I smell food?"

Several family members jumped up at once, including Keen, and a silent arrangement of chores was made quickly between them. Keen, who had already been rinsing dishes, provided a clean cup and plate to Kierra and began quickly washing a set of utensils. Kierra filled the dishes and handed them to her mother, who, once Joran had helped his father sit, began helping him eat. He accepted a piece of bread from his own mother while his father stood silently behind her looking down on him with clear love and concern.

Jerith's father woke soon after, and more food and feeding were organized. Eventually, Shavanir Ranic, the one-eyed man he'd heard so much about since meeting Kierra, turned his damaged face around behind him to where Keen was standing, and smiled.

"Ah, you must be the human that stole my Kierra's heart!"

His jovial tone caught Keen off guard. He glanced at Kierra who smiled broadly at him.

"Come here and sit with me…I don't know what I think of you yet," the older man added with mock sternness in his voice.

Keen moved to the side of his bed, between the cots, acutely aware that the other injured elf was watching him from behind. Keen refused to take a chair offered by Kierra's grandfather, and elected instead to squat next to Ranic's shoulder.

"I don't know, Kierra," Ranic teased, shaking his head and turning toward Kierra on his other side, "I don't see it."

"Dad!" she half-squealed like a tickled child, "Be nice."

Ranic turned back to Keen, who wasn't at all sure what his face was doing: half-smiling with raised eyebrows? Maybe. Ranic laughed, "You'd think I'd attacked. She's terribly protective of you, you know."

Keen looked over at Kierra who was shaking her head. "Don't let him get to you," she warned, "He teases everybody."

Ranic looked back to his daughter, "You're not supposed to warn him! It's my prerogative to interrogate...I mean, get to know him."

Kierra narrowed her eyes playfully at him, still shaking her head and enunciated, "Be. Nice."

Ranic laughed and turned back to Keen, who was painfully aware that he still hadn't said a word, though he was clearly the center of all attention in the room at this point.

"I hear you saved her," Ranic confessed seriously, "Thank you for that. I can't imagine having come home to..." He began to choke on his words, but recovered himself, "I'm grateful."

"She saved me, too, you know. You have an amazing daughter. I couldn't have survived without her."

Keen checked his words back over in his head and decided that, yes, that had been a good response. He let out a breath he had apparently been holding. Ranic laughed.

"Do I make you nervous?" he mused, "You know you could probably break me in half."

At that, Keen decided to smile and play along. He replied, "Nah. Kierra would kill me. I think I like her better when she likes me."

And at that, they all laughed. Keen willed himself to relax as much as he could. He really REALLY wanted to make a good impression, but how in the world could he, Keen, failed soldier who had invaded this country, possibly impress such a tried and honorable military man? Because it was clear to Keen, even if Ranic's family didn't see it yet, that the man laying before him was not broken like Krieg had been, but ready and anxious to get on with his life and his family. Keen smiled at him.

Ranic lowered his voice conspiratorially, "Life IS usually better that way." Then he laughed a hardy laugh that had his whole family smiling.

It was dark before Keen, Kierra, Rana and Nira left to return to the shack where they would be staying that night. Keen had also been introduced to Shavanir Pellen. Kierra had sung for her father and uncle. What conversation had ensued had been light, mostly Ranic asking questions about Keen and his family. Then both men had been given additional medicine and fell back to sleep.

"It's odd," Kierra mused on their way back through the still-busy pathways through the Myandei Mar, "Shadowelves did this to him, but Shadowelves saved him, too. I can't wrap my brain around it."

"Shadowelves saved them?" Rana chimed in, startled.

Kierra nodded. "Apparently while they were there, a shadowelf woman got imprisoned with them. Dad and Uncle Pellen felt sorry for her because she seemed young, and uneducated and poor, and really scared. So, they tried to protect her from the guards, which got them into extra trouble apparently..." Kierra's voice trailed off into thought, but Rana broke in again.

"And?"

As Kierra jolted out of her short reverie, Keen noticed how utterly exhausted she looked.

"And then some shadowelf man came to rescue her. Dad said he'd never seen anything like this man. He called him the scariest shadowelf he'd ever encountered, which really must be saying something. He slaughtered the whole prison camp by himself...all the guards, the torturers, even the cooks. But he helped my dad and my uncle and their men get away, out of gratitude apparently, for helping the woman. Arjina was her name. Dad asked us to pray for her."

"What was the man's name? Did he say?" asked Nira.

"Kavren. I've never heard of him, have you?"

Both other women shook their heads, and Keen asked, perplexed, "Why would you have?"

"Because any shadowelf that much more violent or powerful or whatever he was....you'd think he'd be well known."

"Do you think he's part of the secret leadership of Adrienmark?"

Kierra turned fully around and gazed at Nira following this question. Keen was lost.

"I wasn't..." she stammered, "I mean, I doubt...Why would anyone from Adrienmark help our soldiers?"

Keen glanced at Nira, who shrugged. Then she responded, "They're about the only ones whose names we really don't have yet. Are the shavanira reading anything into this?"

"Like what?" Kierra asked, clearly dumbfounded.

Rana looked unusually thoughtful, then suggested, "Someone with that level of prowess: who could kill Darkwald soldiers indiscriminately...you know, having both the skill and the umbridge to do it...You don't think there's a schism in the Wald, do you?"

Keen thought he was starting to catch on. He didn't know anything about a secret leadership, or anything called Adrienmark, but he had to admit, this Kavren sounded like a big problem for his government.

He turned to Kierra, "Did your father say why the woman was imprisoned?"

She shook her head, "No. He didn't."

"Had you ever heard of her?"

"No, but she sounded, well, common. I hate to say that, but shadowelf culture is highly stratified, and Dad made her sound like one of any number of oppressed, well, peasants, essentially, that presumably live and work all over the Darkwald."

Keen knew something about stratified society. His own culture had four distinct classes, five if you counted the people that no one counted. "Could he be some kind of rebel leader?" Keen asked.

"We haven't heard any rumors of rebellion in the Wald," Nira quickly countered.

"But would we?" Rana mused, "Kajiri would want to keep a tight lid on that!"

"Why would you think that?" Kierra asked thoughtfully.

"Well, why else would a man from a warrior caste and a peasant woman have any association with each other?" Keen asked, "Assuming he isn't just a well-trained soldier…"

"I don't know," Kierra admitted, "I don't really know how those things work, honestly."

"One way or another, the Treesinger's Council is going to be very interested in finding out who these two people are," Rana interjected happily, "This could be big!"

Nothing more was discovered through idle conversation, and by the time the group reached their new quarters outside of the Mar, most of Keen's family had turned in. Only Keen's mother and Lara had waited up to wash the dishes returning from Kierra's family.

That night was peaceful. Everyone felt safe. The forest noises around them seemed dreamlike. There was still a lot of activity going and coming from the Myandei Mar on and off, but it faded into the background as sheer exhaustion learned to ignore it. Kierra slept cuddled up in Keen's arms, which was exactly where he liked her to sleep. Already he felt so accustomed to her presence, that his arms felt empty and strange when she wasn't in them at night. He smiled, as he often did, into her brown mop of hair, and once again thanked whatever benevolent spirits were out there for her.

The following morning, Keen awoke to something of a small commotion. A messenger from the Treesinger's Council had come looking for Joran, and had left rather quickly upon hearing that Joran was still in the Mar. Kierra and especially Rana looked worried. Nira was occupying the children while Lara and Keen's mother heated breakfast for everyone, so she was stoically ignoring the hubbub.

Keen cast his usual furtive glance toward Kierra who was biting her lower lip. She shook her head at him, and indicated that he should follow her outside. Glancing surreptitiously at Krieg, Keen noticed that he was following all of this like a restless hawk.

"Kethran came into town last night," Kierra admitted once they were out on the street, "Rana didn't tell us because of everything going on, but I'm afraid he's here to make more trouble for my brother."

"And for us?"

"I don't know how much he knows yet…or has heard."

"Kierra, even with everything going on in this city, my family's a favorite rumor for most people."

Kierra smiled at him, "How would you know that?"

"Oh, you know, the number of people who see one of us and says, ooo look, there's one now!" he grinned back at her, "And Rana told us."

She giggled briefly, then turned worried again.

"I know things will never go back to what they once were," she stated solemnly, "That's just not how nature heals, but I'd really like to find a pocket of normalcy, even new normalcy, for a while. This constant being on edge is wearing on me."

Keen put his arm around her. She was wise beyond his own ability, and he knew she was right. There was no going back from all of this, but the world would heal. It would be scarred; nothing would ever be the same, but it would heal and move forward again. He, too, was anxious to get there.

"Every generation has its upheaval," he quoted from something Krieg had once said he'd heard from their father.

Kierra looked up at him, "But does every generation think their own upheaval is the worst it's ever been?"

Keen shrugged. He'd never had the chance to ask his father that question.

Despite the restlessness of the morning, the day itself was largely quiet. They visited Kierra's father, but he did little more than sleep. They continued to gather supplies to set up a long-term home in the three shacks they'd been provided; Keen wasn't sure where the elves were getting all of the wool yarn, iron cookware, extra stove, leather and crafting tools they were bringing for them, or how they were paying for it all, but Keen's family was happily busy replacing some of what they'd lost. Krieg was the only one who couldn't seem to join in the pleasant rhythm that was developing. Keen understood his brother's angst. He didn't want charity. He wanted to work. He wanted to provide for the needs of the family, or to have he and Keen and Kaith all providing. Everything the elves brought them made Krieg visibly tenser.

But Krieg said nothing. He and Kaith spent much of the day turning wood and flint and obsidian into the household tools the women needed, while the women sewed and cooked and cleaned. Keen helped where he could, but he spent more time in the Myandei Mar than at "home," such as it was becoming. Joran, however, did not reemerge until after lunch.

Keen and Kierra were just bringing back dirty dishes from her father's tent to be washed. Rana and Nira had been assigned archer duty in the city and were elsewhere. Joran burst into the hovel looking agitated and immediately summoned Kierra and Keen out to talk to him. Kaith watched the exchanged curiously. Krieg was immediately on edge.

Outside, Joran wasted no time explaining.

"It's worse than we thought, worse than we knew," he began, seeming almost out of breath, "The encampments are running out of everything. The city is well over capacity and more refugees keep flooding in. The front lines are ill-equipped to keep defending their positions and food shortages are everywhere. The Treesingers' Council doesn't think the city will stand on its own much longer."

"What do you mean?" asked Kierra in alarm.

"I mean that we can't fight a war on two fronts on our own. We've been foolish to try for so long. If we don't get help soon, Elanra believes that Willowmark will fall before next spring. We might make it a little longer if the humans bunker for the winter and stop pressing their attack, but the shadowelves won't, and we know that."

"What are we going to do?" Kierra asked desperately.

"How can my family and I help?" Keen added.

"The Treesinger's Council is sending me back to Runeheim. We've spent so much time alienating everyone, they fear that my own relationship with Captain Marik may be our best hope for reinforcements for the city."

"What's Runeheim?" Keen asked.

"The Great Rune Library of the Morrowelves. They call it Felwater. The halflings and faeries that helped get dad and the others home have told us that it's fallen to the Darkwald, though. Last I knew, Marik was in charge of its defense. There's no telling what's become of him, but I've agreed to try to find him."

"So this has nothing to do with Kethran?" Kierra inquired.

"Not exactly. He's been brought back to help defend the city."

Keen's face paled. Joran caught it, and placed a hand on Keen's shoulder.

"They're going to ask my father to oversee the defenses. Kethran will have to answer to him. Your family will be safe, in fact…" and here he paused as if trying to find the right words, "How would you feel about teaching my people to make cannons…for the city's defense?"

Keen didn't even have to think about it. If Willowmark fell, his own family, especially his own unborn child, would be lost.

"I have no problem with it, but it's Krieg you should ask," he responded.

"Why?" asked Joran.

"Because he's the one who taught me."

"Who's going with you?" Kierra interrupted.

"So, far, one faerie has volunteered: one of the ones that came from there in the first place."

"A single faerie?" Kierra exclaimed, "That's hardly a fighting force!"

"I haven't spoken to him yet, but I'm sure Jerith will go, and I have permission to take Rana and Nira if they're willing," and at this he looked seriously at his sister, "And I hoped you might, too."

"Me?"

"Then I'm going, too," Keen insisted.

Joran looked at him and nodded.

"Do you think your brother would answer to my father and help us build cannons?"

"I think my brother would jump out of this tree if someone would pay him for it," Keen mused.

"Pay?" asked Joran and Kierra together.

"You know, allow him to provide a living…"

"Oh, right," Joran interjected, "I forgot humans operate with coinage."

"We do things in trade," Kierra explained, "They'll work out a contract with him for goods in exchange for his service."

"That'll work," Keen mused, "I can sell my brother on that, especially since it will also mean protecting our family. When are we leaving?"

Joran looked more serious than Keen had ever seen him. "Tomorrow," he replied.

Jesp

It was shortly after daybreak when Thomas roused Jesp from her saddlebag. He'd brought some dried fruit, and Jesp ate it gratefully.

"How's Tollie?" she asked.

Thomas sighed, "About the same. She's engrossed in one of those books we brought with us, which should tell you something. It's almost like she's determined to become Tallie and her father on their behalf instead of being herself anymore." He shook his head, "I don't know how to help her out of it."

From the crowded street behind Thomas, Jesp caught sight briefly of a small human child who promptly exclaimed, "Look! That short person is talking to a faerie! See?"

Jesp raised her eyebrows and smirked up at Thomas who was rolling his eyes. "She thinks *you're* short?" Jesp mused.

"Apparently," Thomas responded wearily.

"I didn't know there were humans in Willowmark."

Thomas paused a moment while considering her, "I didn't either. I haven't seen any others yet, I don't think."

"You don't think?" Jesp laughed, "You wouldn't notice?"

"Frankly, Jesp, I feel like I'm walking through a fog. I'm not sure I'd notice a dragon."

"Fortunately," Jesp mused, "I don't think a dragon would notice *me*. I had to run from a hawk yesterday. That was enough."

"A hawk? Oh Allura, Jesp! What happened?"

Jesp swallowed. She hadn't meant to mention her little nighttime adventure to anyone but Kyrt, but Thomas had become almost family. She just didn't guard herself around him or Tollie anymore. She immediately felt guilty.

"I went flying around the city last night," she admitted and then realized that she'd have to tell him why. If he was going to guard the ponies while she visited Tollie, he'd notice that the crown was missing. She tread carefully, "I found a hiding place for the crown…"

"Oh, good. Do I need to move it for you?"

"No…it's….done. It's hidden and safe. For now I think."

"Have you made contact with any other faeries about it?"

Relief flooded Jesp. Thomas wasn't going to ask. She felt even more immensely grateful to her friend than she already had, "No, that's something I had hoped Kyrt and I could do together."

"Does Kyrt know then? Because someone needs to know, Jesp. I hate to think that something might happen to you, but if losing Tallie has taught me one thing, it's that anything can happen to any of us. Someone else needs to know where you put it, and I assume you'd have told me first thing if you'd wanted me to know," he grimaced at her.

Jesp gave him an apologetic look. "I plan to tell Kyrt today. I didn't know where I was going to put it until I did…"

"I hope you found somewhere off the beaten track, but not isolated," Thomas suggested.

"I did."

"High rather than low this time? Because anyone looking for it will dig…"

"I did."

Thomas nodded, and Jesp had to concede that being able to run her idea by him would have been very helpful, but she had to go back to thinking like a faerie who was keeping a faerie's charge. Even Thomas could, in his old age, decide to write it down. Jesp couldn't let that happen again.

Thomas changed the subject, "Well, I want to see Kyrt, and I want you to visit Tollie. If the crown's not here anymore, maybe we could just relocate the books to Tollie's tent rather than taking turns guarding the ponies."

"OK, but we should take turns caring for the ponies. I feel terrible that you've been left to do that all by yourself."

Thomas shrugged, "It's no big deal. Caring for the animals is what I do, and these three have been charges of mine since they were born."

Thomas loaded himself up with three of the books. He admitted he could carry more, but didn't want to draw attention to himself. Then he went to Tollie's tent with Jesp riding on his shoulder.

Tollie was in a small tent squashed between two larger ones. It was large enough to house an elf on a cot, but only just. Tollie herself was lying in an elf-sized cot reading. Her damaged foot was bandaged and propped up on pillows. Her cot lay along the back of the tent and was so long by comparison that it pushed the sides of the tent out. In front of it were crammed 2 small stools, one of which sported a wash basin on top. Jesp noticed a neatly folded bedroll tucked up under the cot, and realized that was probably where Thomas had been sleeping. The warm glow of the potbelly stoves the Willowelves used for warmth was visible through the tent walls on both sides providing an emanating coziness from the larger tents around it. For her part, Tollie didn't even look up from her book when they entered.

"I brought you a visitor!" Thomas exclaimed with forced joviality.

Tollie shot an expressionless glance over at Thomas that made Jesp's heart sink. But her eyes caught Jesp's and she immediately tried to sit up.

"Jesp! Thank Allura! How's Kyrt?"

Her clumsy attempt to sit had left her propped on her elbows instead, but her face looked more alive, and Thomas looked relieved. He moved to prop her pillows under her for which she thanked him almost dismissively.

"He's hurting, but he's healing," Jesp answered, coming to rest on Tollie's knees. "He's worried about you, though. We both are," she added quickly.

Tollie waved a hand at that and insisted she was fine, returning to her book as if neither of them were there. Thomas and Jesp exchanged concerned glances.

"Um," tried Jesp, "What are you reading?"

Jesp had to admit to herself that she didn't care; the new location of the crown wasn't written in there, and that's all that mattered, but she recognized immediately why Thomas had wanted her to come so badly. This was not Tollie.

Jesp had certainly seen Tollie read before, but not like she was engaged in it. Jesp had always thought that the sight of Tollie reading was rather akin to a child taking bitter medicine for the promise of a sweet. This looked, well, downright *elven.*

"It's the lineages of elven noble houses from the Andarraine period," Tollie answered simply, "Tallie had noticed that our Papa had made notes in a couple of these books, especially this one."

"Why?" To Jesp, this seemed like completely disturbed behavior. She could not think of one single reason that such an activity would be either useful or interesting.

"He seemed to be trying to figure out what became of the larger families, especially the royal house. What's weird to me is why they would even have a royal house. Andarraine dominated everything, and it was ruled by humans."

"*That's* what seems weird to you?" Jesp looked to Thomas for mutual alarm, but his eyes were dancing at her in amusement. She wasn't sure what that was about, either.

"One of the things he wrote that I'm trying to figure out is the word 'Adrienmark,' which, of course, is the capital of the Darkwald, and the equals sign and 'Elevar,' which I don't get. But I thought it might be important to the war, if it had something to do with Adrienmark..." her voice trailed off and she bit her lip contemplatively.

"OK?" Jesp questioned, though without any real interest.

"Well, the only thing I've been able to put together really at all is that the ancient royal family of the elves apparently led 'a mighty host' of elven nobility up to the Gatewell where they apparently 'traded their souls for transformative power.' But I have no real clue what that means. It seems like it's the end of that royal house, though..."

She trailed off again, and Jesp watched her for a moment, wondering if there was anything at all Jesp could say that would bring back her friend and banish this crusty elf that had apparently possessed her body. Thinking of nothing useful, Jesp aimed at the problem, as she often did when she was confused, from the side.

"You know," she began tentatively, casting a wide net for another topic, "We should bring Kyrt in here. He's all by himself."

"All by himself?" Tollie retorted stunned, "I thought you were with him!"

Offended, Jesp explained, "Well, I have been, *mostly*, but obviously I'm not right now, am I? I wanted to come and see you. But, seriously, if we put the wash basin on the ground, Kyrt's bed could go on that stool. Then we could all stay together," Jesp finished with a vocal flourish of enthusiasm, designed to keep the topic of conversation changed.

"That's a great idea," Thomas agreed. He, too, looked relieved at the change of topic. Jesp could only imagine how bored the poor man had become if this is what Tollie had been like since their arrival. "I can go and get him."

"Do you know where he is?" Jesp asked, not really wanting to be left alone with Tollie in case some ancient elf came up in conversation again. Already she was casting her mind around for a ready list of off-topics she could throw out if necessary: did you know there are humans in the city? We should try and find the elves we helped save and see how they're doing; and, look I can do back flips in the air again: wing's all better, were her top three. It was rather like sneaking weapons into a diplomatic meeting, Jesp mused.

Thomas had nodded and indicated that he'd been told where the two of them were shortly after they arrived. He simply hadn't wanted to leave Tollie for any longer than the care of the ponies required. So, he left, and Jesp looked over at Tollie whose expression had gone from dazed to almost manic. Jesp was weighing the human topic against the backflip when Tollie spoke up again.

"You know, I don't think the scepter was at Alderbrook."

Jesp's thought train fell into her lap, "What?" she stammered.

"One of the other books I have looked at recently suggested that Alderbrook itself may have been a decoy. In which case, I have no idea where it is."

"I do," Jesp admitted as the realization hit her as hard as the question it answered had when she dreamed it, "It's in Brewhall."

"Brewhall? Why would you think that?"

"Because the faeries there recognized the crown and knew exactly what it was. That's why they brought it back to us, remember? If they don't have the scepter itself, they certainly know something."

By the time Thomas returned with a grinning Kyrt, the treesingers had brought lunch, and news.

"The Treesinger's Council is meeting today. They were hoping one or more of you might come to speak with them about the situation at Runeheim."

"Runeheim?" came the confused question from several of them.

"The Rune Keep. The Library. Felwater. In the Morrowlands."

"Ah."

"Oh."

"OK?" This last response was Jesp, who really wanted to point out that they were 2 faeries and 2 halflings, one of whom wasn't from the area at all. Although what Jesp *really* wanted to do was to ask for a tour of the armory since, being elves, they were sure to have one. But she kept all of this to herself because, more than anything, she really wanted to be useful if she could, so she'd try to answer whatever questions they had, even if she had to make it up. After all, the books all seemed to contradict each other; surely the elves expected that sort of thing.

Thomas and Jesp were the only two able to go. Jesp thought this was a poor choice, but what else could they do? Kyrt fell back to sleep after he drank a potion from his healers after lunch. Tollie couldn't walk and wasn't ready to try the crutches. Jesp wasn't entirely sure why. She thought the fresh air could only do Tollie some good, but she seemed inclined to stay behind and read of all things. Thomas made several more trips back and forth to the ponies for the rest of the books, which Tollie seemed uncharacteristically glad to see. Jesp tried to find a way to talk to Kyrt about the new location of the crown, but he had begun snoring, so Jesp left the topic alone.

The journey up to the citadel at the top of the city was a fascinating one. There was more military up here for one thing, and these were officers, which were even better in Jesp's opinion. The public buildings were large and ornate, and very open. Shrines were set up inside what must have been ancient temples. Judicial structures, of which there were 3, were open on three sides and supported by dried pillars made of intertwined vines so that the public could gather in the square outside and watch. And then there was the treesinger school complex which, as far as Jesp could see, housed not one single book, and Jesp could see a lot because these buildings, too, were open to the street. The music coming from teachers and students was some of the most beautiful Jesp had ever heard, even compared to the constant, ongoing, calling to the city that the Treesingers on all of the lower levels perpetuated continuously.

At the top of the city was a large round citadel situated right in the heart of the canopy itself. It was so entwined into the treetop that it looked like little more than a mass of natural vines hanging from the uppermost branches except for one high, railed platform that extended out over the city below like a porch. Its edifice was gilded, and large golden horns were affixed to either side. Jesp thought that if even one of these was blown, it might be heard across the whole of the forest.

But inside, the smooth wooden floor held aloft an open expanse so immense, Jesp thought the whole of the garden could have fit inside it. The ceiling was ornate with painted wooden woodland scenes and was held up by the occasional tree branch that had been allowed to grow through the floor like pillars. Treesingers milled about, congregating at desks, at shelves which seemed to hold scrolls rather than any books, and in open spaces all around the edge. The outermost edges were concealed in leafy green, growing vines, and archers stood at posts all around the outside, facing out.

In the center sat an immense round wooden table shined to an almost mirror finish like the floor. Its edges were carved into gilded images of every woodland creature Jesp could think of, and several she had certainly never even heard of. The entire table was surrounded by high backed chairs made from thick vines that were gilded and then further adorned with soft dark green upholstery.

At the far side of this table sat Lady Elanra in the tallest of the chairs. Additional treesingers sat in two pairs on either side of her: three of them male and one female. Standing at attention off to the side and speaking in low tones to the seated figures was a single officer whose weapons immediately grabbed Jesp's attention. Their escort had to stop her from flying over for a better look. Thomas and their escort had stopped politely several feet from the table on the side opposite from where the officer was having his audience. One of the seated male treesingers, the one closest to them, glanced over and nodded at them once before returning his attention back to the officer.

Jesp sat as patiently as she could on Thomas' shoulder, where she'd returned to after her attempt at flying around to see the officer's sword. She was swinging her feet impatiently which caused Thomas to reach up and press his hand against her legs to make her stop. She supposed she had technically been kicking him.

After what seemed like an hour to Jesp, but probably was nowhere near, the officer bowed politely to Lady Elanra and turned to leave. Passing by Jesp and Thomas, he noticeably sneered in their direction, which made Jesp want to fly after him and give him a piece of her mind. But Thomas started moving forward toward the place where the officer had last been standing, so Jesp stayed put, still fuming.

"Welcome, Thomas of Brewhall and Jesp of Felwater Garden," Elanra greeted them formally as their escort left, "We appreciate you taking the time to come and speak with us. Please, have a seat."

Thomas nodded and climbed up into a chair two away from the nearest Treesinger. Jesp, unwilling to be made to feel unimportant by a bunch of elves, flew herself to a few feet in front of the priestess, and sat crosslegged on the table. Elanra smiled at her, but said nothing.

"We won't take much of your time," Elanra began, "First, we want to thank you again for rescuing our soldiers. We know you paid a terrible price for your intervention on their behalf, and we are immensely grateful to you. How are your wounded companions?"

Jesp looked down at her hands in her lap. Terrible price indeed, she thought, as images of Tallie raced through her mind. She brushed a tear away as Thomas answered, somewhat hoarsely, "They are healing, Lady."

Elanra nodded and went on, "We understand that you traveled from Runeheim to get here. Is that true?"

Jesp looked up and looked back at Thomas. This time she answered, "I came from the Garden, which is next to the Library, or Rune Keep, whatever. Thomas joined us in Brewhall, which was our initial destination."

"Ah, apologies then. Would you happen to know anything about the existing leadership of the Keep?" Elanra asked Jesp directly.

"Not now," she answered, "Lord Ellerby was killed, and then the shadowelves overran the place."

There was murmuring between the seated figures, then a male directly on Elanra's left asked, "Are you sure? Has it fallen completely?"

Thomas responded, "Yes. I'm afraid so. We passed nearby on our way from Brewhall to here. Shadowelves now control both sides of the river right at the Keep. They would have been overrun by sheer numbers if nothing else."

The elves sat for a moment or two in stunned silence. Eventually, the younger female elf spoke, "That may make our summoning of Wythir Joran pointless."

The others nodded solemnly, apparently lost in disturbed thought. Then Elanra spoke to Jesp again, "Do you know Captain Marik?"

"The captain of the guard at the library?" Jesp asked, maybe a little too excitedly in hindsight. She schooled her tone of glee back and went on, "I certainly know who he is, but I've never met him. The elves of the Library and the fae of the Garden did not interact if we could help it."

Elanra cocked her head to one side and asked, "Why not?"

"We don't get along," Jesp answered truthfully, "We have different priorities."

"And what are your priorities?"

An image of the Crown flashed across Jesp's mind. What to say?

"We believe that our Garden is sacred, and is the highest priority. The elves preferred their books."

"Ah, yes," one of the male elves, to Jesp's astonishment, agreed, "We have that same problem with the morrowelves. They abandoned the Sacred Trust of the Forest to attend to those books. It's been a source of deep resentment between them and us for countless generations."

Elanra went on, "We have found in recent years that we share this disposition with faerie kind. You seem to guard your natural places as we do our forest. I can only imagine what the loss of so many of your lands must mean to you. I am sorry."

Jesp returned her gaze to her hands. She had been trying hard not to think of that, especially as it pertained to the Garden.

Thomas spoke up at this point, and Jesp was happy for the subject change, such as it was, "When we passed near to the Library and its grounds, we could see fires. It appeared that the fighting was still going on. Someone must be there still trying to defend it, or to get it back."

"That Library," began Elanra again, "In the hands of shadowelves could mean the death of us all. The morrowelves have long been careless about the things they choose to record and study."

Jesp looked up in shock. Did she really just hear such a *fae* thing come out of the mouth of an *elf*?

Thomas and the elves continued to discuss the likely fate of the Library, while Jesp's mind wandered. Should she tell these elves that the Crown was in their city? Would they guard it like a faerie would? Did they protect their forest simply for the forest or for other secret reasons known only to them such as the fae did? Eventually she decided that, having not even told the other faeries in the city, she certainly couldn't say anything to the elves. Thomas, for his part, said nothing about it or the books. Jesp appreciated having his wisdom to follow.

The group was waiting on someone named Joran to arrive. Thomas agreed to wait for him in case anything he knew might seem relevant to this other elf. Jesp didn't know why. Jesp, however, excused herself and agreed to return.

Jesp left and flew straight down over the city, dodging several birds along the way. She dove headlong towards the Myandei Mar, and then for the small, familiar tent she needed. Thomas was right: someone other than Jesp needed to know what she'd done, and she was only willing to talk to one person.

She entered the tent, and was relieved to find that Tollie had fallen asleep reading, this time another of her ridiculous books. She lighted silently on the stool next to Kyrt's bed, and gently shook him awake.

"Kyrt," she whispered.

Kyrt's bleary eyes opened slightly, then became more alert when he recognized Jesp.

"I need to talk to you. Privately," she pleaded.

Kyrt glanced over at Tollie's sleeping form, then back at Jesp. "This is as private as it gets, unless you think you can carry me," he grinned, "I'm not going walking about in this nightmare of big feet they call a healers district."

Jesp grimaced. He was right. Two faeries on the ground were a muddy smear waiting to happen.

So, Jesp got as close to Kyrt's ear as she could and whispered.

"I've hidden the crown."

She could sense Kyrt tense. His alertness was almost electric in that moment.

"From the ponies, fly to the closest bridge to the south, cross it and turn left. When you find the school, look for the kitchen building in the back. Above that, there's a support beam for the upper city with a hawk's nest on it."

"A hawk's nest??" Kyrt repeated in alarm.

"Yeah, 'fraid so. It's hidden in a hollow in the tree behind the nest, under a loose piece of bark, wrapped in Tollie's elf-dress."

She pulled away and looked at him. He looked solemnly into her eyes and nodded. "Does anyone else know?"

Jesp shook her head.

"Let's keep it that way for now," he suggested. She nodded and took his hand in hers. She began absentmindedly stroking his hair. He closed his eyes enjoying her touch, and soon fell back to sleep.

When Jesp returned to the citadel, the elven officer was there. He was everything Jesp liked about elves, and to his credit, didn't sneer at her like the first one had. They were introduced, and then the conversation they had been having when she came in resumed.

"The only way to know for sure is to go," he was saying to the assemblage.

"We agree," Elanra assured him, "Does that mean you'll agree to it?"

The officer paused and considered the question a moment. Jesp noticed that Thomas seemed to be watching him intently, so she tried to do the same.

"I have conditions," he replied.

The gathered elves clearly didn't care for the sound of that, but they said nothing as the officer went on.

"First, is that this council reigns in Kethran. His actions against my sister's mate should not have been tolerated by this Council, and I can't leave in good conscience if I don't know that my family will be protected by the law as they should have been."

The young man didn't wait for a response, plowing on with his demands, "Second, I will choose my company, and it will not include any of your so-called diplomats."

Jesp was starting to like this elf. The Council, however, was clearly uncomfortable.

"Third, last, and most importantly, I want to offer an apology on behalf of this Council for our behavior of which I was a witness."

"An apology?" exploded a male treesinger.

"You can't be serious!" shouted the female.

"What is it that you feel we should be apologizing for, exactly?" came Elanra's curt reply.

"We marched into their country under the guise of reviving diplomacy and did nothing but demand that they change their way of life, their whole culture," the officer explained.

Another male stood up and pounded his fist on the table, causing Jesp to leap into the air. The officer caught her gently in his hand and sat her back down, almost without thought. It reminded Jesp painfully of Harold, and she decided that whatever these demands of his meant, she was on his side.

The angry elf exclaimed, "Their culture is our culture!"

Patiently, the officer explained, "It may once have been, but it hasn't been for a very long time. You are asking me to go to them with my hand out. The last time I was there, we almost started another war. If I can't offer a simple apology, even just for having misunderstood the gravity of what we were asking, then I can't ask them for aid."

"Oh, we understood the gravity of what we asked of them," Elanra assured them, her usual pleasant demeanor now gone, "And in light of the new dangers, we will likely ask it again in the future."

The officer began to protest, but the priestess held up her hand and silenced him, "If you must offer an apology, and only if you absolutely must, you may apologize for the misunderstanding over why we had asked to talk in the first place. Clearly, they were expecting concessions we would never have given, and possibly, maybe, we played some role in that misunderstanding."

The standing elf stammered, "But!"

"Silence!" Elanra chastised him, "And do sit back down, Elrin. If Joran is right about one thing, it's that we are begging for help from people we have recently offended. And we *need* the *help*." She turned her attention back to the officer named Joran, "As for Kethran and your family, we have spoken to him just today and informed him that he is being reassigned to the defense of this city, under your father's command, and that he will not interfere with any of the people we have allowed to remain here. That will include your sister's mate. And his family. In fact, we were hoping you might persuade your sister's mate to assist."

"Assist Kethran?" Joran asked incredulously.

"Assist your father. He was the one that taught you about the cannons, correct? We could certainly use that technology."

Joran stared at the priestess for a moment before conceding, "Yes, Lady

Elanra. I will ask him."

"And you will need to put your party together quickly, Joran. You have just become this city's last and best chance."

"May I take others from the military?"

"I assume you want your mate, your cousin and his mate?"

"I do."

"Of course. Take who you need, but take as few as you can. Everyone who goes with you is one less person we have left here, and everyone is critical now."

"I understand."

"Then, you are excused."

"Wait," Jesp cut in, dizzy from all of the back and forth. The whole room turned to consider her.

"If you're going back to the Library, I want to go with you."

Joran considered her briefly, and Thomas spoke up, "Don't underestimate her. I've personally seen her fell shadowelves, including some of those who were chasing your father."

"His father?" Jesp asked Thomas quizzically.

"His father was one of the elves we found in the woods. He was the one, if I'm not mistaken, who helped Tollie walk back after her foot was injured. I remember him mentioning your name." This last statement he directed at Joran, who looked suddenly pale.

"You are the ones that rescued those men?" he asked quietly.

Thomas looked sheepish, but Jesp didn't feel that way. They'd risked their lives, lost Tallie, and brought back two friends with serious wounds.

"Yep," she replied to Thomas' apparent surprise.

"Then I'd be honored to have you accompany me," Joran answered simply, "We leave tomorrow."

"But…" Jesp stammered, "My own mate won't be able to go that quickly!"

"I'm sorry," Elanra cut in, "But Joran is right. He cannot wait."

"Tomorrow," he repeated, "Meet me at the entrance to the Myandei Mar at daybreak if you still wish to come."

Jesp was horrified, but she nodded anyway. "Tomorrow," she agreed.

Brody

Adrik raced forward to catch Arisa, even though she seemed to be descending slowly. It was clear that she was still unconscious. Brody bent down and picked up his rock. It seemed so innocuous again, even if it was still warm. He had no idea what this new breakthrough might mean, but he knew Adrik was about to explode at him, so he braced for it.

He didn't have to wait long. As soon as he had Arisa safely laid out on her blankets, Adrik rounded on Brody.

"Queen Lorilaze Andarraine?" he practically shouted, and then got even louder, "QUEEN LORLIAZE ANDARRAINE???? Are you kidding me??"

Brody stared as calmly as he could into Adrik's eyes. He knew the shadowelf wouldn't harm him, but he often had to remind himself of that fact in these moments.

"Is Arisa ok?" he asked Adrik patiently.

Adrik glanced back down at Arisa, who appeared to be sleeping peacefully at the moment.

"I don't know," he fumed, "Your GIRLFRIEND is the litch queen herself!"

"She's not my girlfriend."

"Who knows what she's done to her!"

"I would never intentionally harm Arisa, Adrik. You know that."

"Throw that damned thing back into the pit where you found it!"

"No, please!" came the desperate voice in Brody's head. Brody closed his eyes.

"I agree we should keep it away from Arisa," Finn chimed in quietly, "But we came here for answers, and Brody may now be able to get them."

Adrik stood between Brody and Arisa's prone form heaving with each breath. Brody, for his part, was intensely aware that he didn't care to ever meet any other shadowelf. Adrik's wild white hair and bulging, angry violet eyes would be the stuff of nightmares if Brody didn't already know how quickly his anger could deflate, and how utterly noble the man really was.

Brody thought silently in his head, "Why did you do that?"

Lorliaze's voice came to him tearfully. She sounded so incredibly small in that moment, "I didn't mean to. She…she…has a connection to the prophecy, like I do. And I'm not a litch….I don't think."

"You don't think?" Brody mistakenly said aloud.

Adrik, who had seated himself down next to Arisa by the time Brody opened his eyes, responded, "Is she talking again? You tell her she's on thin ice, Brody. Arisa better be ok when she wakes up, or I'll find some way to hurt that rock!"

Brody fought a chuckle. Finn's amused eyes reached Brody's before he carefully cleared his expression. Adrik hadn't realized how silly that had sounded. He was just too angry.

Brody understood, though. It was obvious to anyone that Adrik was in love with Arisa, and that her wellbeing was what he really cared most about. Brody found it sweet.

Fletch had begun to lick Arisa's face behind Adrik while he fumed, and she was beginning to stir and to moan. Adrik's attention was immediately drawn back to her. Strangely, though, he petted the dog rather than chastising him for a change.

"Yes," Brody answered again, "She's talking. She didn't mean to hurt Arisa."

Adrik whipped back around, "So *she* says!"

"She says she has a connection to the prophecy like Arisa does, and…" Brody paused and sighed. His first loyalty had to be to his companions, even if he had developed a soft spot for the weeping disembodied woman, "She doesn't think she's a litch."

"She doesn't *think* she's a litch?" asked Finn as Adrik loudly harrumphed.

"The legend in the Darkwald," Adrik continued, "Was that Lorliaze Andarraine destroyed and replaced a powerful litch."

"I thought you didn't know any more about her," Brody protested.

"If she's the one that unleashed the Gatewell, then I guess I do. I didn't know that Lorliaze Andarraine was the same person as the young girl whose story we had been following. On the list of hair-raising schemes that members of the shadowelf royal family has concocted over the centuries is a desire to find the litch queen and do to her what she did to him."

"That would be bad," said Lorliaze's quiet voice, "A shadowelf litch would be very very bad."

"Are you a litch then?" Brody asked her again.

"I don't really know what I am. I'm little more than nothing, truthfully."

"What did she say?" Adrik demanded and Brody told him.

"Did she destroy a powerful litch and take his place? In any sense of that statement?"

Brody waited. He knew Lorliaze could hear Adrik.

"I guess so. The Storm Litch, the Storm Titan, the Lord of this fortress, *he* was a litch. He would entrap the souls of my people here, and feed off of their remaining nightmares and fears. I meant to release them onto him, and only him, but I didn't realize that they'd go farther afield, which they did, and still do, when anyone uncovers it again."

Brody repeated all of this to the room dutifully. Arisa opened her eyes, and stared blankly around at them all. Adrik began stroking her hair, but continued to speak, albeit more calmly now, to Brody.

"What does that mean?" he asked.

"In my day, my kingdom had been overrun by two powerful litches from the north. During Andarraine's expansions, someone uncovered their lairs and woke them up. They took control of my kingdom and imprisoned my family. My father, my grandfather, and my great grandmother were little more than puppets at their command. My people were suffering, so I tried to do something that might destroy at least one of them."

After repeating all of this, he then asked her out loud what happened next. She went on:

"My father had tried to undermine the Titans. As punishment, they killed my brother, and forced my father to send me and his crown and scepter here. It was supposed to keep my father in line. It did sort of. He committed suicide."

"I'm sorry," said Brody before repeating this to the others.

"I was here for two years, and I spent the time learning what I could about the well. Eventually I realized that I could release the trapped spirits, or at least, I thought I could, if I sacrificed myself willingly to the well itself. So I did."

Brody repeated, then asked, "Did it work?"

"Yes, and no. I didn't die completely. I've been stuck ever since. The spirits did destroy the Storm Titan, but then they apparently flooded into the southernmost forest of Elevar and decimated an elven army there. And then they returned to the well again. I hadn't really freed them at all. And in all the time since then, I haven't been able to figure out how to die."

She continued, "I do have some control over things here. Minor control really. I can sense the territory, the region. I can wake the Bramblemen on the mountain and send them out, which I do everytime I sense a shadowelf in the area. Most of the Bramblemen are descended from the first shadowelf army that amassed here. I attacked them with the trees, but either the trees were cursed from their time on this mountain, or the shadowelves had become something that couldn't tolerate the anger of nature. I'm not really sure how it happened, but I can control them somewhat. Not reliably, which is why I only wake them rarely.

"I can somewhat understand where the spirits have been when they leave and what they've been up to, though I can't really communicate with them... or with the bramblemen. Not meaningfully."

"So the spirits leave occasionally?" asked Arisa from her sick bed, causing Finn and Adrik both to jump, "Were do they go?"

"It's only happened two other times since I've been here. Both times, someone came down here and, like me, willingly sacrificed themselves to the well, releasing the army of spirits. But they only ever go to one place: it's a battlefield that was already ancient in my time where the last great war between the humans of Andarraine and the elves of Elevar fought before the great treaty. It's a cursed place in the middle of the forest where no trees can grow. The last time it happened was really recently. The shadowelves came in numbers too great for my bramblemen to stop."

"How long ago?" asked Adrik after Brody finished repeating her words.

"Time is strange for me down here. Days? Weeks? Maybe months? I don't think it's been a year, but I'm not really sure."

"And the storms?" asked Finn, "Are you doing that, too?"

"Me? No. That's the energy being released from the well."

"And they went to the same place again? This last time?" Arisa asked.

"Yes. There were humans and elves gathered there apparently. I don't really know anything else."

"What about the comet? The thing we've been calling the Titan?"

"The comet? Have the comets returned?" Lorliaze asked in alarm.

"Two have. One seemed to come from here."

"In my day we were taught that magic ebbed and flowed in our world, like a great tide. The comets herald its flow back into the world, but they have to be called. Each is summoned by breaking runic seals in certain sacred places, and only after a certain amount of time has passed. I can't sense the runes, though; not in this state.

The power ebbs again at the time that the great lights can be seen in the sky to the south. That happens once magic has built up to a certain level that overwhelms…something…the natural order maybe? I don't entirely understand it. But, if the last litch is awake, he'll try to use the return of energy to come back to power. Brody, whatever you do, you can't let that happen."

"So, why did you suggest that you might be a litch?" asked Brody curiously.

"I didn't mean to. I just can't say for sure, really. I mean, I did, technically, kill the guards that were down here and sacrifice myself to the well. My spirit *is* bound to a material object, apparently. But I don't have a body anymore. I'm not sure *what* that makes me."

"Is there anyway we can help her?" asked Arisa.

"Whoa, wait a minute," Adrik insisted, "We don't even know if we can trust her. She could be lying her head off."

"I can't lie in this form," Lorliaze said quietly, "But I can't prove that either."

"She says she can't lie, but she admits she can't prove that."

"Convenient," muttered Adrik.

"*Is* there anything we can do?" Brody asked.

"Hang on!" Adrik insisted.

"Finding out what she wants isn't the same thing as agreeing to it," Brody reasoned calmly.

Adrik nodded solemnly, but looked like he'd just bitten into a lemon.

"For one thing, the Gatewell *must* be destroyed. The evil that's been allowed to continue here is just another catastrophe waiting to happen to your world once the wrong person figures out how to use it."

"Do you mean the pit or the whole mountain?" Brody asked without repeating her request first.

"The fortress. The Great Castle of the Breaking Mountains. The Mountain that isn't a mountain. The Un-Breaking. It must be destroyed! No matter what happens to me, or any other long dead spirit, this place will be a blight on the living again. It cannot be used for anything good."

When Brody repeated this request, Adrik had only one thing to say, "How?"

"I wish I knew," came Lorliaze's reply.

Dawn was breaking hazily overhead. It's light barely penetrated into the gloom of the Unbreaking, but penetrate it did. The friends realized that they had been up all night talking, but they were learning so much, they had all but forgotten the sudden revelation of the Prophecy itself. Arisa was dozing off, and the others agreed that at least a nap was in order before trying to brave their way back up and out of the mountain. Still, Brody's head was spinning with so much new information, and the excitement that came along with it, that he doubted he would be able to sleep at all. Instead, he offered to take the first watch.

"I can watch with you if you like," Lorliaze offered, "I don't really sleep, and I can let you know if there's any trouble."

"Ask her if we're alone in here," Finn suggested, and Brody didn't have to repeat the request.

"At the moment, yes, but there are shadowelves camped on top of the fortress. My bramblemen are engaged with them now. Too many of them willingly exposed themselves to the magic here. I don't want to let them leave, though that is what they're trying to do."

"Kill them if you can," came Adrik's dark reply from his sleeping place he had laid out next to Arisa, "Kill them *all* if you can."

"Does he admire none of his own kind?" Lorliaze asked Brody.

"He's mentioned a little sister before," Brody answered her silently, so that the others could get to sleep, "But I know very little about her."

"Hmmmm. He's different than the shadowelves I remember. Perhaps the corruption they suffered here did not pass to future generations like I assumed."

"Oh, he's different than the shadowelves now, too, believe me."

"But in my day, the corruption of the noble houses of the elves was absolute and inherent: insurmountable by the indiviuals involved. Perhaps the corruption they passed on was learned rather inherited, taught rather than infused."

"I wouldn't know," Brody answered.

Brody never bothered to wake the others for another watch. He let them sleep most of the day. He was too busy learning all he could from Lorliaze who seemed to be just pleased to have someone to talk to at long last. She told him about great ancient cities, both human and elven: Andarraine, Adrimar, Dannaire, Blanfeld, Freyensei, and Fyremark for the humans, Elevar, Willamar, Tonneth and Perithon for the elves, along with the Sacred elven sites of Runheym and Hallowmar. She taught him about the treaties that protected those twelve locations and bought an often uneasy peace between elves and humans for countless centuries, maybe millenia. There had been other smaller kingdoms, too. The Freehills kingdom of the halflings, the series of coastal free cities that were built by elflings, the faerie kingdoms of Alderbrook and Glen Hills, and even an orcish kingdom far to the north of the Barrow Hills that had been called Fargreb. It was a world Brody couldn't have dreamed of: so alien and so exotic. He wondered how much of the world currently was similar and how much it had changed. Never before had he lamented his lack of knowledge about his own world, but staying awake listening to tales of everything Lorliaze had once loved, he sadly had to admit that, without an education, he was hardly even a part of his world.

Eventually, the others stirred.

They ate quickly and began hatching their plan of escape, which largely involved moving across and up the landing as quickly as possible and ducking into side rooms periodically before Adrik became overwhelmed. Adrik, for his part, bristled at the idea that he was the reason they would need to stop occasionally, but he didn't argue. They intended to leave the way they came, since any other options would require further exploration, and they just weren't interested in that. Lorliaze suggested that she knew other ways in and out, but not exactly how those egresses may have fared the passage of time. She knew the shadowelves were using another means of entry and exit, which she suspected was a window on a level below, and across the fortress from, the balcony they themselves had used.

The journey took the rest of the day, but more because of Arisa's health than Adrik's mental stability, though both were questionable. Arisa had become extremely sick in the stomach after eating, and kept alternating between vomiting and dizzy spells as they climbed.

During one pause, a new idea had occurred to Arisa.

"Brody," she whispered, her latest bout with dizziness having rendered her voice weak, "Didn't Lorliaze say something about her father's crown and scepter having been here, too? Do we need to worry about that?"

Brody waited for Lorliaze to respond.

"No. Although, I suppose it's possible that the crown could help me out of my predicament. I hadn't considered that."

Brody dutifully repeated her answers as a new back and forth broke out between her and Arisa.

"What do you mean?" Arisa asked weakly.

"There was another prophecy, one that was already ancient in my own time, that had said that Andarraine would fall when the last of the royal line became soul-trapped. I hadn't thought about that story since I was little. It never occurred to me that I became that last ruler."

"What does that have to do with with the crown?"

"The crown was designed by elven sorcerors in Elevar for my family. It binds our souls to our bodies. It has had the effect over many many generations of causing my ancestors to live unnaturally long lives, but the purpose of it was to prevent exactly what happened to me. I don't know if its magic would fix anything, though. But I suppose it might."

"What happened to it?"

"Well, I knew the crown wouldn't let me just die. Not from simply jumping into the welldeep part of the fortress, though it never occurred to me that by getting rid of it, I was dooming myself to be one that was soul-trapped."

"So, you got rid of it?"

"Yes. I wasn't the only one imprisoned here. There were two faeries here, too. Well, there were several of us, but the two faeries and I had become good friends. Like me, they were being held so that their respective kingdoms could be controlled. I gave one of them my crown and one of them my scepter and helped them to escape. It was only after that that I could sacrifice myself."

"So, you have no idea where they went?"

"Oh, no, I know where they went. I just don't know what may have happened since then. I gave my scepter to Kiki, who was from Alderbrook. She was going home to hide it there. Nyllie, who was from Glenn Hills, though, was afraid to go home. Glenn Hills was right at the base of the Breaking, practically at the foot of this mountain, just before the Willa borders emerge from the hills. I had suggested that she head Runheym. The elves had a River Fortress there that was still free. She took the crown."

"Is Runheym the same thing as Rune Heim? As in the Runic Library?"

"I don't know. It wasn't a library then. It was a Sacred site built over the place where the Ashana were said to have once touched the world. Supposedly there's a cavern underneath that houses the star matter where the elves believed that life began."

"Well, Arisa," Adrik chimed in, "I guess it's time to take you home. If that crown's still there, it may be in grave danger, all things considered."

"Will it work for anyone else?" Arisa asked.

"Presumably," came Lorliaze's reply.

As night fell like ink into the deep well of the fortress, they were only about two levels below their destination. They had ducked briefly into a small, empty room that Lorliaze thought had once been a servant's room, and were about to leave again when Brody had to stop them.

"Wait," he cautioned. Lorliaze had just said the words they were all dreading, "She says they're coming back."

"The shadowelves?" Arisa whimpered.

Brody nodded solemnly and put a finger to his lips to indicate that they needed to be quiet.

Within minutes they could hear commotion overhead. An argument of some sort had apparently broken out between the shadowelves that had re-entered the structure. They could hear the commotion heading their way, and were suddenly struck by the reality that if they left the room, they could be seen, but that within the room, there was nowhere to hide. If the shadowelves were to peer in at all, they would see them without question. And from the sounds of the growing argument, there were at least a dozen of them.

They each looked frantically around at each other. The argument, now that they could hear it, apparently amounted to a sense that several of them did not feel that they had yet acquired enough treasure from the fortress to carry home to their queen. Others, apparently rattled by how many had already been lost on the expedidition, did not wish to be venturing back into the mountain. Nonetheless, the group was clearly moving down the landing, looking into the chambers they passed as they went. The group of friends were stuck and exposed and most certainly about to be caught.

They sat huddled, terrified, just inside and behind an old door that, except with exceptional luck, would not hide them all from view. Even Fletch was cowering between Brody's legs and was unusually silent.

"I have an idea," Adrik whispered so quietly, Brody almost didn't catch his words. They all looked at him.

"Give me a minute," he instructed, "But if you get your chance to escape, go for it."

"No!" protested Arisa. Finn was also shaking his head at the elf. Brody joined him.

"Don't worry," Adrik insisted, "If the opportunity presents itself, I'll head up, too, just don't linger here if you can help it."

"What are you going to do?" Arisa asked fearfully.

Then Adrik did something unusual; he kissed Arisa's forehead gently. Then he smiled at her, and deftly slipped out of the doorway and onto the landing.

Arisa's eyes were wide with fear.

"Can you still see him?" Brody asked Lorliaze in his head.

"See?" she asked, bewildered, "I can't *see* anything. I can sense, though, and he's moving down, not up."

Brody looked at his remaining companions, unsure what to do. What if Adrik got caught? How could they do anything about it? Then again, none of them had Adrik's ability at stealth. If they tried to follow him, they would surely *get* him caught. To Brody, every one of his breaths sounded too loud, and the fear was threatening to engulf him in utter black despair.

"Oh no," Lorliaze whispered, as if she, too, needed to be quiet.

"What?" asked Brody silently.

"He's…he's…"

And then there was the sound they had all been dreading.

"Who's that?"

"Get him!"

And the sound of a chase ensuing.

Arisa gasped. Finn leaped out from behind the door, but Brody had beaten him to threshold. The elves were chasing Adrik down, down and out of sight.

"He did that on purpose," Lorliaze lamented, "He's leading them away."

Brody repeated this pronouncement solemnly and added, "But how can he think he won't get caught?"

"I don't think he plans to escape," choked Arisa, "That's what the kiss was about."

Finn bowed his head. Brody sank against the wall. Soon enough, the triumphant sounds of capture reached their ears. They listened, in solemn, tearful silence, as Adrik, a captured traitor and the last treasure the shadowelves needed to be able to return home, was marched back up and out the way they had come.

"He saved us," Arisa sobbed, "He sacrificed himself to save us."

"I understand that impulse," Lorliaze sighed, "And I understand its foolishness. But without him, there would have been no tomorrow…for any of you."

Pronunciations & Translations

i. Pronounced "Why-theer:" literally "Guardian." A low-ranking officer; leutinent

ii. Pronunciation Guide:

 Eh vahn too eel, ah vahn eel too

 Ahn too sheel feel, eel sheel wahn roo

 may fahra vahn, may willa shy

 en-dye-ah lahn, en-dye-ah thy

 Feel sheel, dye-ah too

 hah-lah treel, trilla voo

 wah ell ell wah, wah ell wah ell

 Vahn too eel, Ahn too sheel pahr eel vahn-ee

iii. Literal Translation:

 If sing you me, then sing I you

 What your heart hears, my heart once cries

 As birds sing, as trees rise

 Over/out-reach the deep, over/out reach divide

 Hear my heart reach you

 Feel the beat beating through

 All/we all/we are, all/we are all/we (all and we are the same word)

 Sing you I, what your heart for/on behalf of me sang.

iv. Pronunciation Guide:

 Ah-nah shohn nah-lah par too

 As kin shan doh ah-shoo shale (long a like ale)

 Ah-nah throo-vin nahn may troo

 Shah-vah thah-lah thee-lah kale

 As sh-doh lye kee neel rah nay

 As nah-too thee-lah too lah-shay

 Ee-ale too more-nah lah more-noo

 Ah-nah nah-sheel-yah theel-ah too

Ah-nah too-thee-lah lah-shay mye

Ee trahth kin throo-vin i-Lah

Ah-nah sheel-sah sahn shahnd too drye

Ee-nah mye too shahnd-ee shee-lah

Loo leh-yehn kin loo-ahn lahn loo

Ah-shah-nah, too-ah-loor meer soo

Ah-shahn-dee wye, ee-lah too wye

Loo loo-ahn-tah-ee ee mye.

v.   Literal Translation:

May here always be for/on behalf of you

That with/in darkness light shines

May the future hold as true

Ills seek finding never

That shadows stalk but lose their prey

That always you find your way/path/road

And ever your skies be blue

May always hope find you

May you find a way/path/road to heal/fix/mend

And blessed in/with future days

May love loosen the pain you feel

And always heal/fix/mend your darkened hearts

Rest/sleep/peace now, in peace/rest-ful dream- rest/sleep/peace

The Ashana (the sacred stars of the Kingdom of Elevar, believed to be where prophetic dreams came from) your spirit safe keeps

Life (Darkened stardust, literally) guards/shields and is your guard/shield

Rest/sleep/peace rest/peace-fully and heal/fix/mend

Pronounced "Shah-Vahn-eer:" Literally "Lead Warrior" or "Leader of War"

vi.   Shavanir plural

vii.   Wythir plural

viii.   Pronounced "MYE-en-day MAR" Literally Healers Village (plural) not Healers' Village (possessive)

Notes

Each year is named for one of the 30 Timeless Beings and each cycle of 30 years is named for one of the 200 Runes. Ancient scholars believed that Morroan, god of the Open Land, would return once the entire cycle of 6000 years was complete. 4000 have past. The world is currently 10 years into the Rune cycle of Adamon, the Rune of Change. At the beginning of our story, we are at the end of the year of Kylaer, in the Cycle of Adamon. The years follow this order:

Herta

Zol

Isil

Trezen

Shilir

Rinet

Willa

Vestana

Morroan

Kylaer

Ceru

Borroaz

Amuzenna

Roth

Andarraine

Wocata

Isilzen

Anupi

Arzen

Mikaz

Wynn Talley Perkins

Allura

Rinlira

Brigana

Sellir

Shilirin

Brath

Elevar

Mila

Lila

Jynin

The Kingdoms of Andarraine and Elevar fell in the Year of Mikaz, in the Cycle of the 66th Rune, Jorna, the Rune of the Ages.

The Days of the Week: Year:	**The Months of the**	
Wocatsday (Oct31-Nov27)	*Winter*	Selliris
Rothsday (Nov28-Dec25)		Zolas
Amusday (Dec26-Jan22)		Isilis
Kylarsday (Jan23-Feb19)		Brathis
Arzenday	*Spring*	
Cerusas(Feb20-Mar19)		
Isilsday		Mikas

(Mar20-Apr16)

Anupday

Rinliras(Apr17-May14)

Summer   Hertas

(May15-Jun11)

Alluras

(Jun12-Jul09)

Trezens(Jul10-Aug06)

Autumn   Rinets

(Aug07-Sep03)A

Shilirs

(Sep04-Oct01)

Vestanas(Oct02-Oct30)

(Each is 28 days plus an extra "Harvest Day" at the beginning of Vestanas, which although considered Vestanas 1st, is not given a day of the week. So, the year always begins on a Wocatsday, and always ends on an Anupday. Every 4 years, Harvest Day is 48 hours long. This is one of those years.)

Chapter One begins on Rinets 24, which is an Amusday. In our world, it is the last day of August.

The Prologue begins on Mikas 28 (April 16), an Anupday, in the Year of Shilir, although the villagers in Luring don't know that.

<<<<>>>>

488

www.ingramcontent.com/pod-product-compliance
Lightning Source LLC
Chambersburg PA
CBHW032154180726
48284CB00001B/47